VIZ GRAPHIC NOVEL

CERES™
Celestial Legend
VOL. 4 CHIDORI

Story and Art by
YÛ WATASE

CERES™
Celestial Legend
VOL. 4: Chidori

This volume contains the CERES: CELESTIAL LEGEND installments from
Part 4, issue 1 through Part. 4, issue 4 in their entirety.

STORY & ART BY YÛ WATASE

English Adaptation/Gary Leach

Translaton/Lillian Olsen
Touch-Up Art & Lettering/Bill Schuch
Cover Design/Hidemi Sahara
Graphic Design/Carolina Ugalde
Editor/Andy Nakatani

Managing Editor/Annette Roman
Editor-in-Chief/Bill Flanagan
Director of Licensing and Acquisitions/Rika Inouye
Sr. Vice President of Sales & Marketing/Rick Bauer
Sr. Vice President of Editorial/Hyoe Narita
Publisher/Seiji Horibuchi

© 1997 Yuu Watase/Shogakukan. First published by SHOGAKUKAN, Inc in Japan. as "Ayashi no Ceres."
(New and adapted artwork and text © 2003 VIZ, LLC.) All rights reserved.

Printed in Canada

Published by VIZ, LLC
P.O. Box 77010 • San Francisco, CA 94107

10 9 8 7 6 5 4 3 2 1
First printing, May 2003

store.viz.com

www.viz.com

Ceres

Long long ago a tennyo (celestial maiden) named Ceres descended to earth. A mortal man stole her hagoromo (feathered robe) without which she could not return to the heavens. The man forced Ceres to bear his children, beginning the Mikage family line. Awakened after aeons of waiting, Ceres wants her hagoromo back and vows to use all her celestial powers to get revenge against the descendents of the man who wronged her ages ago.

Aya Mikage

Ceres is taking over 16-year-old Aya Mikage's mind and body. To prevent Ceres from destroying the Mikage clan, Aya's own family is trying to kill her. Despite all the turmoil, Aya finds herself falling in love with Tōya—a man hired by Kagami to keep an eye on her.

Aki Mikage

Aya's twin brother. While the consciousness of Ceres is taking over Aya, Aki is showing signs of bearing the consciousness of the founder of the Mikage family line. He has been put under confinement by the Mikage family to keep him separated from Aya.

Suzumi Aogiri

An instructor of traditional Japanese dance and a descendent of a tennyo. Suzumi has welcomed Aya into her household and provides Aya with all the protection, assistance, and support that she can. In the last volume, Kagami's goons trap Suzumi in a hallucinatory dream-state. While Ceres manages to save her, Suzumi's psyche may be forever trapped in a world of illusions.

Yūhi Aogiri

Suzumi's 16-year-old brother-in-law. Yūhi is an aspiring chef and a proficient martial artist. Suzumi has ordered Yūhi to be Aya's watchful protector and guardian.

Mrs. Q. (Oda Kyu)

Bizarre but faithful servant of Suzumi's household.

Tōya

A mysterious man who has come to Aya's aid on numerous occasions. Tōya has lost his memory and he works for Mikage International in exchange for their help in getting his memory back.

Kagami Mikage

Although the Mikage family wants to kill off Ceres through Aya, Kagami, the head of Mikage International's research and development department, intends to use the power of the tennyo for his own agenda.

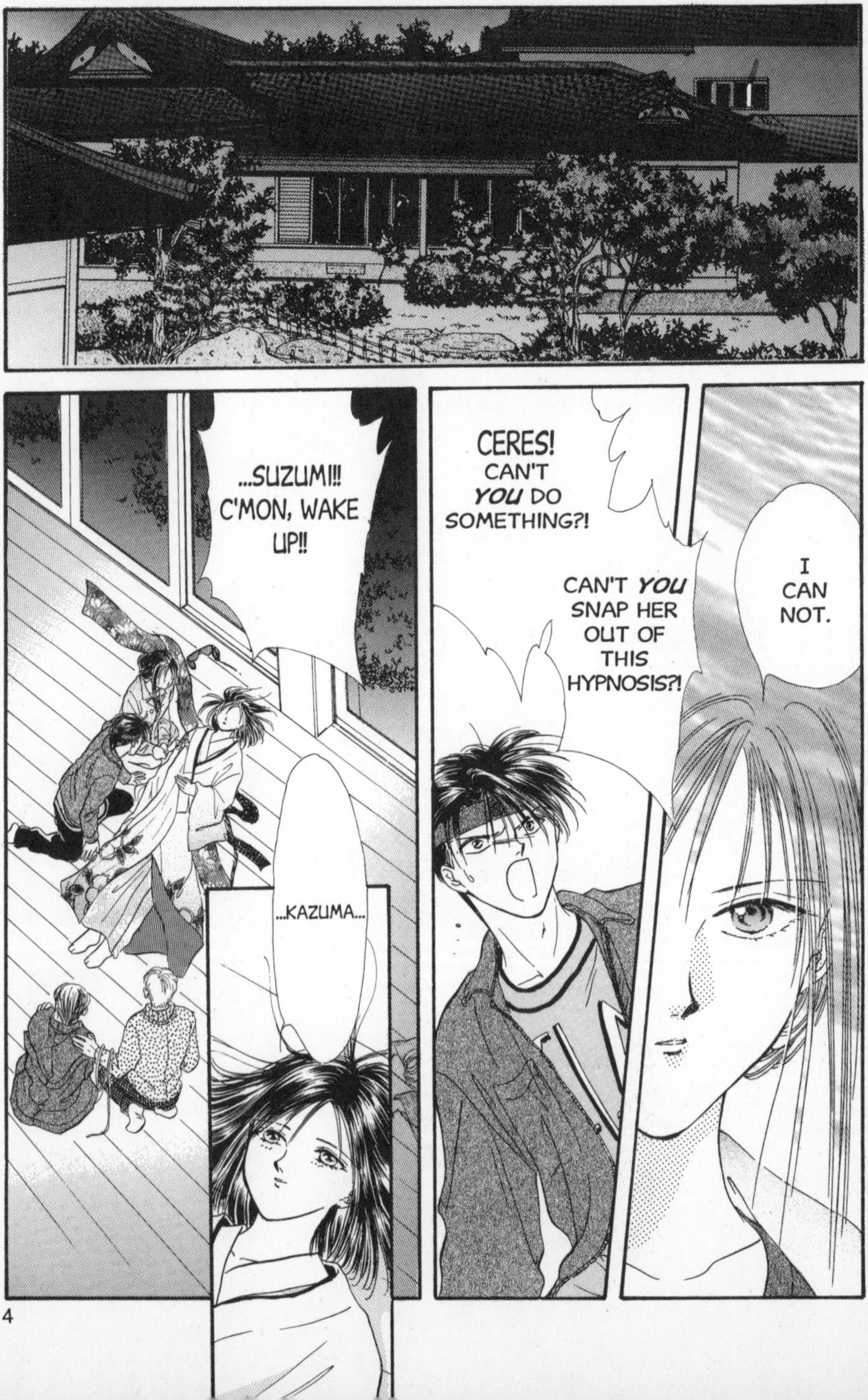

...SUZUMI!! C'MON, WAKE UP!!
...KAZUMA...
CERES! CAN'T *YOU* DO SOMETHING?!
CAN'T *YOU* SNAP HER OUT OF THIS HYPNOSIS?!
I CAN NOT.

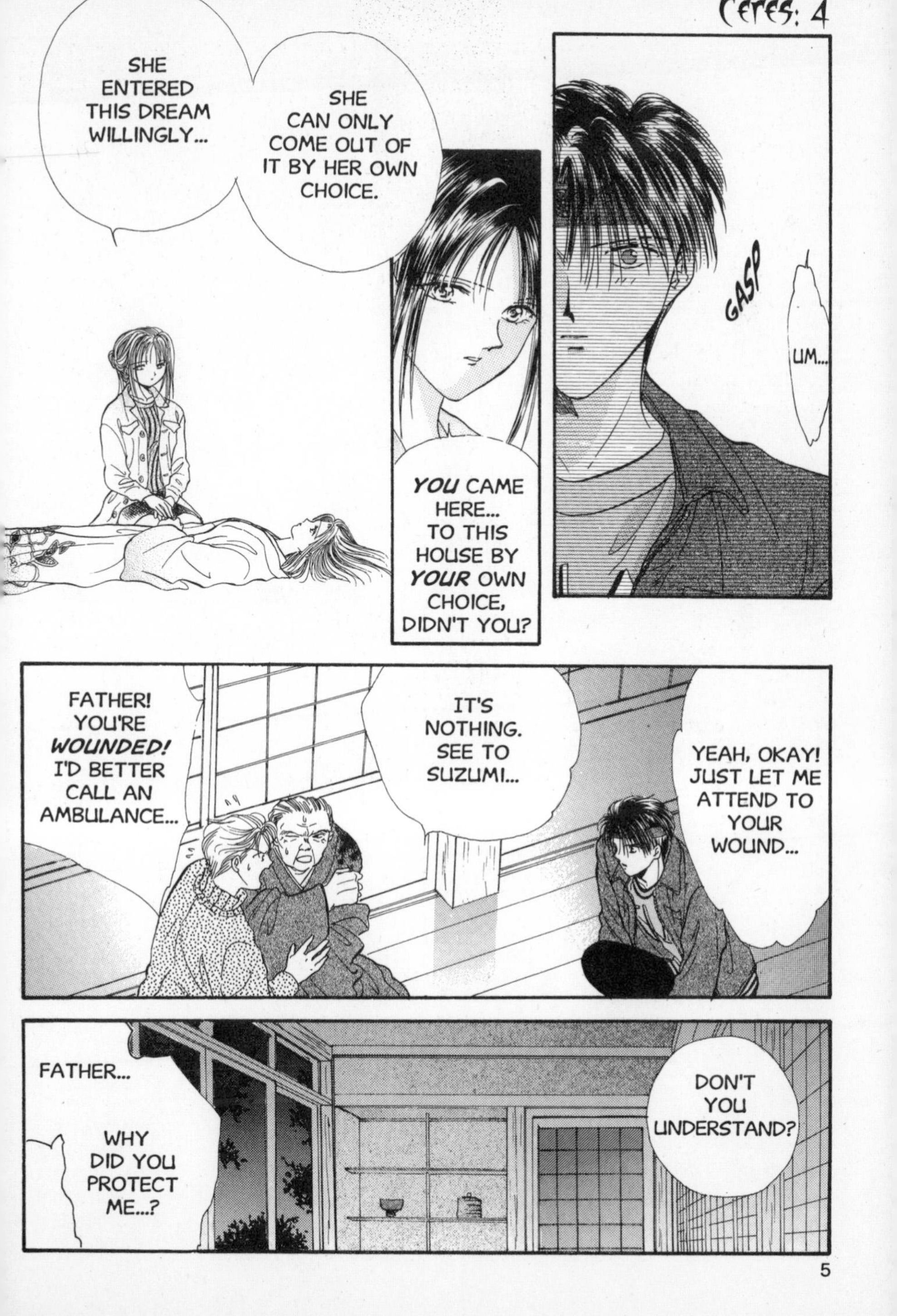
SHE ENTERED THIS DREAM WILLINGLY...
SHE CAN ONLY COME OUT OF IT BY HER OWN CHOICE.
YOU CAME HERE... TO THIS HOUSE BY YOUR OWN CHOICE, DIDN'T YOU?
GASP
UM...
FATHER! YOU'RE WOUNDED! I'D BETTER CALL AN AMBULANCE...
IT'S NOTHING. SEE TO SUZUMI...
YEAH, OKAY! JUST LET ME ATTEND TO YOUR WOUND...
FATHER...
WHY DID YOU PROTECT ME...?
DON'T YOU UNDERSTAND?

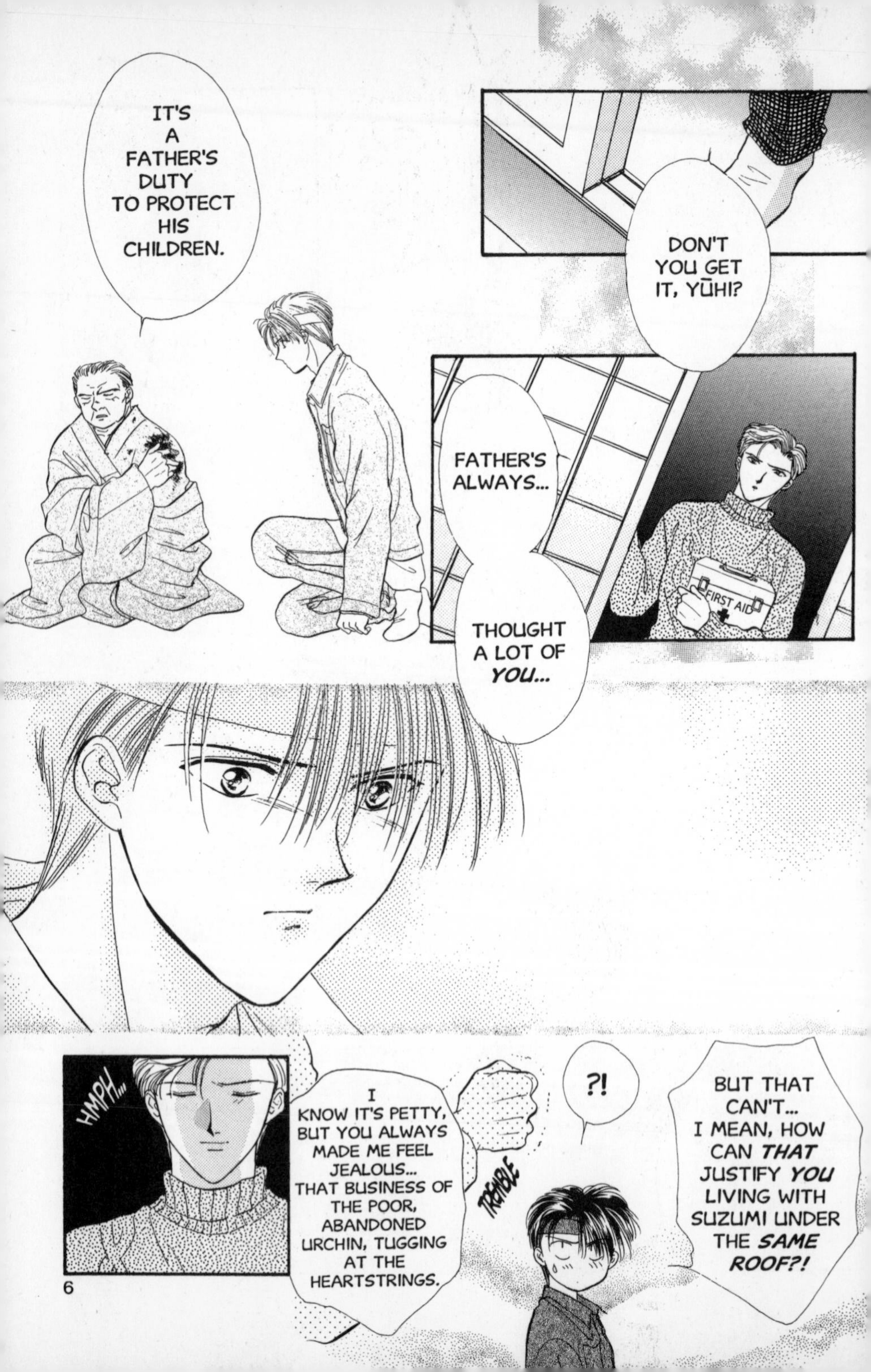
DON'T YOU GET IT, YŪHI?
FATHER'S ALWAYS...
THOUGHT A LOT OF *YOU*...
IT'S A FATHER'S DUTY TO PROTECT HIS CHILDREN.
BUT THAT CAN'T... I MEAN, HOW CAN *THAT* JUSTIFY *YOU* LIVING WITH SUZUMI UNDER THE *SAME ROOF?!*
?!
TREMBLE
I KNOW IT'S PETTY, BUT YOU ALWAYS MADE ME FEEL JEALOUS... THAT BUSINESS OF THE POOR, ABANDONED URCHIN, TUGGING AT THE HEARTSTRINGS.
HMPH...

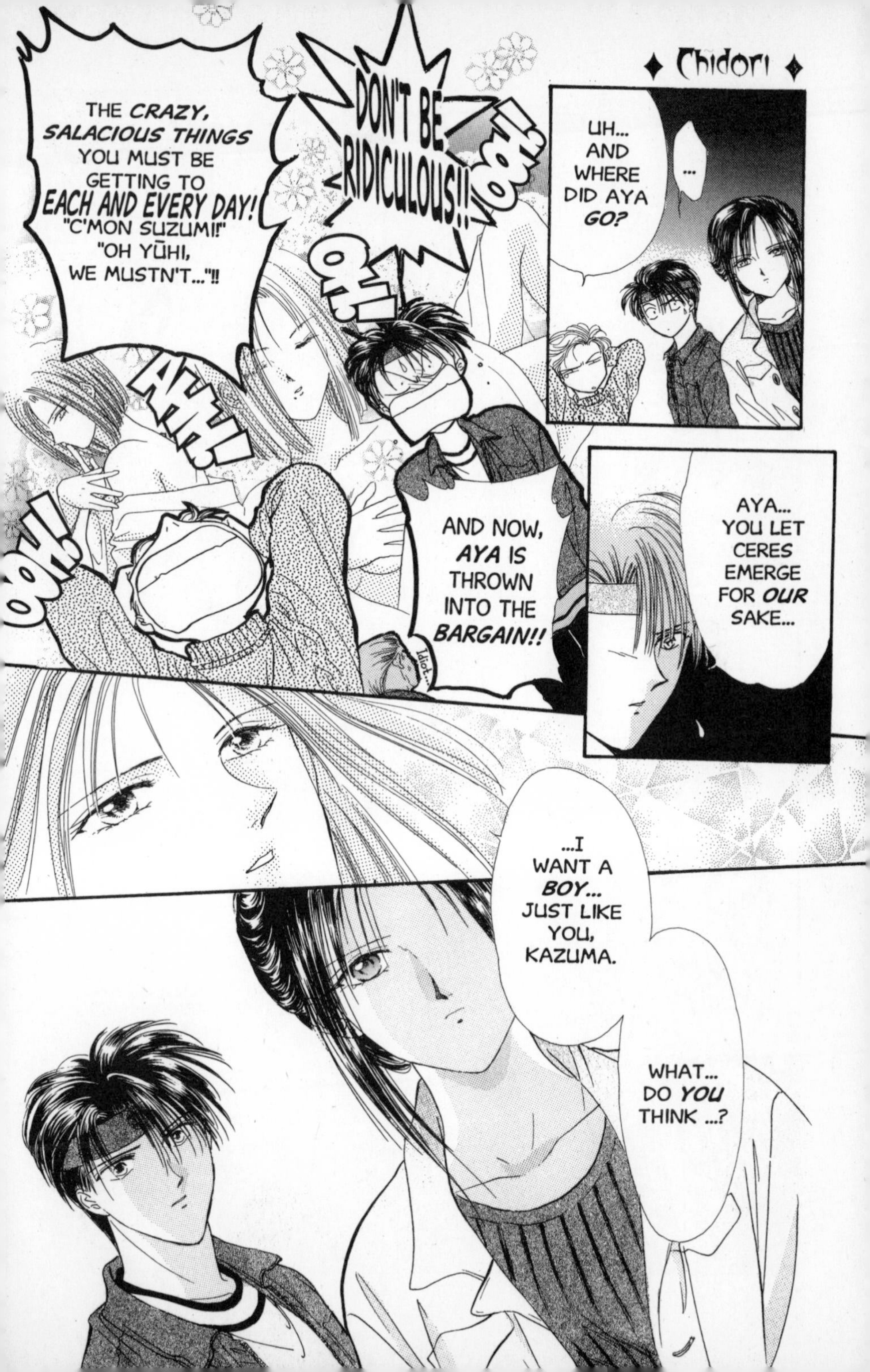
UH... AND WHERE DID AYA GO?
...
THE CRAZY, SALACIOUS THINGS YOU MUST BE GETTING TO EACH AND EVERY DAY! "C'MON SUZUMI!" "OH YŪHI, WE MUSTN'T..."!!
DON'T BE RIDICULOUS!!
OF!
AHH!
OOH!
AND NOW, AYA IS THROWN INTO THE BARGAIN!!
Idiot...
AYA... YOU LET CERES EMERGE FOR OUR SAKE...
...I WANT A BOY... JUST LIKE YOU, KAZUMA.
WHAT... DO YOU THINK ...?

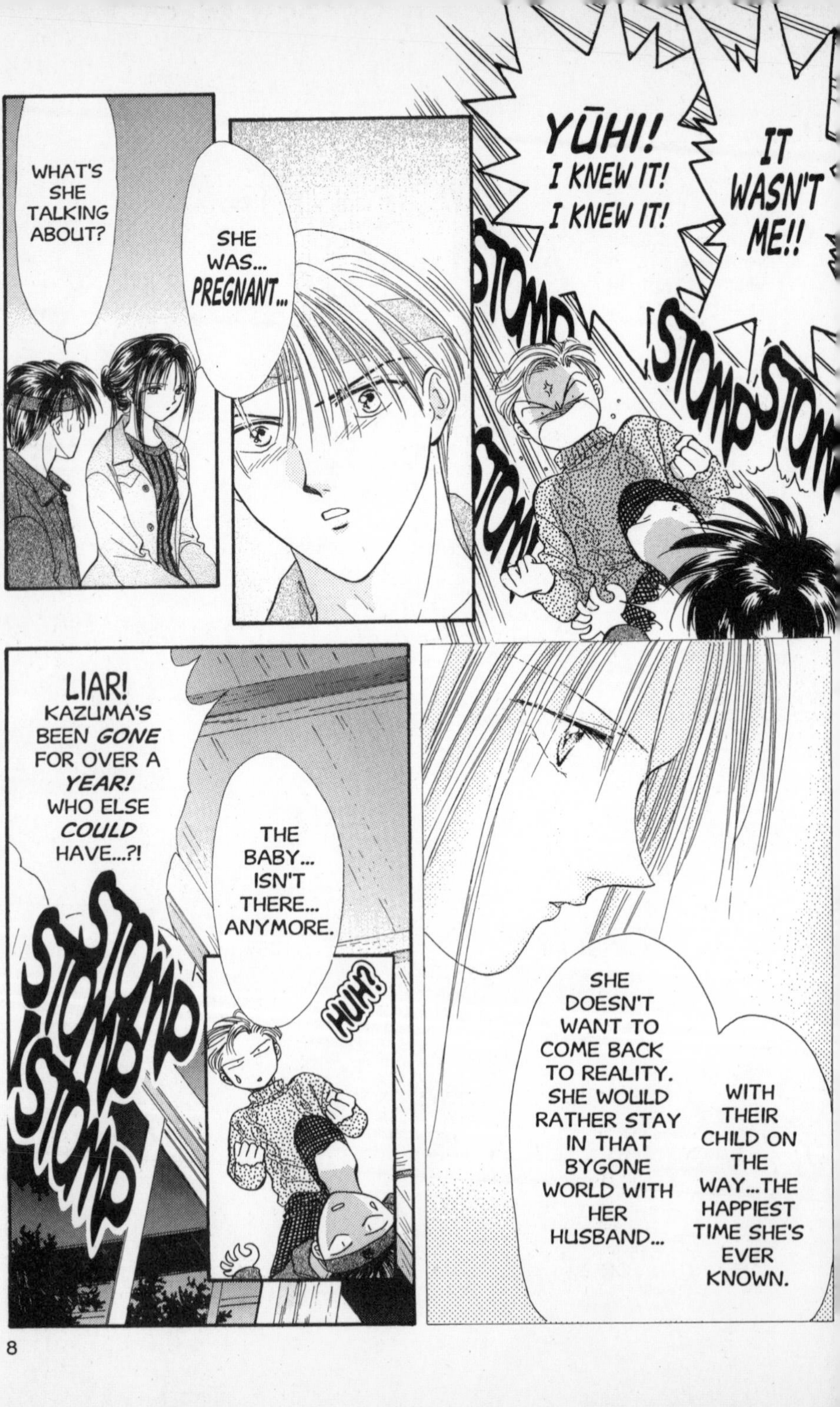
YŪHI! I KNEW IT! I KNEW IT!
IT WASN'T ME!!
STOMP STOMP STOMP STOMP STOMP
SHE WAS... PREGNANT...
WHAT'S SHE TALKING ABOUT?
SHE DOESN'T WANT TO COME BACK TO REALITY. SHE WOULD RATHER STAY IN THAT BYGONE WORLD WITH HER HUSBAND...
WITH THEIR CHILD ON THE WAY...THE HAPPIEST TIME SHE'S EVER KNOWN.
LIAR! KAZUMA'S BEEN *GONE* FOR OVER A *YEAR!* WHO ELSE *COULD* HAVE...?!
THE BABY... ISN'T THERE... ANYMORE.
HUH?
STOMP STOMP STOMP

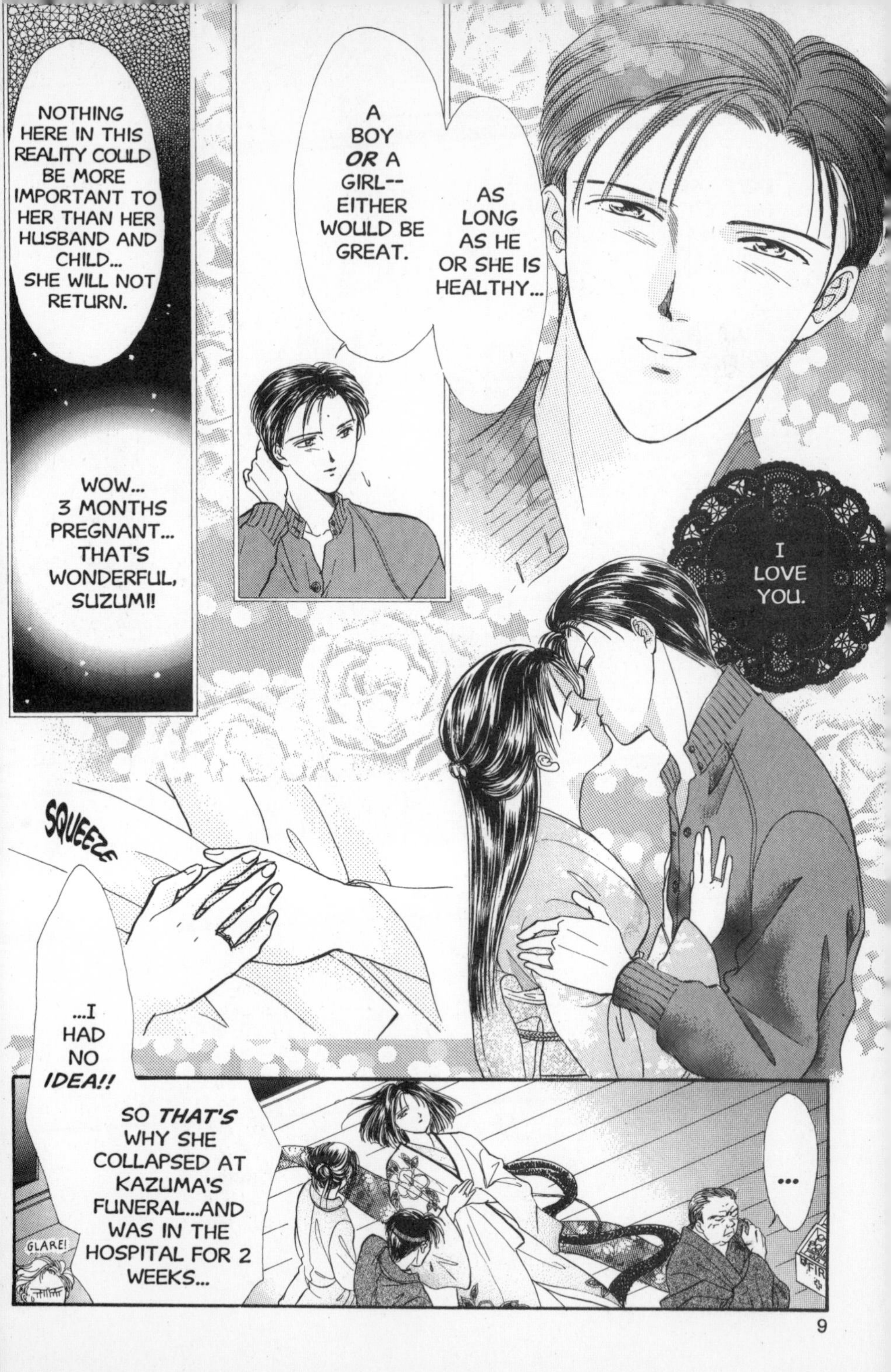

A BOY *OR* A GIRL-- EITHER WOULD BE GREAT.
AS LONG AS HE OR SHE IS HEALTHY...
NOTHING HERE IN THIS REALITY COULD BE MORE IMPORTANT TO HER THAN HER HUSBAND AND CHILD... SHE WILL NOT RETURN.
WOW... 3 MONTHS PREGNANT... THAT'S WONDERFUL, SUZUMI!
I LOVE YOU.
SQUEEZE
...I HAD NO *IDEA!!*
...
SO *THAT'S* WHY SHE COLLAPSED AT KAZUMA'S FUNERAL...AND WAS IN THE HOSPITAL FOR 2 WEEKS...
GLARE!

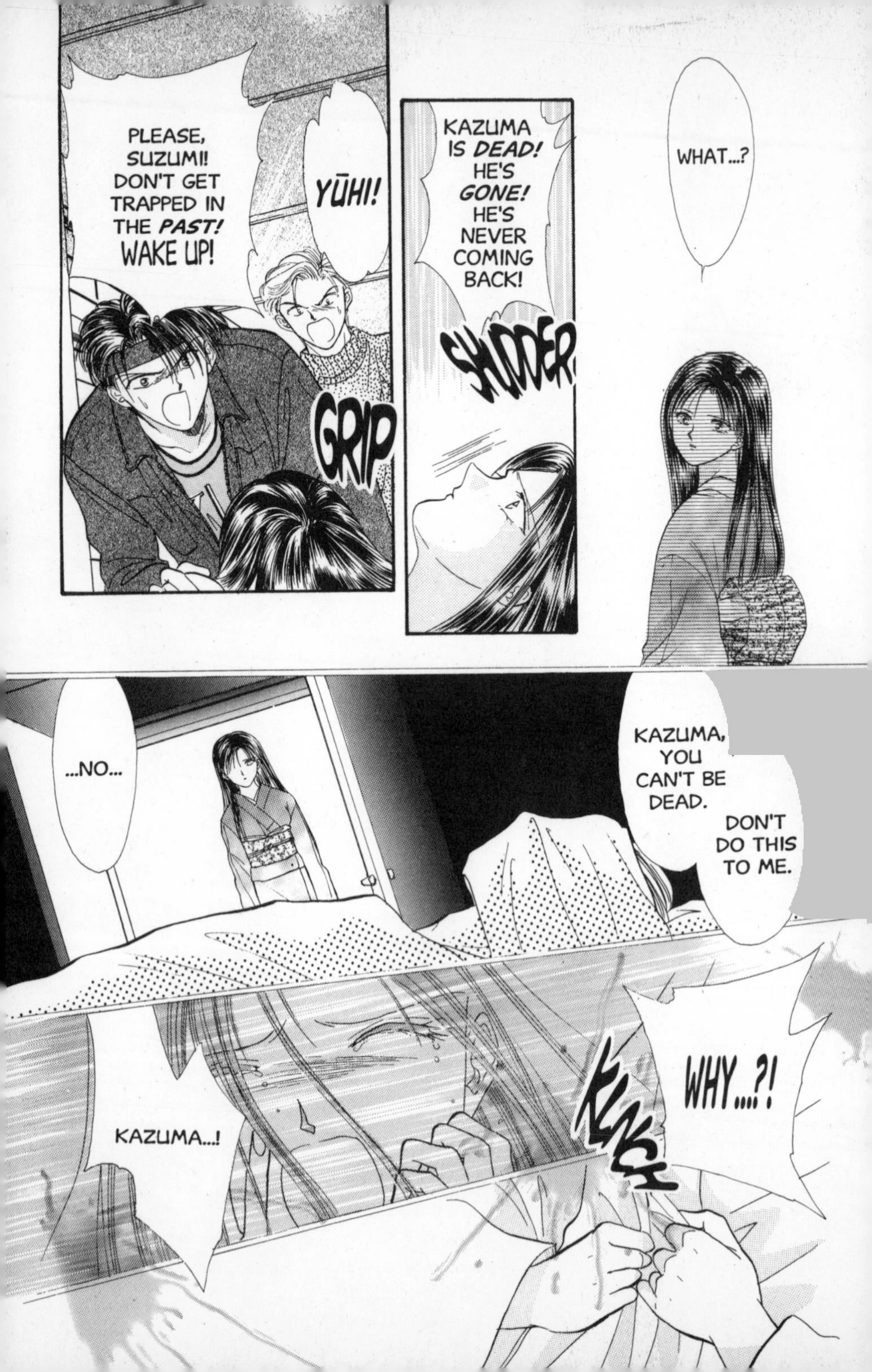
WHAT...?
KAZUMA IS DEAD! HE'S GONE! HE'S NEVER COMING BACK!
SHUDDER!
PLEASE, SUZUMI!! DON'T GET TRAPPED IN THE PAST! WAKE UP!
YŪHI!
GRIP
KAZUMA, YOU CAN'T BE DEAD.
DON'T DO THIS TO ME.
...NO...
WHY...?!
KLINCH
KAZUMA...!

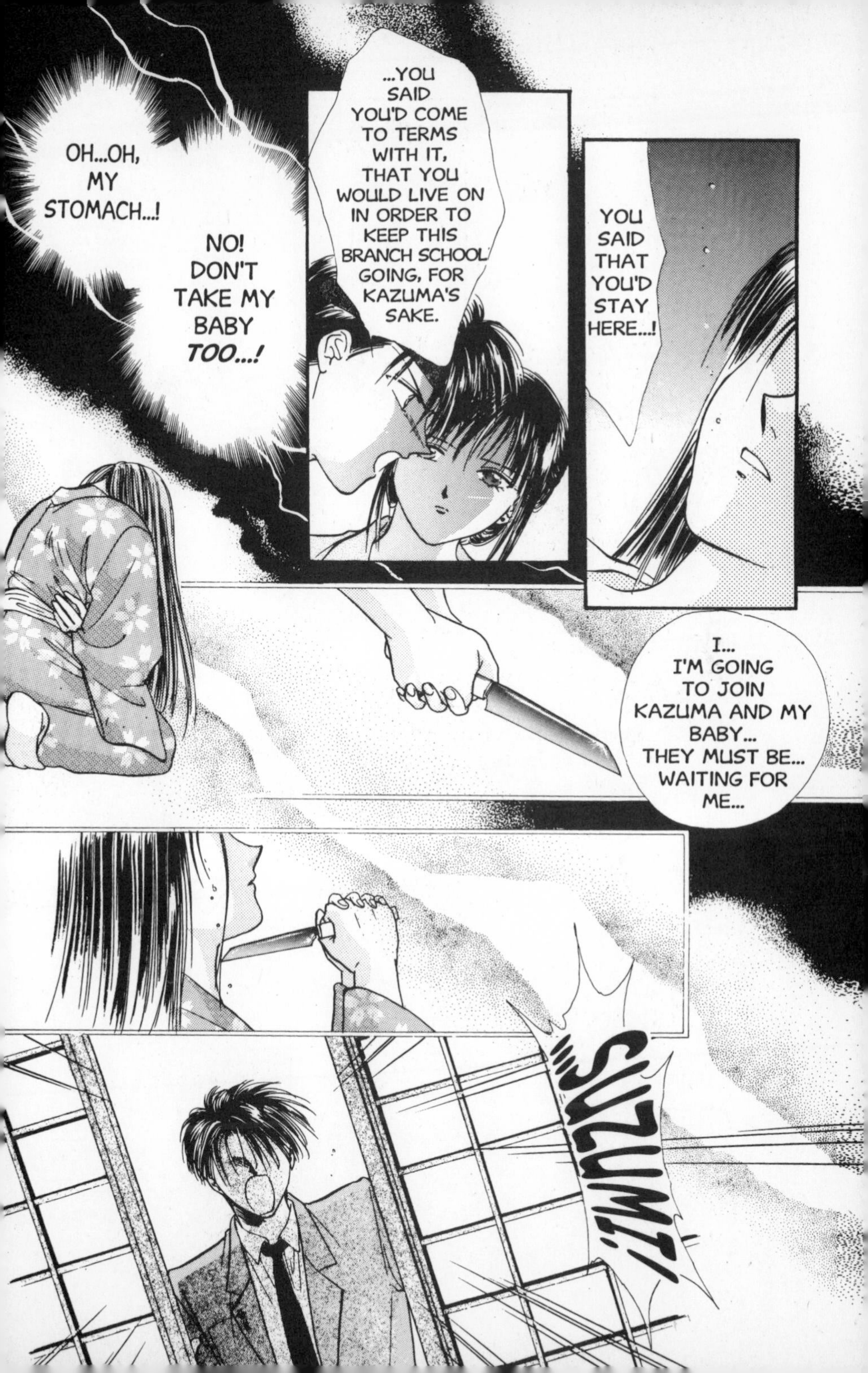
YOU SAID THAT YOU'D STAY HERE...!
...YOU SAID YOU'D COME TO TERMS WITH IT, THAT YOU WOULD LIVE ON IN ORDER TO KEEP THIS BRANCH SCHOOL GOING, FOR KAZUMA'S SAKE.
OH...OH, MY STOMACH...!
NO! DON'T TAKE MY BABY *TOO...!*
I... I'M GOING TO JOIN KAZUMA AND MY BABY... THEY MUST BE... WAITING FOR ME...
SUZUMI!!

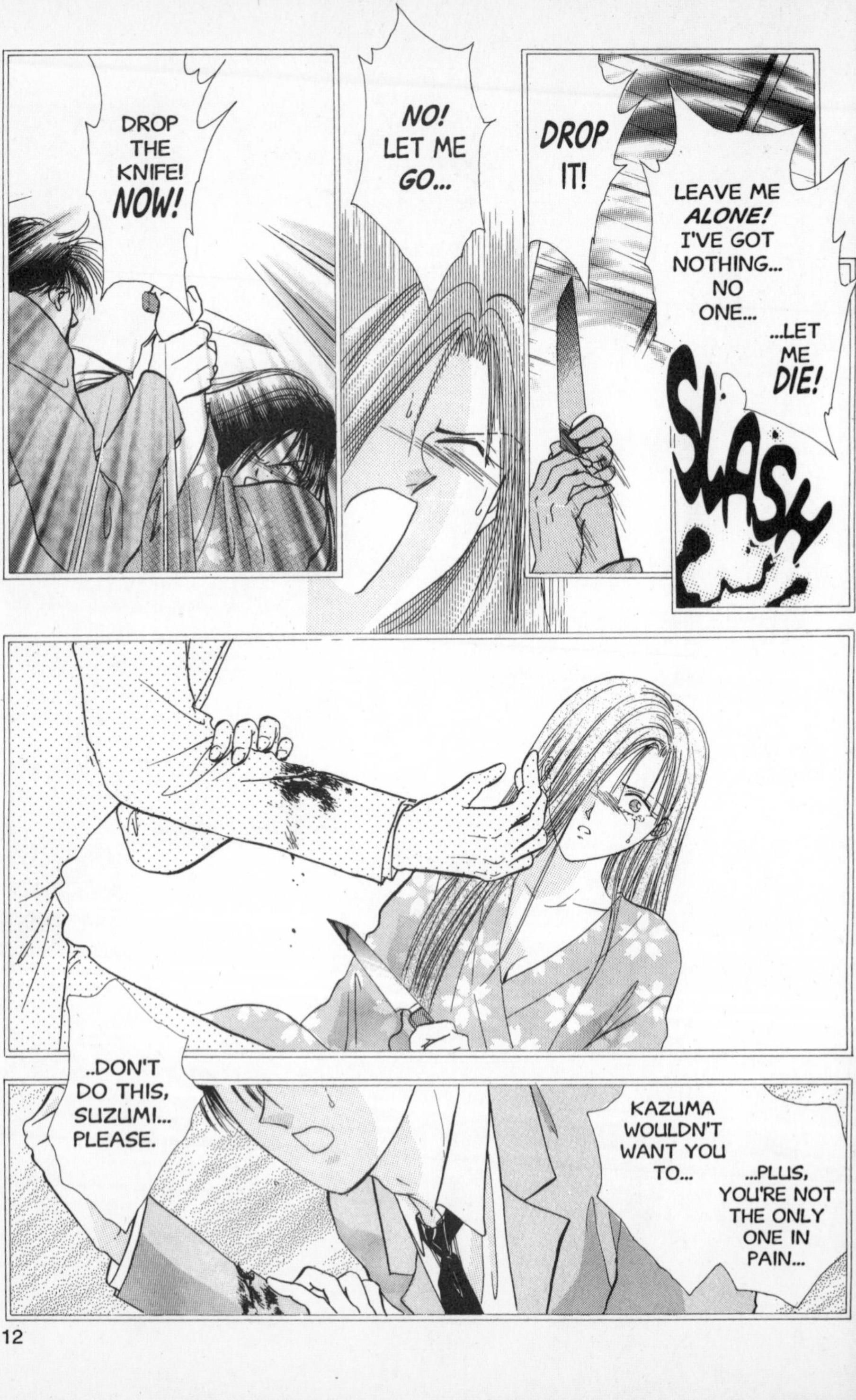
DROP THE KNIFE! NOW!
NO! LET ME GO...
DROP IT!
LEAVE ME ALONE! I'VE GOT NOTHING... NO ONE...
...LET ME DIE!
SLASH
..DON'T DO THIS, SUZUMI... PLEASE.
KAZUMA WOULDN'T WANT YOU TO...
...PLUS, YOU'RE NOT THE ONLY ONE IN PAIN...

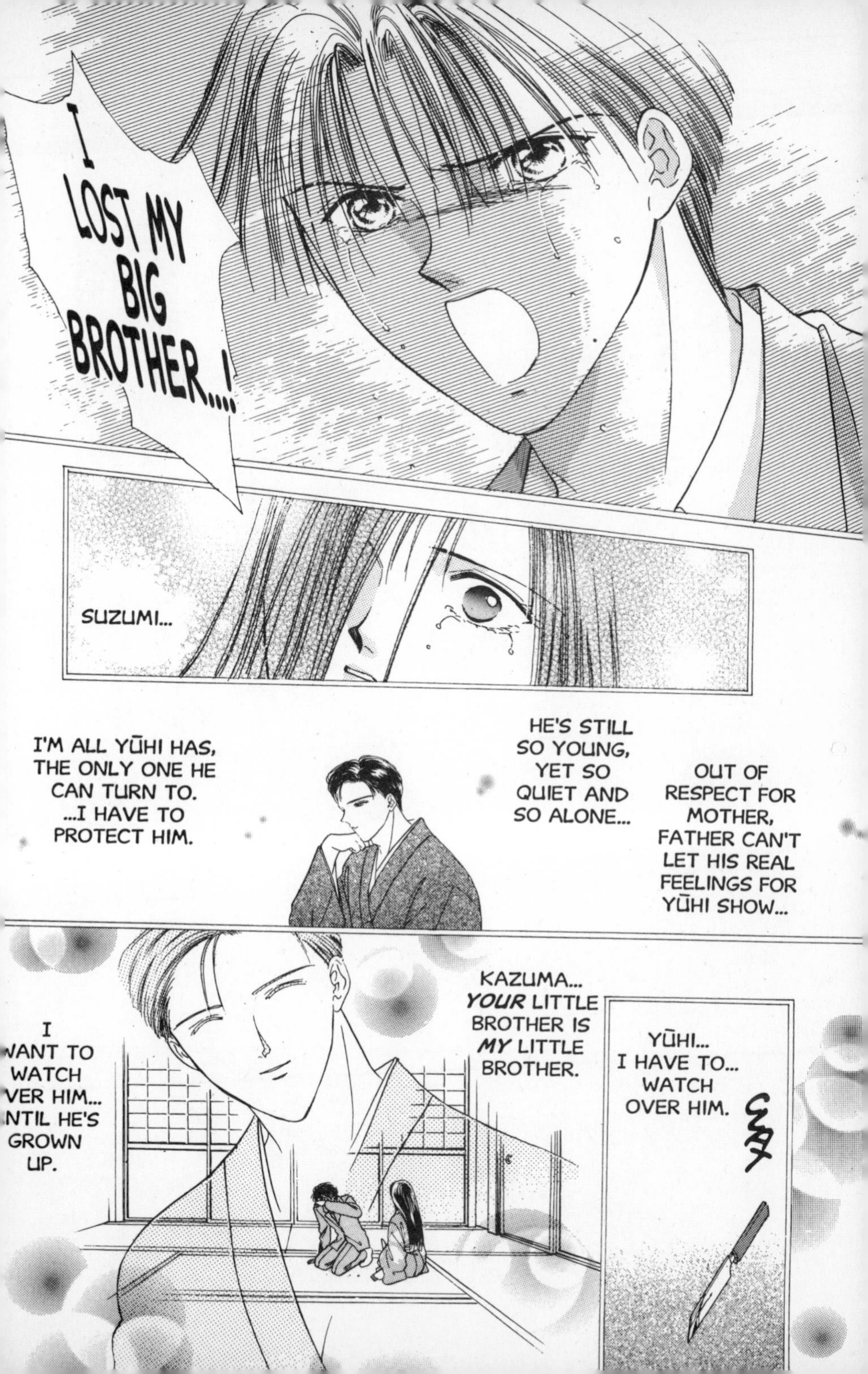
I LOST MY BIG BROTHER...!
SUZUMI...
OUT OF RESPECT FOR MOTHER, FATHER CAN'T LET HIS REAL FEELINGS FOR YŪHI SHOW...
HE'S STILL SO YOUNG, YET SO QUIET AND SO ALONE...
I'M ALL YŪHI HAS, THE ONLY ONE HE CAN TURN TO. ...I HAVE TO PROTECT HIM.
YŪHI... I HAVE TO... WATCH OVER HIM.
KAZUMA... *YOUR* LITTLE BROTHER IS *MY* LITTLE BROTHER.
I WANT TO WATCH VER HIM... NTIL HE'S GROWN UP.

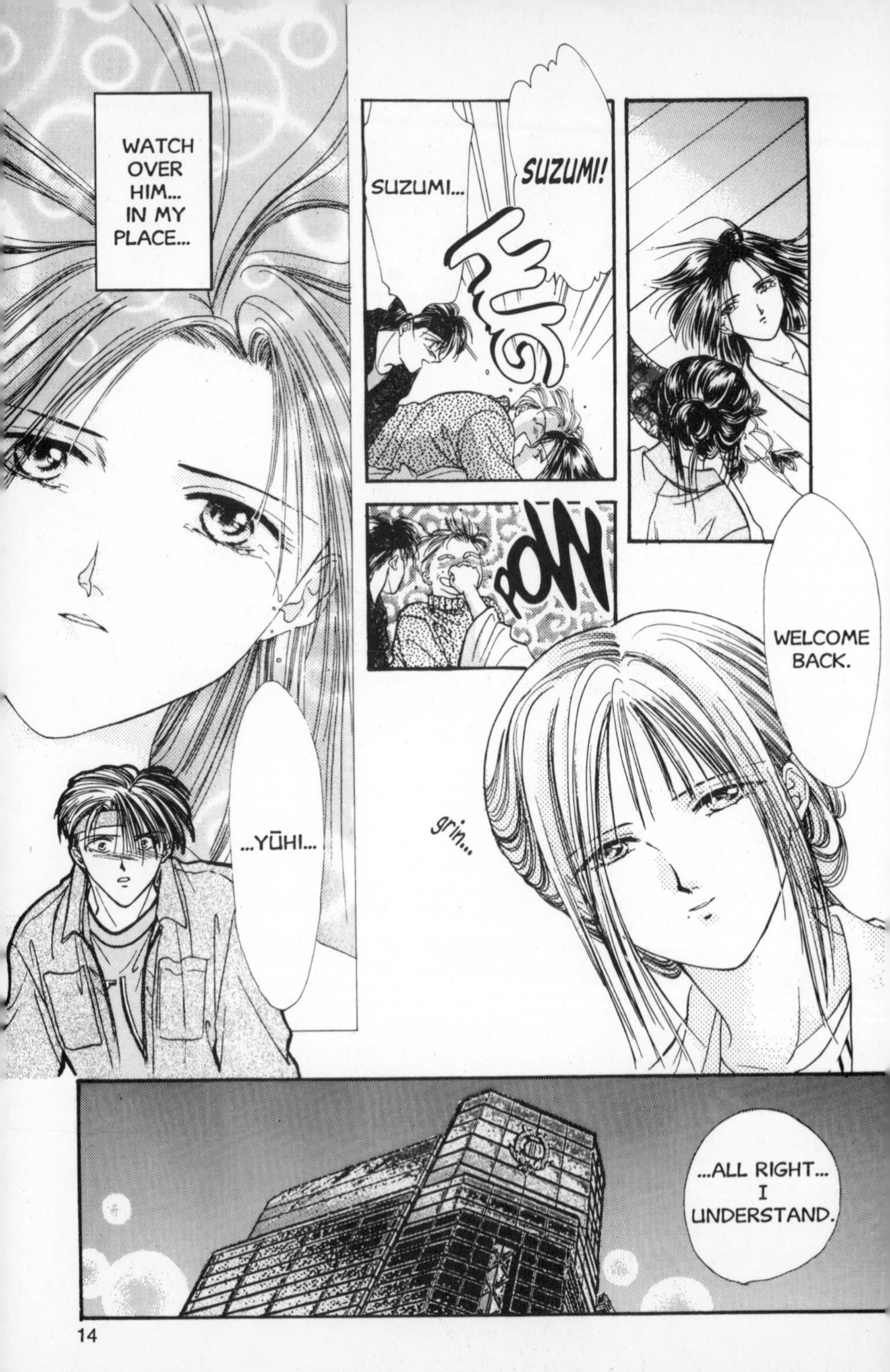
SUZUMI!
SUZUMI...
POW
WELCOME BACK.
grin...
WATCH OVER HIM... IN MY PLACE...
...YŪHI...
...ALL RIGHT... I UNDERSTAND.

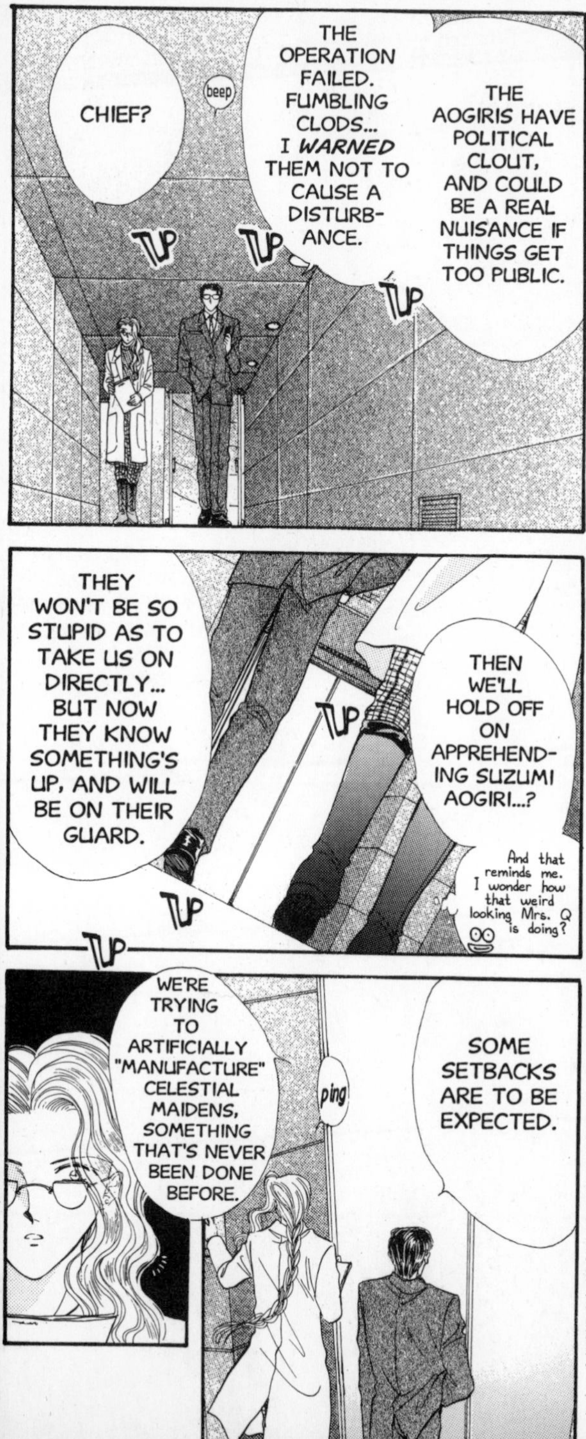
CHIEF?
beep
THE OPERATION FAILED. FUMBLING CLODS... I *WARNED* THEM NOT TO CAUSE A DISTURB-ANCE.
THE AOGIRIS HAVE POLITICAL CLOUT, AND COULD BE A REAL NUISANCE IF THINGS GET TOO PUBLIC.
TUP
TUP
TUP
THEY WON'T BE SO STUPID AS TO TAKE US ON DIRECTLY... BUT NOW THEY KNOW SOMETHING'S UP, AND WILL BE ON THEIR GUARD.
TUP
THEN WE'LL HOLD OFF ON APPREHEND-ING SUZUMI AOGIRI...?
And that reminds me. I wonder how that weird looking Mrs. Q is doing?
TUP
TUP
WE'RE TRYING TO ARTIFICIALLY "MANUFACTURE" CELESTIAL MAIDENS, SOMETHING THAT'S NEVER BEEN DONE BEFORE.
ping
SOME SETBACKS ARE TO BE EXPECTED.

Hello and welcome to the 4th volume of Ceres! Little by little, I'm giving out hints of foreshadowing here and there, but don't mind them - just keep reading. And while I'm working on this series, some sad incidents have been happening, a child has murdered other children, and I feel so bluer than blue... I'm feeling dark blue. So I was talking about it all with my assistants, and our opinion was that "it's unreasonable for adults to try and understand what a child is thinking." People forget as they get older that they had unexpected dark sides to themselves when they were in middle school and high school. That's because as adults we're too concerned with making a living. As I was talking with my assistants about how we ourselves used to think back when we were children, I remembered that I wanted psychic powers. I wanted powers others didn't have that would let me get back at people I didn't like. I wanted to become a completely different person, and I really wished that there could be someone who could truly understand me, even if it were a ghost or goblin. I had totally forgotten about all that. After I realized that psychic powers wouldn't bring me happiness, I turned those ideas into concepts for manga. Maybe that's what it means to grow up? Anyway, now I wonder where all that middle school anger swirling inside me like hot magma came from. Last time, I said, "you should go to school"... but I can say that in retrospect, because I don't have to go to school anymore. I **hated** school. I liked studying -well, I didn't mind it- but the social life just wasn't my thing. Is that just because I don't like to cooperate with others? They do say that people with blood type B aren't the best team players... Why am I talking about such heavy stuff...? Well, I'll continue in the next sidebar...

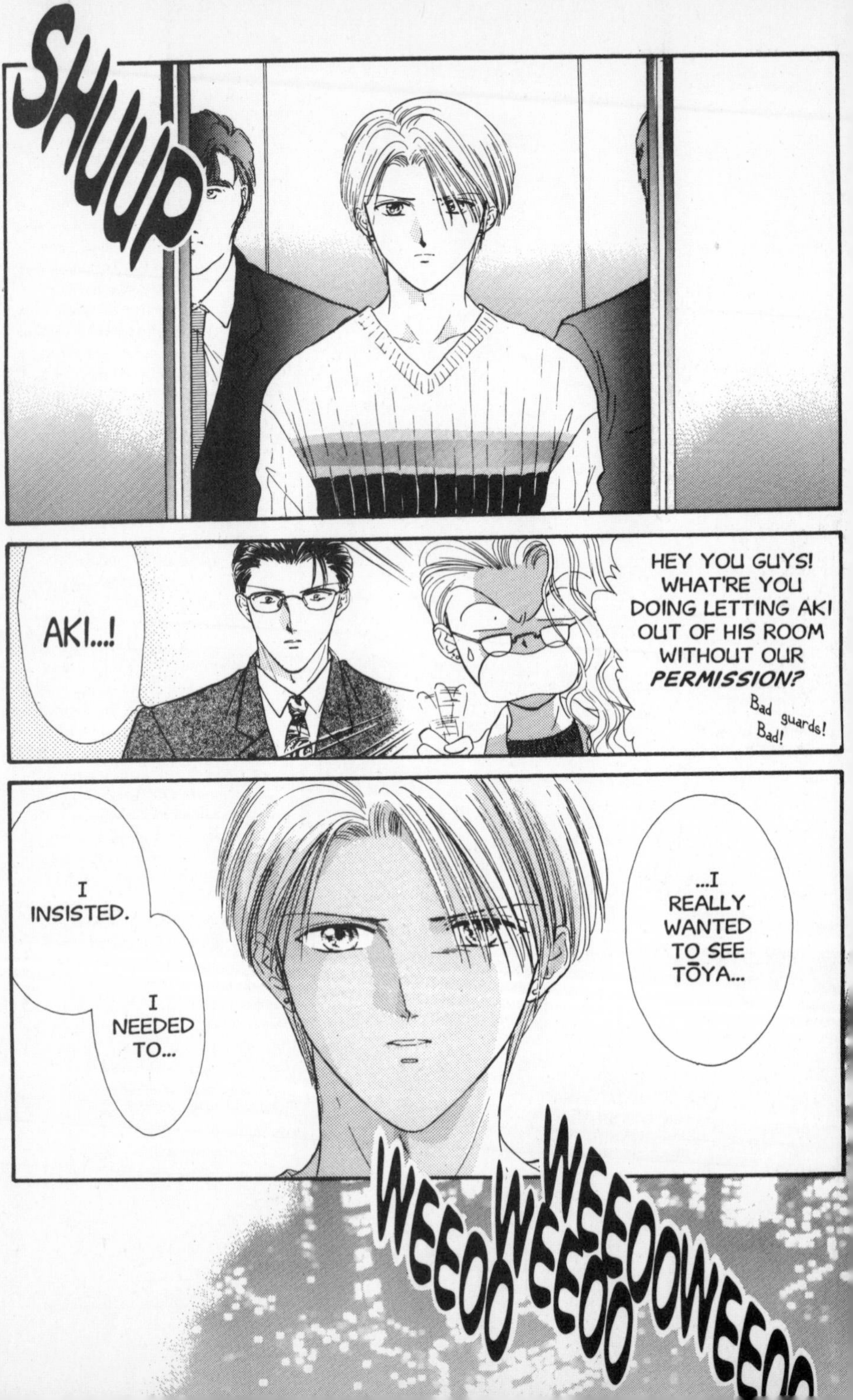
SHUUP
HEY YOU GUYS! WHAT'RE YOU DOING LETTING AKI OUT OF HIS ROOM WITHOUT OUR PERMISSION?
Bad guards! Bad!
AKI...!
...I REALLY WANTED TO SEE TŌYA...
I INSISTED.
I NEEDED TO...
WEEOOWEEOO
WEEOO WEEOO

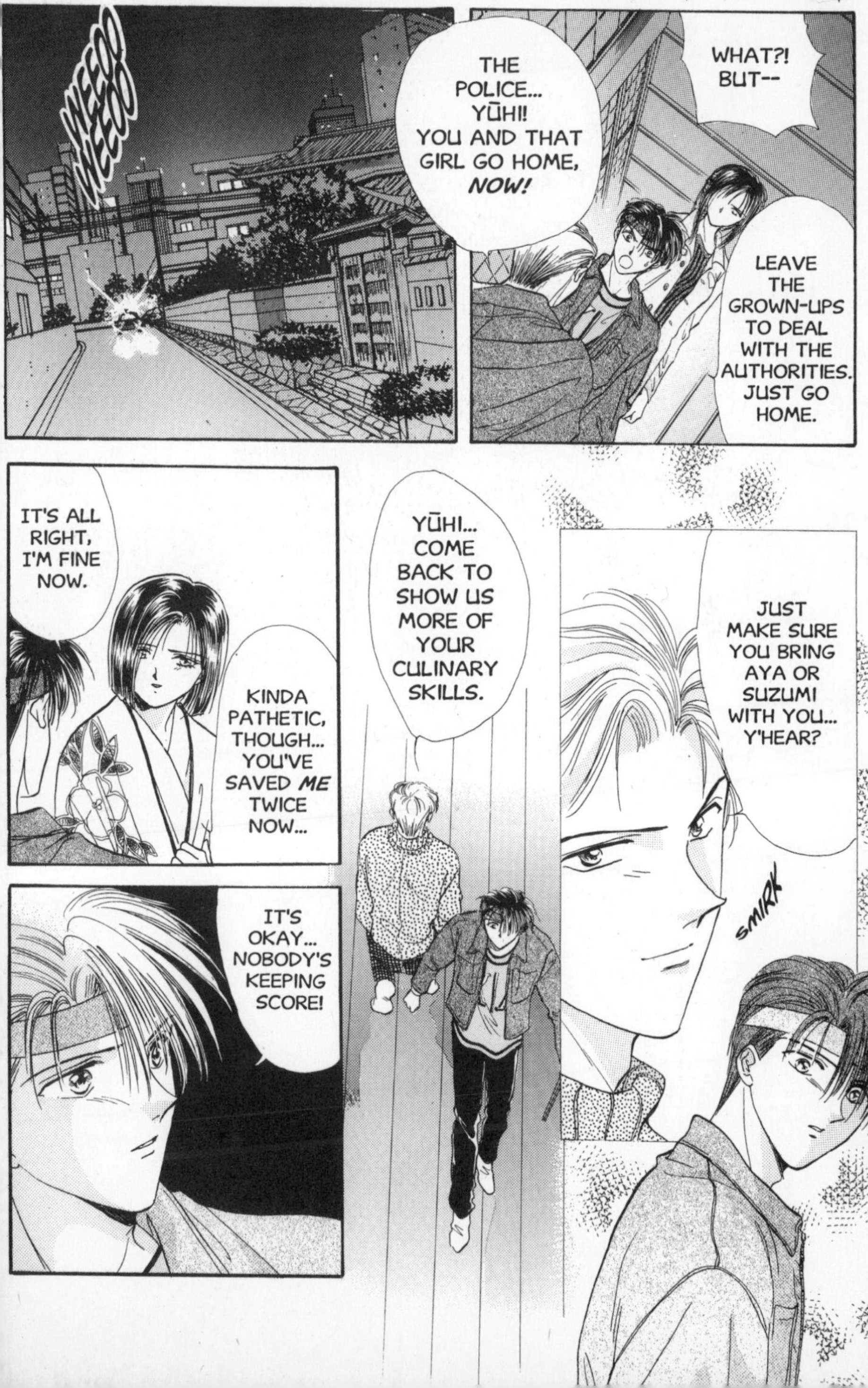
THE POLICE... YŪHI! YOU AND THAT GIRL GO HOME, *NOW!*
WHAT?! BUT--
LEAVE THE GROWN-UPS TO DEAL WITH THE AUTHORITIES. JUST GO HOME.
WEEOO WEEOO
YŪHI... COME BACK TO SHOW US MORE OF YOUR CULINARY SKILLS.
JUST MAKE SURE YOU BRING AYA OR SUZUMI WITH YOU... Y'HEAR?
SMIRK
IT'S ALL RIGHT, I'M FINE NOW.
KINDA PATHETIC, THOUGH... YOU'VE SAVED *ME* TWICE NOW...
IT'S OKAY... NOBODY'S KEEPING SCORE!

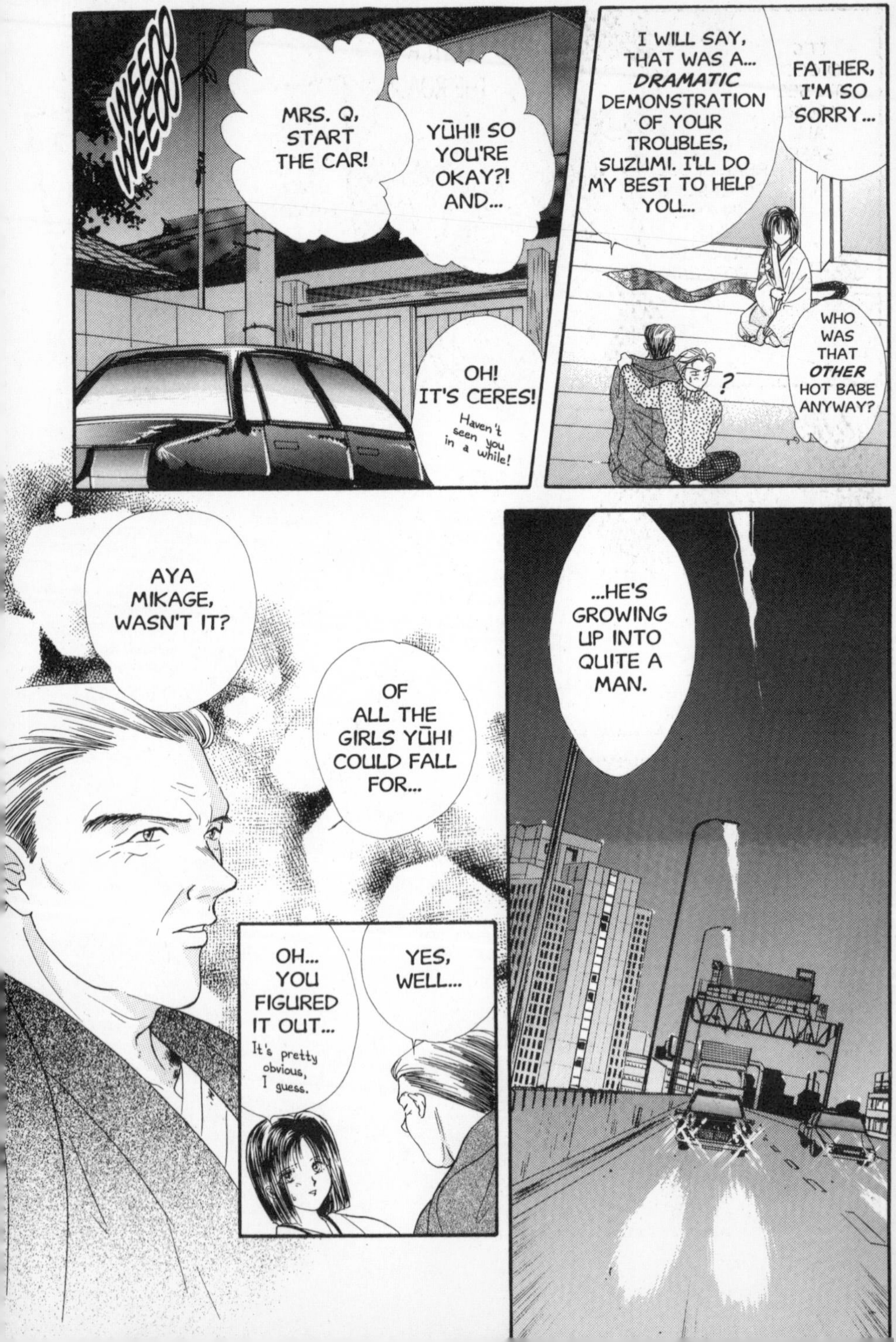
FATHER, I'M SO SORRY...
I WILL SAY, THAT WAS A... ***DRAMATIC*** DEMONSTRATION OF YOUR TROUBLES, SUZUMI. I'LL DO MY BEST TO HELP YOU...
?
WHO WAS THAT ***OTHER*** HOT BABE ANYWAY?
YŪHI! SO YOU'RE OKAY?! AND...
MRS. Q, START THE CAR!
WEEOO WEEOO
OH! IT'S CERES!
Haven't seen you in a while!
...HE'S GROWING UP INTO QUITE A MAN.
AYA MIKAGE, WASN'T IT?
OF ALL THE GIRLS YŪHI COULD FALL FOR...
YES, WELL...
OH... YOU FIGURED IT OUT...
It's pretty obvious, I guess.

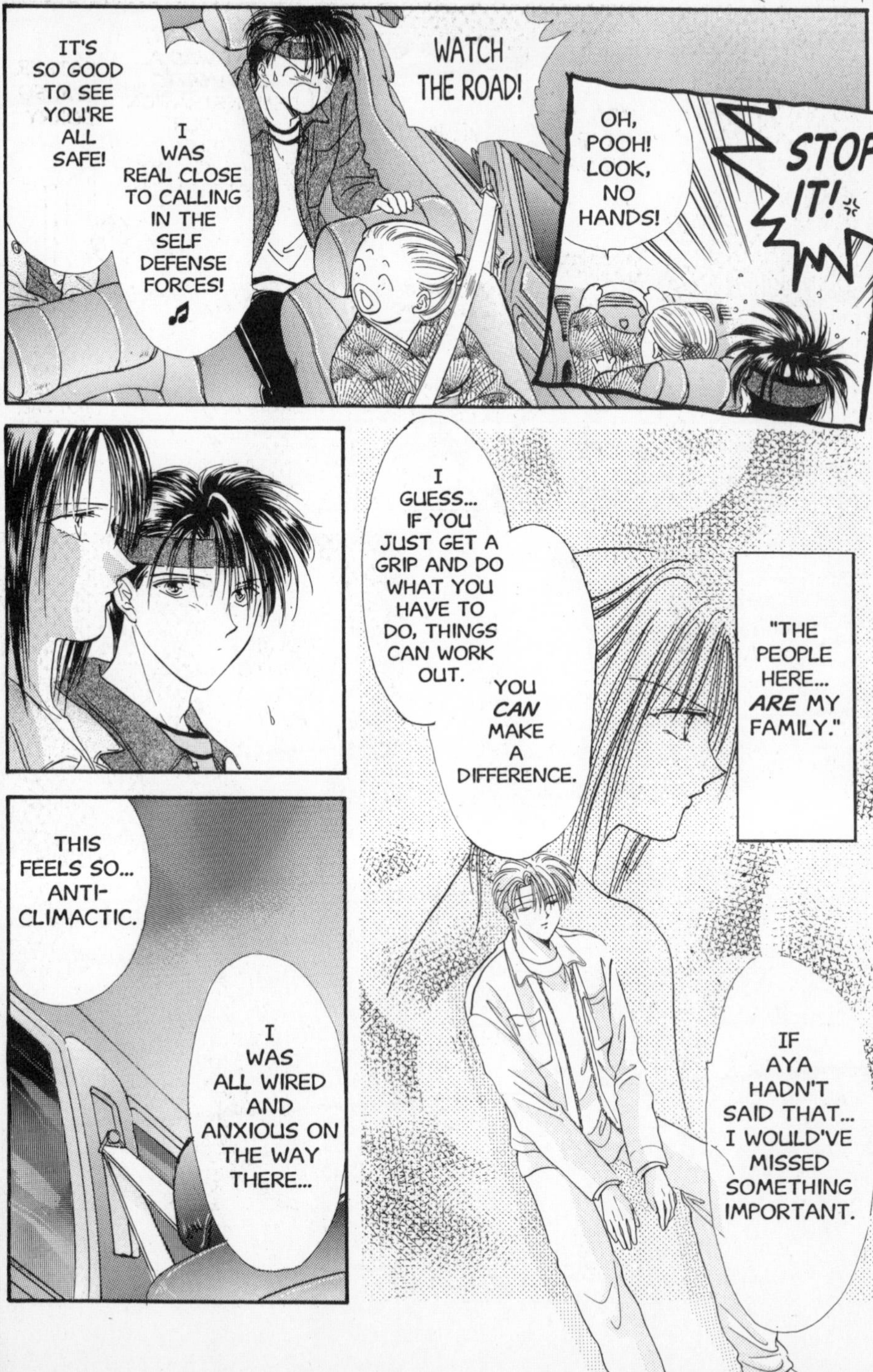
IT'S SO GOOD TO SEE YOU'RE ALL SAFE!
I WAS REAL CLOSE TO CALLING IN THE SELF DEFENSE FORCES! ♪
WATCH THE ROAD!
OH, POOH! LOOK, NO HANDS!
STOP IT!
THIS FEELS SO... ANTI-CLIMACTIC.
I WAS ALL WIRED AND ANXIOUS ON THE WAY THERE...
I GUESS... IF YOU JUST GET A GRIP AND DO WHAT YOU HAVE TO DO, THINGS CAN WORK OUT.
YOU *CAN* MAKE A DIFFERENCE.
"THE PEOPLE HERE... *ARE* MY FAMILY."
IF AYA HADN'T SAID THAT... I WOULD'VE MISSED SOMETHING IMPORTANT.

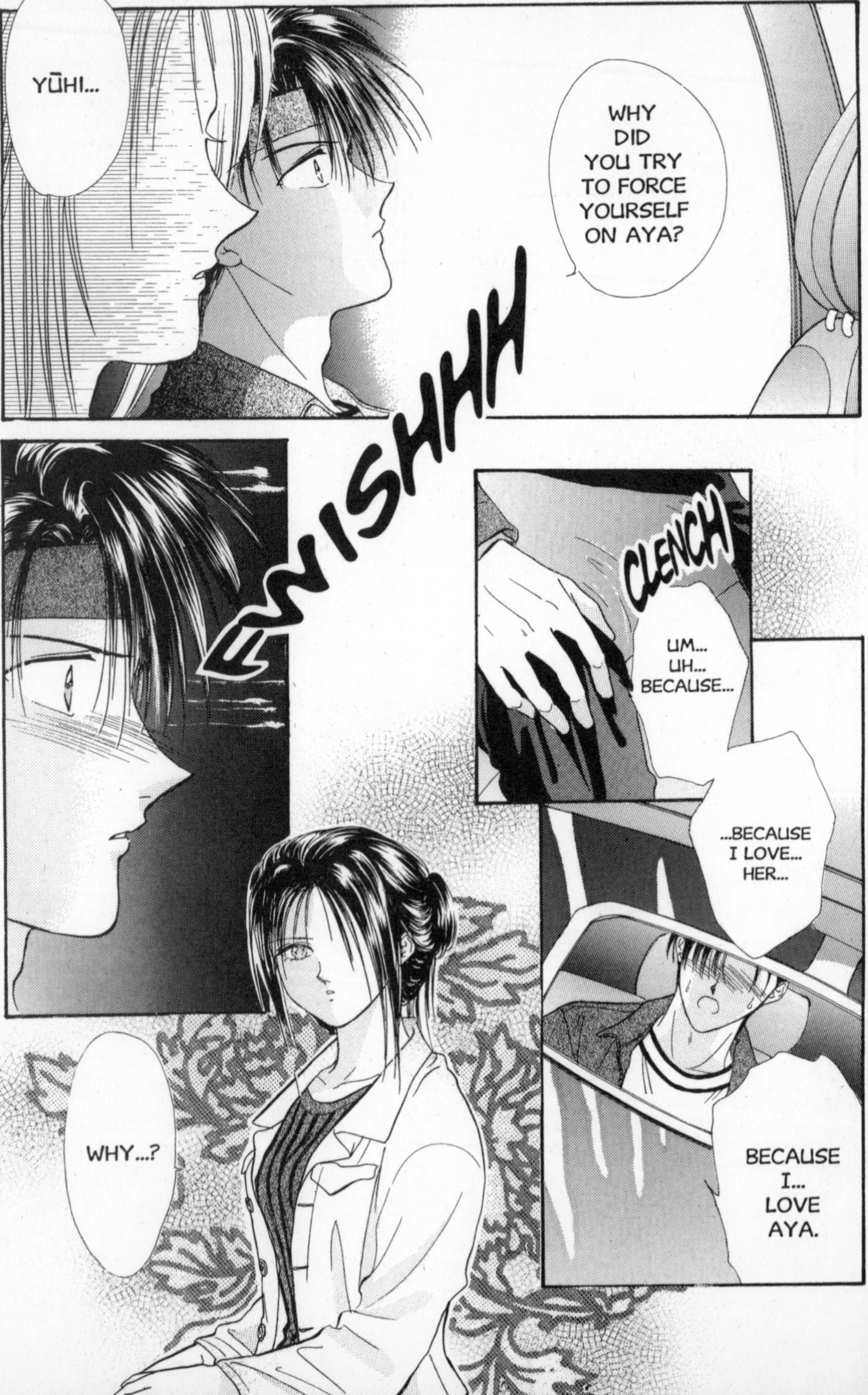
WHY DID YOU TRY TO FORCE YOURSELF ON AYA?
YŪHI...
SWISHHH
CLENCH
UM... UH... BECAUSE...
...BECAUSE I LOVE... HER...
BECAUSE I... LOVE AYA.
WHY...?

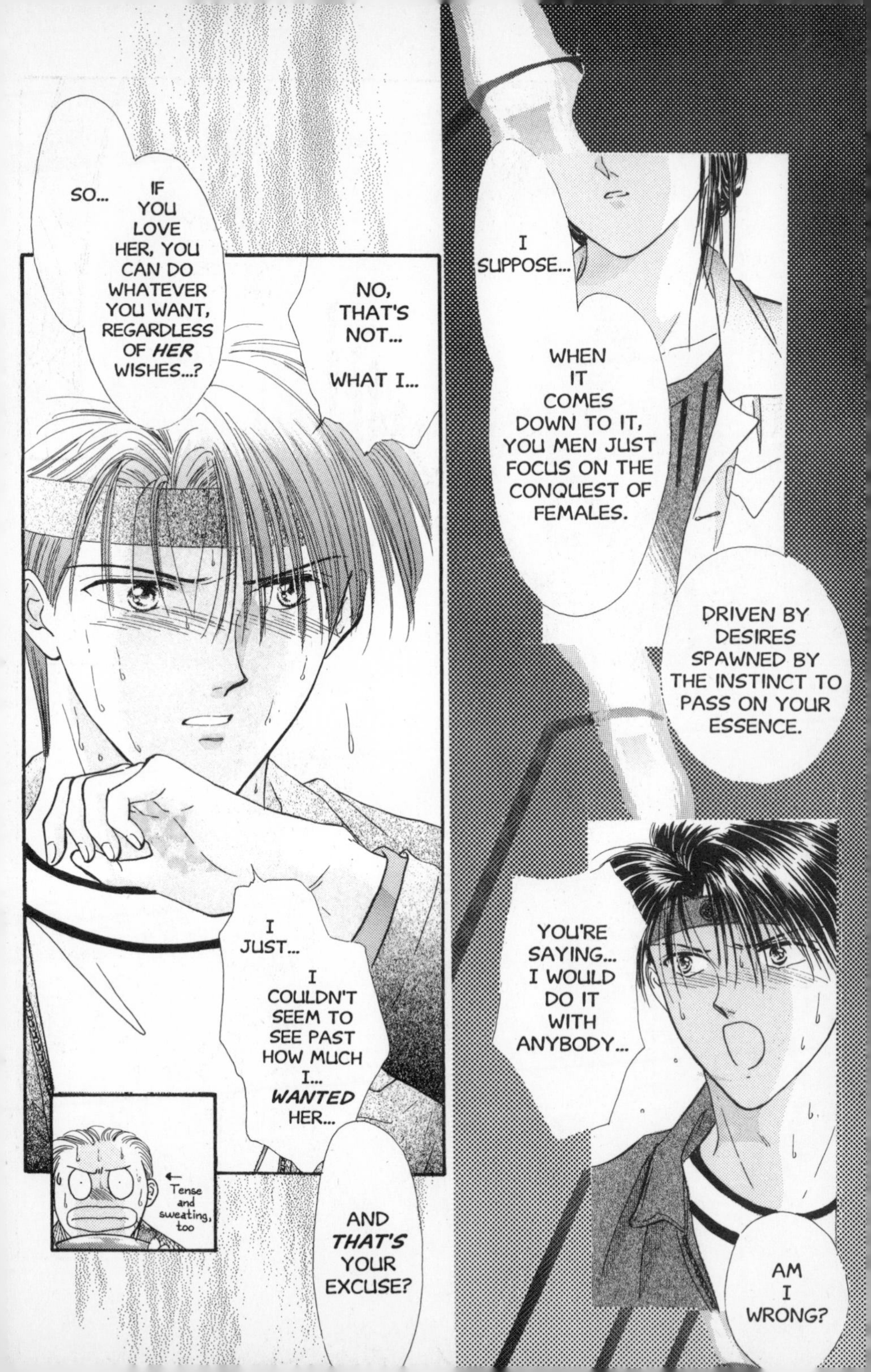
I SUPPOSE...
WHEN IT COMES DOWN TO IT, YOU MEN JUST FOCUS ON THE CONQUEST OF FEMALES.
DRIVEN BY DESIRES SPAWNED BY THE INSTINCT TO PASS ON YOUR ESSENCE.
YOU'RE SAYING... I WOULD DO IT WITH ANYBODY...
AM I WRONG?
SO...
IF YOU LOVE HER, YOU CAN DO WHATEVER YOU WANT, REGARDLESS OF *HER* WISHES...?
NO, THAT'S NOT...
WHAT I...
I JUST...
I COULDN'T SEEM TO SEE PAST HOW MUCH I... ***WANTED*** HER...
AND ***THAT'S*** YOUR EXCUSE?
← Tense and sweating, too

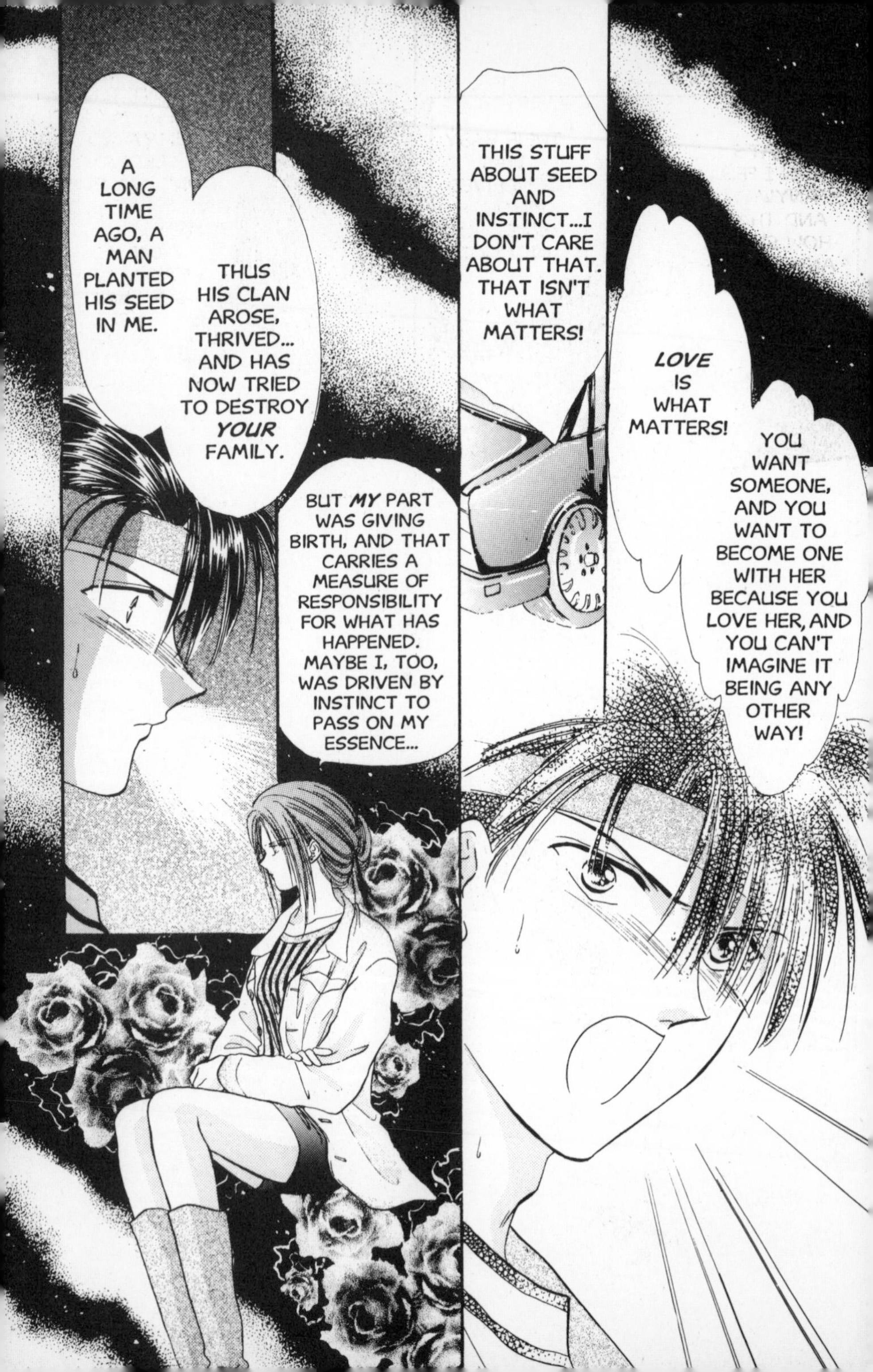
A LONG TIME AGO, A MAN PLANTED HIS SEED IN ME.
THUS HIS CLAN AROSE, THRIVED... AND HAS NOW TRIED TO DESTROY *YOUR* FAMILY.
BUT *MY* PART WAS GIVING BIRTH, AND THAT CARRIES A MEASURE OF RESPONSIBILITY FOR WHAT HAS HAPPENED. MAYBE I, TOO, WAS DRIVEN BY INSTINCT TO PASS ON MY ESSENCE...
THIS STUFF ABOUT SEED AND INSTINCT...I DON'T CARE ABOUT THAT. THAT ISN'T WHAT MATTERS!
LOVE IS WHAT MATTERS!
YOU WANT SOMEONE, AND YOU WANT TO BECOME ONE WITH HER BECAUSE YOU LOVE HER, AND YOU CAN'T IMAGINE IT BEING ANY OTHER WAY!

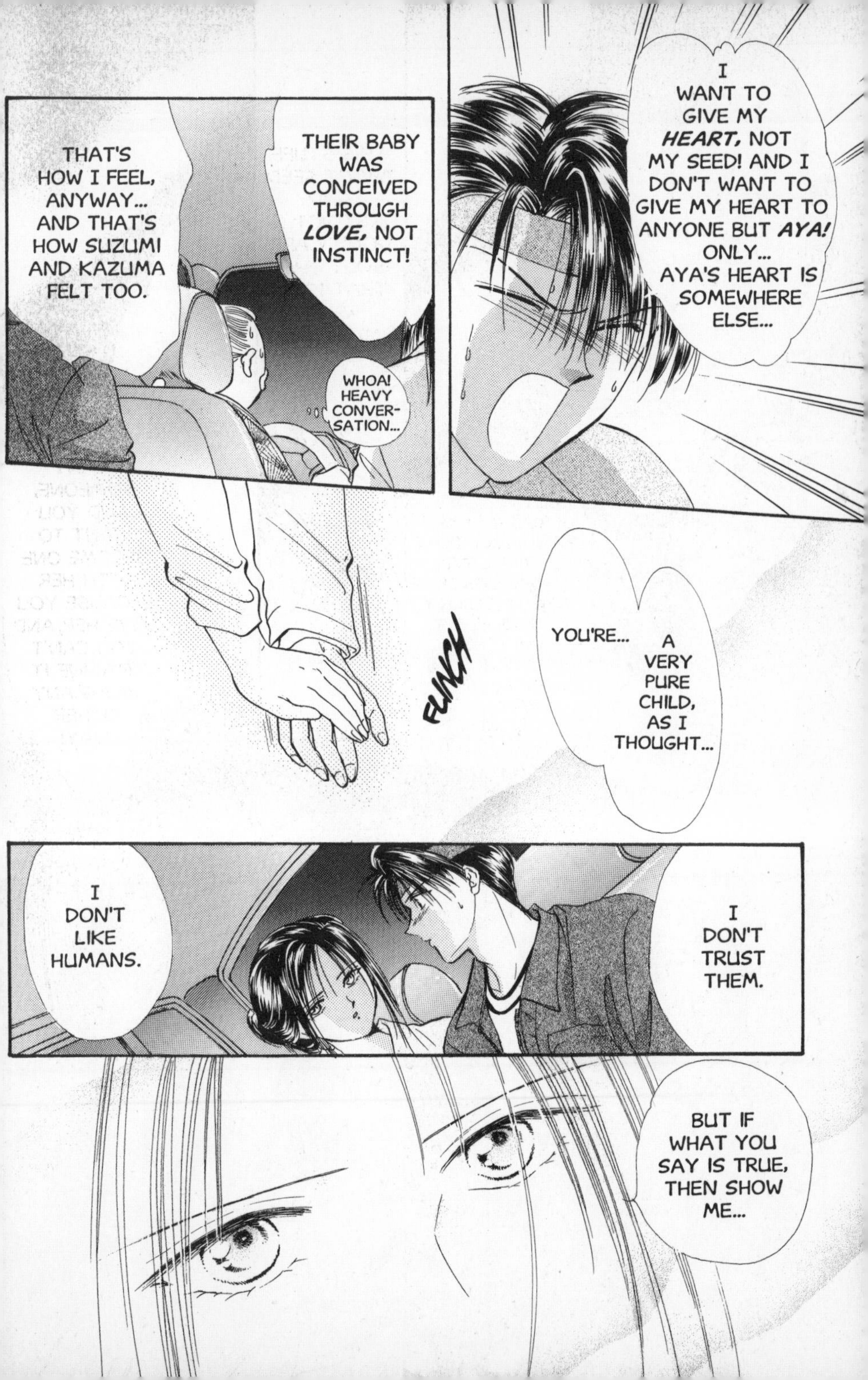
I WANT TO GIVE MY HEART, NOT MY SEED! AND I DON'T WANT TO GIVE MY HEART TO ANYONE BUT AYA! ONLY... AYA'S HEART IS SOMEWHERE ELSE...
THEIR BABY WAS CONCEIVED THROUGH LOVE, NOT INSTINCT!
THAT'S HOW I FEEL, ANYWAY... AND THAT'S HOW SUZUMI AND KAZUMA FELT TOO.
WHOA! HEAVY CONVER-SATION...
YOU'RE... A VERY PURE CHILD, AS I THOUGHT...
FLINCH
I DON'T TRUST THEM.
I DON'T LIKE HUMANS.
BUT IF WHAT YOU SAY IS TRUE, THEN SHOW ME...

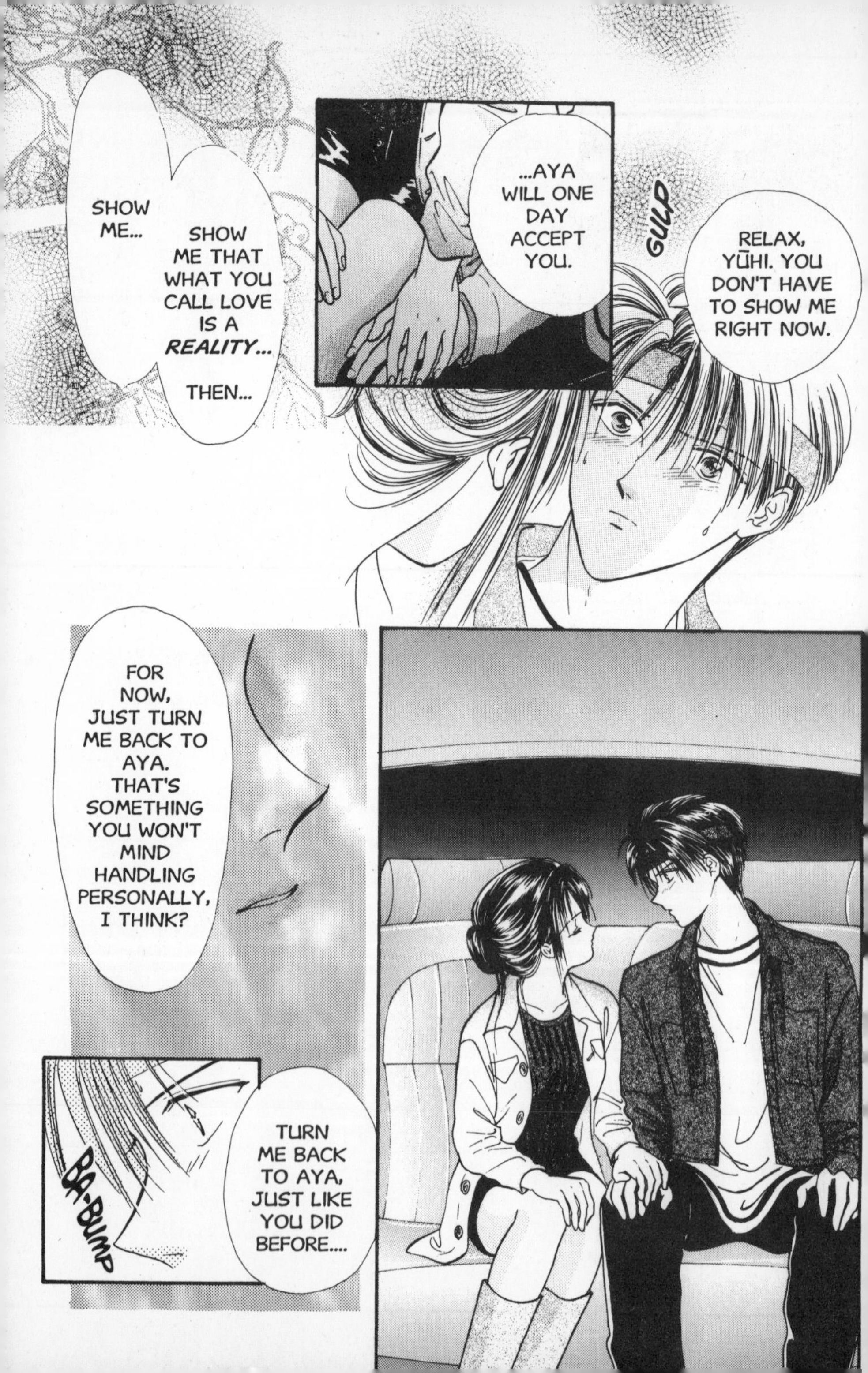
RELAX, YŪHI. YOU DON'T HAVE TO SHOW ME RIGHT NOW.
GULP
...AYA WILL ONE DAY ACCEPT YOU.
SHOW ME...
SHOW ME THAT WHAT YOU CALL LOVE IS A *REALITY*... THEN...
FOR NOW, JUST TURN ME BACK TO AYA. THAT'S SOMETHING YOU WON'T MIND HANDLING PERSONALLY, I THINK?
BA-BUMP
TURN ME BACK TO AYA, JUST LIKE YOU DID BEFORE....

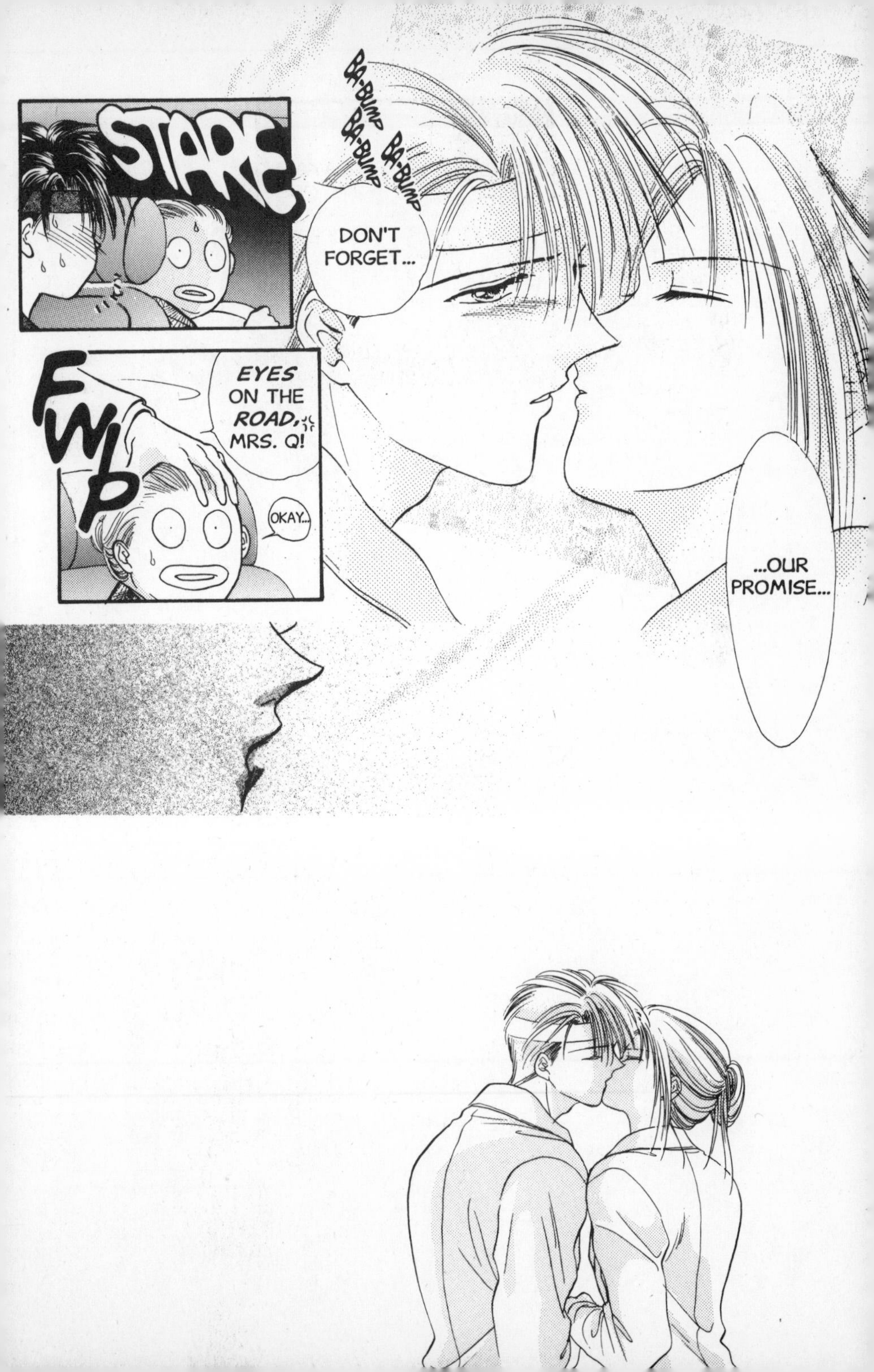
BA-BUMP BA-BUMP BA-BUMP BA-BUMP
DON'T FORGET...
...OUR PROMISE...
STARE
EYES ON THE ROAD, MRS. Q!
FWIP
OKAY...

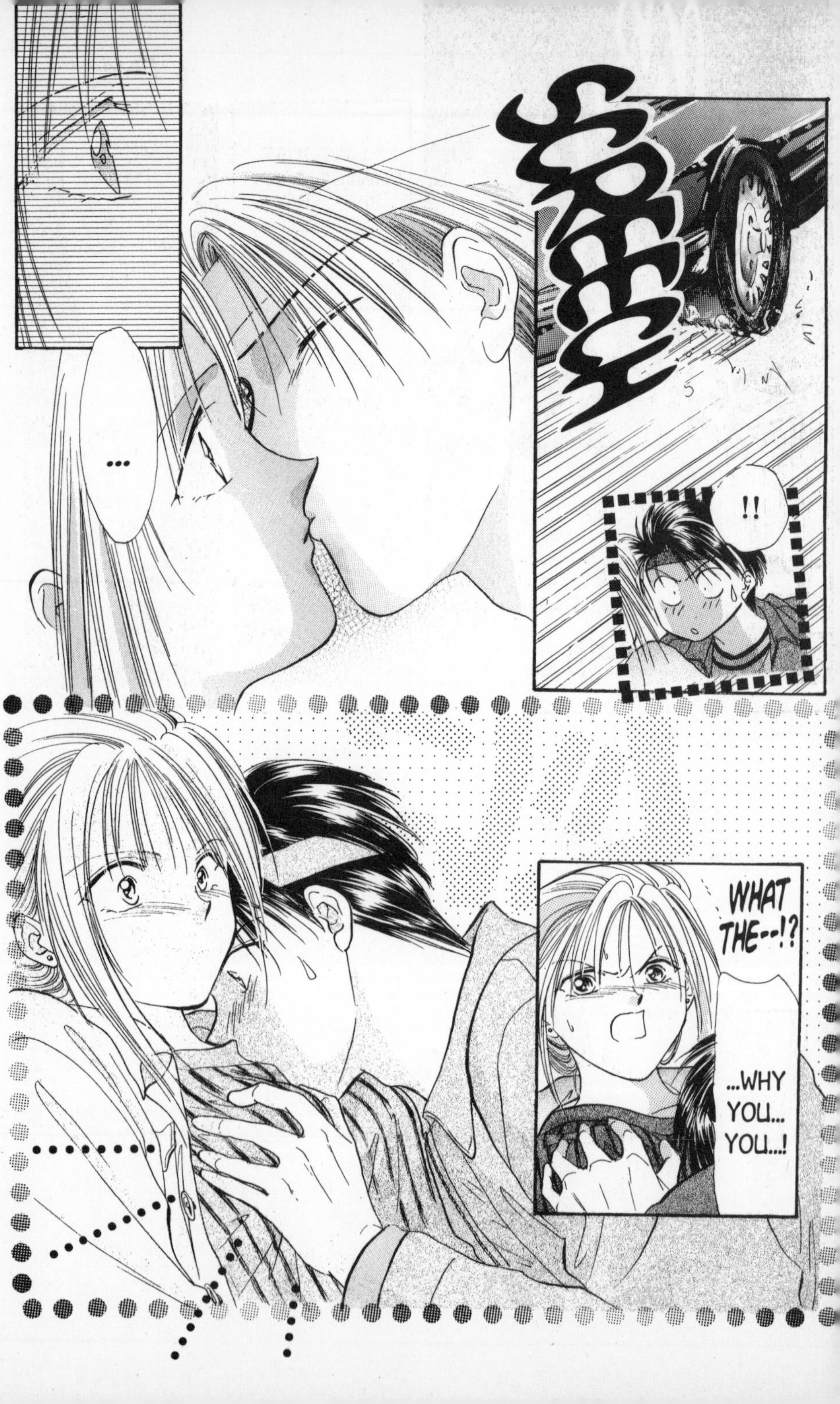
SCREE
!!
...
WHAT THE--!?
...WHY YOU... YOU...!

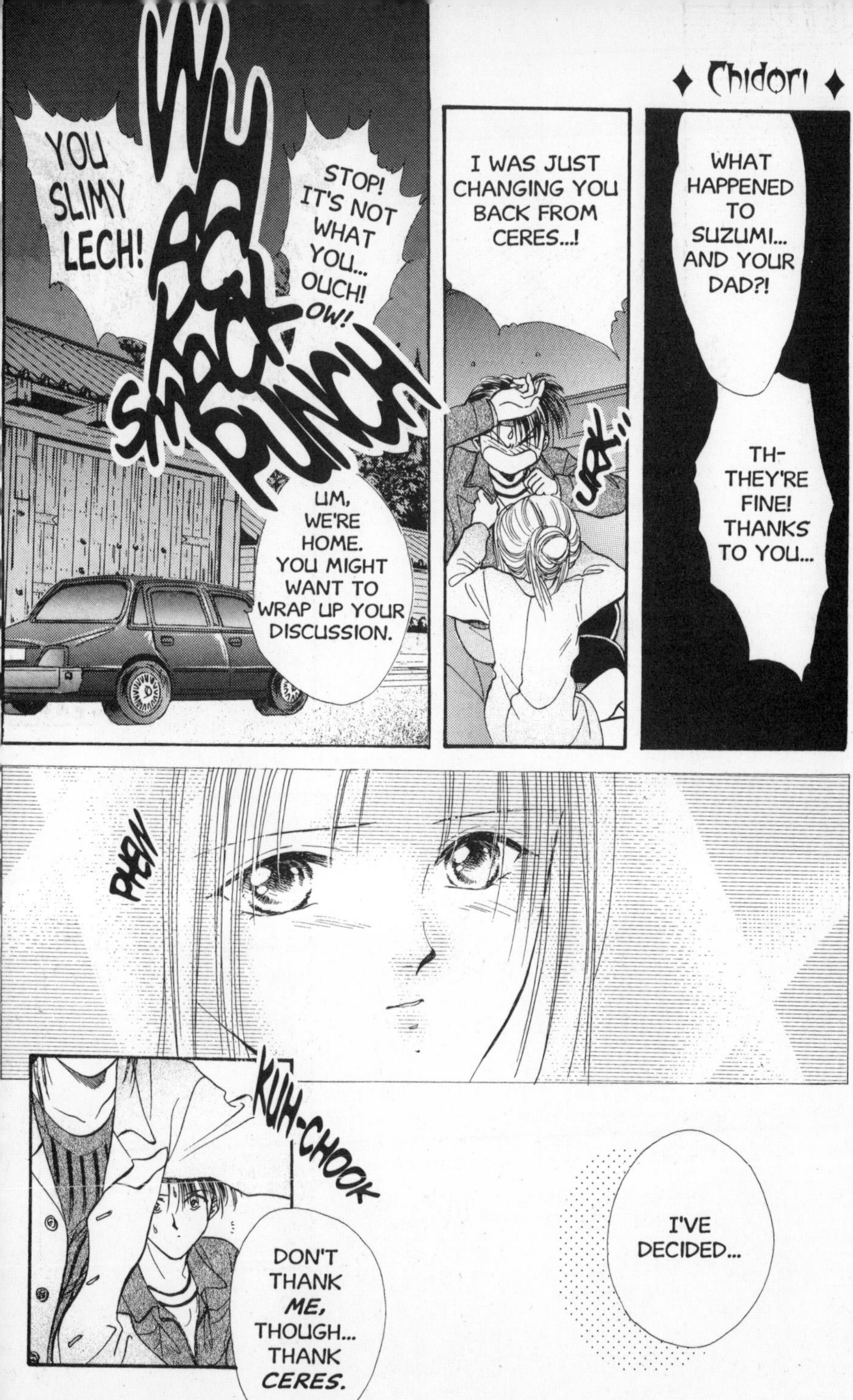
WHAT HAPPENED TO SUZUMI... AND YOUR DAD?!
TH- THEY'RE FINE! THANKS TO YOU...
I WAS JUST CHANGING YOU BACK FROM CERES...!
SPAT
YOU SLIMY LECH!
STOP! IT'S NOT WHAT YOU... OUCH! OW!
PUNCH
UM, WE'RE HOME. YOU MIGHT WANT TO WRAP UP YOUR DISCUSSION.
PHEW
I'VE DECIDED...
KUH-CHOOK
DON'T THANK *ME,* THOUGH... THANK ***CERES.***

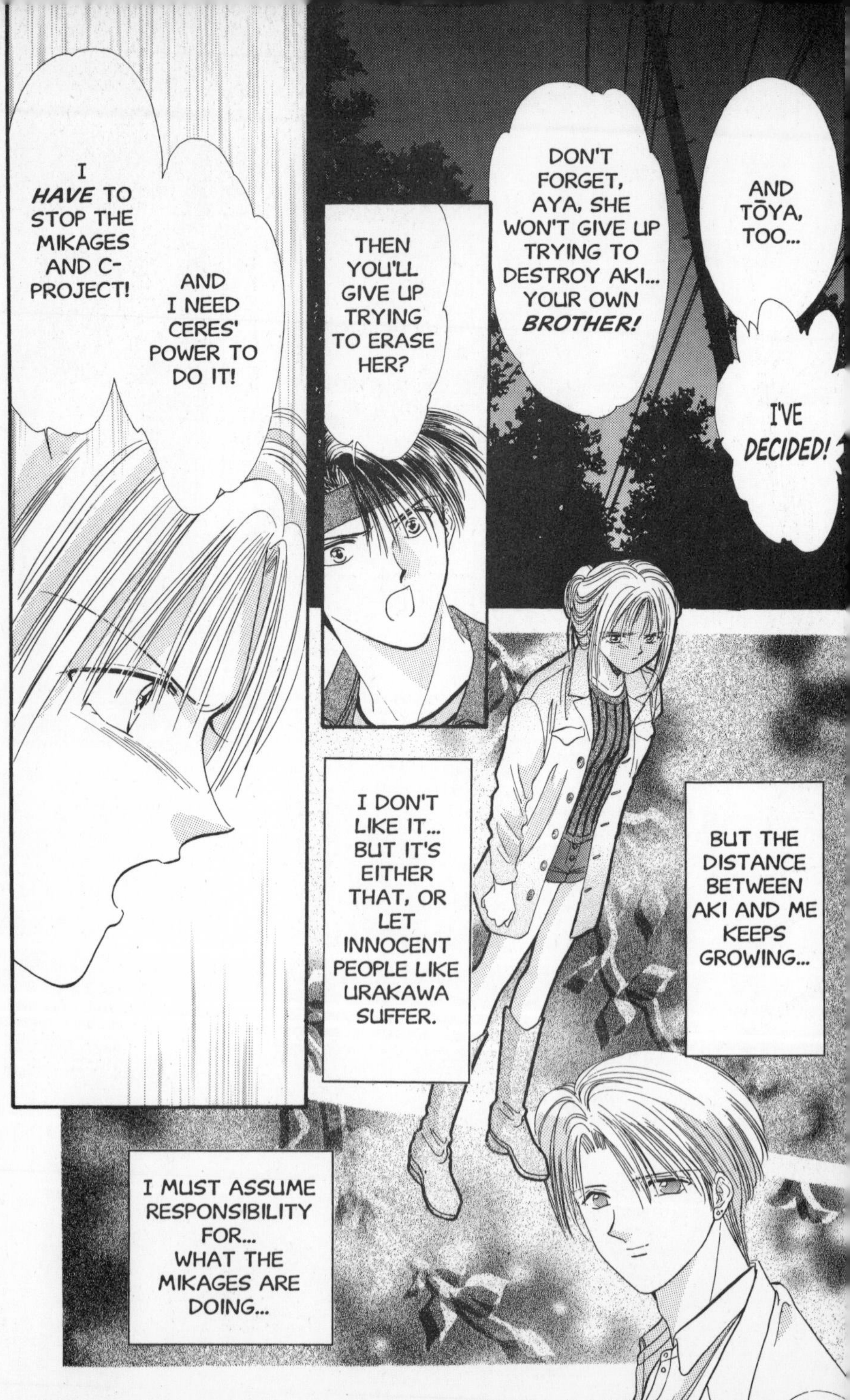
AND TŌYA, TOO...
I'VE DECIDED!
DON'T FORGET, AYA, SHE WON'T GIVE UP TRYING TO DESTROY AKI... YOUR OWN BROTHER!
THEN YOU'LL GIVE UP TRYING TO ERASE HER?
I HAVE TO STOP THE MIKAGES AND C-PROJECT!
AND I NEED CERES' POWER TO DO IT!
I DON'T LIKE IT... BUT IT'S EITHER THAT, OR LET INNOCENT PEOPLE LIKE URAKAWA SUFFER.
BUT THE DISTANCE BETWEEN AKI AND ME KEEPS GROWING...
I MUST ASSUME RESPONSIBILITY FOR... WHAT THE MIKAGES ARE DOING...

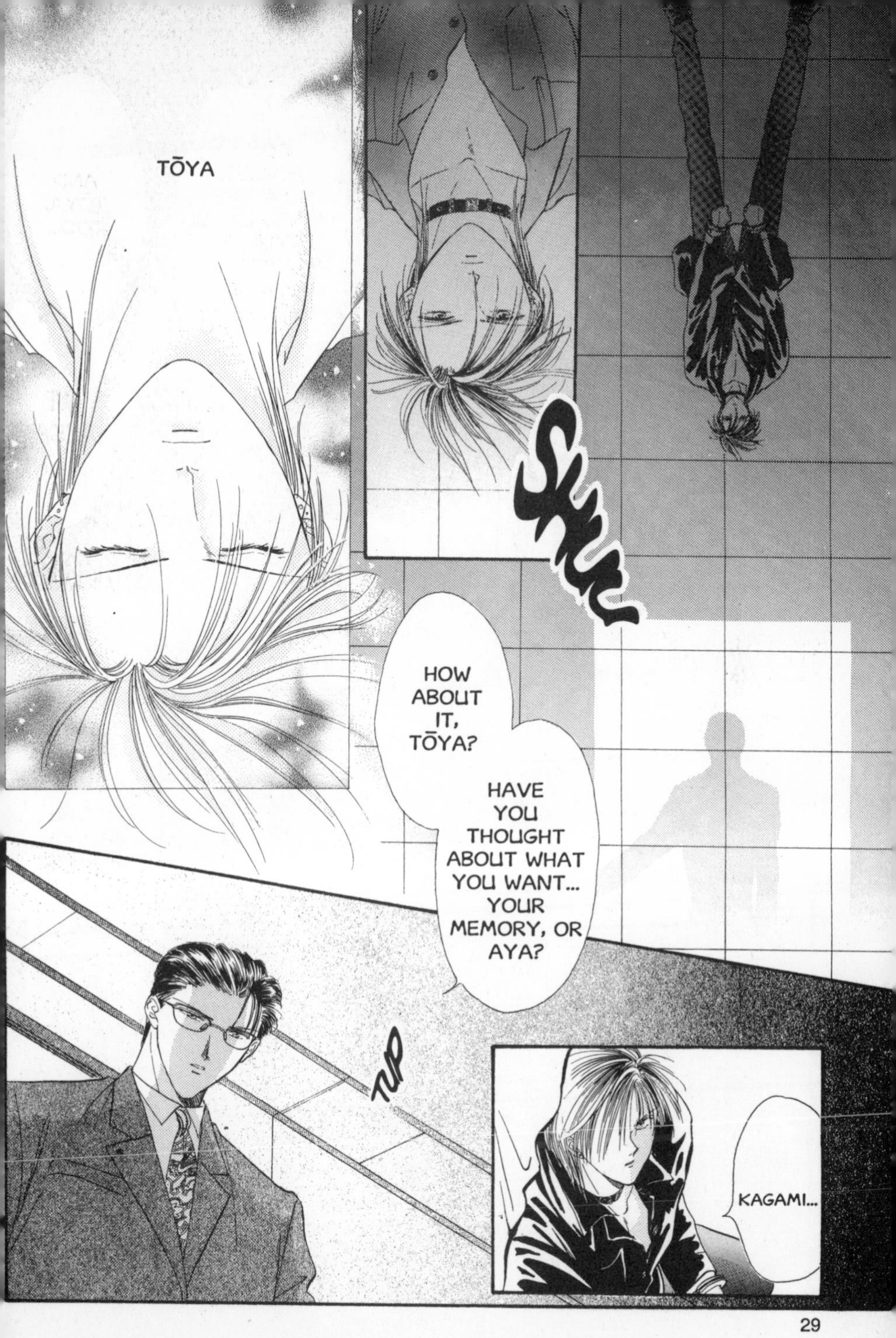
SHUU
TŌYA
HOW ABOUT IT, TŌYA?
HAVE YOU THOUGHT ABOUT WHAT YOU WANT... YOUR MEMORY, OR AYA?
TUP
KAGAMI...

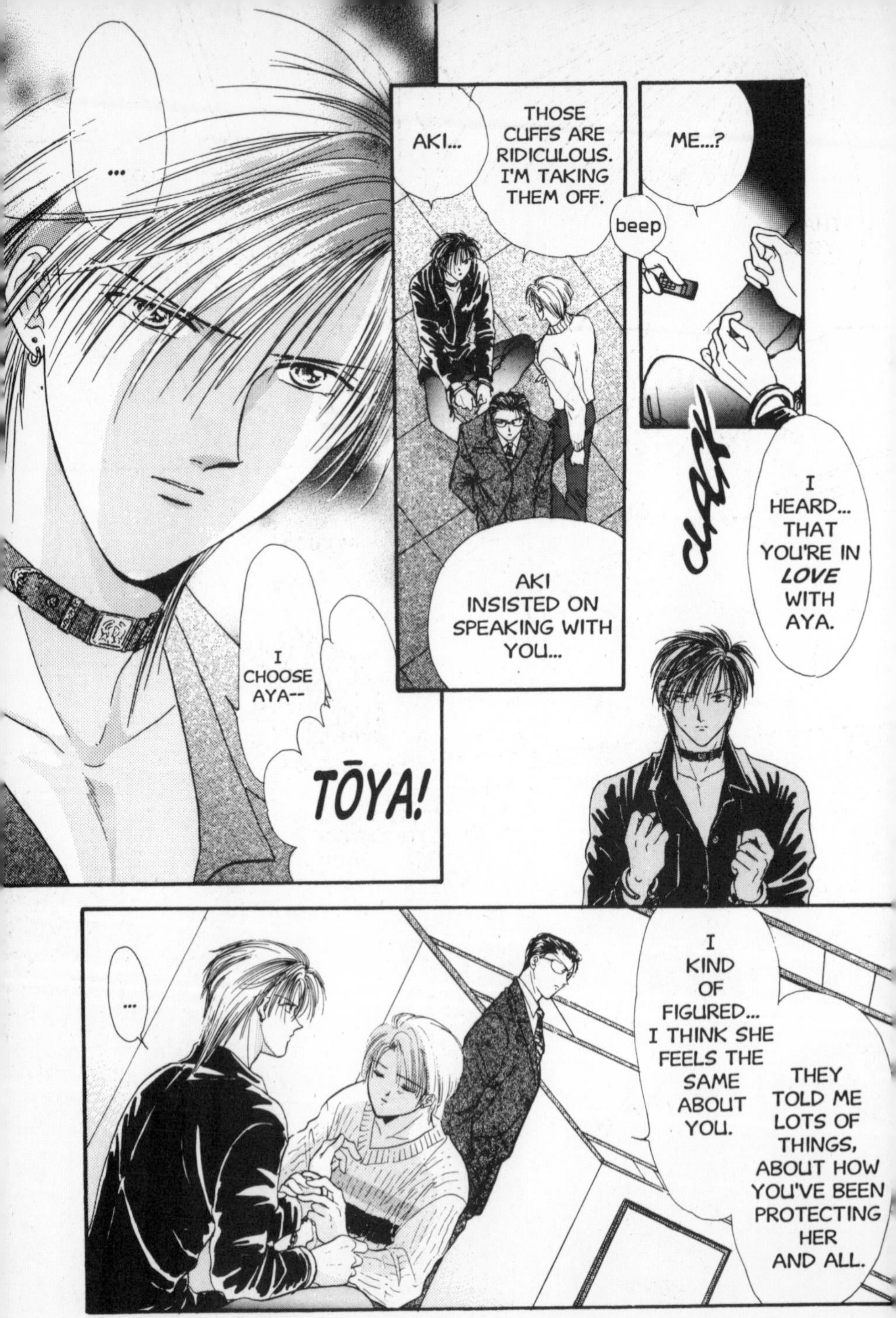
ME...?
beep
CLACK
I HEARD... THAT YOU'RE IN *LOVE* WITH AYA.
THOSE CUFFS ARE RIDICULOUS. I'M TAKING THEM OFF.
AKI...
AKI INSISTED ON SPEAKING WITH YOU...
...
I CHOOSE AYA--
TŌYA!
I KIND OF FIGURED... I THINK SHE FEELS THE SAME ABOUT YOU.
THEY TOLD ME LOTS OF THINGS, ABOUT HOW YOU'VE BEEN PROTECTING HER AND ALL.
...

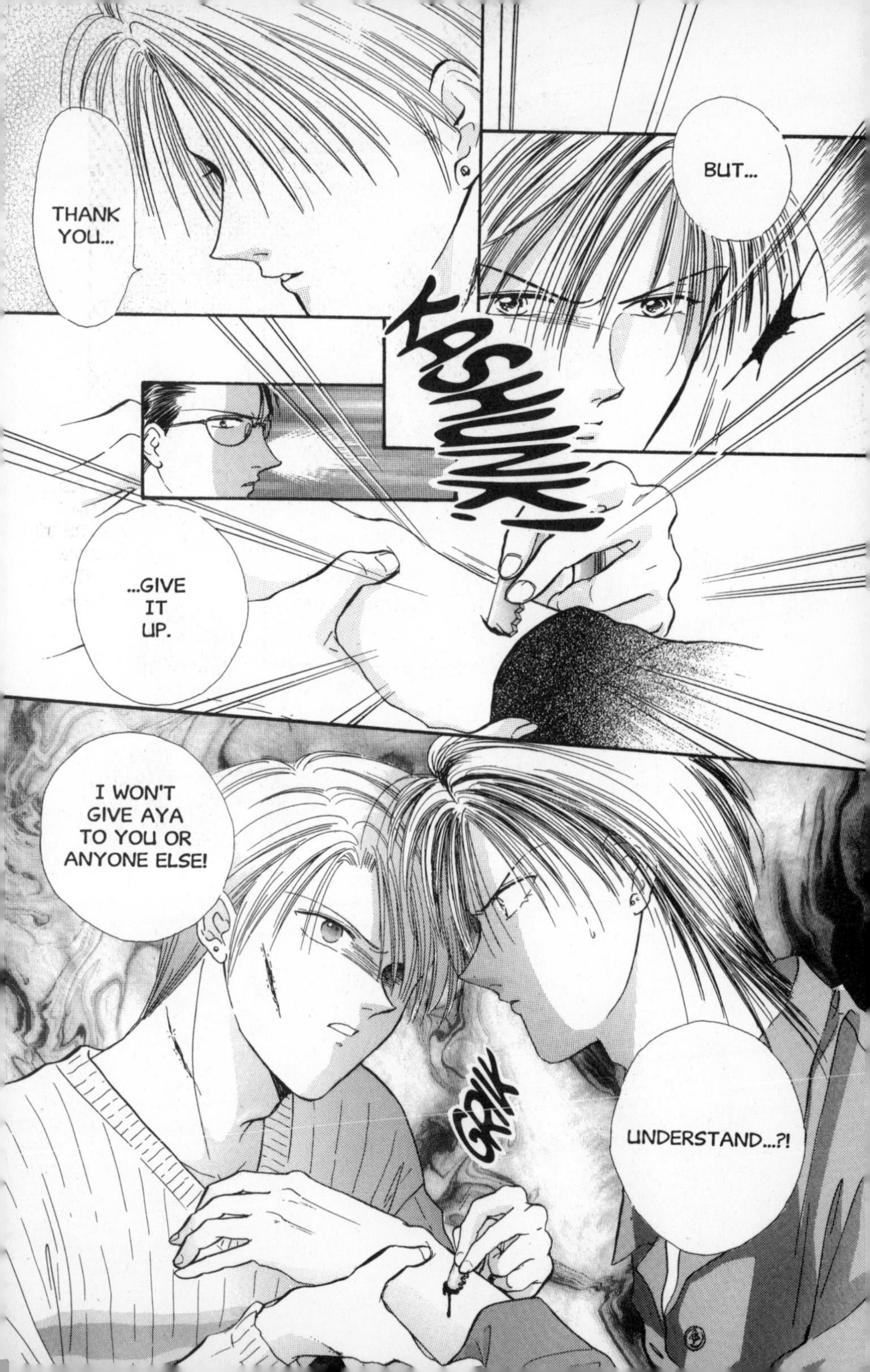
THANK YOU...
BUT...
KASHUNK!
...GIVE IT UP.
I WON'T GIVE AYA TO YOU OR ANYONE ELSE!
GRIK
UNDERSTAND...?!

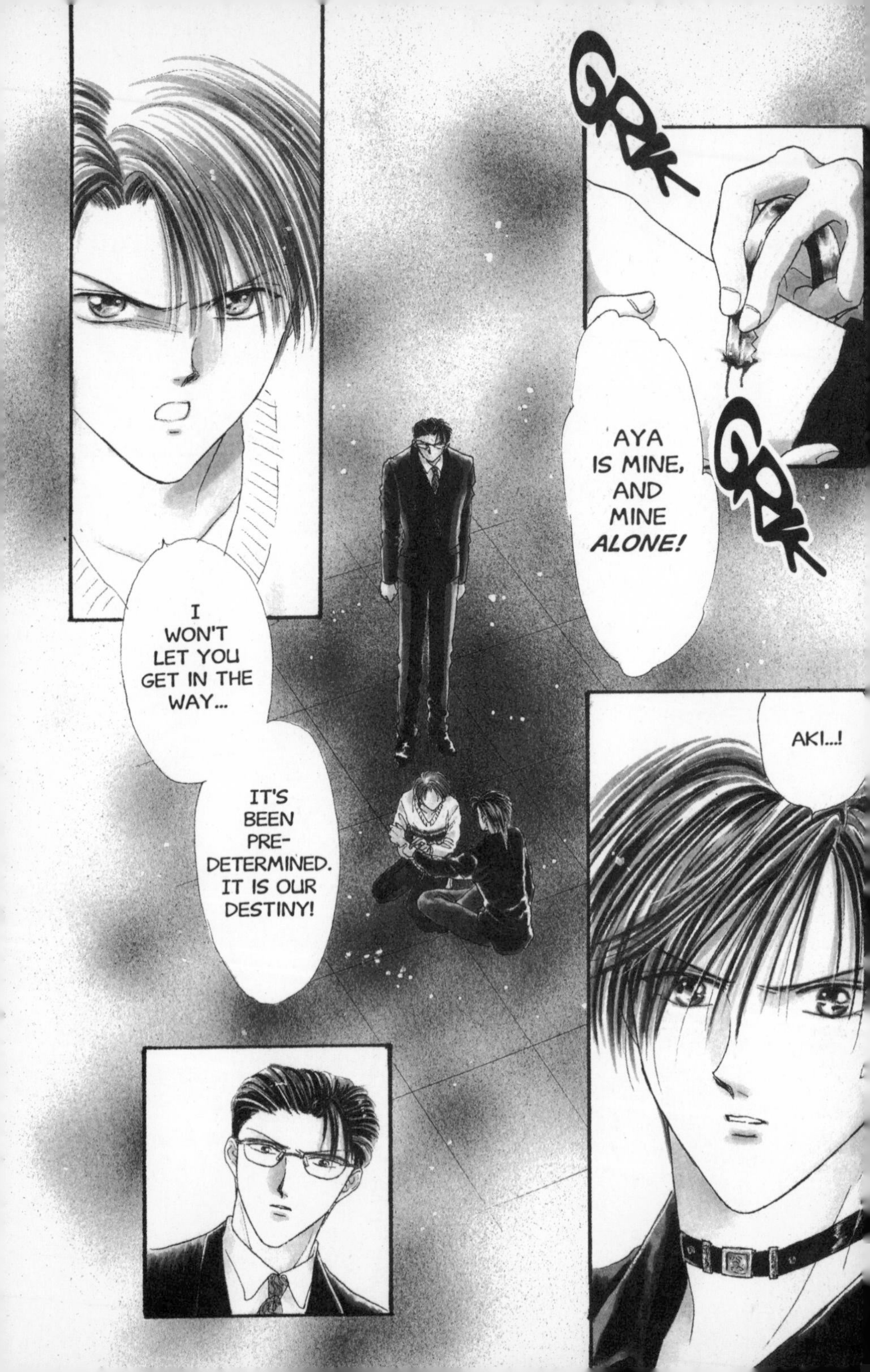
GRAK
AYA IS MINE, AND MINE ALONE!
GRAK
I WON'T LET YOU GET IN THE WAY...
IT'S BEEN PRE-DETERMINED. IT IS OUR DESTINY!
AKI...!

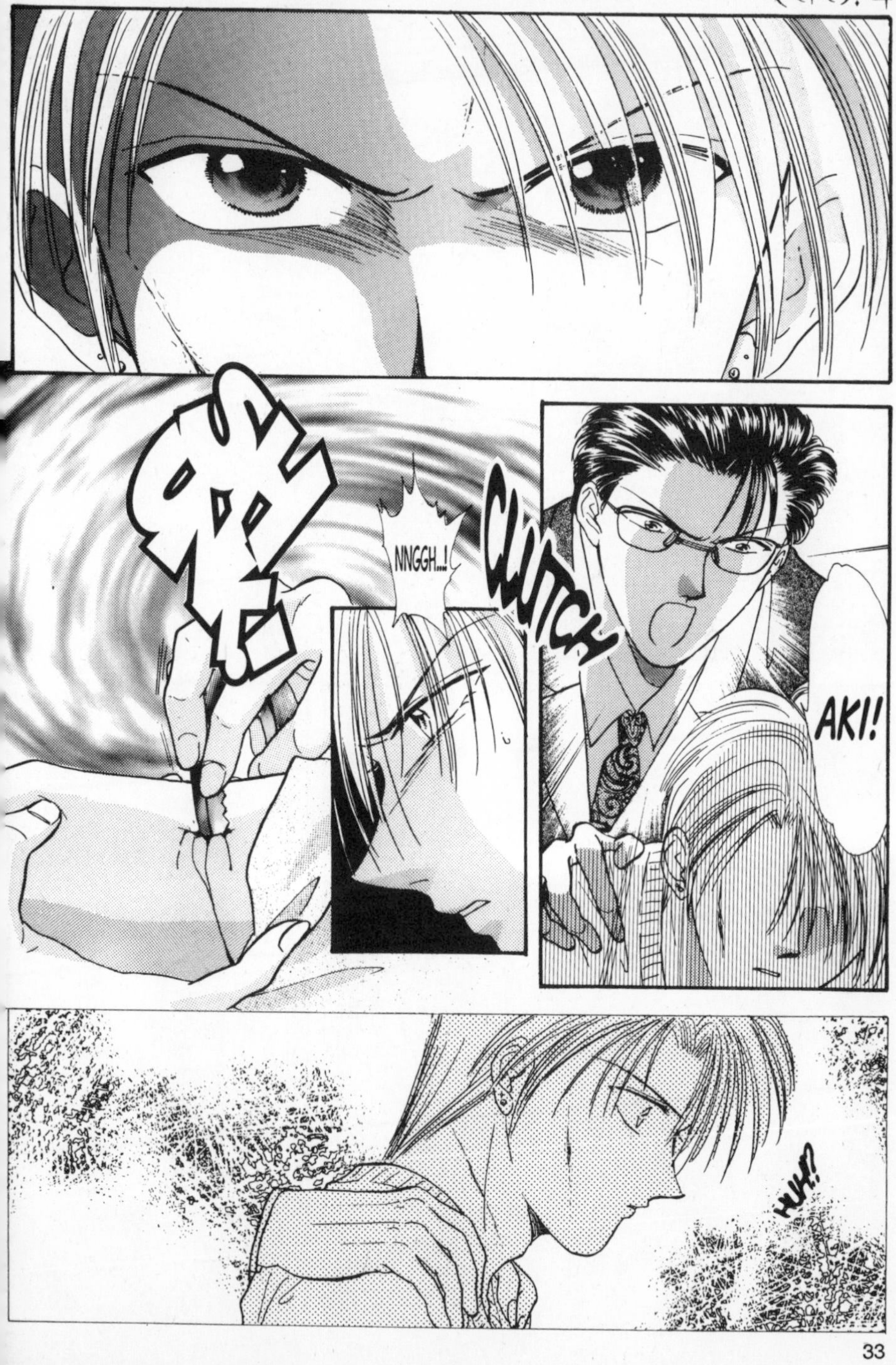
CLUTCH
AKI!
NNGGH...!
HUH?

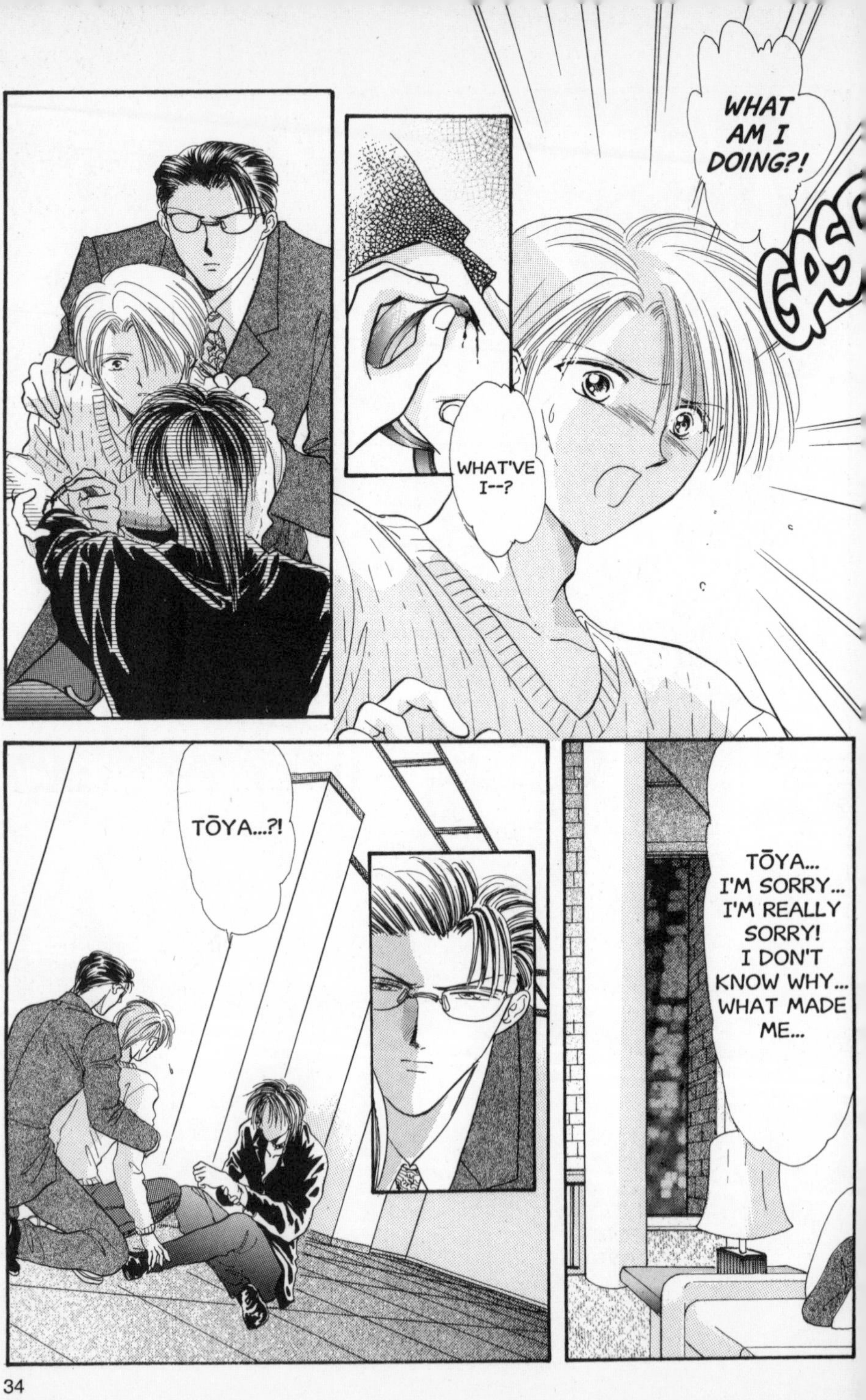
WHAT AM I DOING?!
WHAT'VE I--?
TŌYA... I'M SORRY... I'M REALLY SORRY! I DON'T KNOW WHY... WHAT MADE ME...
TŌYA...?!

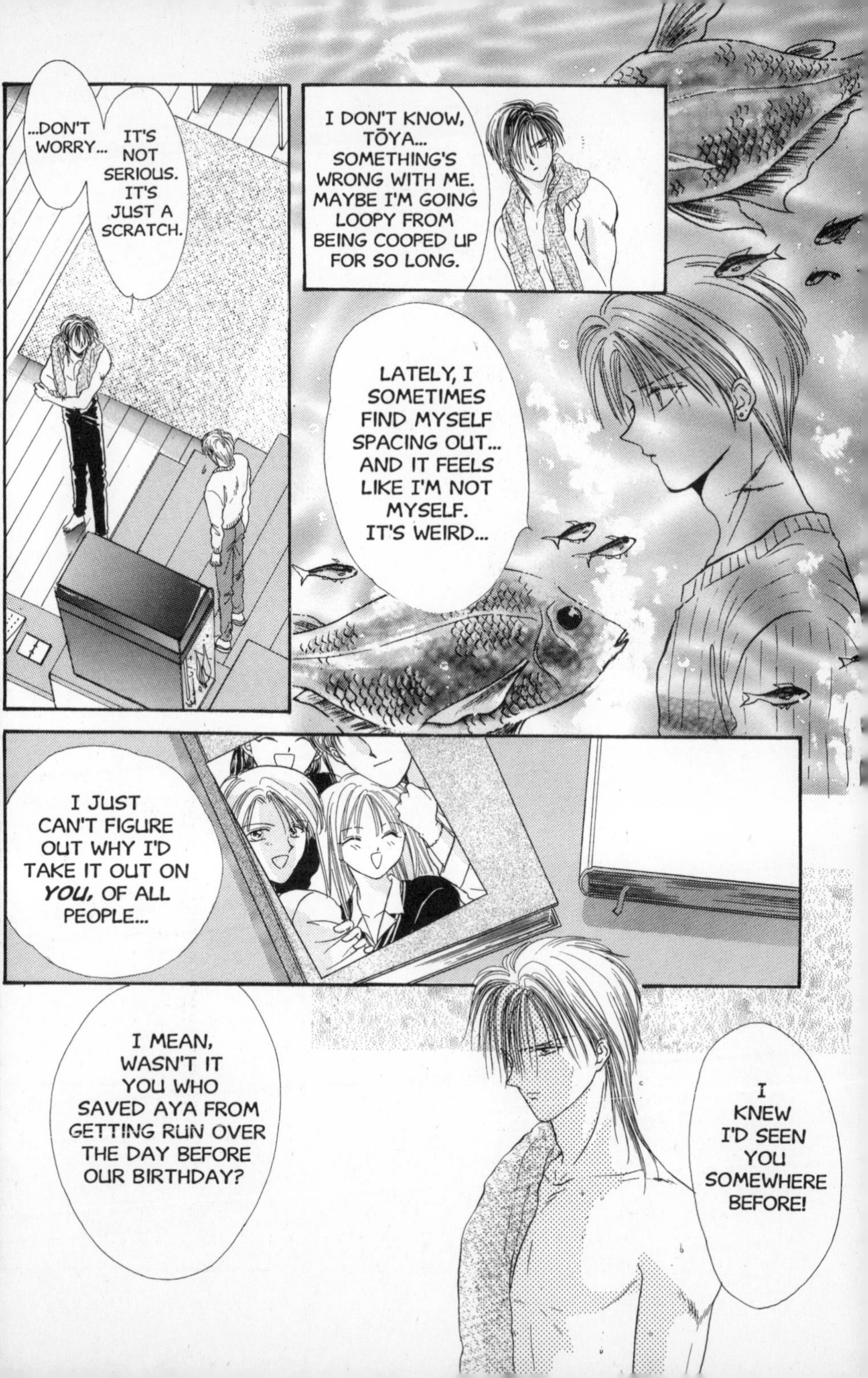
I DON'T KNOW, TŌYA... SOMETHING'S WRONG WITH ME. MAYBE I'M GOING LOOPY FROM BEING COOPED UP FOR SO LONG.
LATELY, I SOMETIMES FIND MYSELF SPACING OUT... AND IT FEELS LIKE I'M NOT MYSELF. IT'S WEIRD...
...DON'T WORRY... IT'S NOT SERIOUS. IT'S JUST A SCRATCH.
I JUST CAN'T FIGURE OUT WHY I'D TAKE IT OUT ON *YOU,* OF ALL PEOPLE...
I MEAN, WASN'T IT YOU WHO SAVED AYA FROM GETTING RUN OVER THE DAY BEFORE OUR BIRTHDAY?
I KNEW I'D SEEN YOU SOMEWHERE BEFORE!

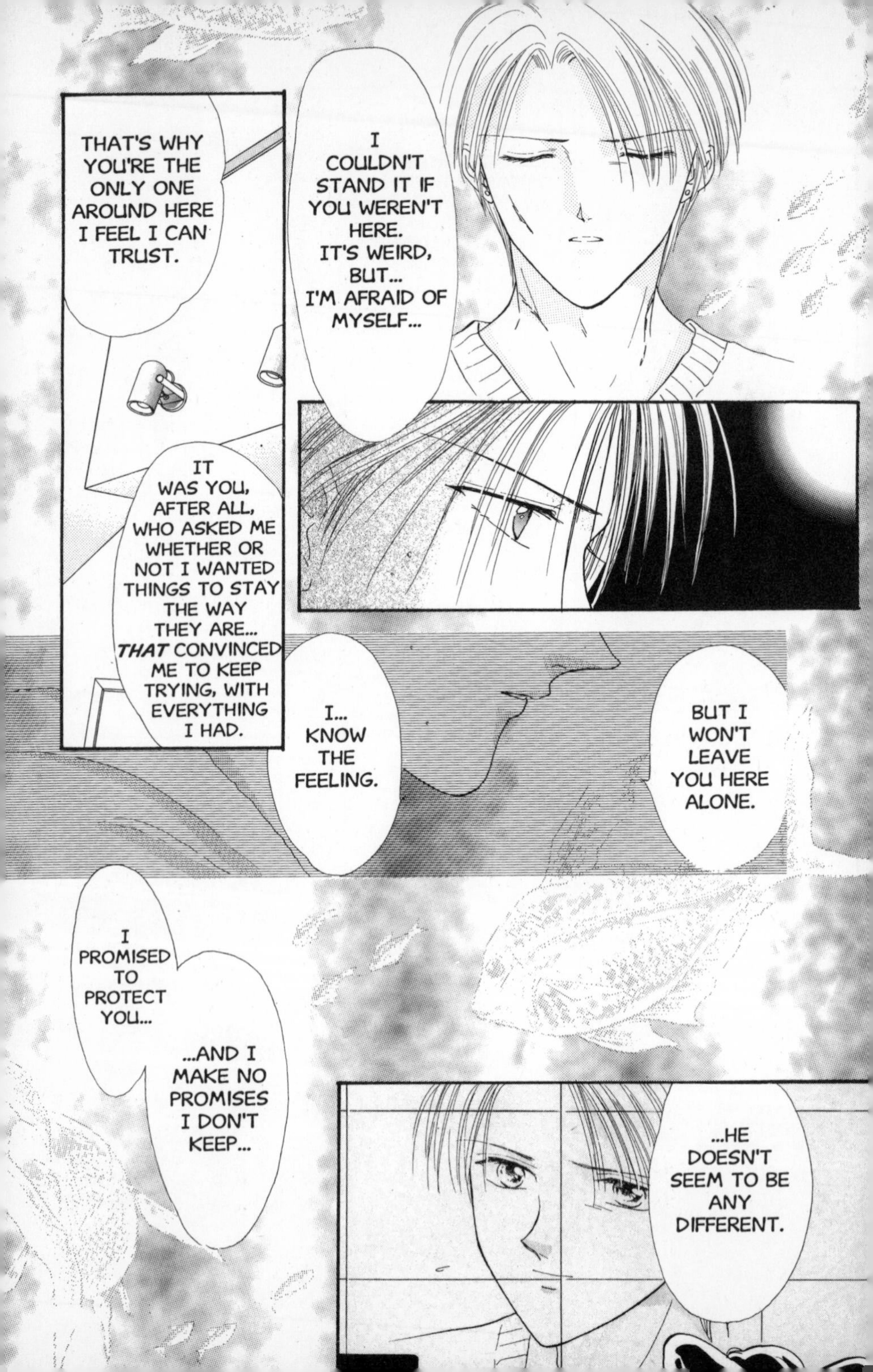
I COULDN'T STAND IT IF YOU WEREN'T HERE. IT'S WEIRD, BUT... I'M AFRAID OF MYSELF...
THAT'S WHY YOU'RE THE ONLY ONE AROUND HERE I FEEL I CAN TRUST.
IT WAS YOU, AFTER ALL, WHO ASKED ME WHETHER OR NOT I WANTED THINGS TO STAY THE WAY THEY ARE... *THAT* CONVINCED ME TO KEEP TRYING, WITH EVERYTHING I HAD.
I... KNOW THE FEELING.
BUT I WON'T LEAVE YOU HERE ALONE.
I PROMISED TO PROTECT YOU...
...AND I MAKE NO PROMISES I DON'T KEEP...
...HE DOESN'T SEEM TO BE ANY DIFFERENT.

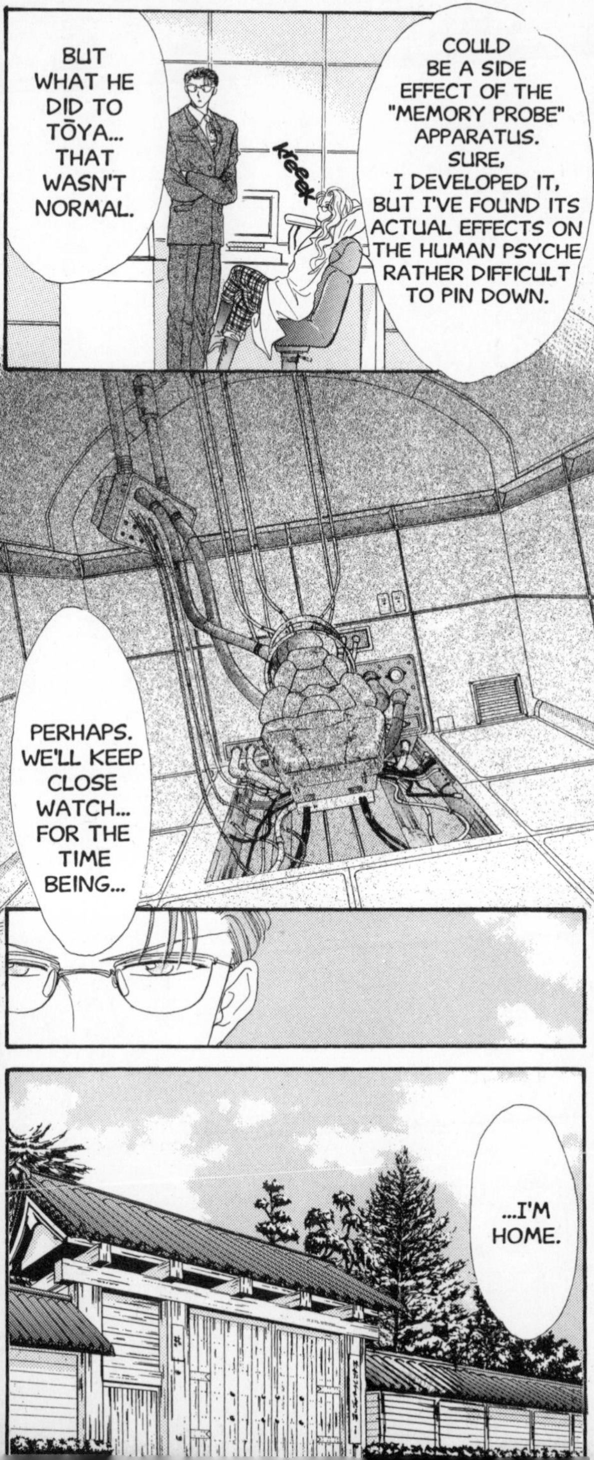
BUT WHAT HE DID TO TŌYA... THAT WASN'T NORMAL.
COULD BE A SIDE EFFECT OF THE "MEMORY PROBE" APPARATUS. SURE, I DEVELOPED IT, BUT I'VE FOUND ITS ACTUAL EFFECTS ON THE HUMAN PSYCHE RATHER DIFFICULT TO PIN DOWN.
kreeek
PERHAPS. WE'LL KEEP CLOSE WATCH... FOR THE TIME BEING...
...I'M HOME.

◆ Chidori ◆

Oh, I'd been thinking about how I said in a previous sidebar that **Ceres** is rather dark, and then I realized - this is a contemporary drama. I guess this is what happens when I try to set the story in the present day. The present day as I see it is gloomy and grey (at least Japan is). People as a whole, even children, are depressed. They look tired. Even high school girls, those hordes of look-a-like clones, who are said to represent the present day, look like they lack spirit to me and my assistants. It's like they're living a lie, without realizing it, by acting so incredibly chipper. But I guess its okay, as long as they're having fun. And if I focus on that, the series is probably going to be really dark, but there are still lots of things that show it's not all bad for mankind. Also, those girls labeled kogals might look flighty on the outside,
but they could be pretty serious inside. Really?
It's not good when people just go by outward appearances. The media is making too much of a big deal. And there are way too many stupid adults around! Still, I hope young boys and girls don't lose heart. You can change the future. Each of you has that power. Wait until you are older to start thinking about the futility of it all. And I'll have Aya keep doing her best, too. This is an age when parents and children kill each other, and people with money and power use underhanded methods to get what they want. The Mikage Family is representative of those things for me. And as you may have realized, the theme is the same as my previous series. My next series will also probably inherit the same theme too. Just like genes.

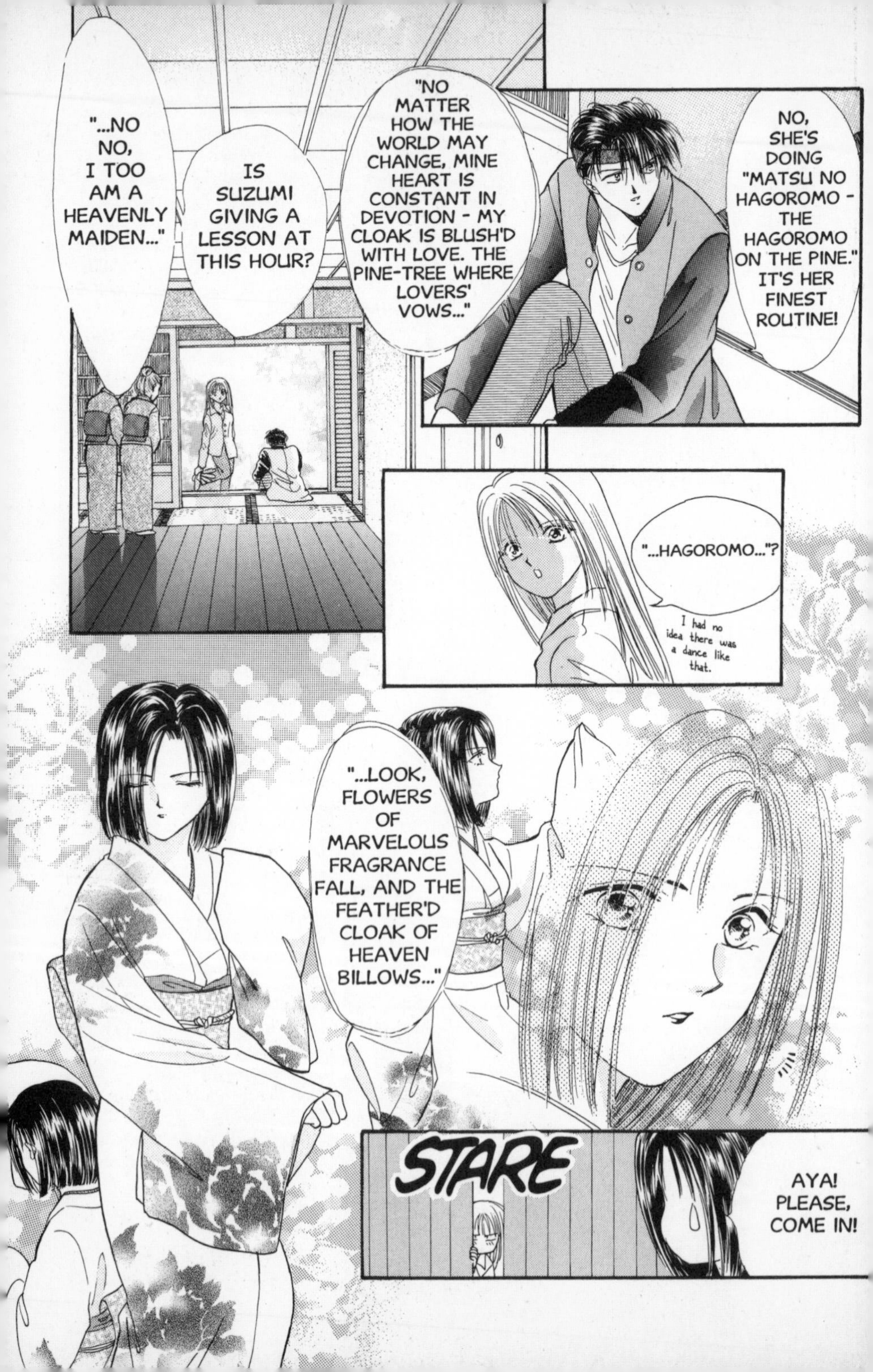
"NO MATTER HOW THE WORLD MAY CHANGE, MINE HEART IS CONSTANT IN DEVOTION - MY CLOAK IS BLUSH'D WITH LOVE. THE PINE-TREE WHERE LOVERS' VOWS..."
"...NO NO, I TOO AM A HEAVENLY MAIDEN..."
IS SUZUMI GIVING A LESSON AT THIS HOUR?
NO, SHE'S DOING "MATSU NO HAGOROMO - THE HAGOROMO ON THE PINE." IT'S HER FINEST ROUTINE!
"...HAGOROMO..."?
I had no idea there was a dance like that.
"...LOOK, FLOWERS OF MARVELOUS FRAGRANCE FALL, AND THE FEATHER'D CLOAK OF HEAVEN BILLOWS..."
STARE
AYA! PLEASE, COME IN!

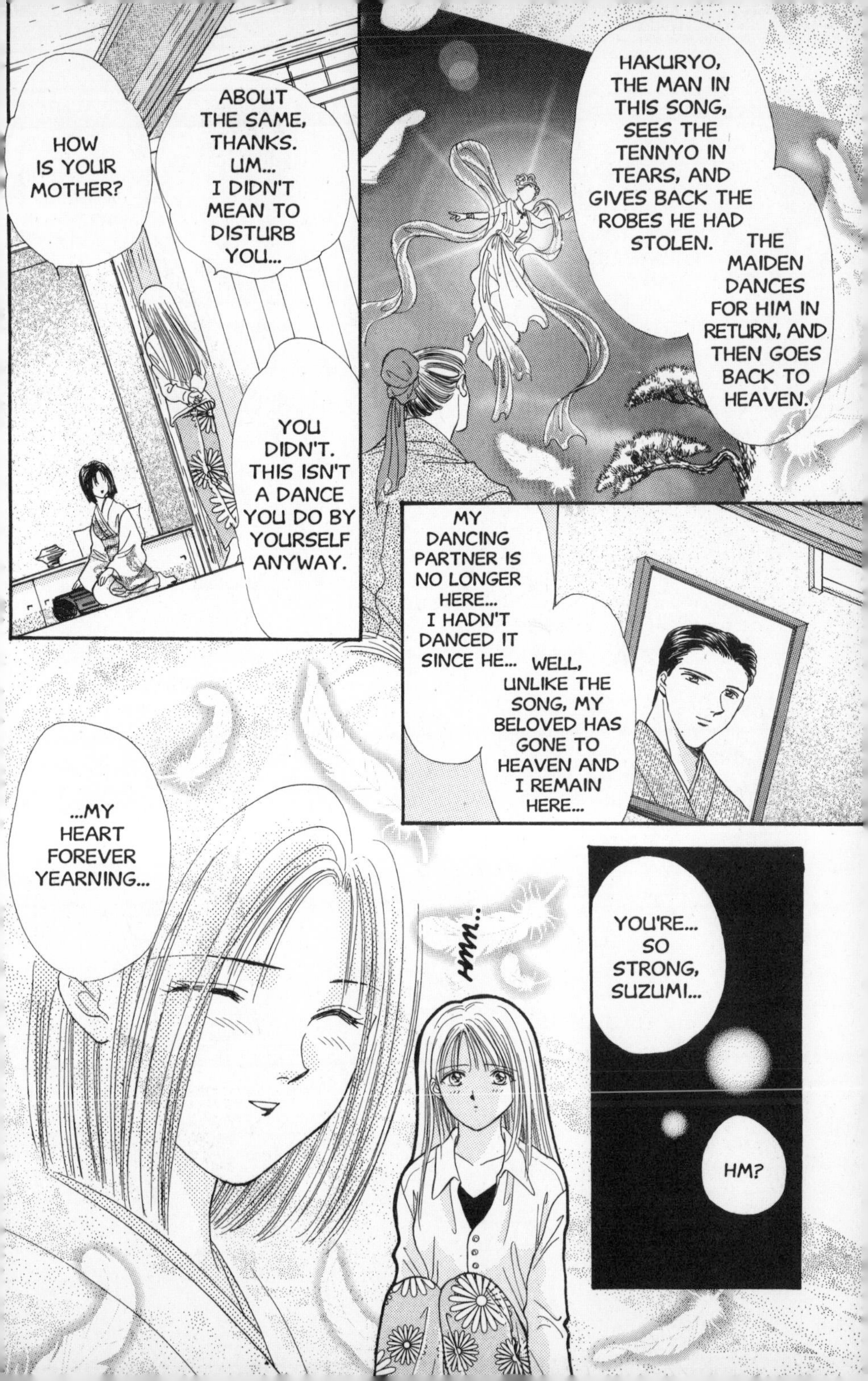
HOW IS YOUR MOTHER?
ABOUT THE SAME, THANKS. UM... I DIDN'T MEAN TO DISTURB YOU...
YOU DIDN'T. THIS ISN'T A DANCE YOU DO BY YOURSELF ANYWAY.
HAKURYO, THE MAN IN THIS SONG, SEES THE TENNYO IN TEARS, AND GIVES BACK THE ROBES HE HAD STOLEN. THE MAIDEN DANCES FOR HIM IN RETURN, AND THEN GOES BACK TO HEAVEN.
MY DANCING PARTNER IS NO LONGER HERE... I HADN'T DANCED IT SINCE HE...
WELL, UNLIKE THE SONG, MY BELOVED HAS GONE TO HEAVEN AND I REMAIN HERE...
...MY HEART FOREVER YEARNING...
YOU'RE... SO STRONG, SUZUMI...
HM?

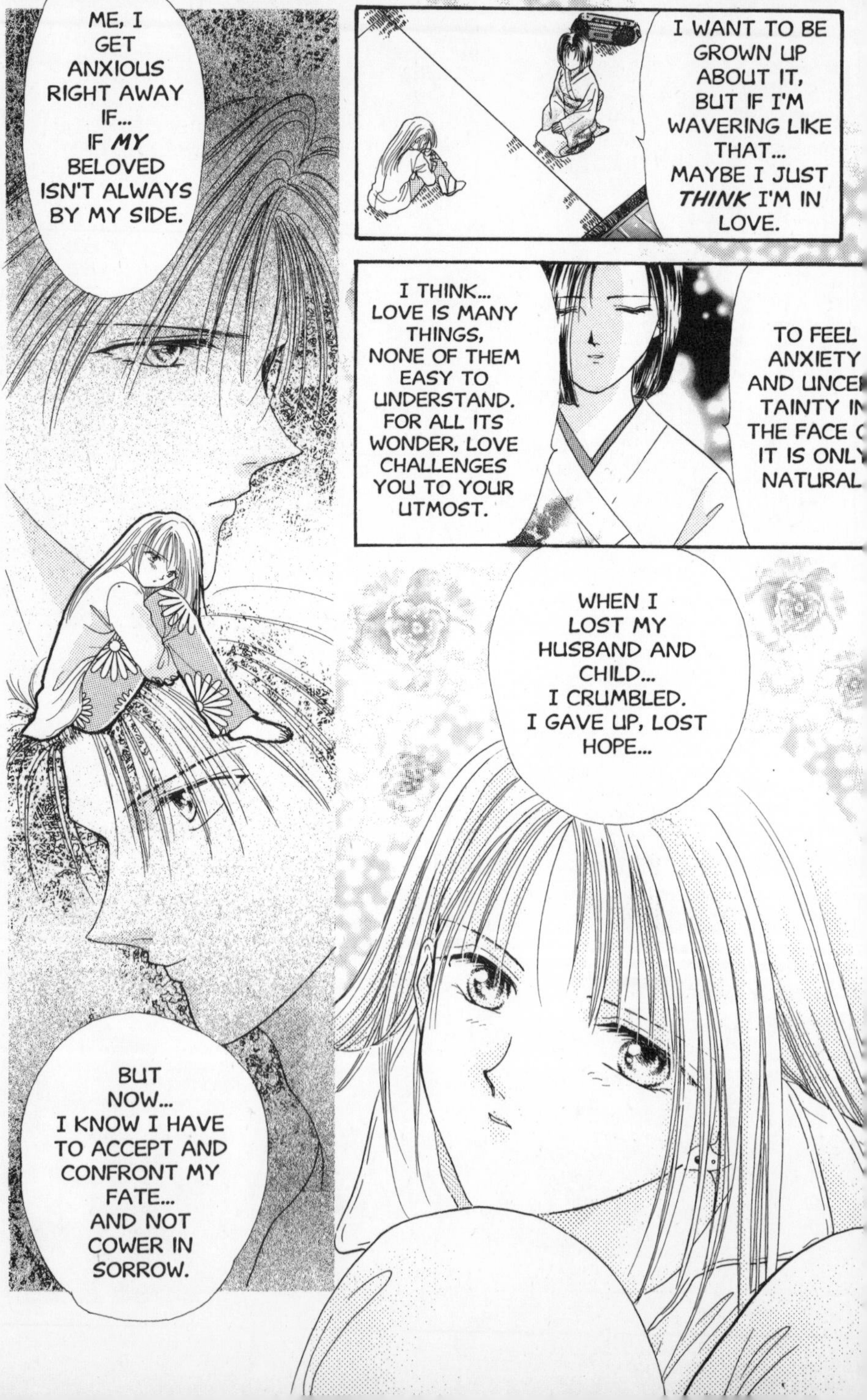
I WANT TO BE GROWN UP ABOUT IT, BUT IF I'M WAVERING LIKE THAT... MAYBE I JUST *THINK* I'M IN LOVE.
TO FEEL ANXIETY AND UNCER TAINTY IN THE FACE O IT IS ONLY NATURAL
I THINK... LOVE IS MANY THINGS, NONE OF THEM EASY TO UNDERSTAND. FOR ALL ITS WONDER, LOVE CHALLENGES YOU TO YOUR UTMOST.
WHEN I LOST MY HUSBAND AND CHILD... I CRUMBLED. I GAVE UP, LOST HOPE...
ME, I GET ANXIOUS RIGHT AWAY IF... IF *MY* BELOVED ISN'T ALWAYS BY MY SIDE.
BUT NOW... I KNOW I HAVE TO ACCEPT AND CONFRONT MY FATE... AND NOT COWER IN SORROW.

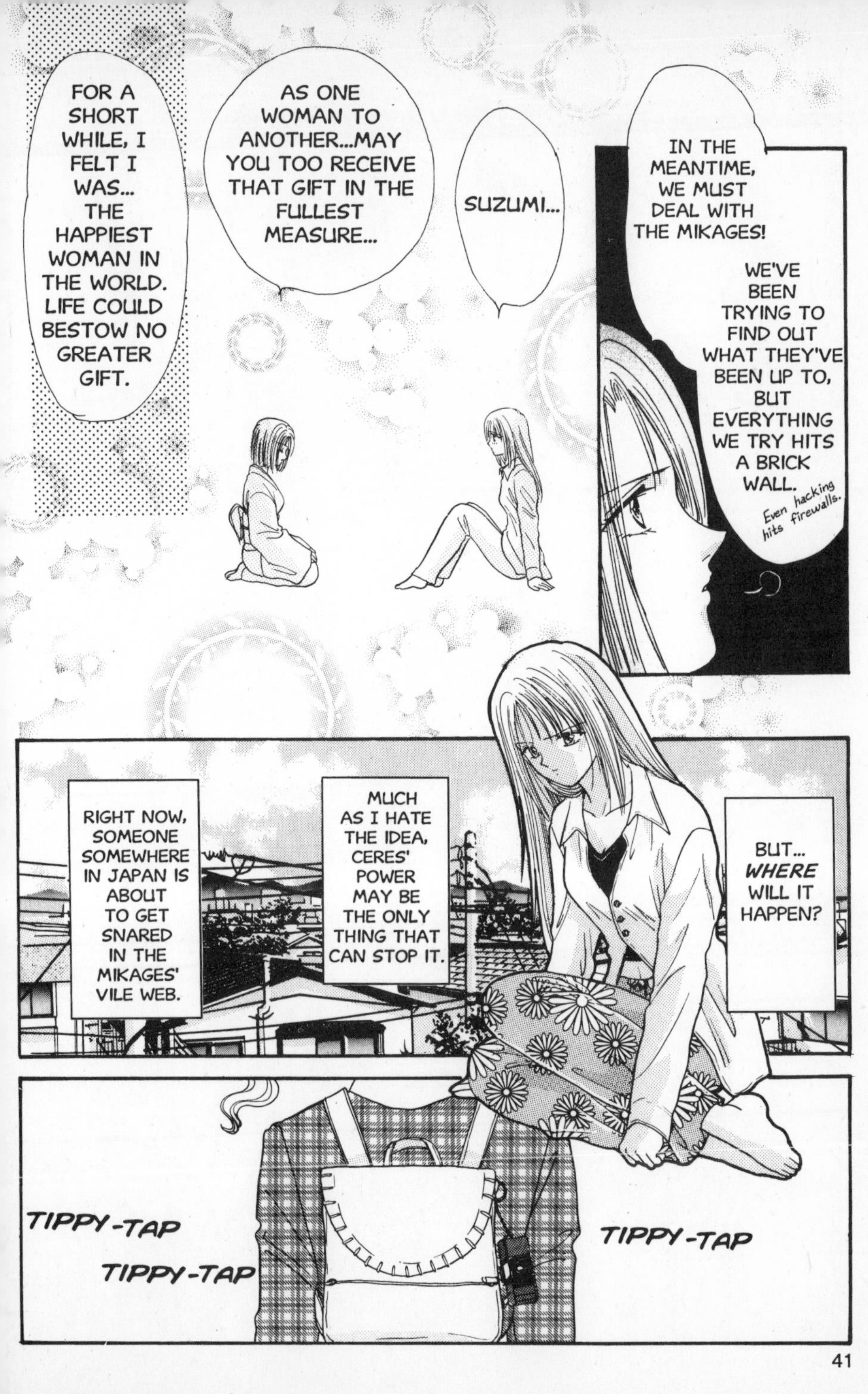
FOR A SHORT WHILE, I FELT I WAS... THE HAPPIEST WOMAN IN THE WORLD. LIFE COULD BESTOW NO GREATER GIFT.
AS ONE WOMAN TO ANOTHER...MAY YOU TOO RECEIVE THAT GIFT IN THE FULLEST MEASURE...
SUZUMI...
IN THE MEANTIME, WE MUST DEAL WITH THE MIKAGES!
WE'VE BEEN TRYING TO FIND OUT WHAT THEY'VE BEEN UP TO, BUT EVERYTHING WE TRY HITS A BRICK WALL.
Even hacking hits firewalls.
RIGHT NOW, SOMEONE SOMEWHERE IN JAPAN IS ABOUT TO GET SNARED IN THE MIKAGES' VILE WEB.
MUCH AS I HATE THE IDEA, CERES' POWER MAY BE THE ONLY THING THAT CAN STOP IT.
BUT... *WHERE* WILL IT HAPPEN?
TIPPY-TAP
TIPPY-TAP
TIPPY-TAP

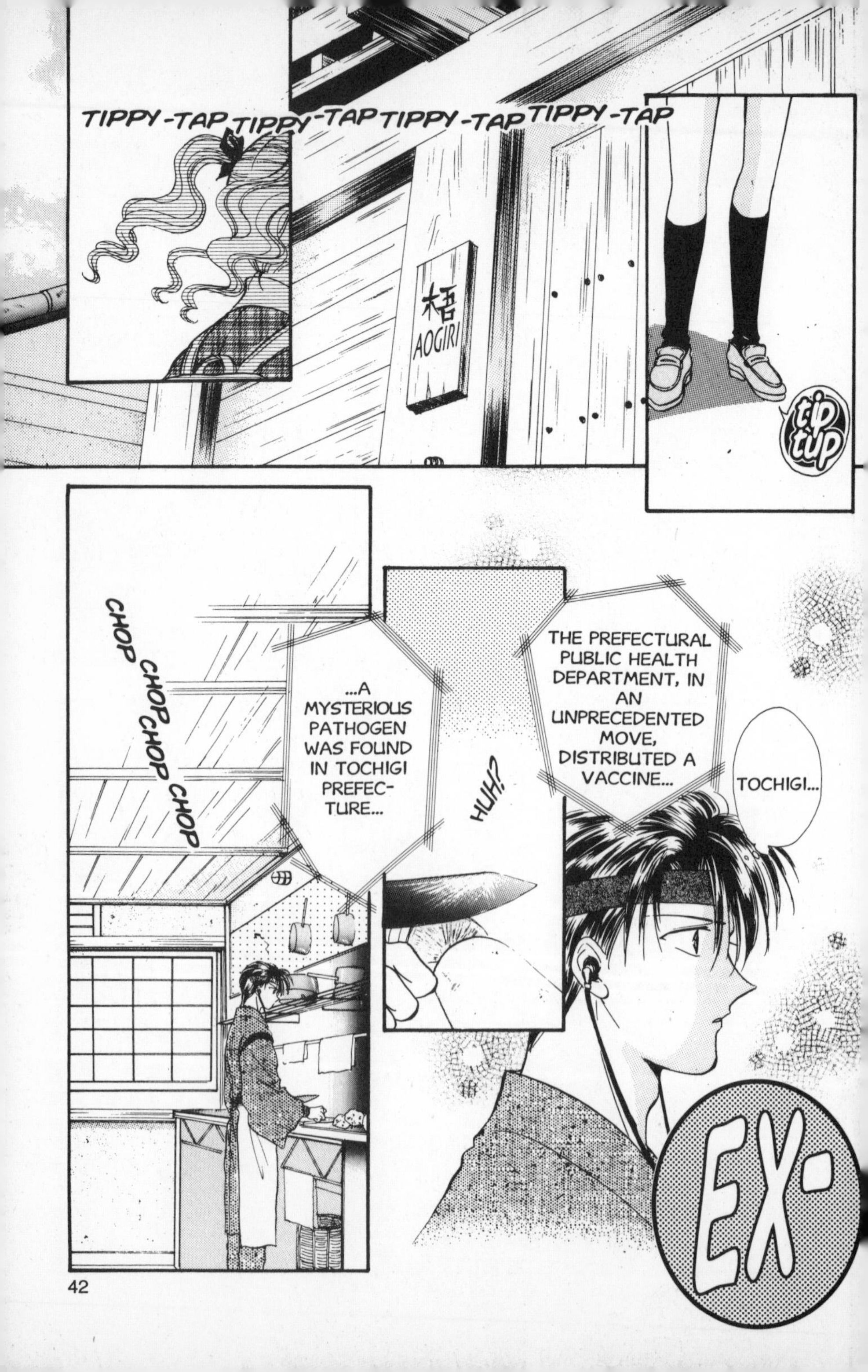

tip tup
TIPPY-TAP TIPPY-TAP TIPPY-TAP TIPPY-TAP
AOGIRI
CHOP CHOP CHOP CHOP
...A MYSTERIOUS PATHOGEN WAS FOUND IN TOCHIGI PREFEC-TURE...
THE PREFECTURAL PUBLIC HEALTH DEPARTMENT, IN AN UNPRECEDENTED MOVE, DISTRIBUTED A VACCINE...
HUH?
TOCHIGI...
EX-

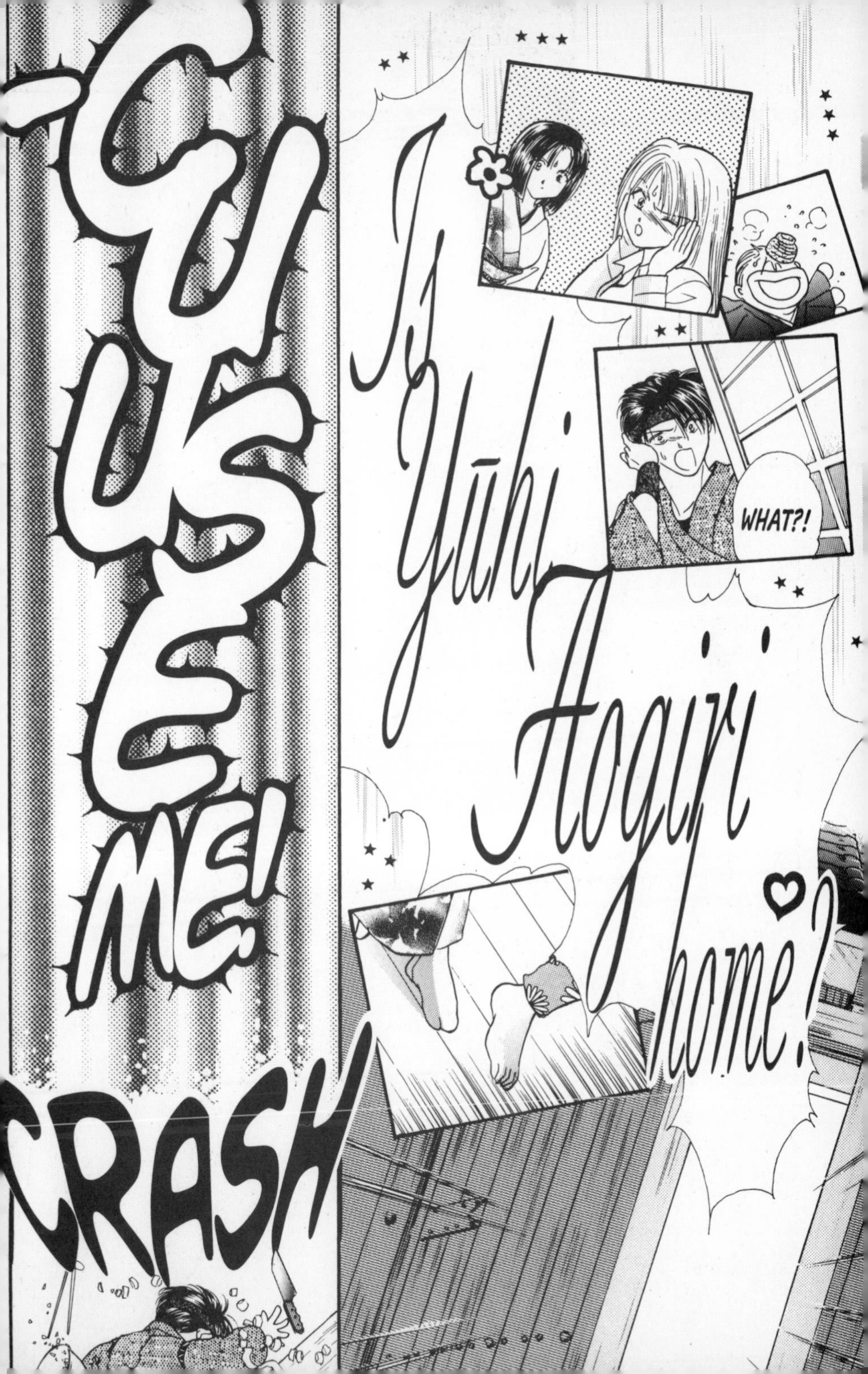
Is Yūhi Aogiri home?
WHAT?!
'CUSE ME!
CRASH

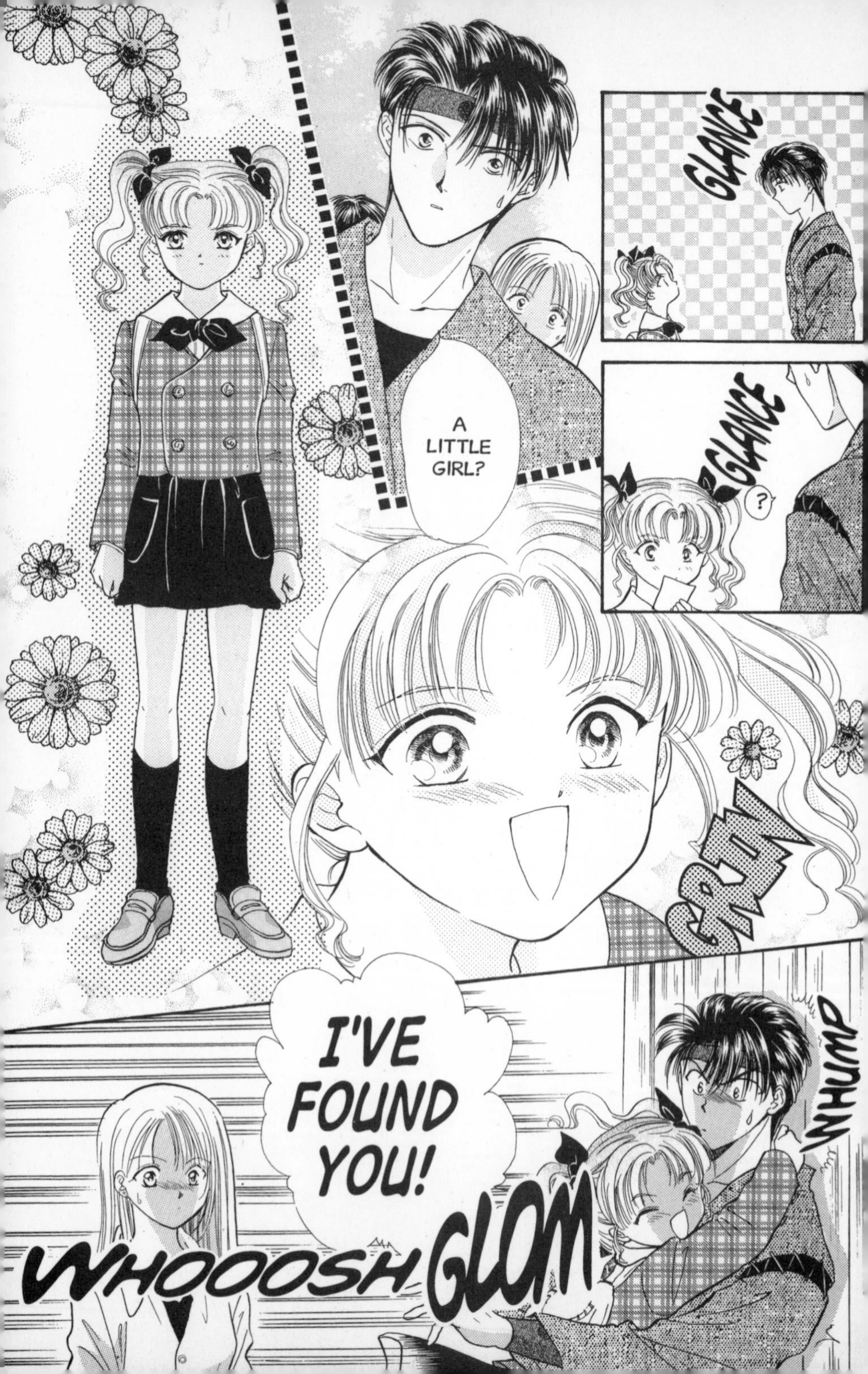
GLANCE
GLANCE
?
A LITTLE GIRL?
GRIN
WHUMP
I'VE FOUND YOU!
GLOM
WHOOOSH

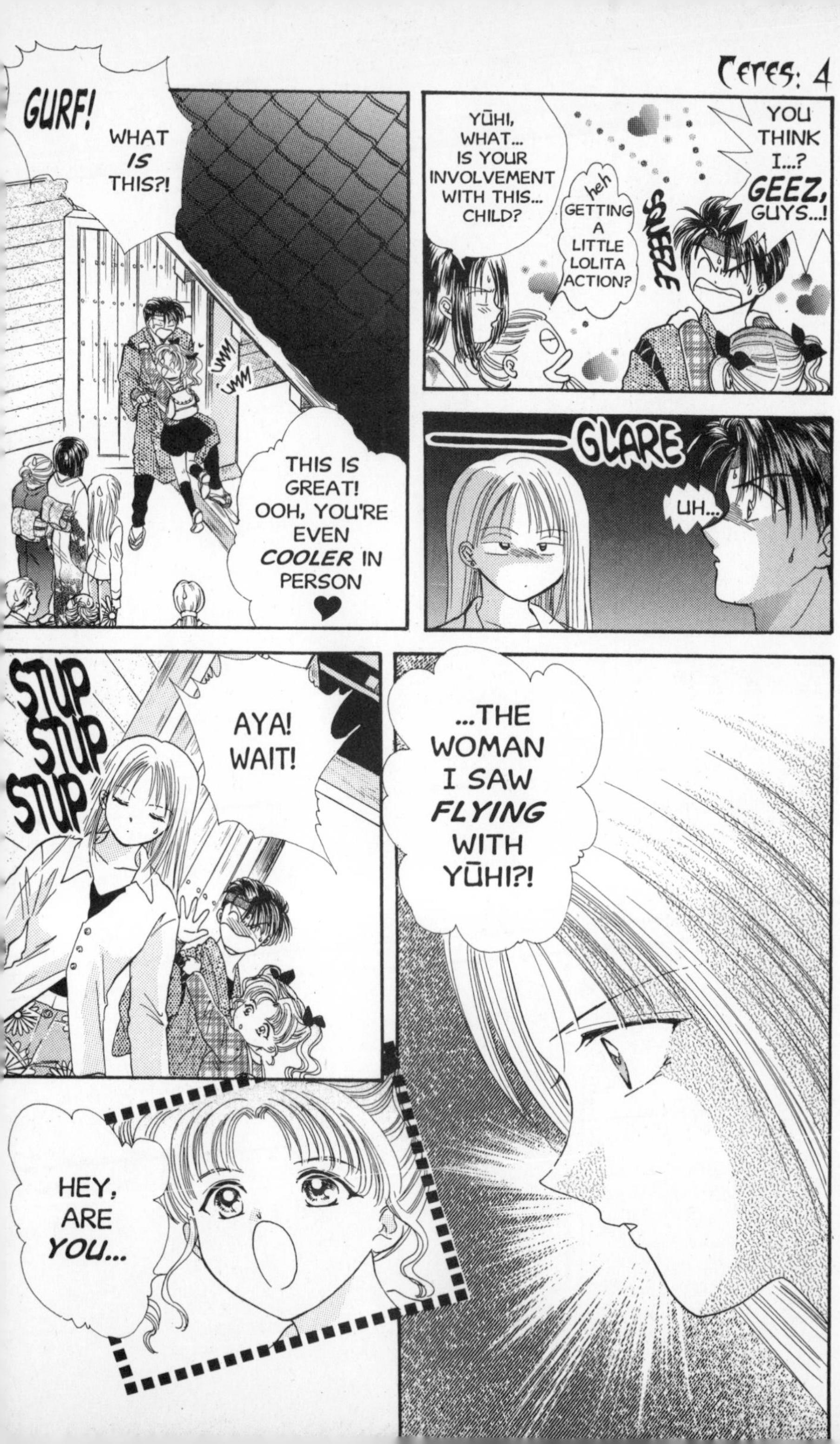
YŪHI, WHAT... IS YOUR INVOLVEMENT WITH THIS... CHILD?
heh
GETTING A LITTLE LOLITA ACTION?
SQUEEZE
YOU THINK I...? GEEZ, GUYS...!
GLARE
UH...
GURF!
WHAT IS THIS?!
UMM
UMM
THIS IS GREAT! OOH, YOU'RE EVEN COOLER IN PERSON ♥
...THE WOMAN I SAW FLYING WITH YŪHI?!
STUP STUP STUP
AYA! WAIT!
HEY, ARE YOU...

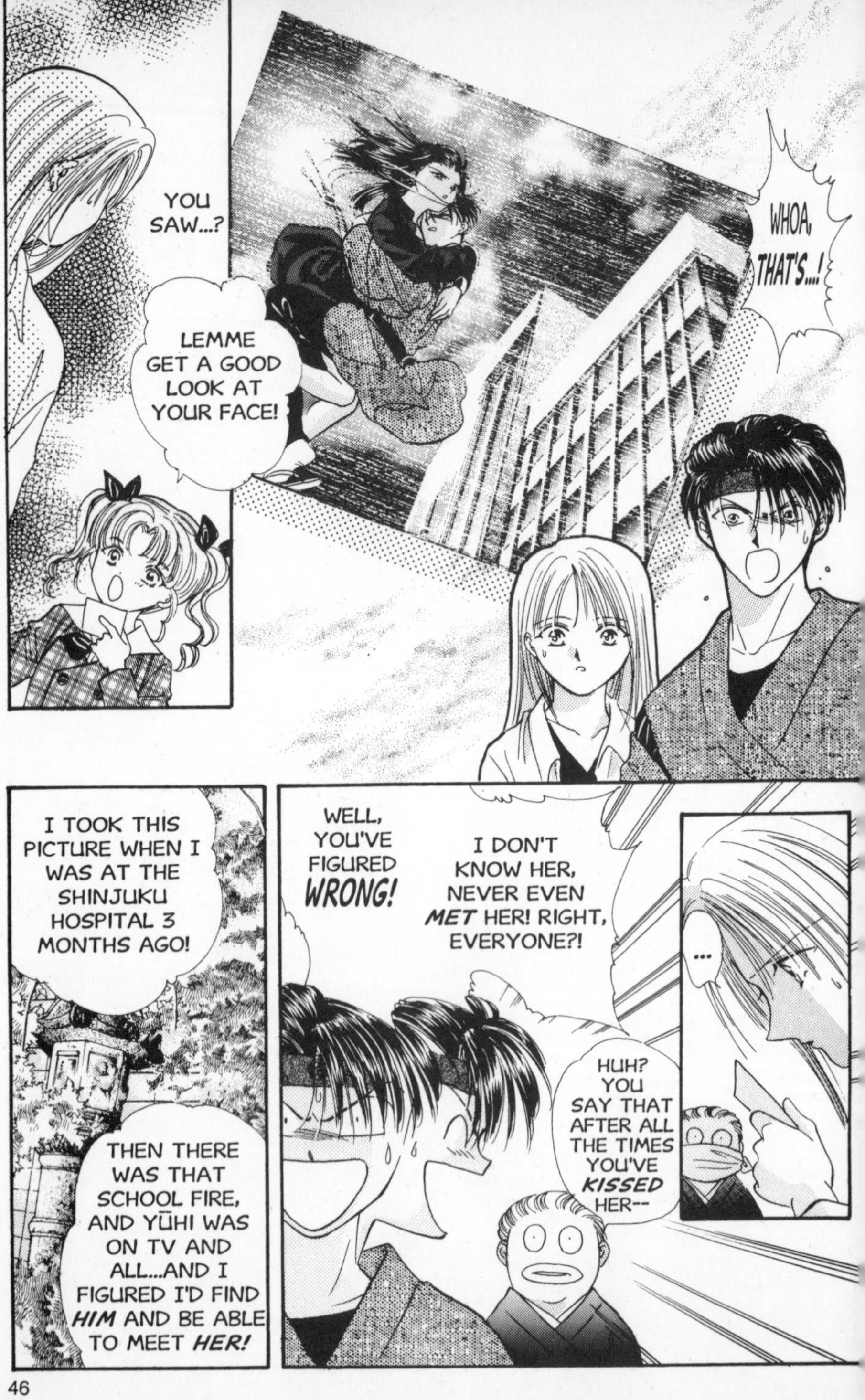
YOU SAW...?
LEMME GET A GOOD LOOK AT YOUR FACE!
WHOA, THAT'S...!
I TOOK THIS PICTURE WHEN I WAS AT THE SHINJUKU HOSPITAL 3 MONTHS AGO!
THEN THERE WAS THAT SCHOOL FIRE, AND YŪHI WAS ON TV AND ALL...AND I FIGURED I'D FIND *HIM* AND BE ABLE TO MEET *HER!*
WELL, YOU'VE FIGURED **WRONG!**
I DON'T KNOW HER, NEVER EVEN *MET* HER! RIGHT, EVERYONE?!
HUH? YOU SAY THAT AFTER ALL THE TIMES YOU'VE *KISSED* HER--
...

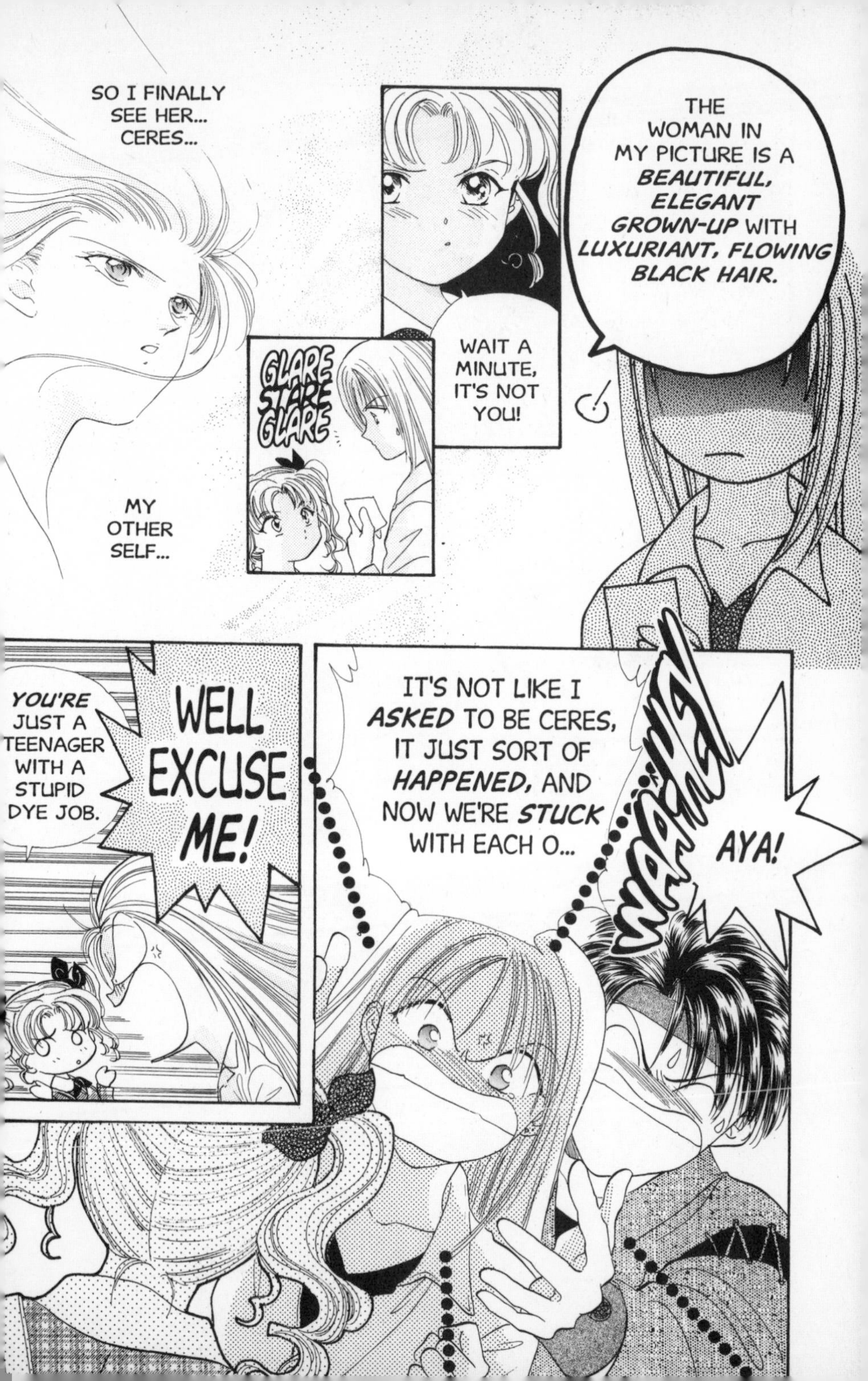

THE WOMAN IN MY PICTURE IS A *BEAUTIFUL, ELEGANT GROWN-UP* WITH *LUXURIANT, FLOWING BLACK HAIR.*
WAIT A MINUTE, IT'S NOT YOU!
GLARE STARE GLARE
SO I FINALLY SEE HER... CERES...
MY OTHER SELF...
IT'S NOT LIKE I *ASKED* TO BE CERES, IT JUST SORT OF *HAPPENED,* AND NOW WE'RE *STUCK* WITH EACH O...
AYA!
YOU'RE JUST A TEENAGER WITH A STUPID DYE JOB.
WELL EXCUSE ME!

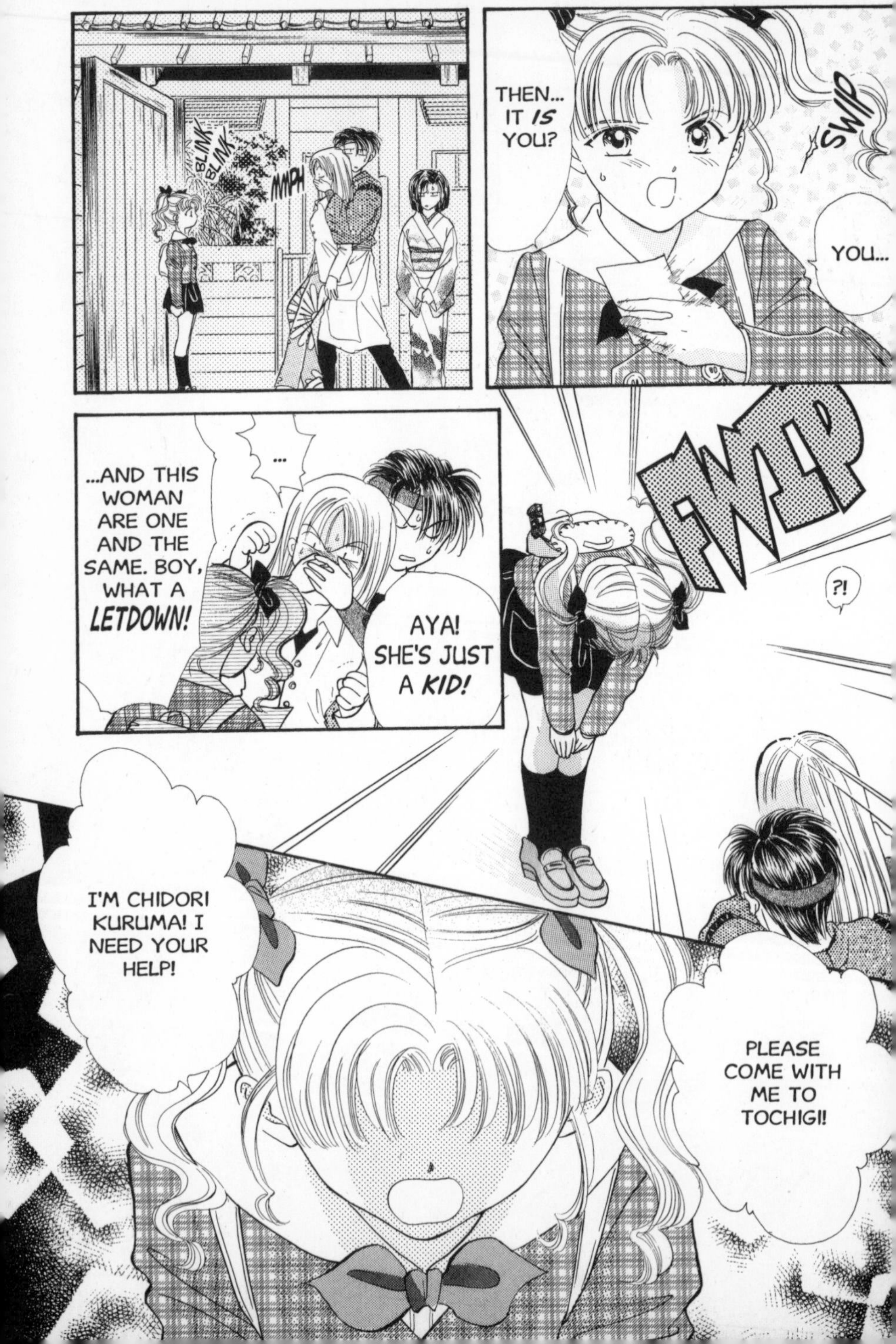
SWIP
THEN... IT *IS* YOU?
YOU...
BLINK BLINK
MMPH
FWIP
?!
...
...AND THIS WOMAN ARE ONE AND THE SAME. BOY, WHAT A **LETDOWN!**
AYA! SHE'S JUST A *KID!*
PLEASE COME WITH ME TO TOCHIGI!
I'M CHIDORI KURUMA! I NEED YOUR HELP!

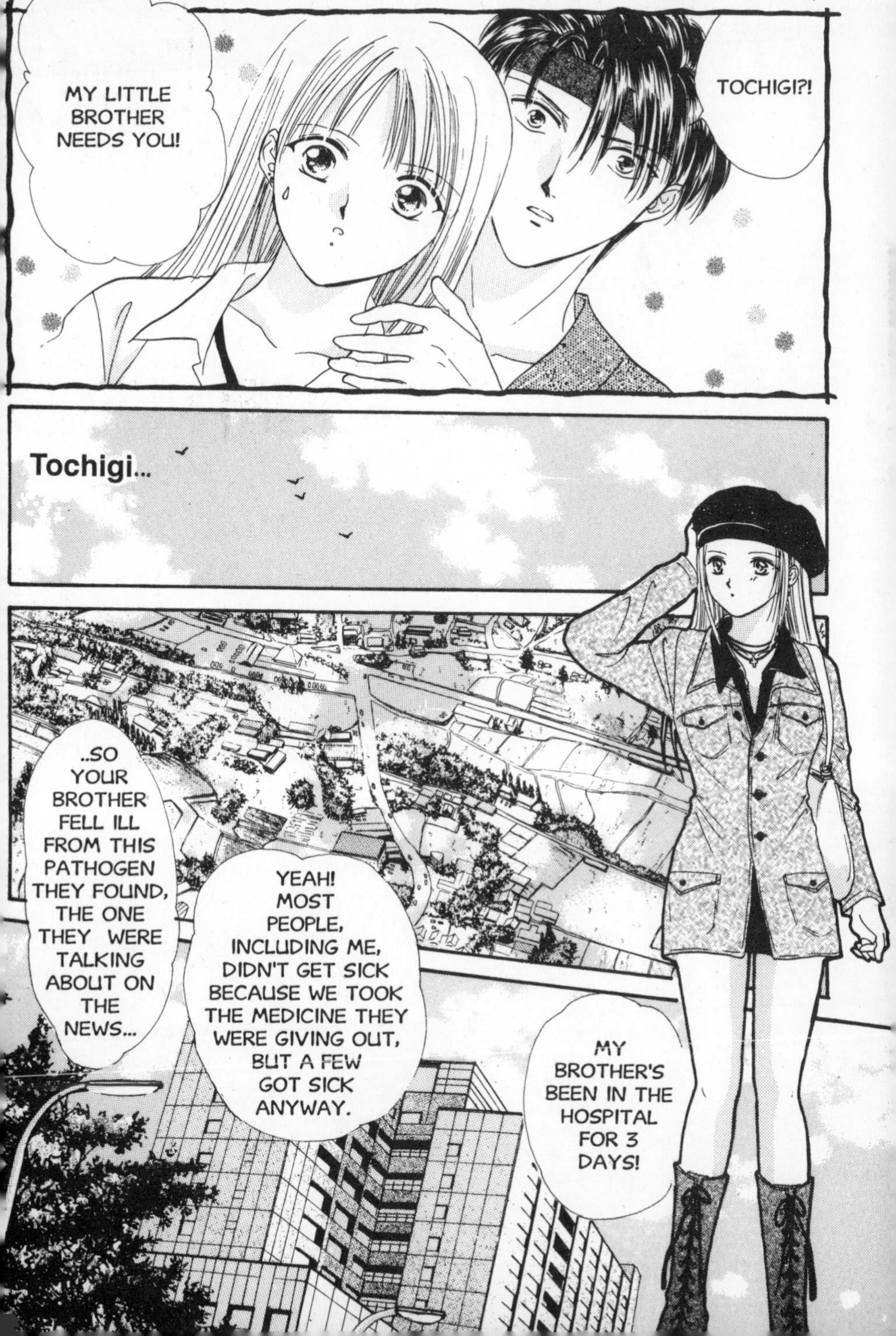
TOCHIGI?!
MY LITTLE BROTHER NEEDS YOU!
Tochigi...
MY BROTHER'S BEEN IN THE HOSPITAL FOR 3 DAYS!
..SO YOUR BROTHER FELL ILL FROM THIS PATHOGEN THEY FOUND, THE ONE THEY WERE TALKING ABOUT ON THE NEWS...
YEAH! MOST PEOPLE, INCLUDING ME, DIDN'T GET SICK BECAUSE WE TOOK THE MEDICINE THEY WERE GIVING OUT, BUT A FEW GOT SICK ANYWAY.

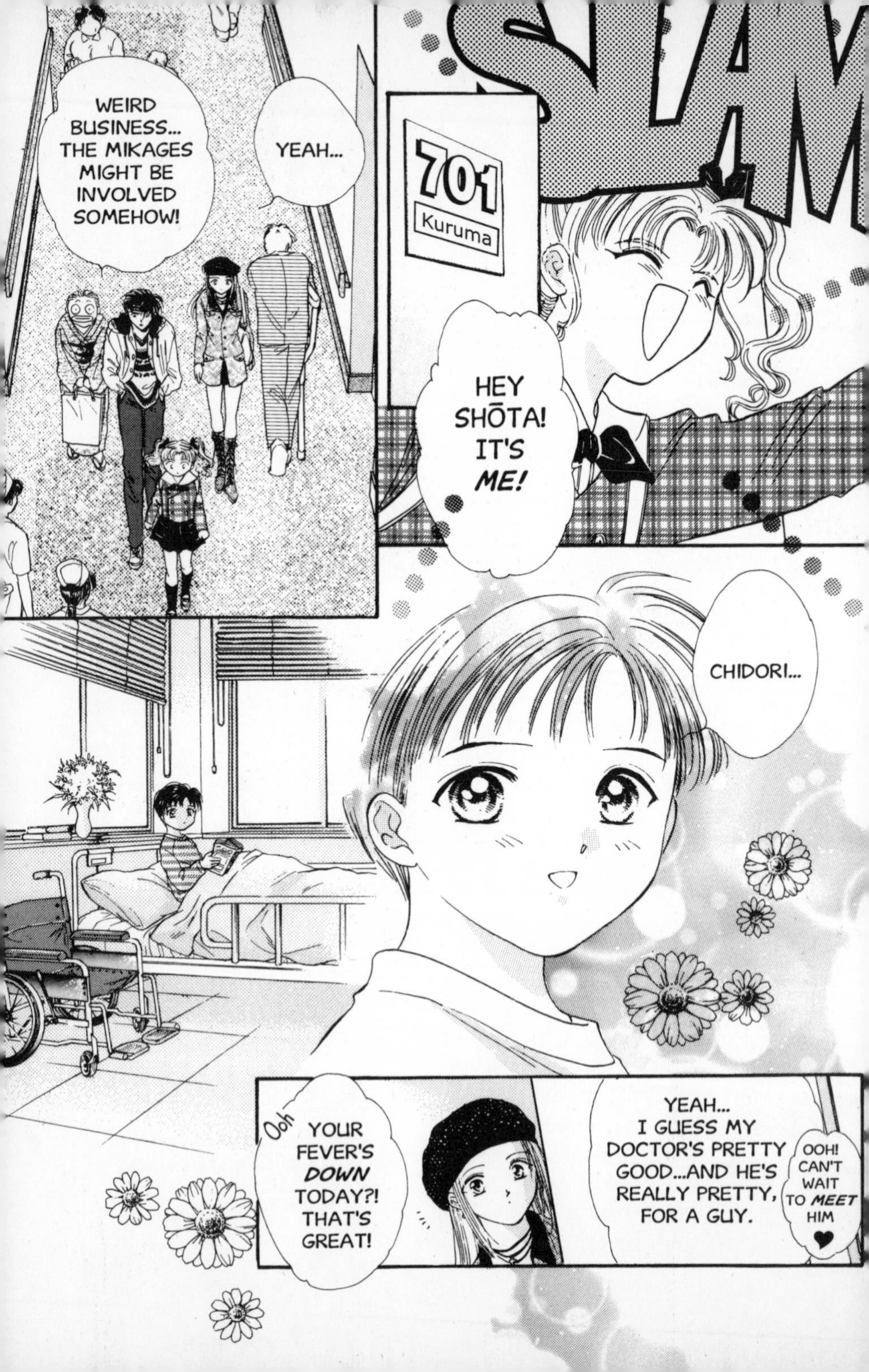
WEIRD BUSINESS... THE MIKAGES MIGHT BE INVOLVED SOMEHOW!
YEAH...
SLAM
701
Kuruma
HEY SHŌTA! IT'S *ME!*
CHIDORI...
Ooh
YOUR FEVER'S *DOWN* TODAY?! THAT'S GREAT!
YEAH... I GUESS MY DOCTOR'S PRETTY GOOD...AND HE'S REALLY PRETTY, FOR A GUY.
OOH! CAN'T WAIT TO *MEET* HIM ♥

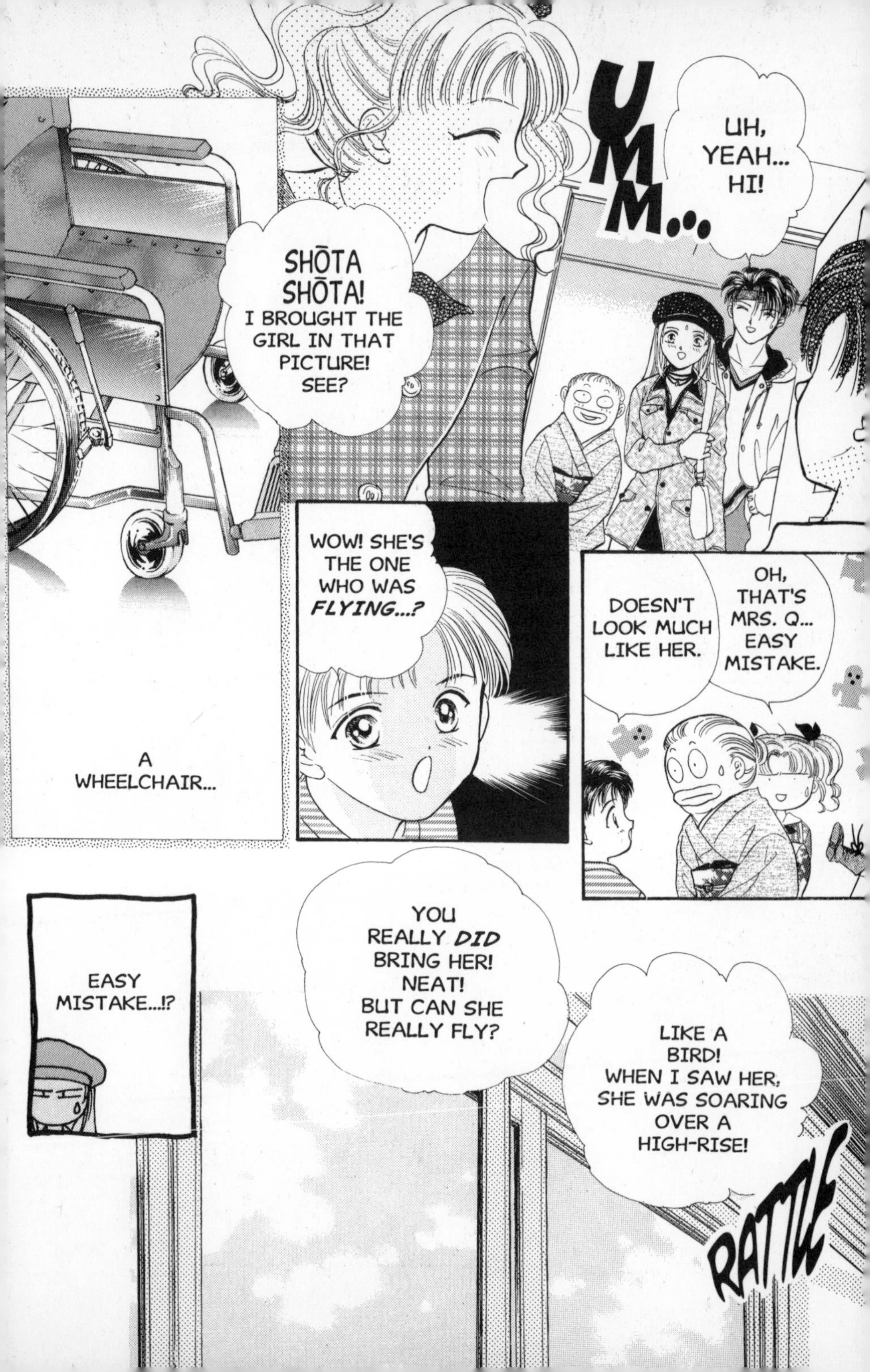
SHŌTA SHŌTA! I BROUGHT THE GIRL IN THAT PICTURE! SEE?
UMM...
UH, YEAH... HI!
OH, THAT'S MRS. Q... EASY MISTAKE.
DOESN'T LOOK MUCH LIKE HER.
WOW! SHE'S THE ONE WHO WAS *FLYING*...?
A WHEELCHAIR...
YOU REALLY *DID* BRING HER! NEAT! BUT CAN SHE REALLY FLY?
LIKE A BIRD! WHEN I SAW HER, SHE WAS SOARING OVER A HIGH-RISE!
RATTLE
EASY MISTAKE...!?

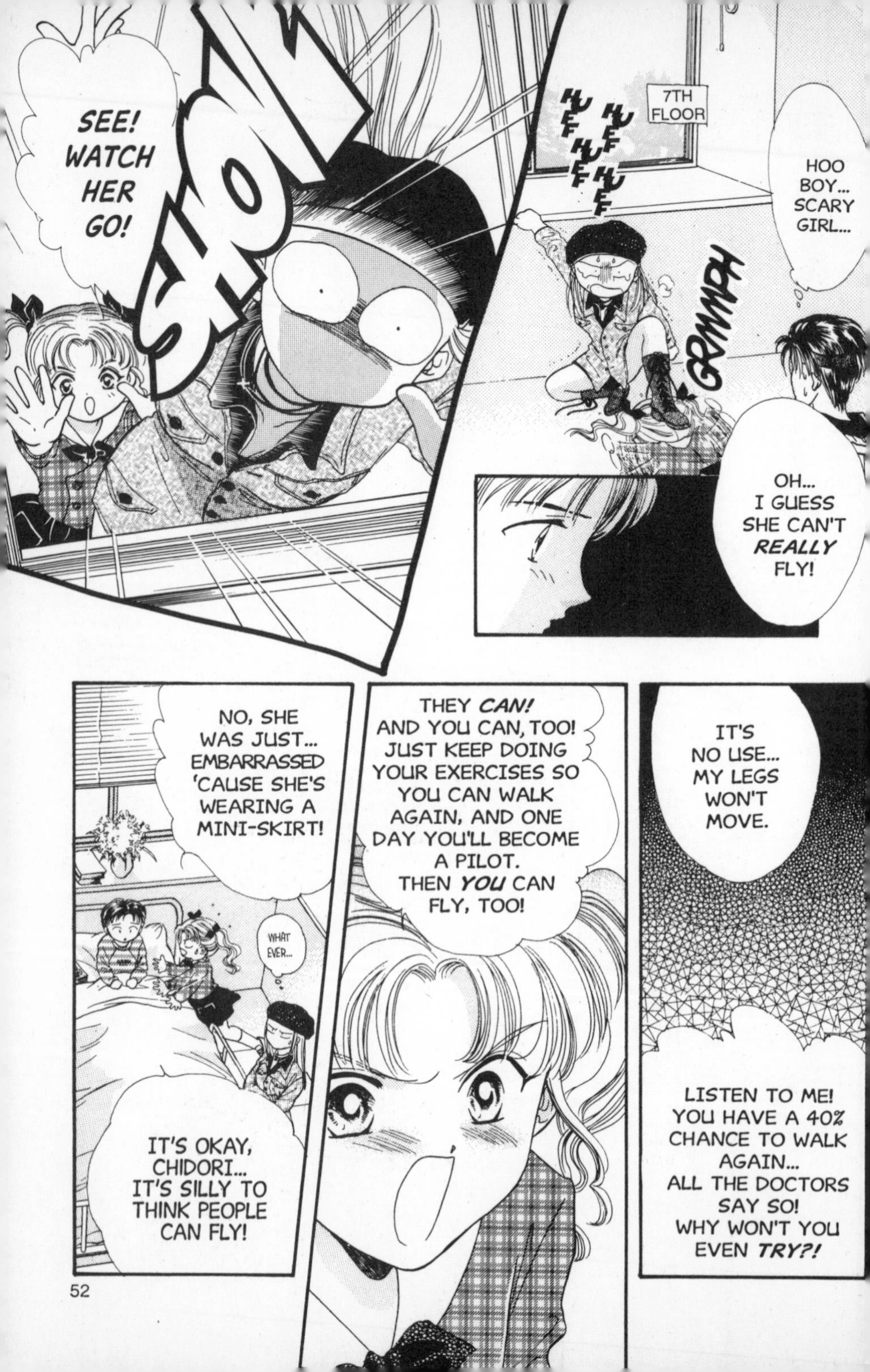
7TH FLOOR
HUFF HUFF HUFF HUFF
HOO BOY... SCARY GIRL...
GRMMPH
OH... I GUESS SHE CAN'T *REALLY* FLY!
SEE! WATCH HER GO!
IT'S NO USE... MY LEGS WON'T MOVE.
LISTEN TO ME! YOU HAVE A 40% CHANCE TO WALK AGAIN... ALL THE DOCTORS SAY SO! WHY WON'T YOU EVEN *TRY?!*
THEY *CAN!* AND YOU CAN, TOO! JUST KEEP DOING YOUR EXERCISES SO YOU CAN WALK AGAIN, AND ONE DAY YOU'LL BECOME A PILOT. THEN *YOU* CAN FLY, TOO!
NO, SHE WAS JUST... EMBARRASSED 'CAUSE SHE'S WEARING A MINI-SKIRT!
WHAT EVER...
IT'S OKAY, CHIDORI... IT'S SILLY TO THINK PEOPLE CAN FLY!

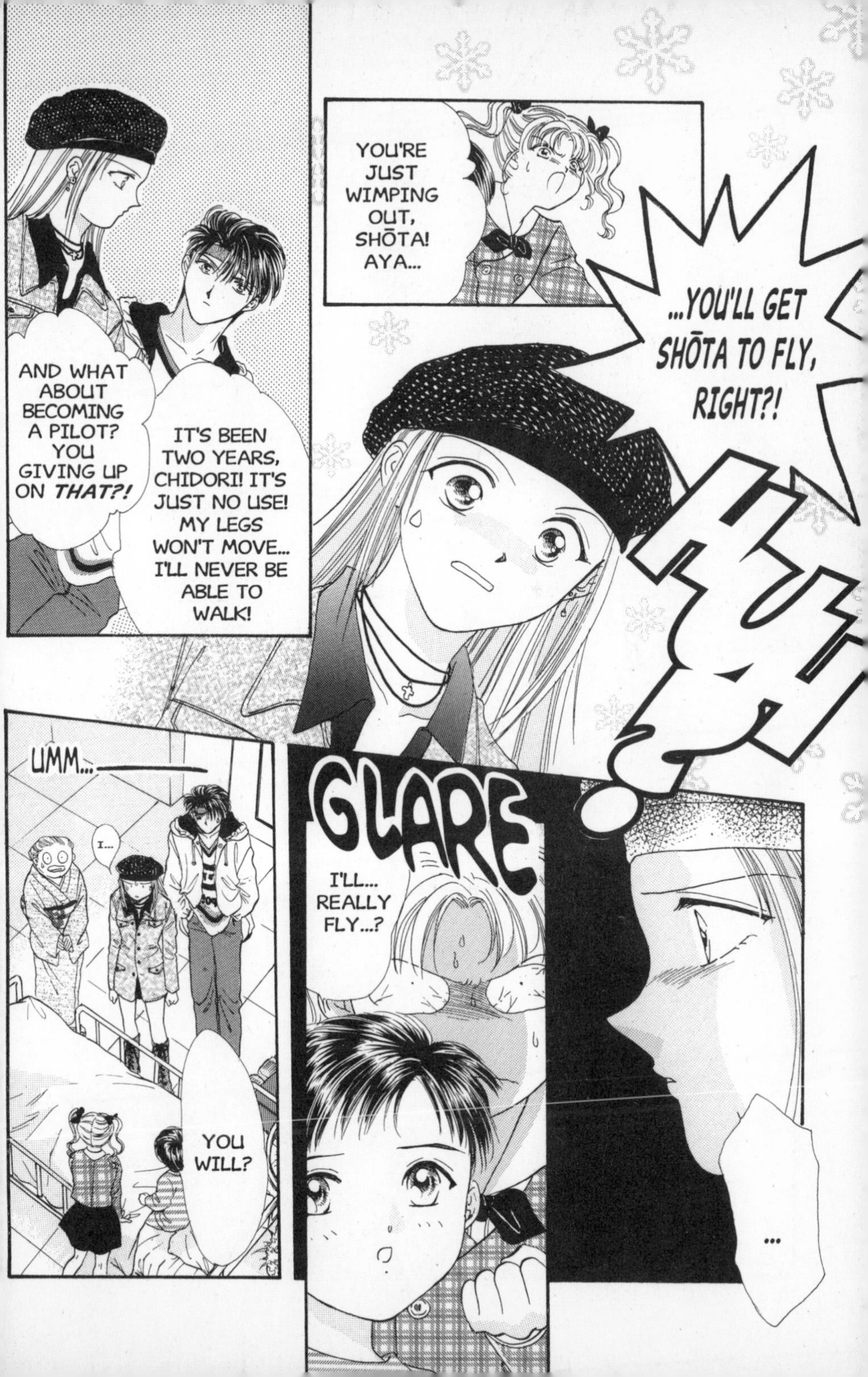
AND WHAT ABOUT BECOMING A PILOT? YOU GIVING UP ON *THAT?!*
IT'S BEEN TWO YEARS, CHIDORI! IT'S JUST NO USE! MY LEGS WON'T MOVE... I'LL NEVER BE ABLE TO WALK!
YOU'RE JUST WIMPING OUT, SHŌTA! AYA...
...YOU'LL GET SHŌTA TO FLY, RIGHT?!
UMM...
I...
YOU WILL?
GLARE
I'LL... REALLY FLY...?
...

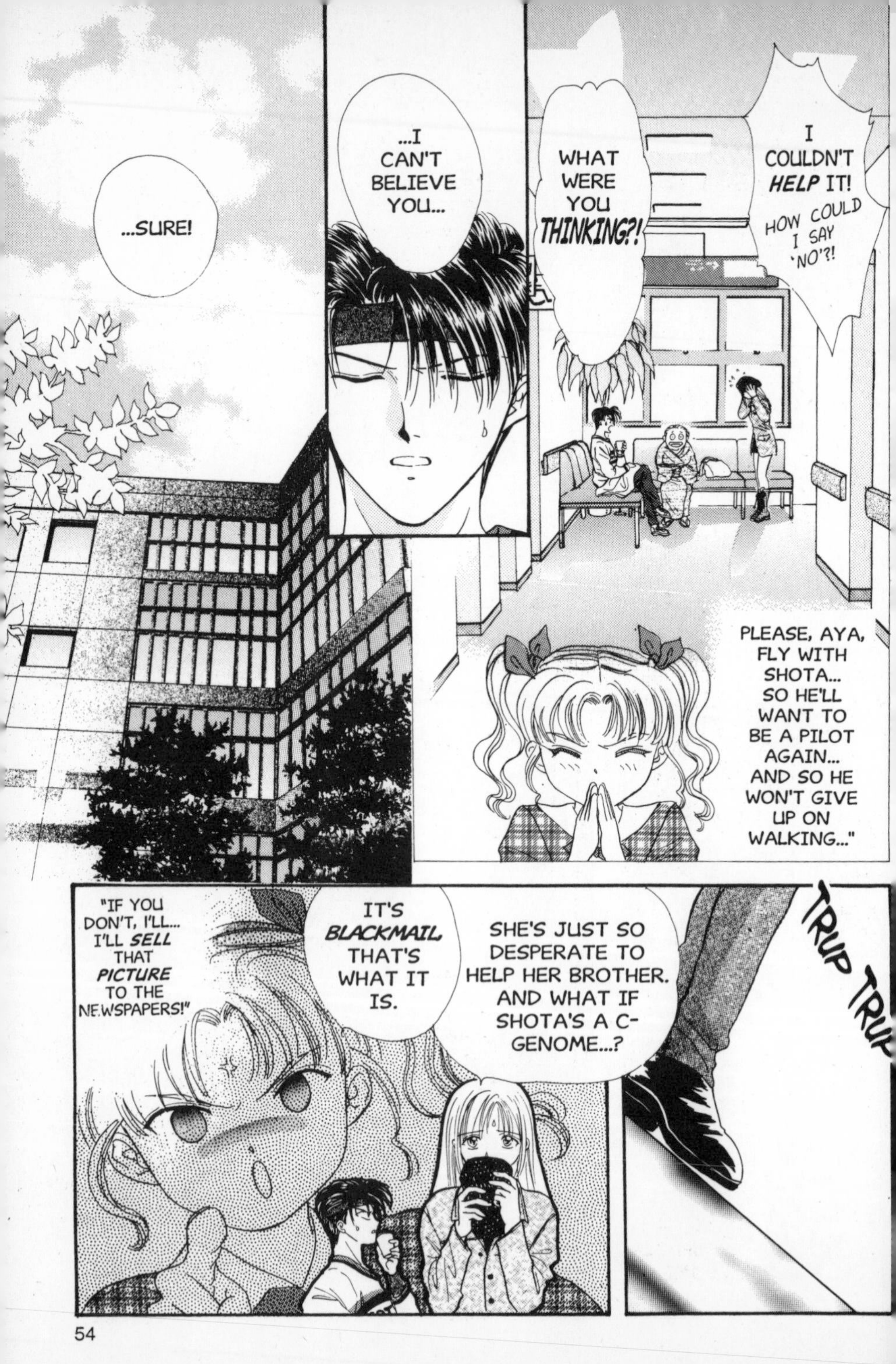
WHAT WERE YOU *THINKING?!*
I COULDN'T *HELP* IT!
HOW COULD I SAY 'NO'?!
PLEASE, AYA, FLY WITH SHOTA... SO HE'LL WANT TO BE A PILOT AGAIN... AND SO HE WON'T GIVE UP ON WALKING..."
...I CAN'T BELIEVE YOU...
...SURE!
TRUP TRUP
SHE'S JUST SO DESPERATE TO HELP HER BROTHER. AND WHAT IF SHOTA'S A C-GENOME...?
IT'S *BLACKMAIL* THAT'S WHAT IT IS.
"IF YOU DON'T, I'LL... I'LL *SELL* THAT *PICTURE* TO THE NEWSPAPERS!"

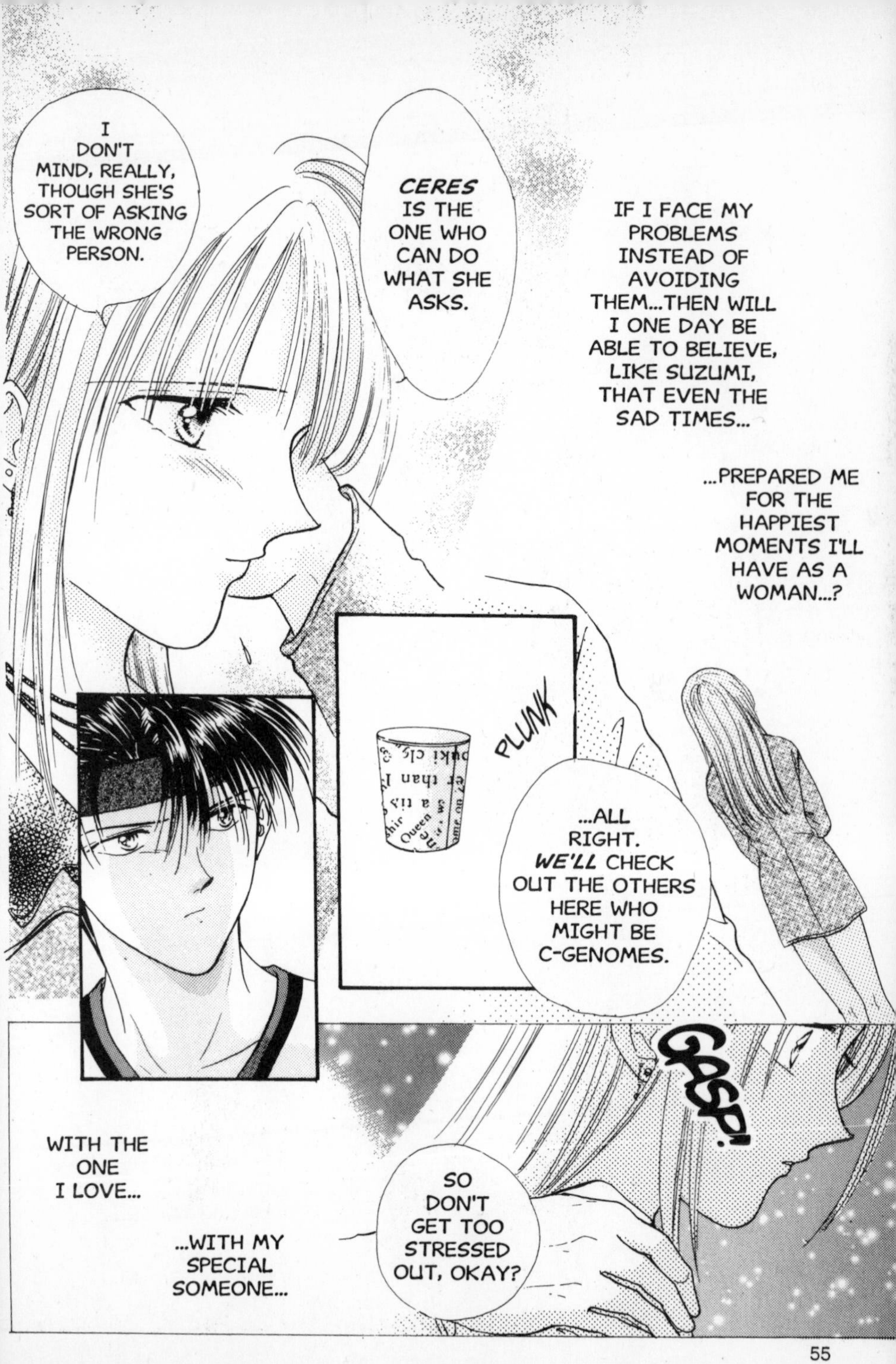
IF I FACE MY PROBLEMS INSTEAD OF AVOIDING THEM...THEN WILL I ONE DAY BE ABLE TO BELIEVE, LIKE SUZUMI, THAT EVEN THE SAD TIMES...
...PREPARED ME FOR THE HAPPIEST MOMENTS I'LL HAVE AS A WOMAN...?
I DON'T MIND, REALLY, THOUGH SHE'S SORT OF ASKING THE WRONG PERSON.
CERES IS THE ONE WHO CAN DO WHAT SHE ASKS.
PLUNK
...ALL RIGHT. *WE'LL* CHECK OUT THE OTHERS HERE WHO MIGHT BE C-GENOMES.
SO DON'T GET TOO STRESSED OUT, OKAY?
GASP!
WITH THE ONE I LOVE...
...WITH MY SPECIAL SOMEONE...

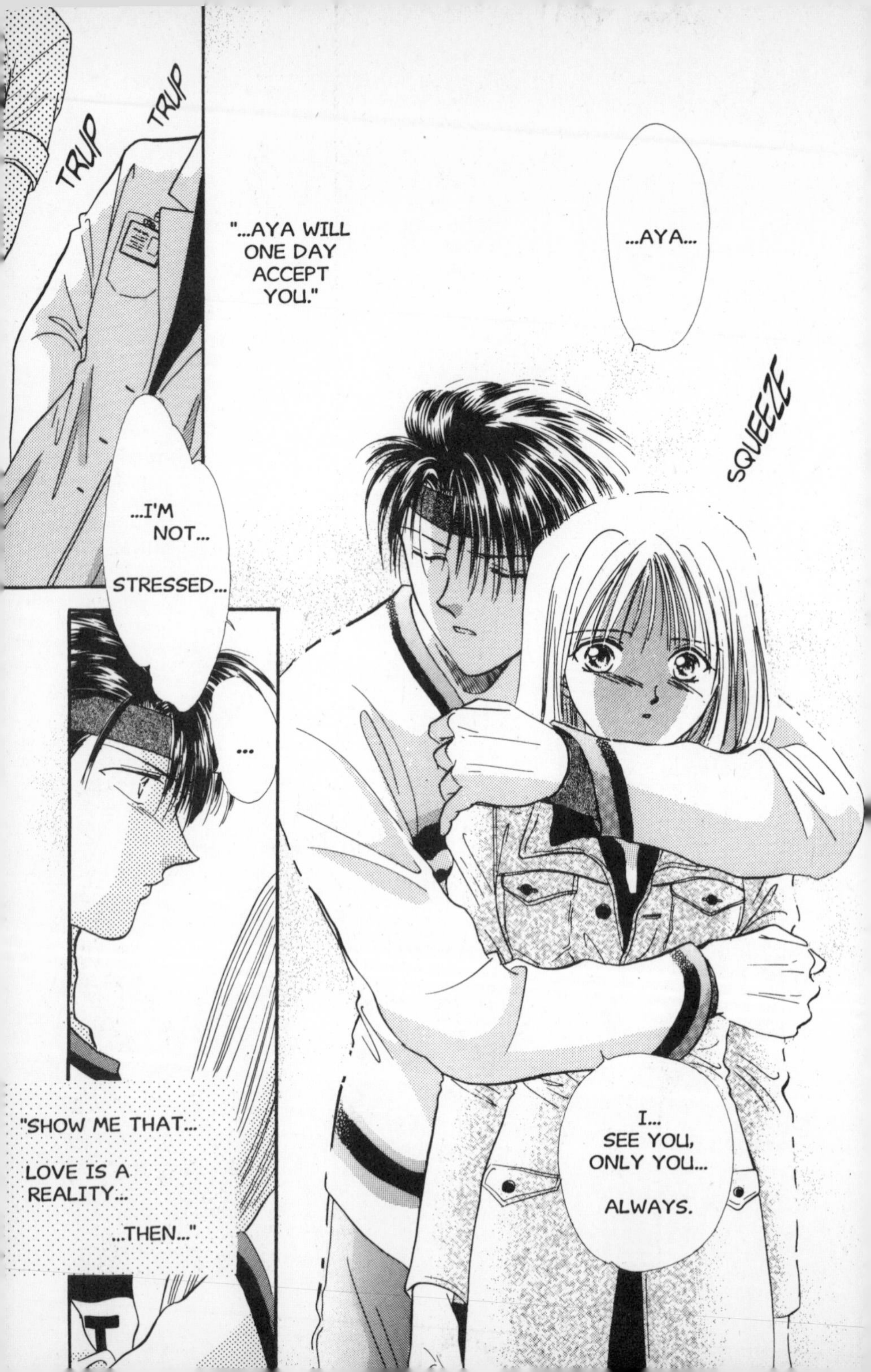
TRUP TRUP
"...AYA WILL ONE DAY ACCEPT YOU."
...I'M NOT... STRESSED...
...
"SHOW ME THAT... LOVE IS A REALITY... ...THEN..."
...AYA...
SQUEEZE
I... SEE YOU, ONLY YOU... ALWAYS.

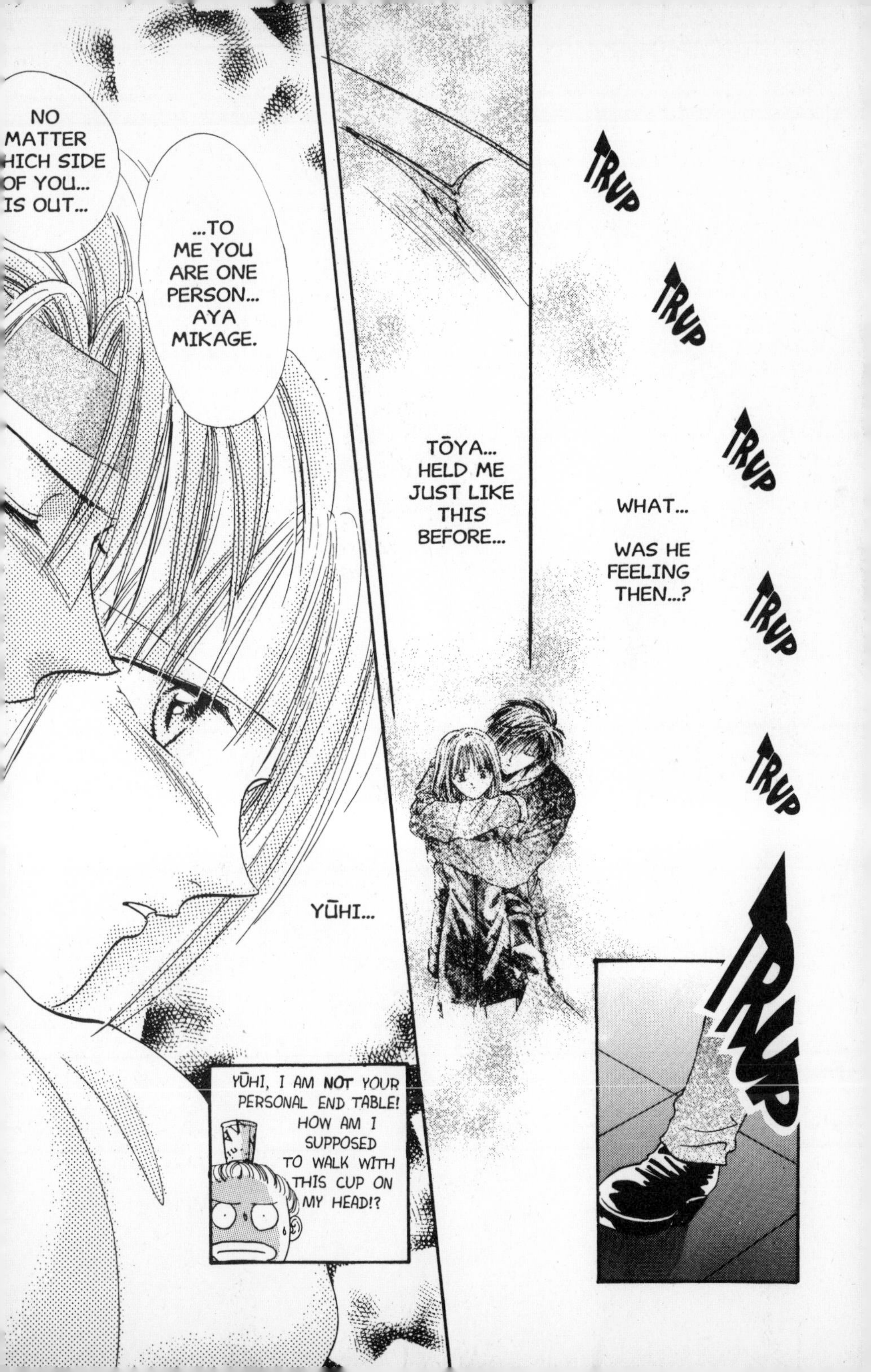
TRUP
TRUP
TRUP
WHAT...
WAS HE FEELING THEN...?
TRUP
TRUP
TRUP
TŌYA... HELD ME JUST LIKE THIS BEFORE...
YŪHI...
NO MATTER HICH SIDE OF YOU... IS OUT...
...TO ME YOU ARE ONE PERSON... AYA MIKAGE.
YŪHI, I AM NOT YOUR PERSONAL END TABLE! HOW AM I SUPPOSED TO WALK WITH THIS CUP ON MY HEAD!?

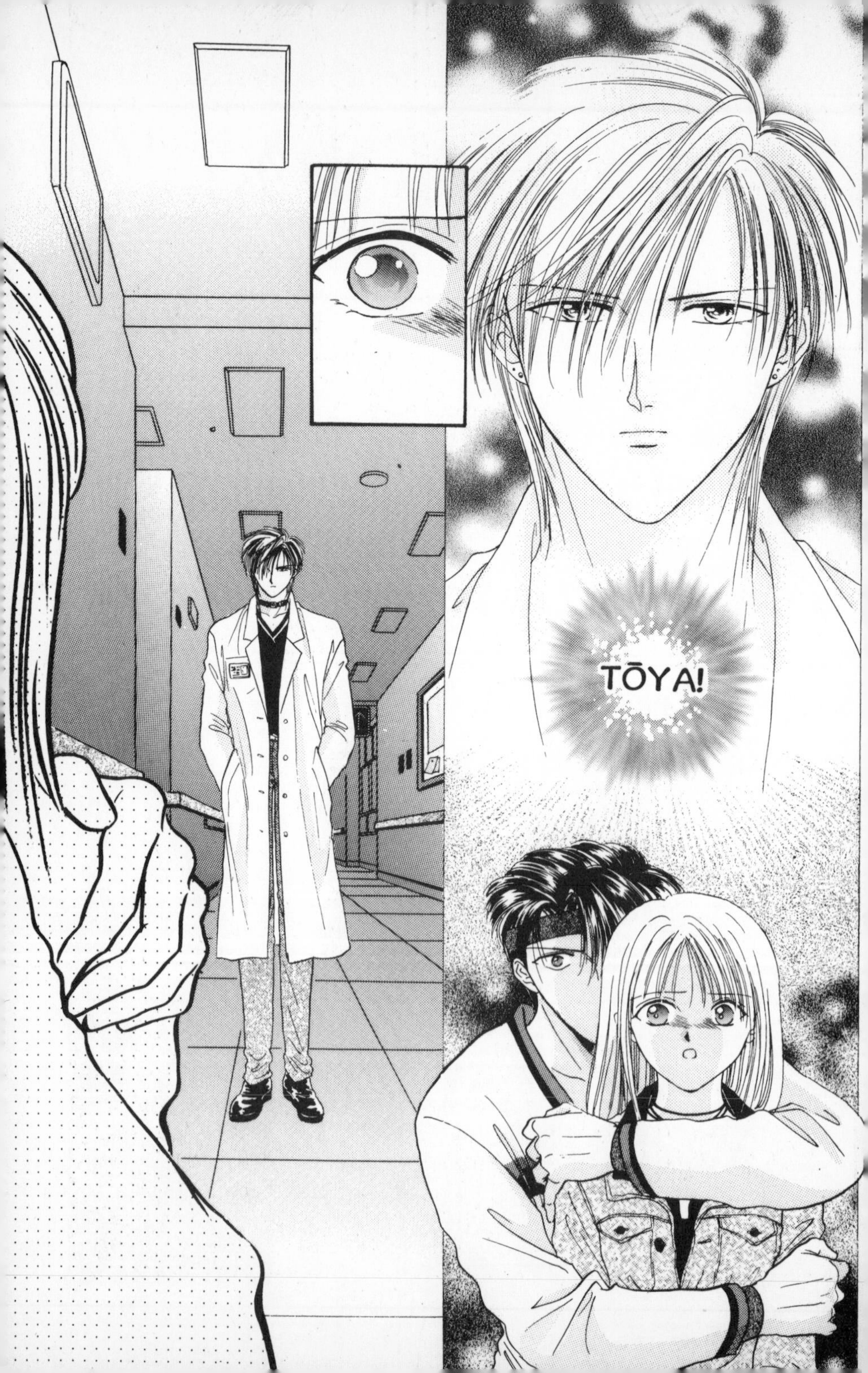
TŌYA!

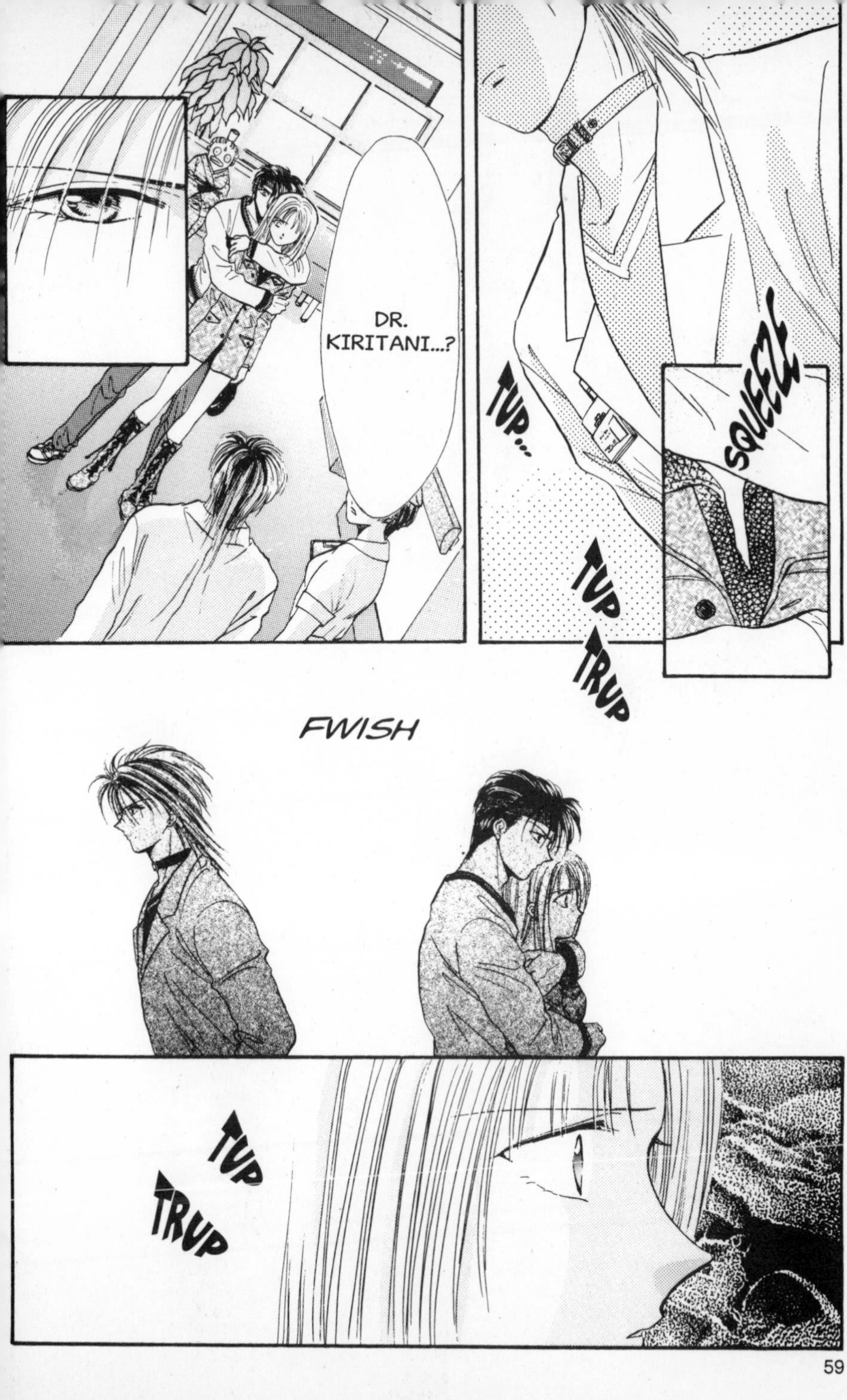
SQUEEZE
TUP...
TUP
TRUP
DR. KIRITANI...?
FWISH
TUP
TRUP

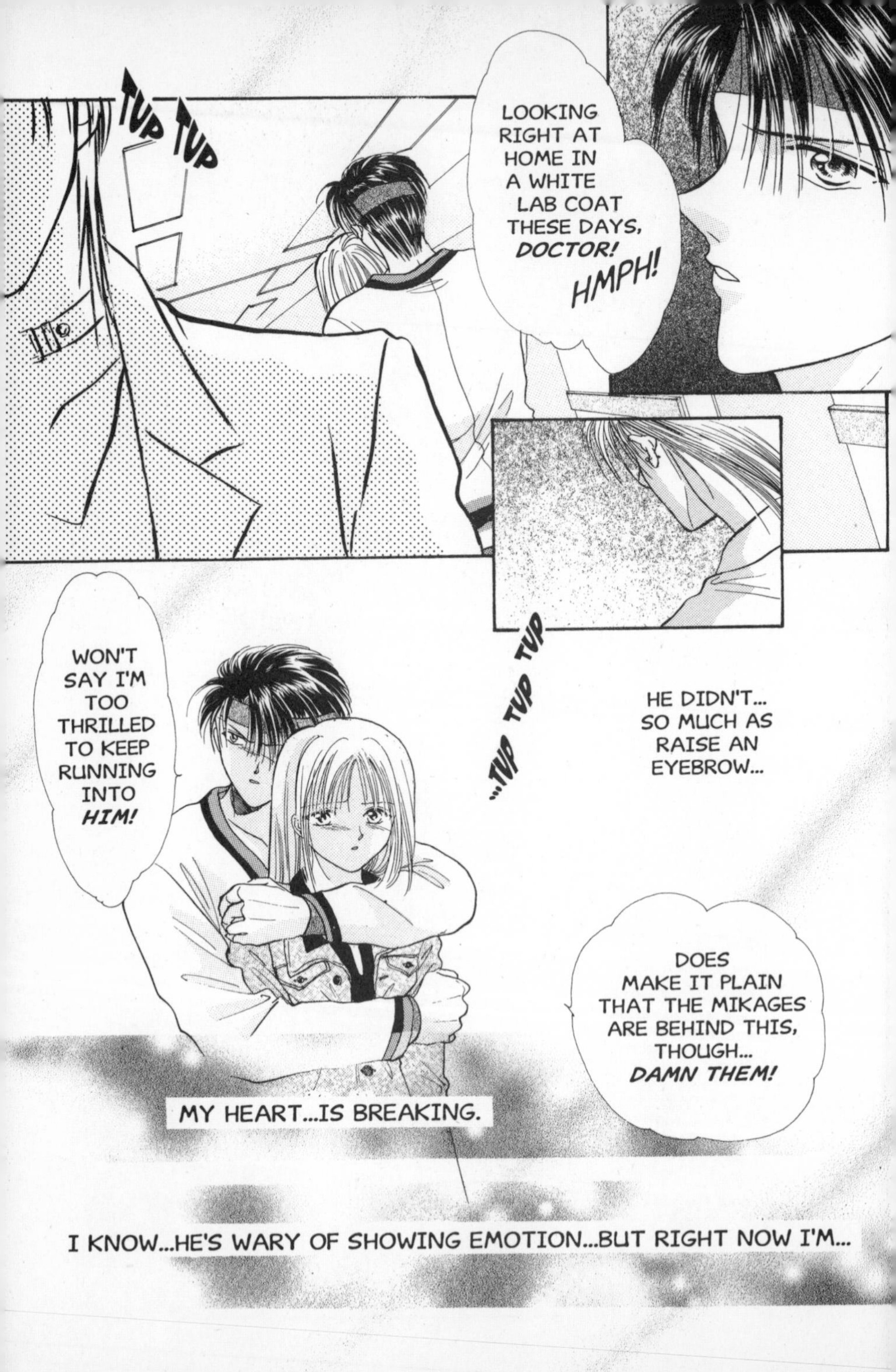
LOOKING RIGHT AT HOME IN A WHITE LAB COAT THESE DAYS, DOCTOR!
HMPH!
TUP TUP
...TUP TUP TUP
HE DIDN'T... SO MUCH AS RAISE AN EYEBROW...
WON'T SAY I'M TOO THRILLED TO KEEP RUNNING INTO HIM!
DOES MAKE IT PLAIN THAT THE MIKAGES ARE BEHIND THIS, THOUGH... DAMN THEM!
MY HEART...IS BREAKING.
I KNOW...HE'S WARY OF SHOWING EMOTION...BUT RIGHT NOW I'M...

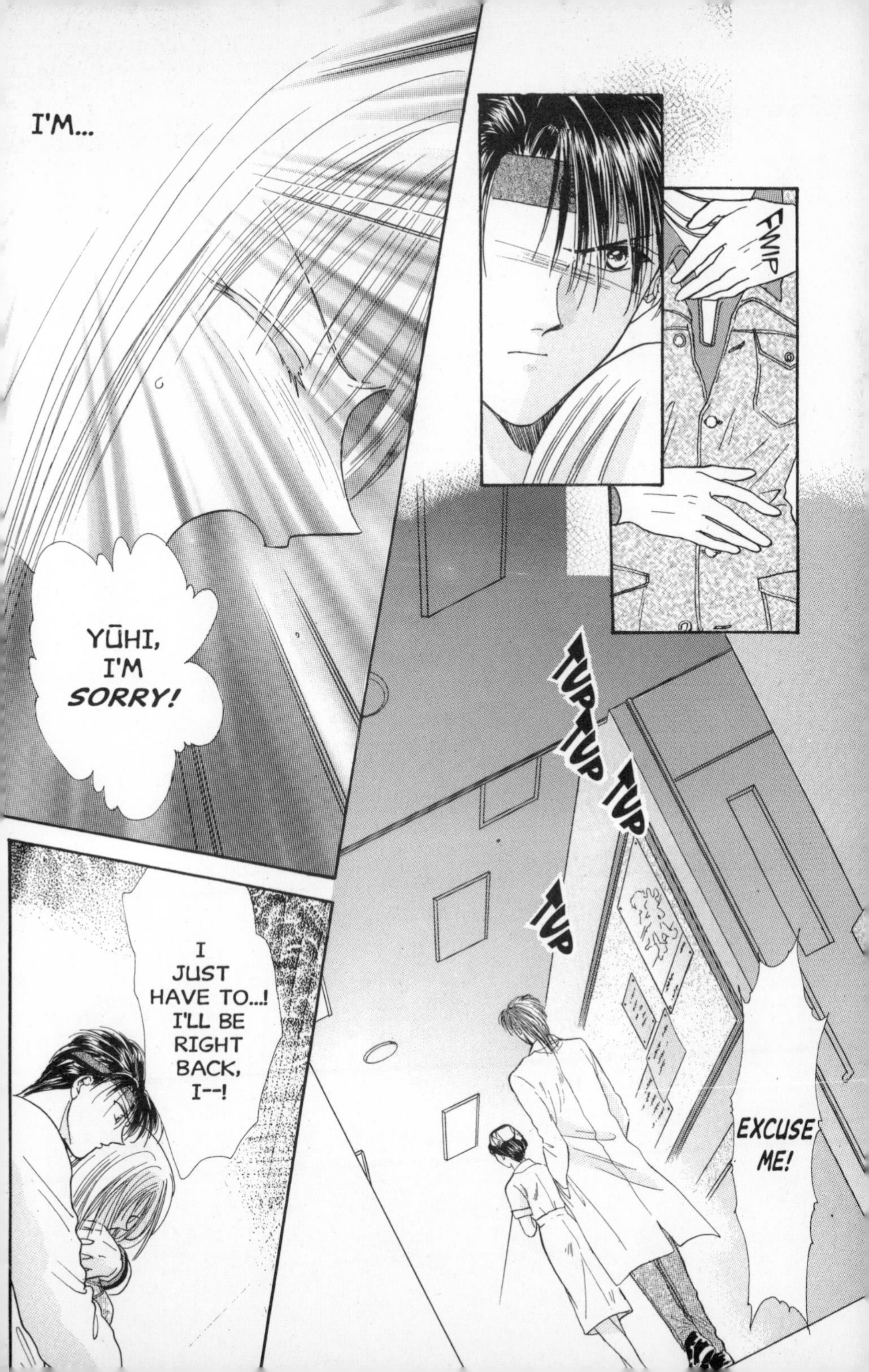
FWIP
I'M...
YŪHI, I'M SORRY!
TUP TUP
TUP
TUP
TUP
EXCUSE ME!
I JUST HAVE TO...! I'LL BE RIGHT BACK, I--!

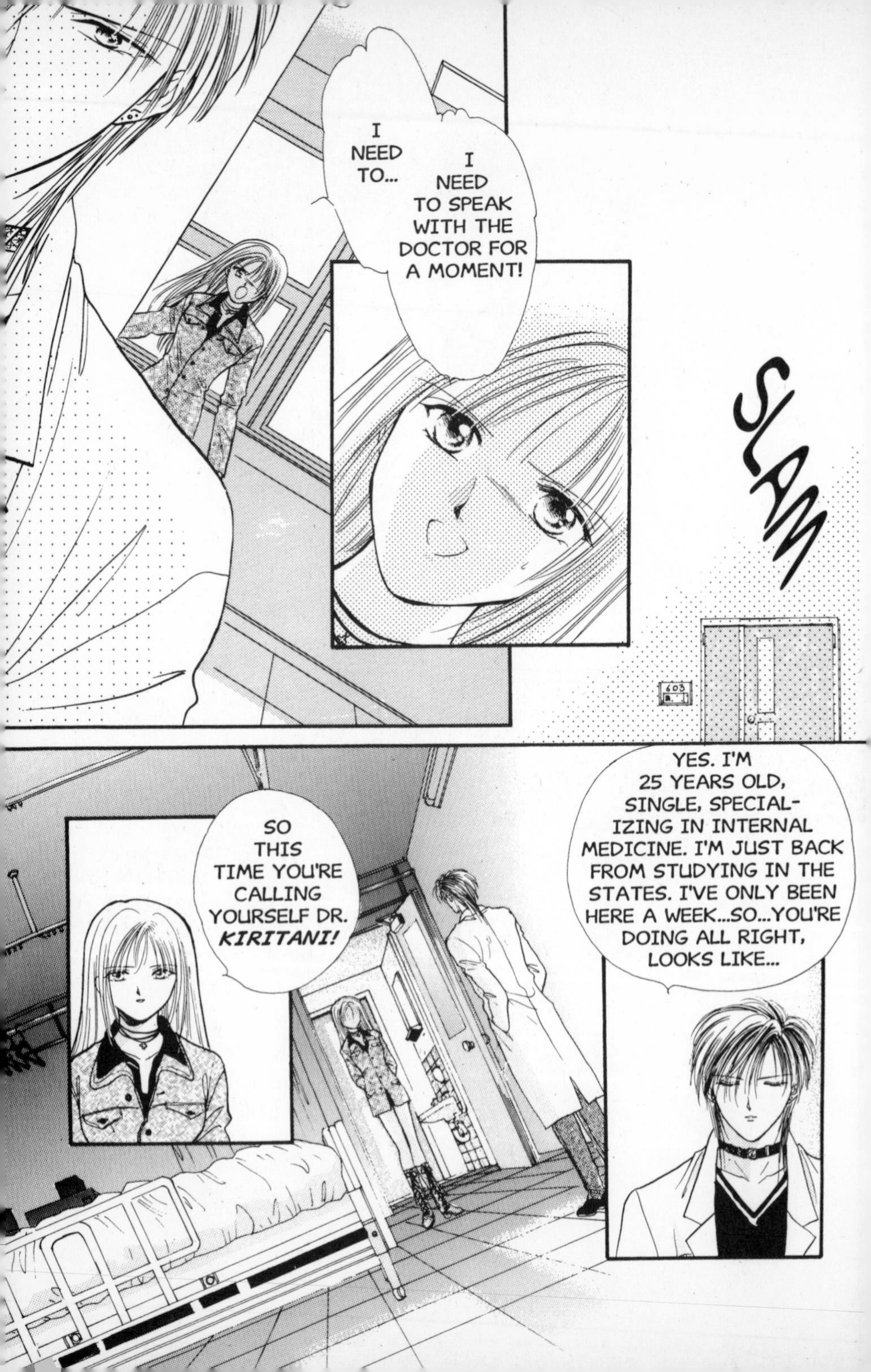
SLAM
I NEED TO...
I NEED TO SPEAK WITH THE DOCTOR FOR A MOMENT!
603
SO THIS TIME YOU'RE CALLING YOURSELF DR. *KIRITANI!*
YES. I'M 25 YEARS OLD, SINGLE, SPECIAL-IZING IN INTERNAL MEDICINE. I'M JUST BACK FROM STUDYING IN THE STATES. I'VE ONLY BEEN HERE A WEEK...SO...YOU'RE DOING ALL RIGHT, LOOKS LIKE...

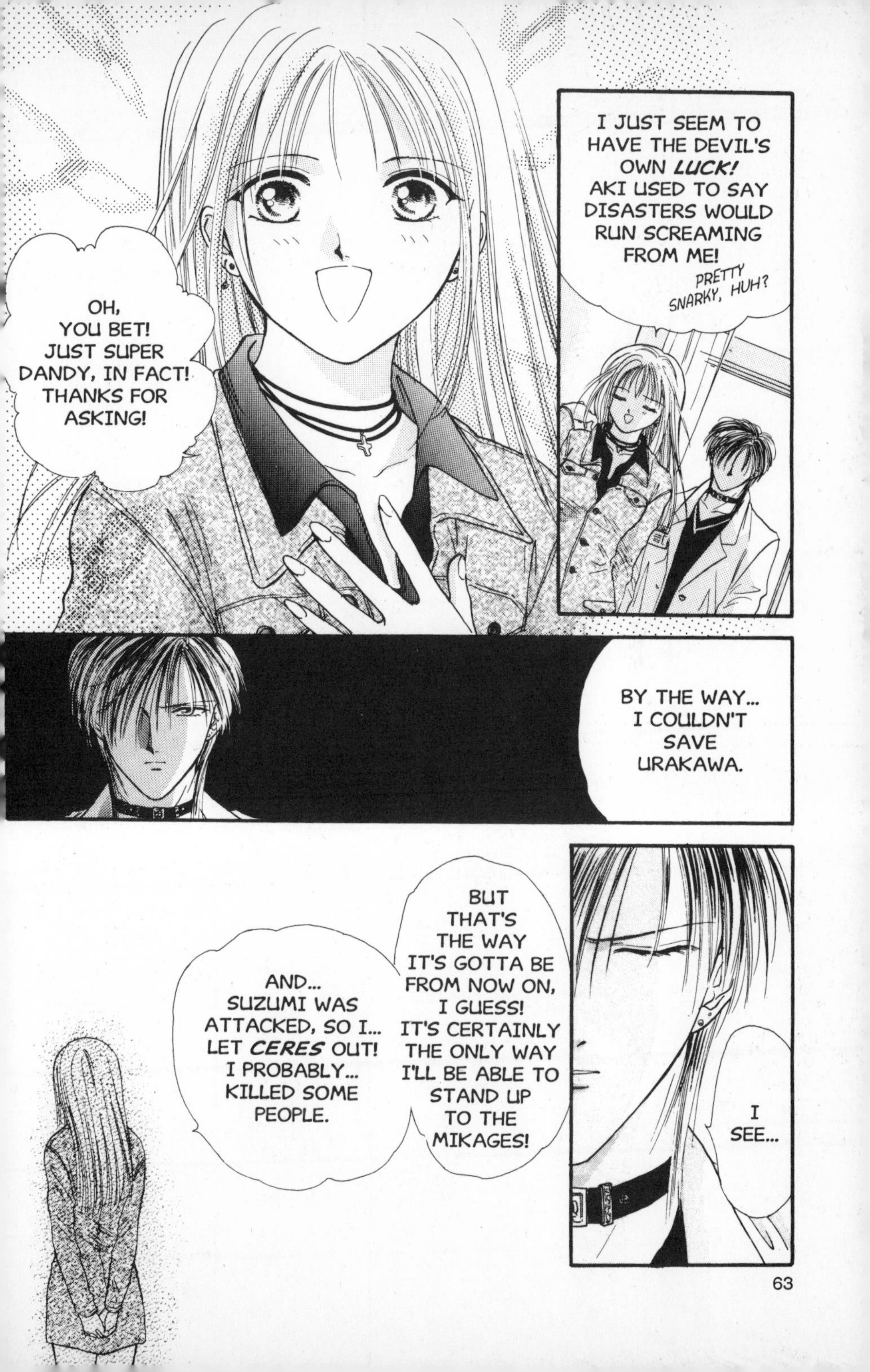
OH, YOU BET! JUST SUPER DANDY, IN FACT! THANKS FOR ASKING!
I JUST SEEM TO HAVE THE DEVIL'S OWN ***LUCK!*** AKI USED TO SAY DISASTERS WOULD RUN SCREAMING FROM ME!
PRETTY SNARKY, HUH?
BY THE WAY... I COULDN'T SAVE URAKAWA.
AND... SUZUMI WAS ATTACKED, SO I... LET ***CERES*** OUT! I PROBABLY... KILLED SOME PEOPLE.
BUT THAT'S THE WAY IT'S GOTTA BE FROM NOW ON, I GUESS! IT'S CERTAINLY THE ONLY WAY I'LL BE ABLE TO STAND UP TO THE MIKAGES!
I SEE...

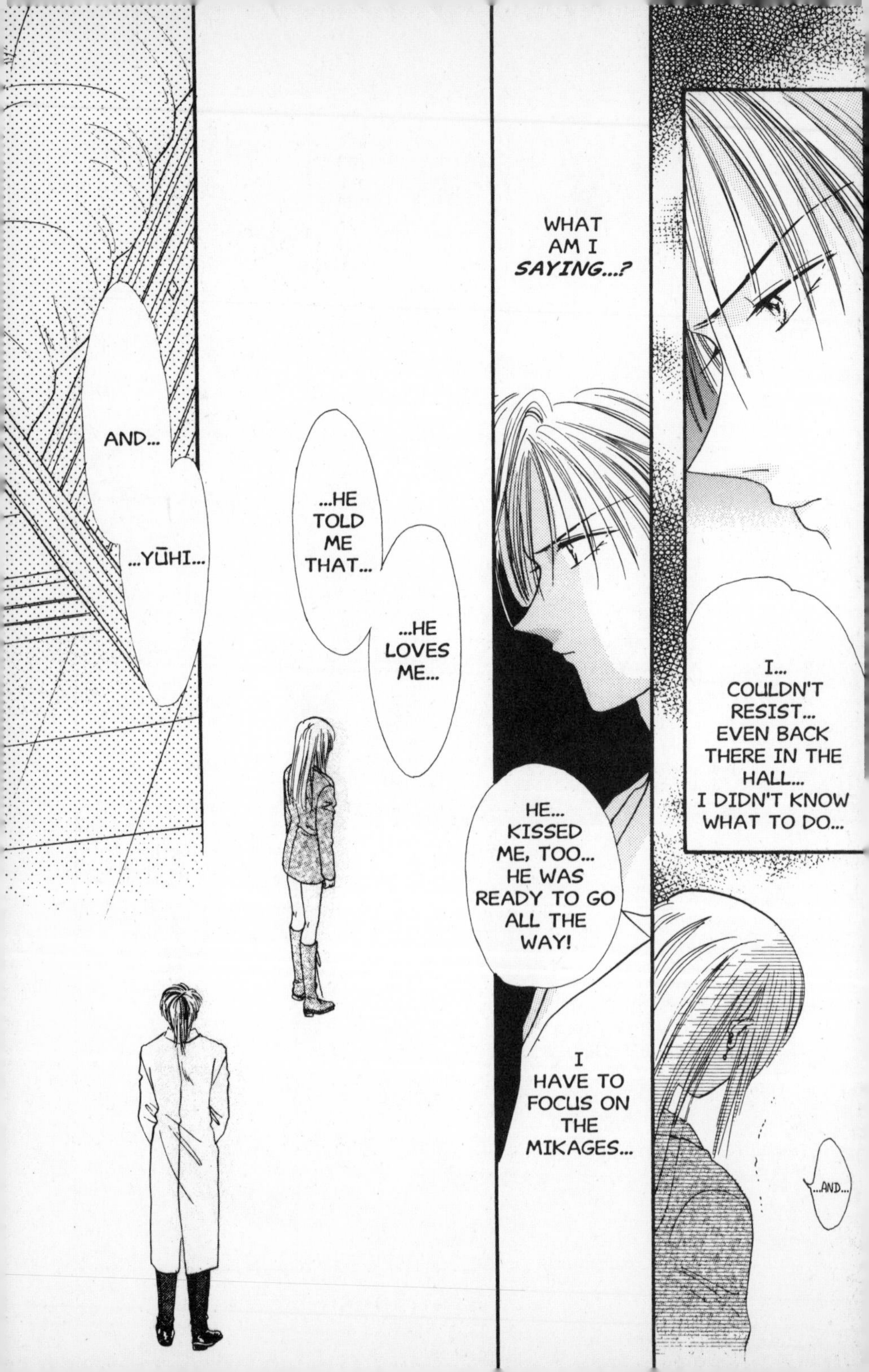
I... COULDN'T RESIST... EVEN BACK THERE IN THE HALL... I DIDN'T KNOW WHAT TO DO...
...AND...
WHAT AM I SAYING...?
HE... KISSED ME, TOO... HE WAS READY TO GO ALL THE WAY!
I HAVE TO FOCUS ON THE MIKAGES...
...HE TOLD ME THAT...
...HE LOVES ME...
AND...
...YŪHI...

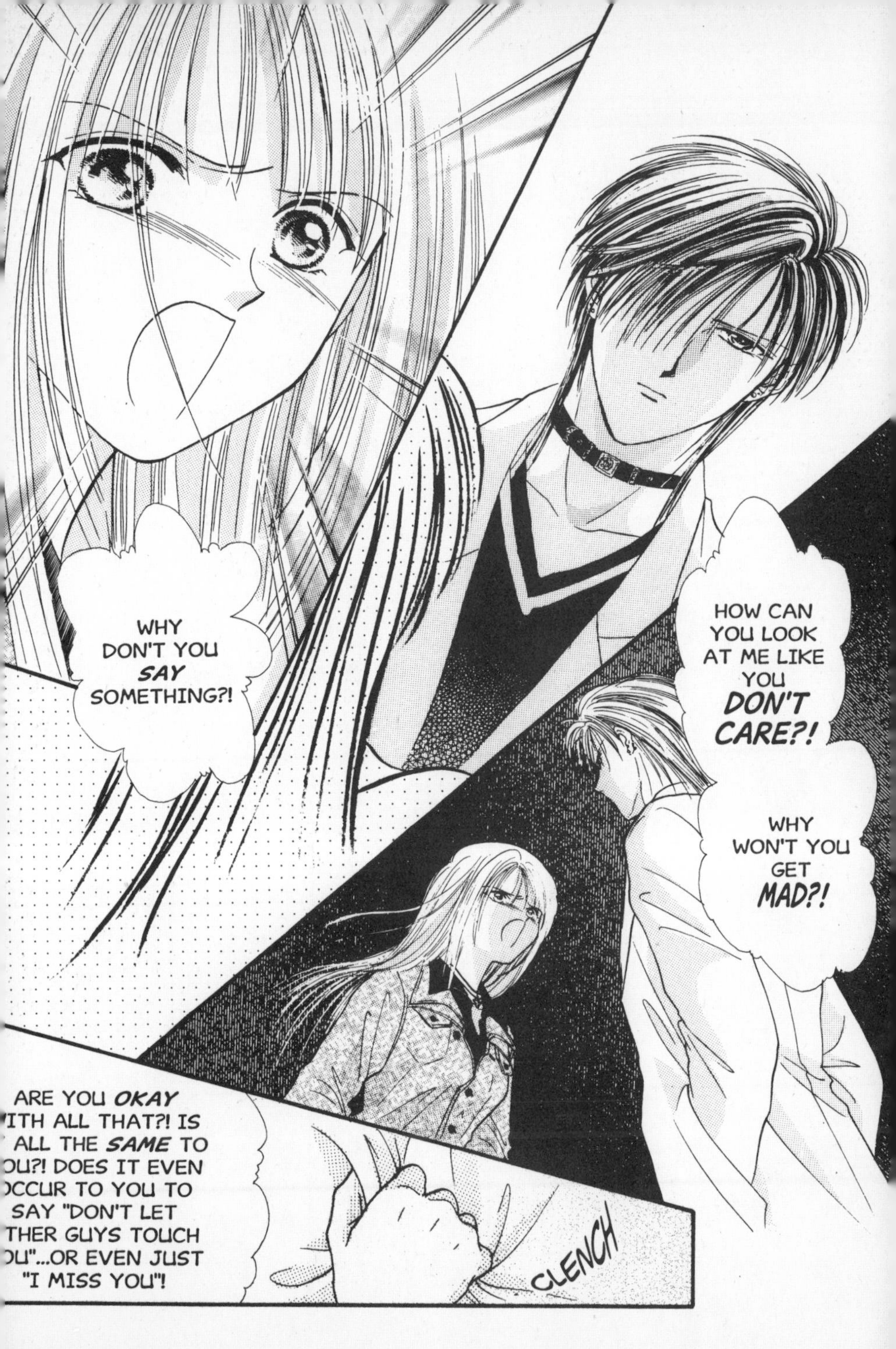
WHY DON'T YOU *SAY* SOMETHING?!
HOW CAN YOU LOOK AT ME LIKE YOU *DON'T CARE?!*
WHY WON'T YOU GET *MAD?!*
ARE YOU *OKAY* ITH ALL THAT?! IS ALL THE *SAME* TO OU?! DOES IT EVEN OCCUR TO YOU TO SAY "DON'T LET THER GUYS TOUCH OU"...OR EVEN JUST "I MISS YOU"!
CLENCH

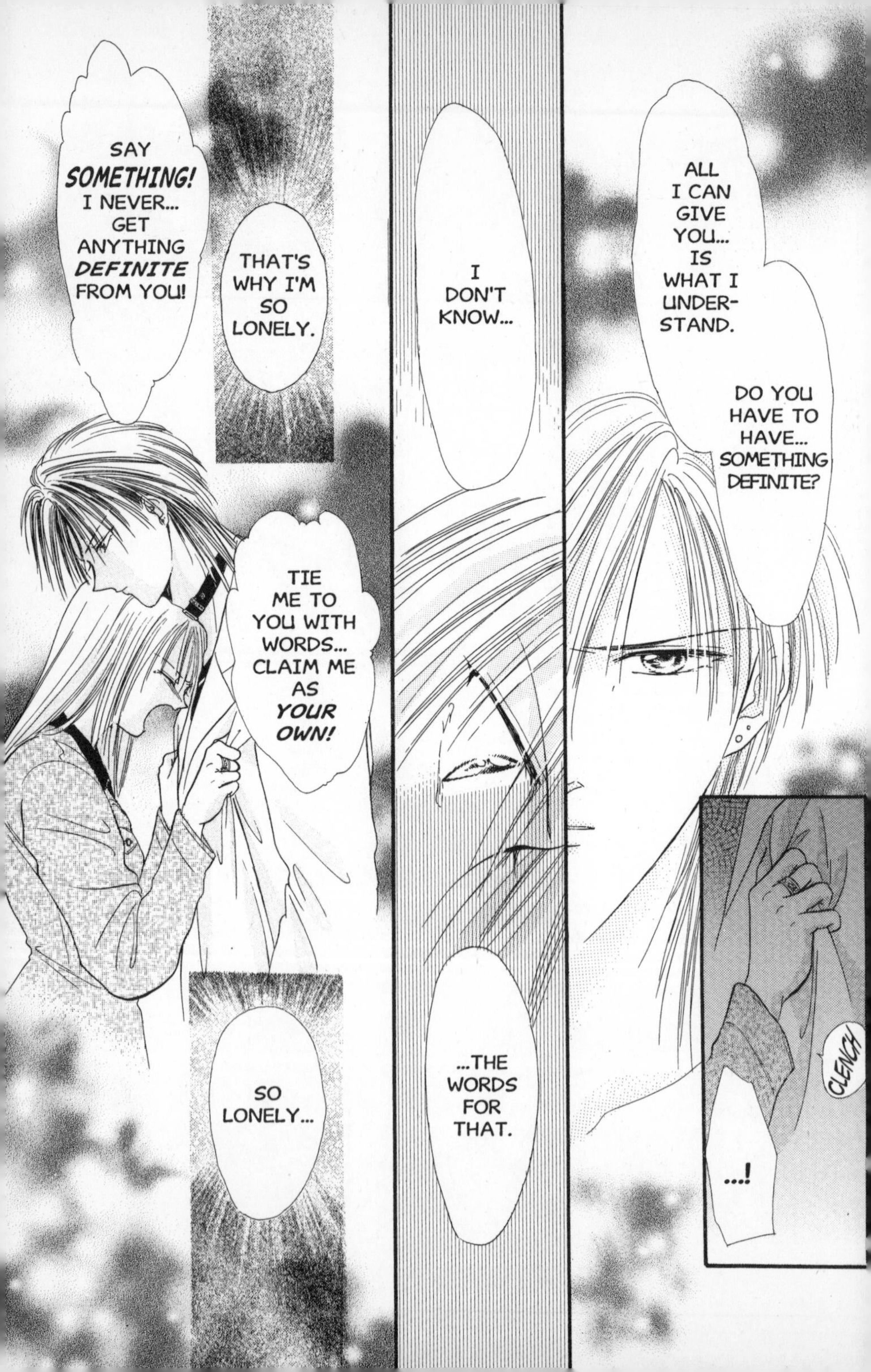
SAY *SOMETHING!* I NEVER... GET ANYTHING *DEFINITE* FROM YOU!
THAT'S WHY I'M SO LONELY.
TIE ME TO YOU WITH WORDS... CLAIM ME AS *YOUR OWN!*
SO LONELY...
I DON'T KNOW...
...THE WORDS FOR THAT.
ALL I CAN GIVE YOU... IS WHAT I UNDER-STAND.
DO YOU HAVE TO HAVE... SOMETHING DEFINITE?
CLENCH
...!

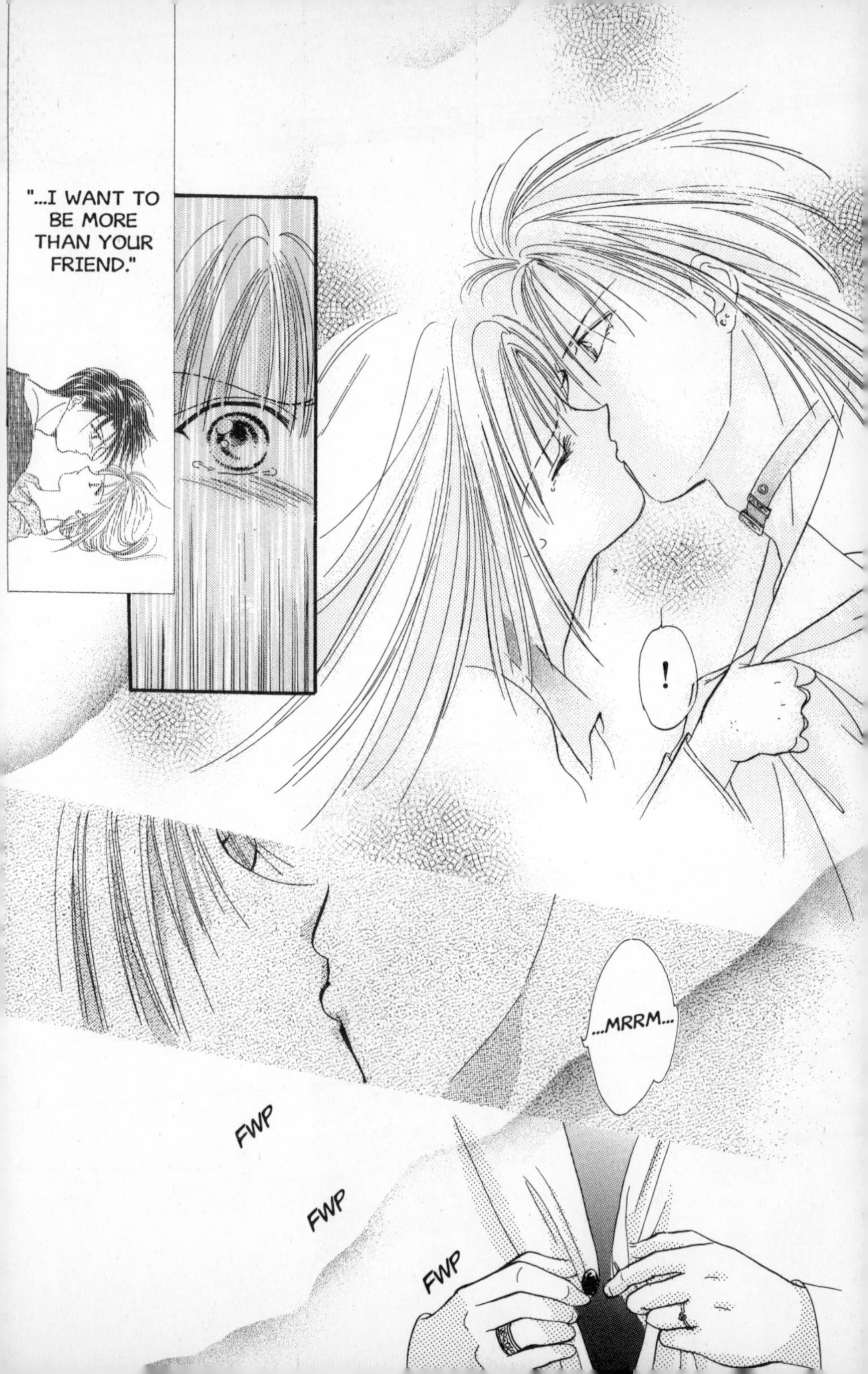
!
"...I WANT TO BE MORE THAN YOUR FRIEND."
...MRRM...
FWP
FWP
FWP

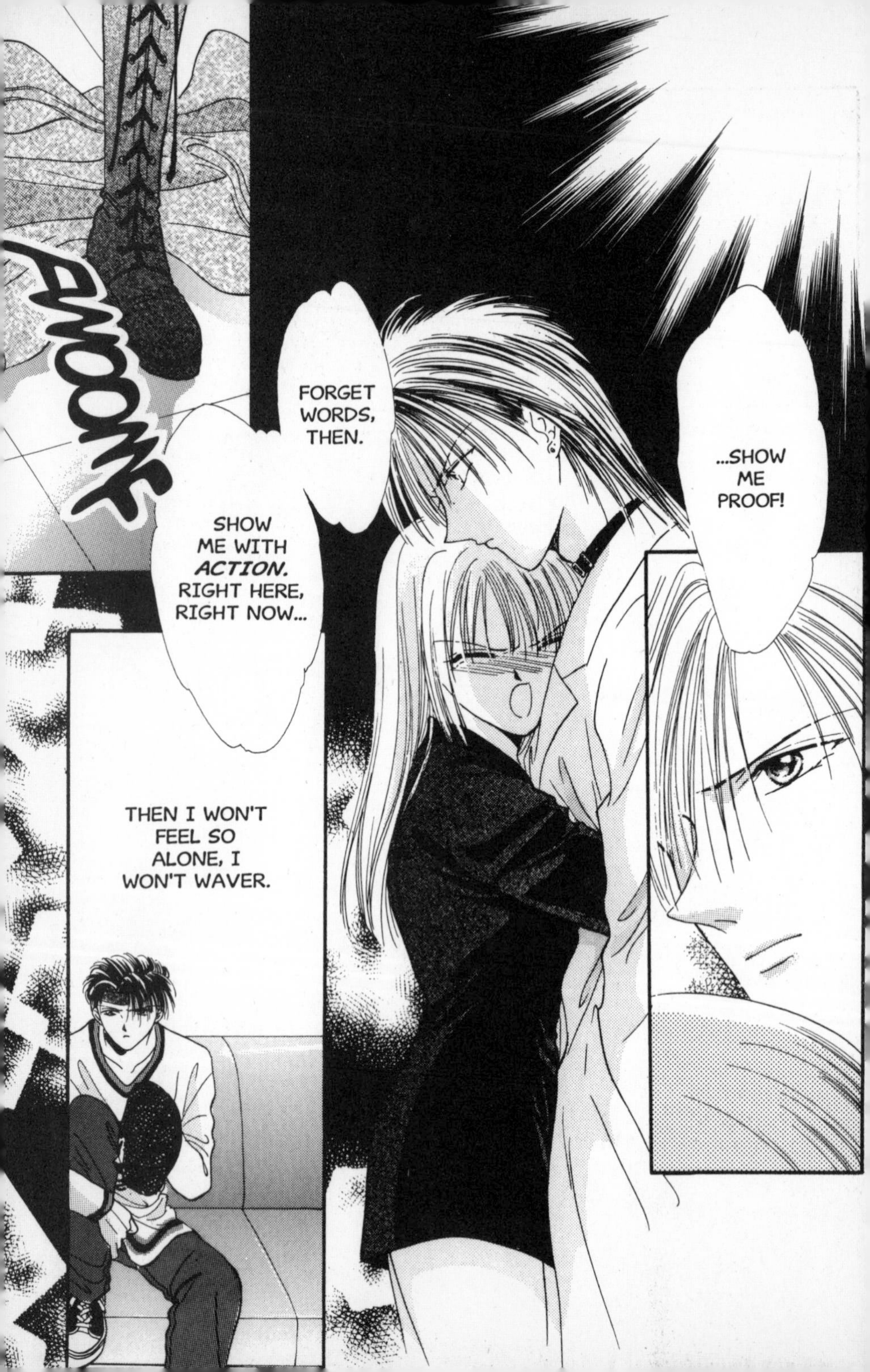
FORGET WORDS, THEN.
SHOW ME WITH *ACTION.* RIGHT HERE, RIGHT NOW...
...SHOW ME PROOF!
THEN I WON'T FEEL SO ALONE, I WON'T WAVER.

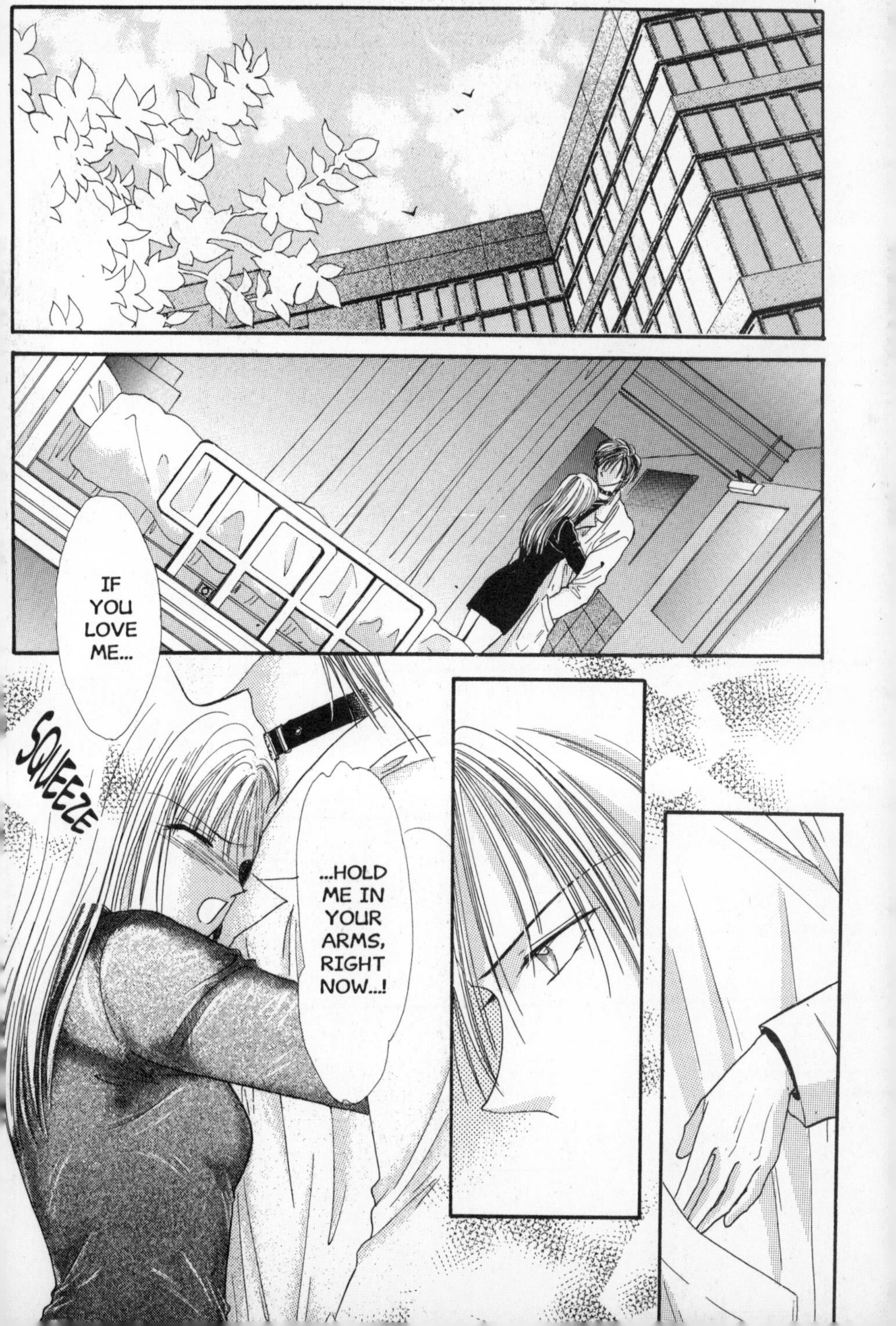
IF YOU LOVE ME...
SQUEEZE
...HOLD ME IN YOUR ARMS, RIGHT NOW...!

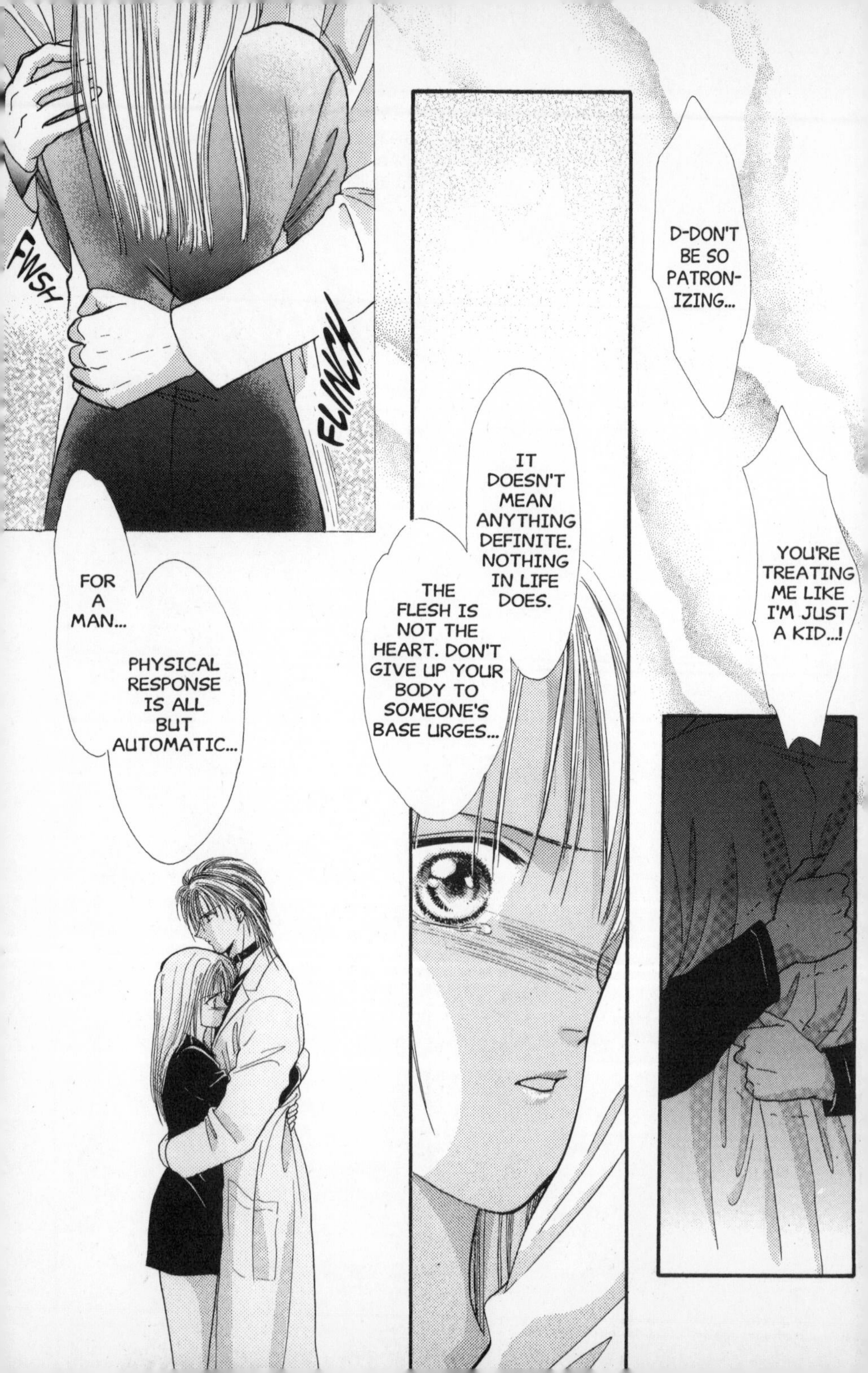
D-DON'T BE SO PATRON-IZING...
YOU'RE TREATING ME LIKE I'M JUST A KID...!
IT DOESN'T MEAN ANYTHING DEFINITE. NOTHING IN LIFE DOES.
THE FLESH IS NOT THE HEART. DON'T GIVE UP YOUR BODY TO SOMEONE'S BASE URGES...
FLINCH
FWSH
FOR A MAN...
PHYSICAL RESPONSE IS ALL BUT AUTOMATIC...

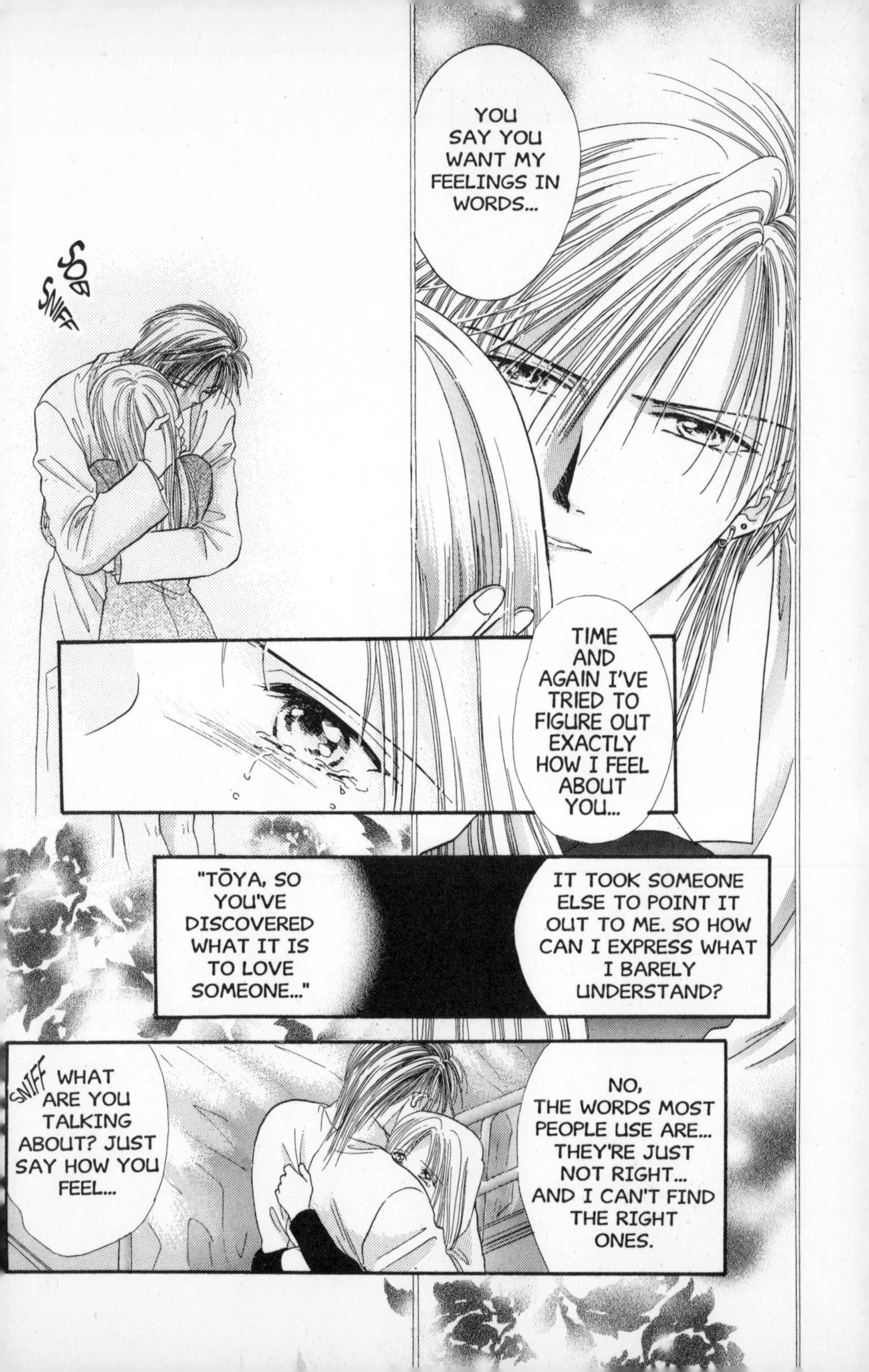
SOB
SNIFF
YOU SAY YOU WANT MY FEELINGS IN WORDS...
TIME AND AGAIN I'VE TRIED TO FIGURE OUT EXACTLY HOW I FEEL ABOUT YOU...
"TŌYA, SO YOU'VE DISCOVERED WHAT IT IS TO LOVE SOMEONE..."
IT TOOK SOMEONE ELSE TO POINT IT OUT TO ME. SO HOW CAN I EXPRESS WHAT I BARELY UNDERSTAND?
SNIFF
WHAT ARE YOU TALKING ABOUT? JUST SAY HOW YOU FEEL...
NO, THE WORDS MOST PEOPLE USE ARE... THEY'RE JUST NOT RIGHT... AND I CAN'T FIND THE RIGHT ONES.

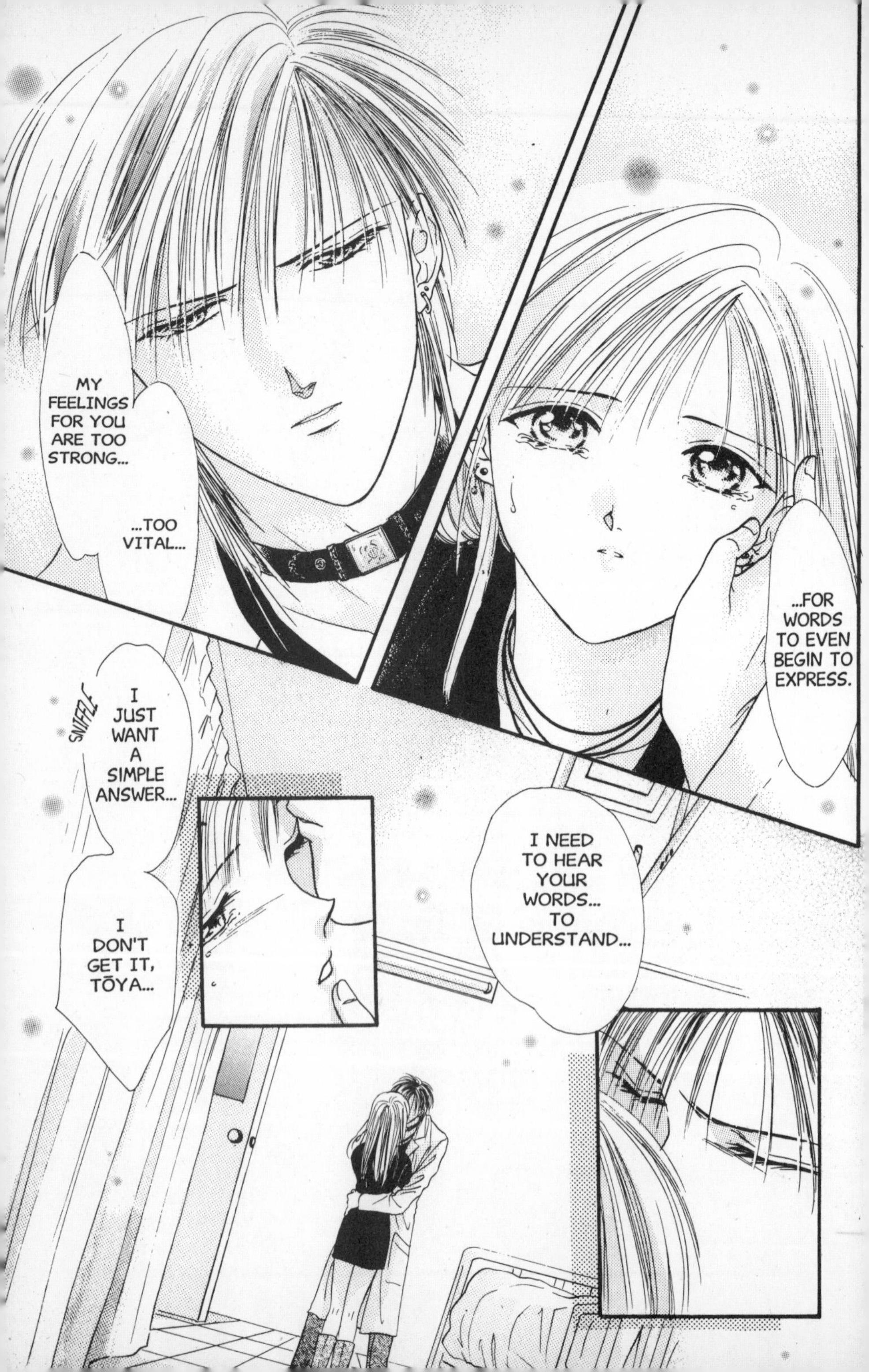
MY FEELINGS FOR YOU ARE TOO STRONG...
...TOO VITAL...
...FOR WORDS TO EVEN BEGIN TO EXPRESS.
SNIFFLE
I JUST WANT A SIMPLE ANSWER...
I DON'T GET IT, TŌYA...
I NEED TO HEAR YOUR WORDS... TO UNDERSTAND...

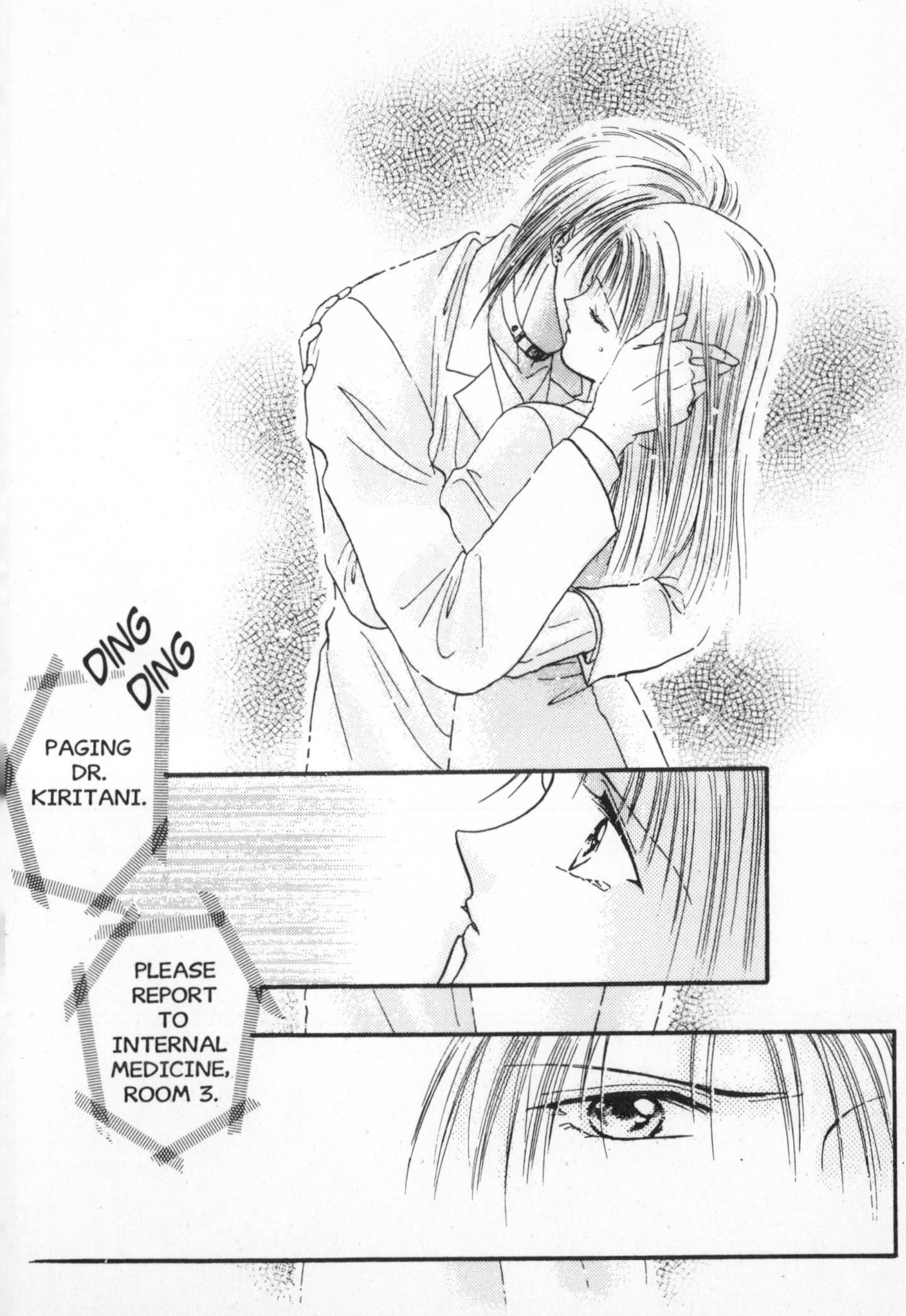
DING DING
PAGING DR. KIRITANI.
PLEASE REPORT TO INTERNAL MEDICINE, ROOM 3.

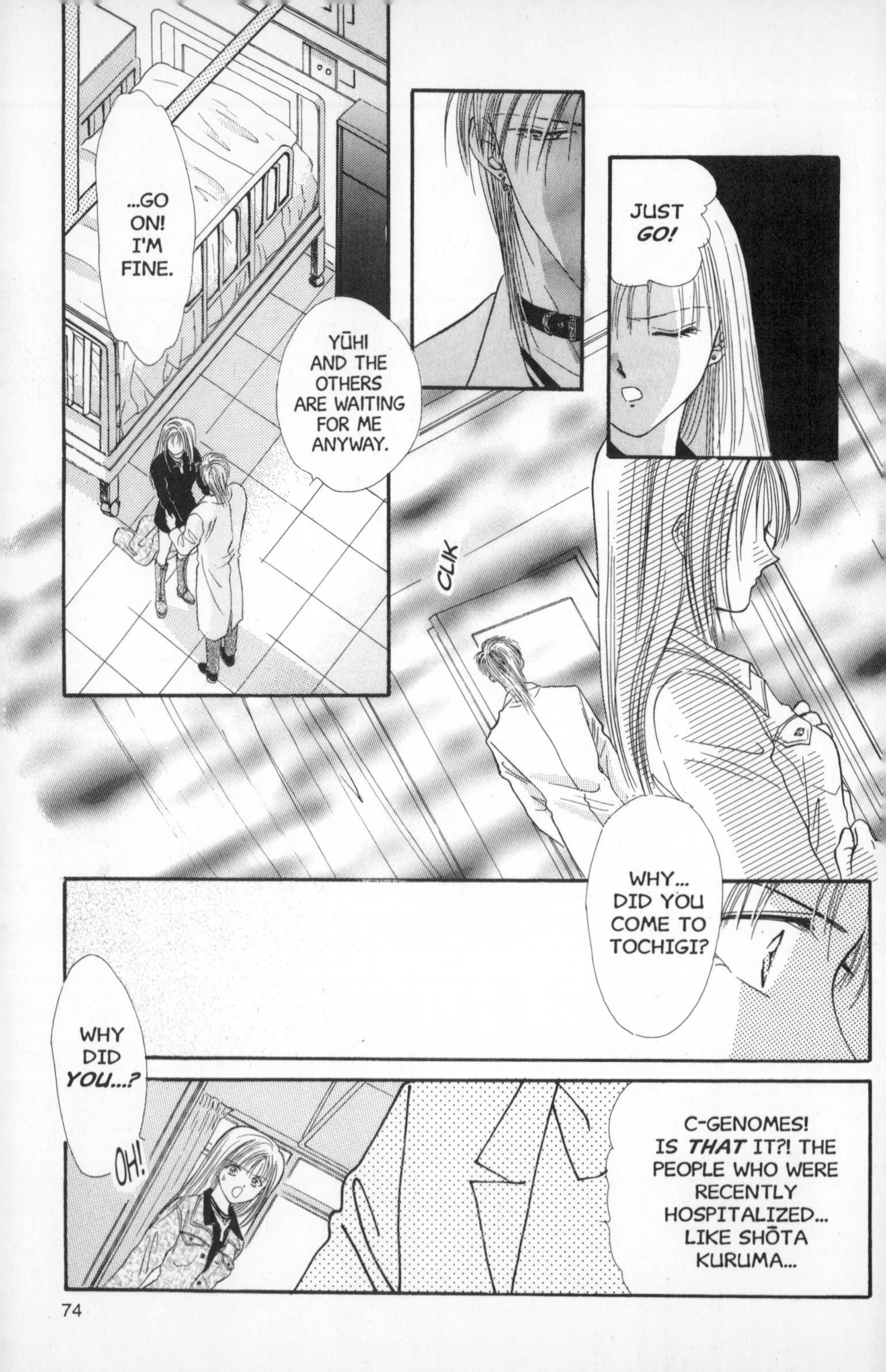
JUST GO!
...GO ON! I'M FINE.
YŪHI AND THE OTHERS ARE WAITING FOR ME ANYWAY.
CLIK
WHY... DID YOU COME TO TOCHIGI?
WHY DID YOU...?
OH!
C-GENOMES! IS THAT IT?! THE PEOPLE WHO WERE RECENTLY HOSPITALIZED... LIKE SHŌTA KURUMA...

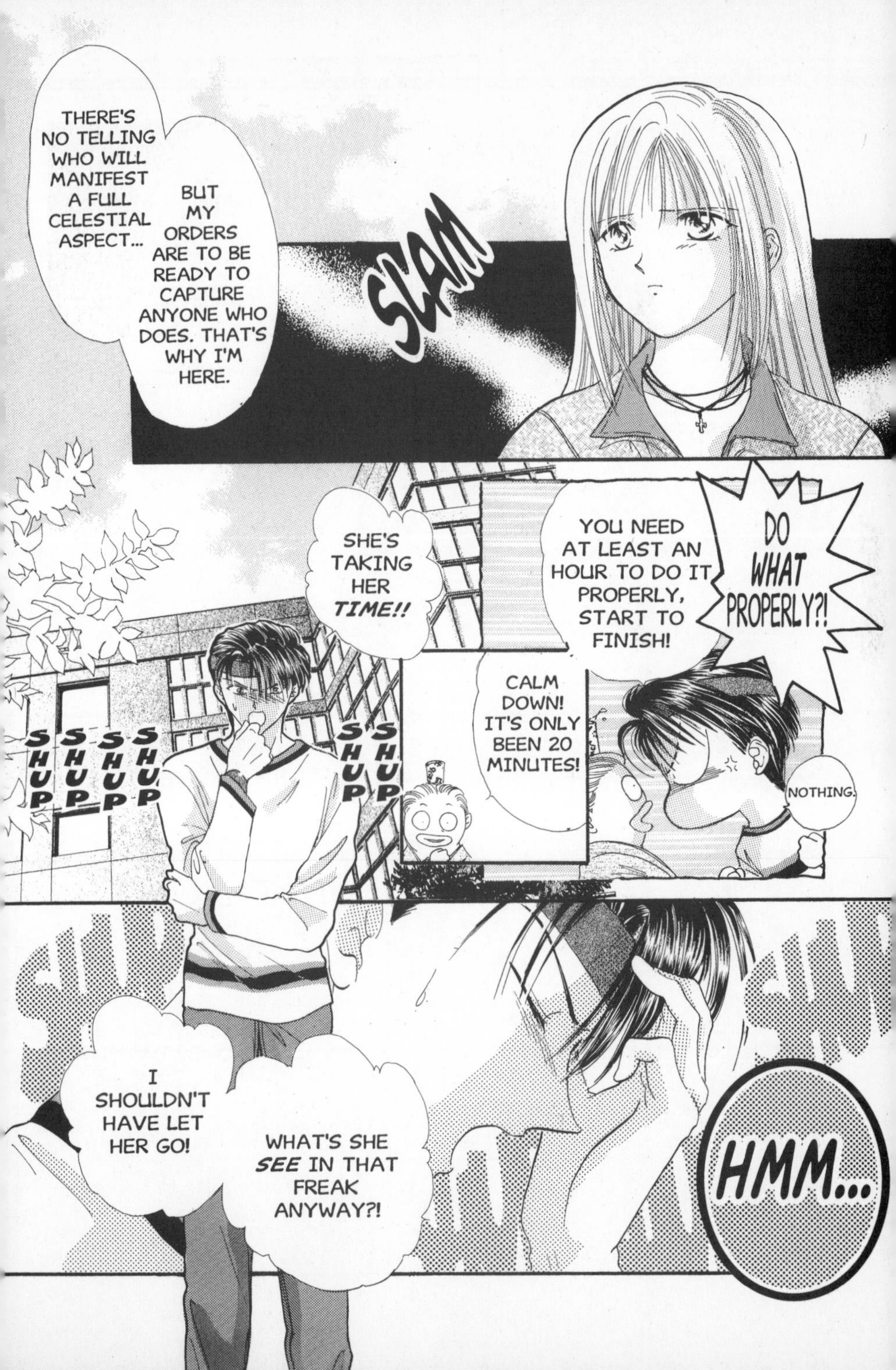
THERE'S NO TELLING WHO WILL MANIFEST A FULL CELESTIAL ASPECT...
BUT MY ORDERS ARE TO BE READY TO CAPTURE ANYONE WHO DOES. THAT'S WHY I'M HERE.
SLAM
YOU NEED AT LEAST AN HOUR TO DO IT PROPERLY, START TO FINISH!
DO WHAT PROPERLY?!
NOTHING.
CALM DOWN! IT'S ONLY BEEN 20 MINUTES!
SHUP SHUP
SHE'S TAKING HER *TIME!!*
SHUP SHUP SHUP SHUP
HMM...
WHAT'S SHE *SEE* IN THAT FREAK ANYWAY?!
I SHOULDN'T HAVE LET HER GO!

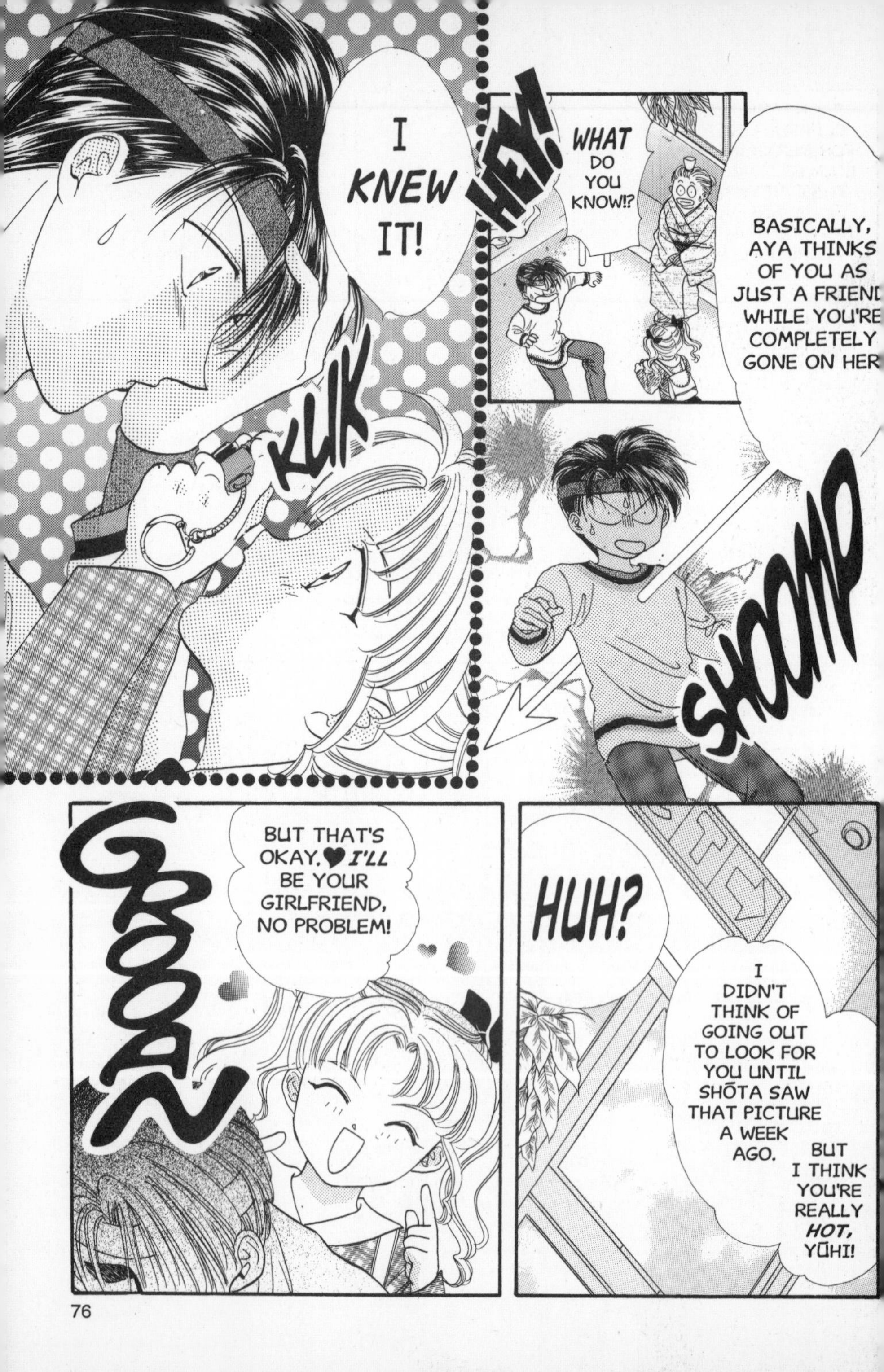
HEY!
WHAT DO YOU KNOW!?
BASICALLY, AYA THINKS OF YOU AS JUST A FRIEN WHILE YOU'RE COMPLETELY GONE ON HER
SHOOMP
I KNEW IT!
KLIK
HUH?
I DIDN'T THINK OF GOING OUT TO LOOK FOR YOU UNTIL SHŌTA SAW THAT PICTURE A WEEK AGO.
BUT I THINK YOU'RE REALLY *HOT,* YŪHI!
BUT THAT'S OKAY.♥ *I'LL* BE YOUR GIRLFRIEND, NO PROBLEM!
GROAN

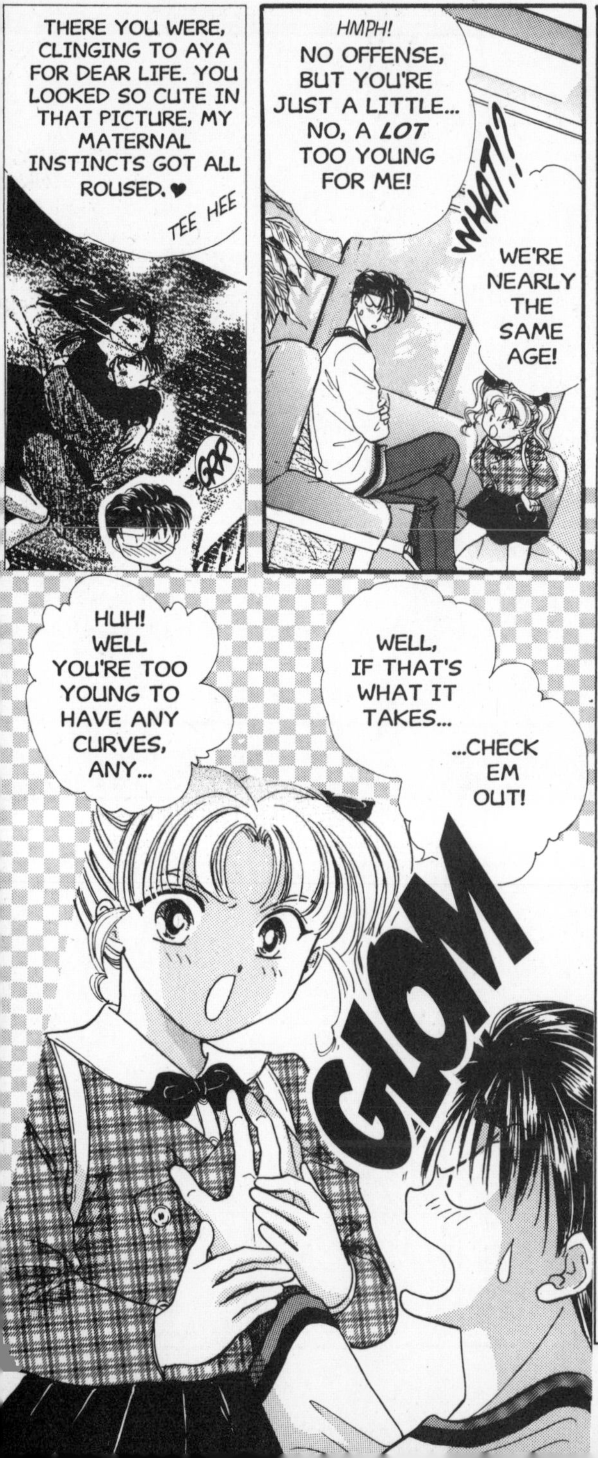
THERE YOU WERE, CLINGING TO AYA FOR DEAR LIFE. YOU LOOKED SO CUTE IN THAT PICTURE, MY MATERNAL INSTINCTS GOT ALL ROUSED. ♥
TEE HEE
GRR
HMPH!
NO OFFENSE, BUT YOU'RE JUST A LITTLE... NO, A *LOT* TOO YOUNG FOR ME!
WHAT!?
WE'RE NEARLY THE SAME AGE!
HUH! WELL YOU'RE TOO YOUNG TO HAVE ANY CURVES, ANY...
WELL, IF THAT'S WHAT IT TAKES...
...CHECK EM OUT!
GLOM

...By the way!
I've finally gotten hooked on Final Fantasy VII. :) When I was in bed with a cold and a high fever around New Years, I got brainwashed (?) by all those commercials on TV, so I pre-ordered F.F. VII. I got it, but I hadn't touched it in six months... What? Why didn't I play it right away? I was busy with work, I moved, I just didn't have the time...and besides, I'd never played an RPG game before! Seriously! I owned F.F. III for the Super Nintendo, but back then, those games were so slow and boring, and I hated all the fighting and item management you had to do all the time. So even though I gave it a try, I gave up on it right away. But this time, I was curious to see the graphics from the point of view of an artist—I thought I could learn something from it. I started playing F.F. VII and... "Hey, this is pretty cool. Ooh...This is interesting, what happens next? ...Geez, I'm totally hooked!"
It was all because I fell in love with Cloud. One of my friends also started playing, and we're both gaga over him. "Could you draw Cloud for me?" "Sure!" ...*Do I really have the time for that?!* Come to think of it, my editors (and my readers) think I'm a hard-core gamer because I've written about video games in my past columns. Sorry - I own very few games, and I don't play much. I have the SNES, PlayStation, and the Sega Saturn (my editor at the time got it for me for my birthday ♥). But I have less than ten games in all. They were just collecting dust. There was a time when I was hooked on Street Fighter II (when it first came out), but I quickly lost interest. (I stopped playing fighting games because they hurt my drawing hand.) I play less than the average person. However, now I have awoken to their splendor! But I have so much work to do! Wh-what should I do...?
So now I just listen to the F.F. soundtrack...

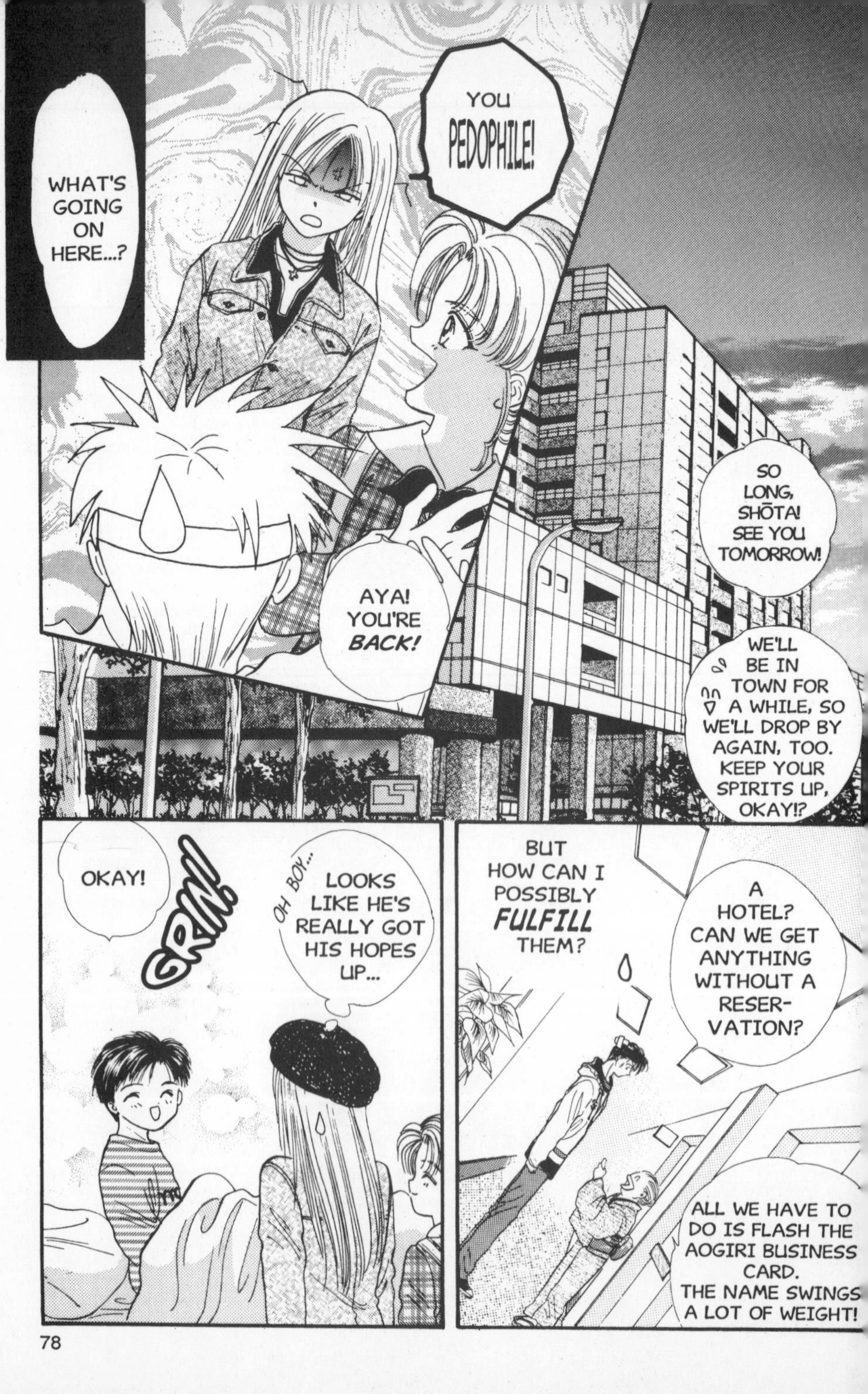
AYA! YOU'RE BACK!
YOU PEDOPHILE!
WHAT'S GOING ON HERE...?
SO LONG, SHŌTA! SEE YOU TOMORROW!
WE'LL BE IN TOWN FOR A WHILE, SO WE'LL DROP BY AGAIN, TOO. KEEP YOUR SPIRITS UP, OKAY!?
OKAY!
GRIN!
OH BOY... LOOKS LIKE HE'S REALLY GOT HIS HOPES UP...
BUT HOW CAN I POSSIBLY FULFILL THEM?
A HOTEL? CAN WE GET ANYTHING WITHOUT A RESER-VATION?
ALL WE HAVE TO DO IS FLASH THE AOGIRI BUSINESS CARD. THE NAME SWINGS A LOT OF WEIGHT!

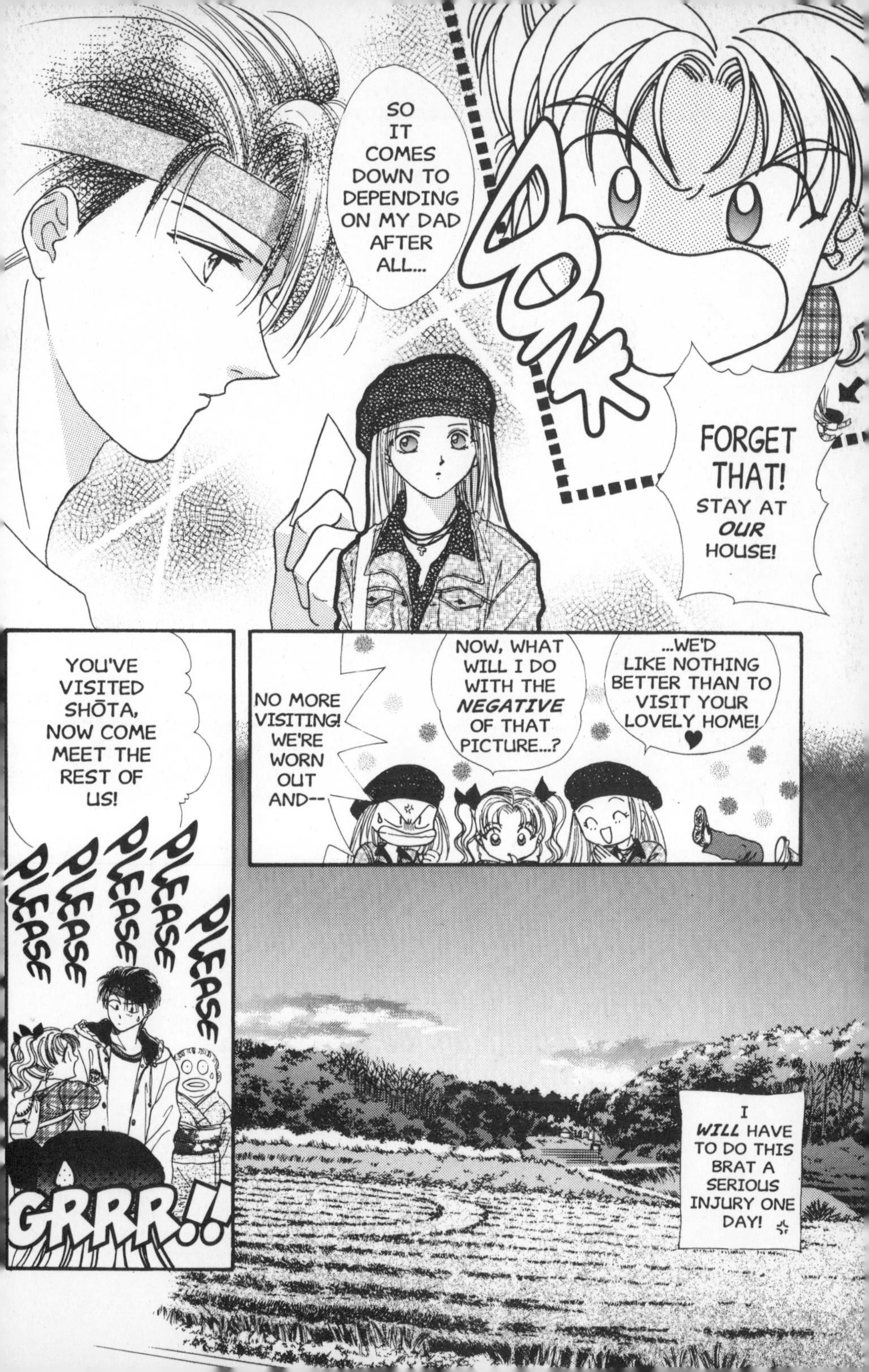
SO IT COMES DOWN TO DEPENDING ON MY DAD AFTER ALL...
BONK
FORGET THAT! STAY AT OUR HOUSE!
YOU'VE VISITED SHŌTA, NOW COME MEET THE REST OF US!
NO MORE VISITING! WE'RE WORN OUT AND--
NOW, WHAT WILL I DO WITH THE NEGATIVE OF THAT PICTURE...?
...WE'D LIKE NOTHING BETTER THAN TO VISIT YOUR LOVELY HOME! ♥
PLEASE PLEASE PLEASE PLEASE
GRRR!!
I WILL HAVE TO DO THIS BRAT A SERIOUS INJURY ONE DAY!

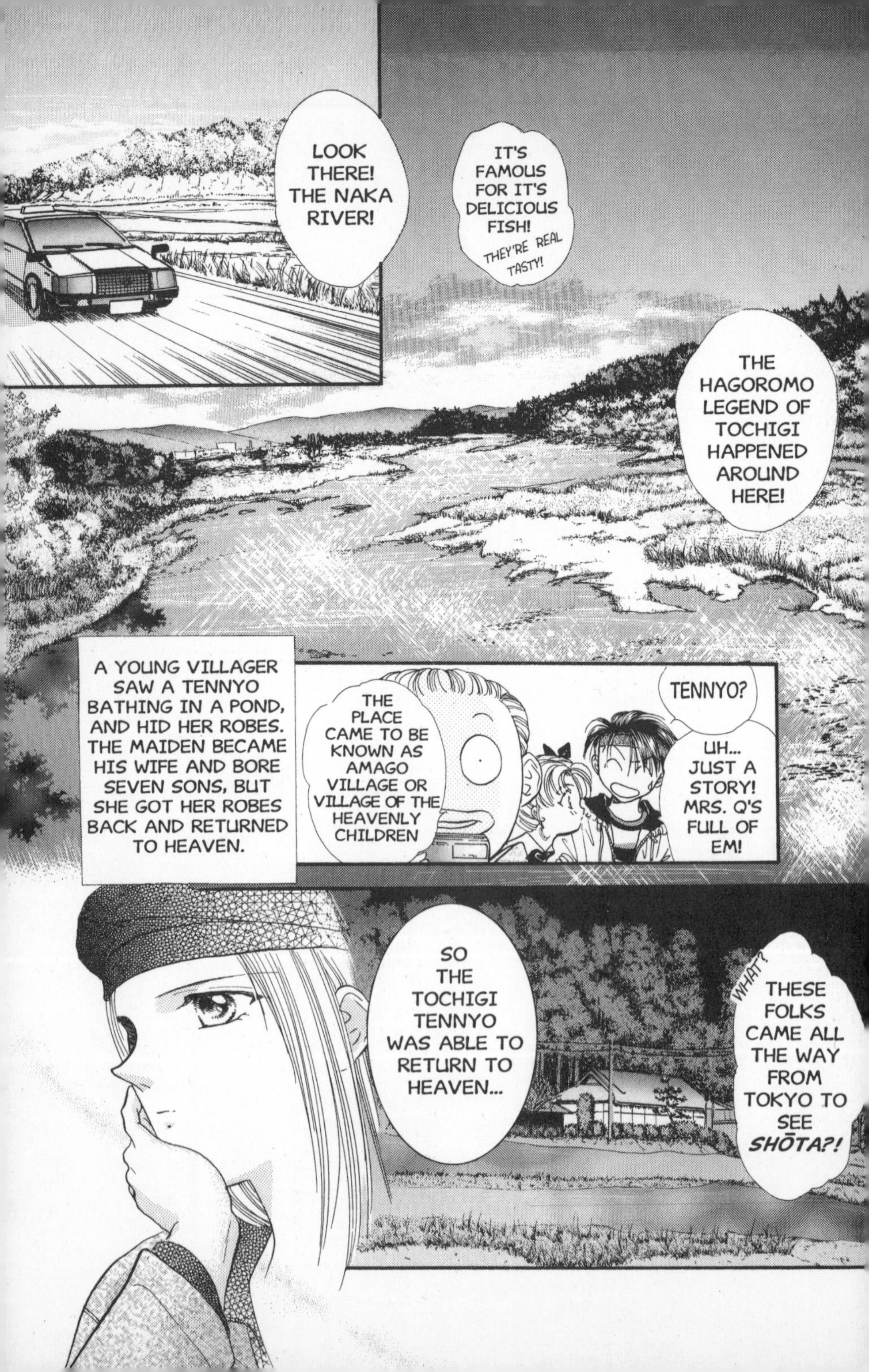

LOOK THERE! THE NAKA RIVER!
IT'S FAMOUS FOR IT'S DELICIOUS FISH!
THEY'RE REAL TASTY!
THE HAGOROMO LEGEND OF TOCHIGI HAPPENED AROUND HERE!
TENNYO?
UH... JUST A STORY! MRS. Q'S FULL OF EM!
THE PLACE CAME TO BE KNOWN AS AMAGO VILLAGE OR VILLAGE OF THE HEAVENLY CHILDREN
A YOUNG VILLAGER SAW A TENNYO BATHING IN A POND, AND HID HER ROBES. THE MAIDEN BECAME HIS WIFE AND BORE SEVEN SONS, BUT SHE GOT HER ROBES BACK AND RETURNED TO HEAVEN.
WHAT?
THESE FOLKS CAME ALL THE WAY FROM TOKYO TO SEE *SHŌTA?!*
SO THE TOCHIGI TENNYO WAS ABLE TO RETURN TO HEAVEN...

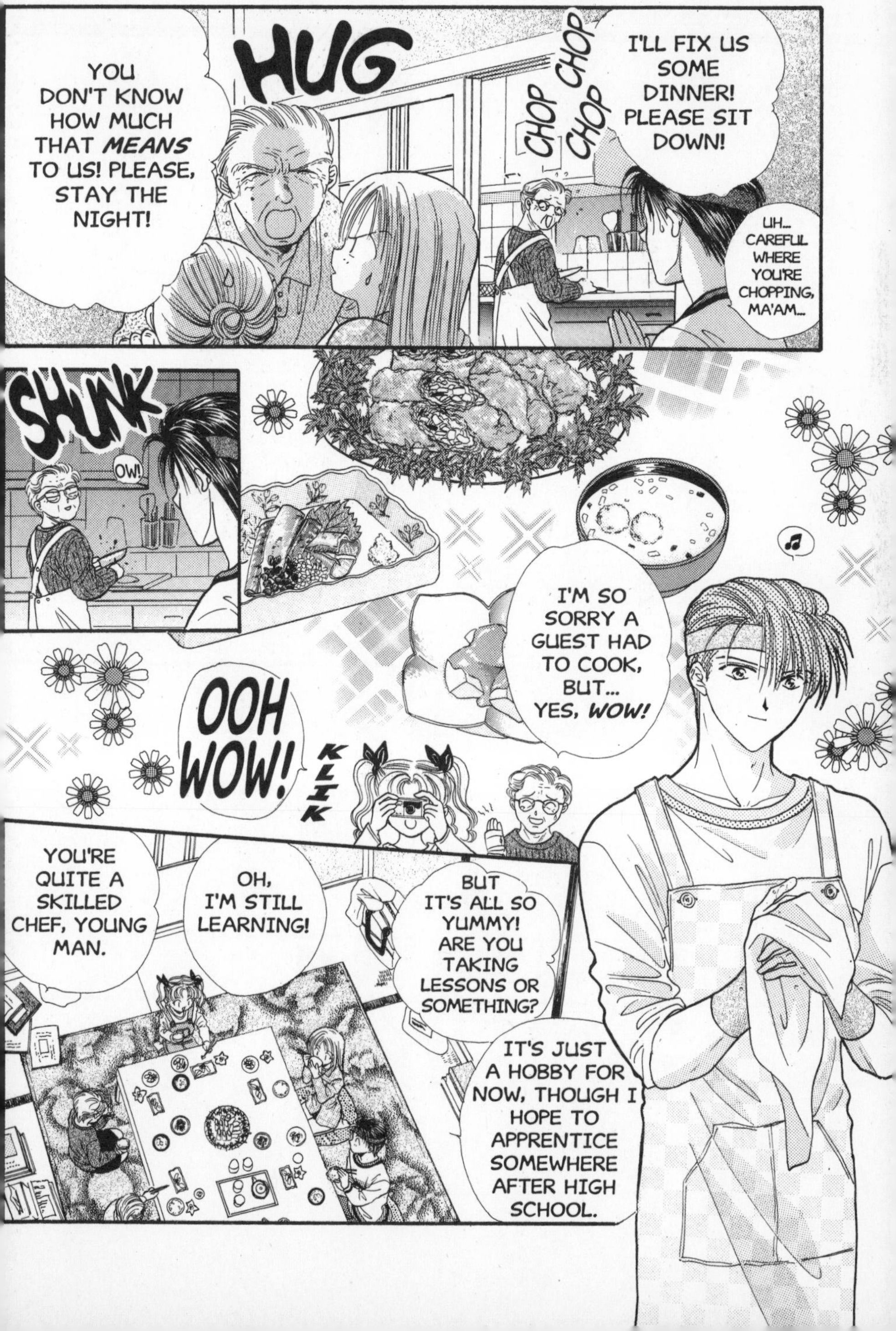
YOU DON'T KNOW HOW MUCH THAT *MEANS* TO US! PLEASE, STAY THE NIGHT!
HUG
CHOP CHOP CHOP
I'LL FIX US SOME DINNER! PLEASE SIT DOWN!
UH... CAREFUL WHERE YOU'RE CHOPPING, MA'AM...
SHUNK
OW!
OOH WOW!
KLIK
I'M SO SORRY A GUEST HAD TO COOK, BUT... YES, *WOW!*
YOU'RE QUITE A SKILLED CHEF, YOUNG MAN.
OH, I'M STILL LEARNING!
BUT IT'S ALL SO YUMMY! ARE YOU TAKING LESSONS OR SOMETHING?
IT'S JUST A HOBBY FOR NOW, THOUGH I HOPE TO APPRENTICE SOMEWHERE AFTER HIGH SCHOOL.

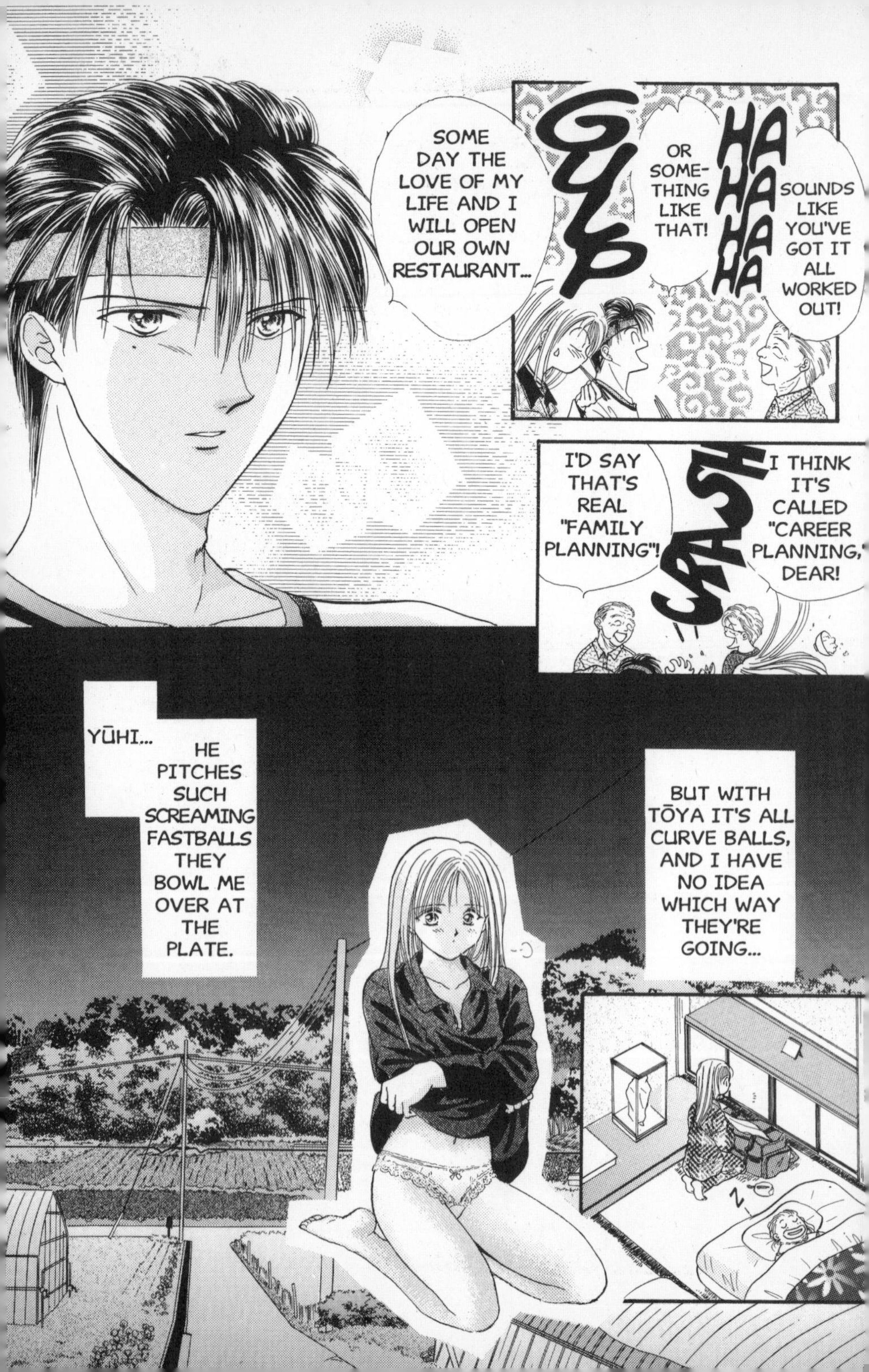
SOME DAY THE LOVE OF MY LIFE AND I WILL OPEN OUR OWN RESTAURANT...
OR SOMETHING LIKE THAT!
GULP
HA HA HA HA
SOUNDS LIKE YOU'VE GOT IT ALL WORKED OUT!
I'D SAY THAT'S REAL "FAMILY PLANNING"!
CRASH
I THINK IT'S CALLED "CAREER PLANNING, DEAR!
YŪHI... HE PITCHES SUCH SCREAMING FASTBALLS THEY BOWL ME OVER AT THE PLATE.
BUT WITH TŌYA IT'S ALL CURVE BALLS, AND I HAVE NO IDEA WHICH WAY THEY'RE GOING...

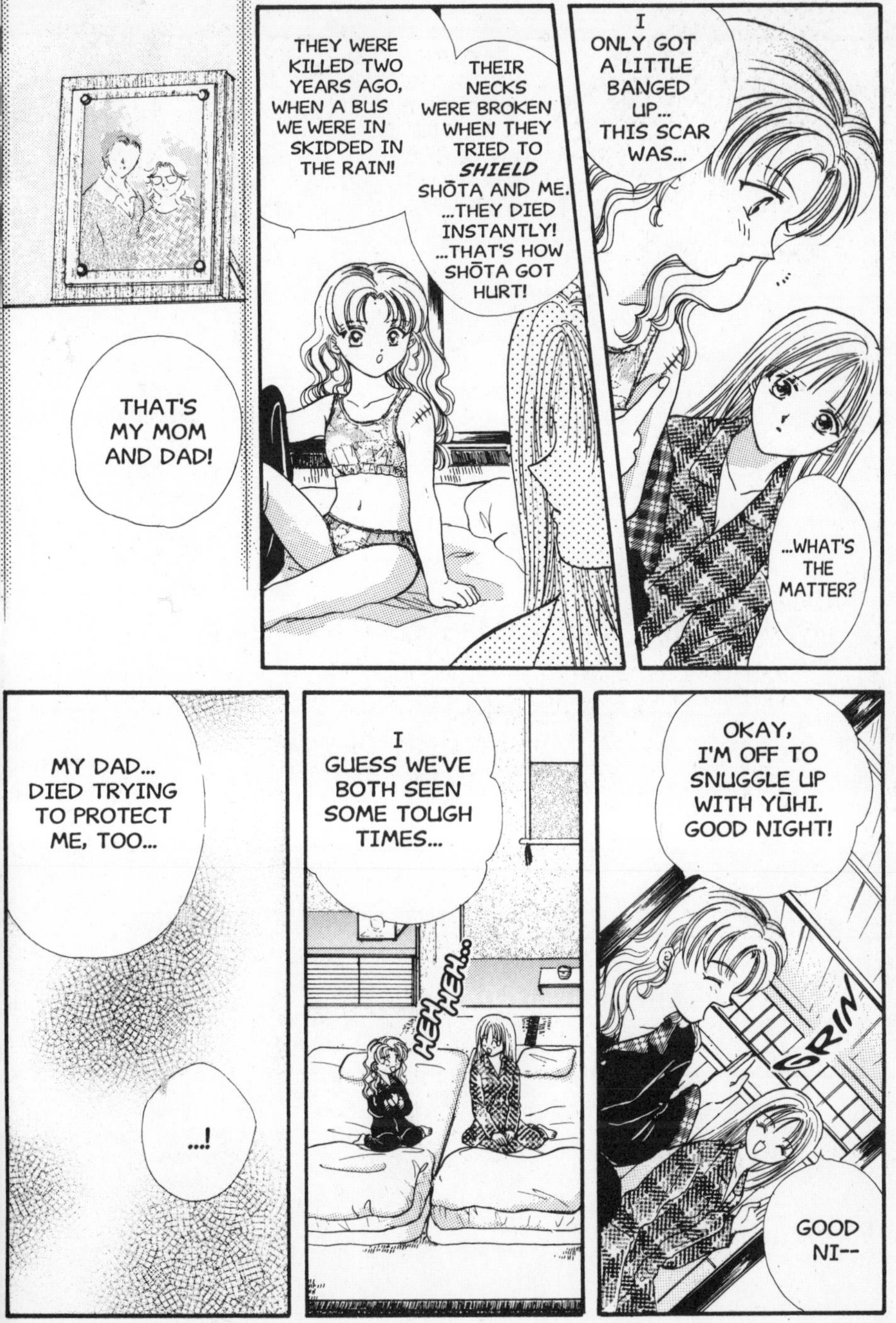
THAT'S MY MOM AND DAD!
THEY WERE KILLED TWO YEARS AGO, WHEN A BUS WE WERE IN SKIDDED IN THE RAIN!
THEIR NECKS WERE BROKEN WHEN THEY TRIED TO SHIELD SHŌTA AND ME. ...THEY DIED INSTANTLY! ...THAT'S HOW SHŌTA GOT HURT!
I ONLY GOT A LITTLE BANGED UP... THIS SCAR WAS...
...WHAT'S THE MATTER?
MY DAD... DIED TRYING TO PROTECT ME, TOO...
...!
I GUESS WE'VE BOTH SEEN SOME TOUGH TIMES...
HEH HEH...
OKAY, I'M OFF TO SNUGGLE UP WITH YŪHI. GOOD NIGHT!
GRIN
GOOD NI--

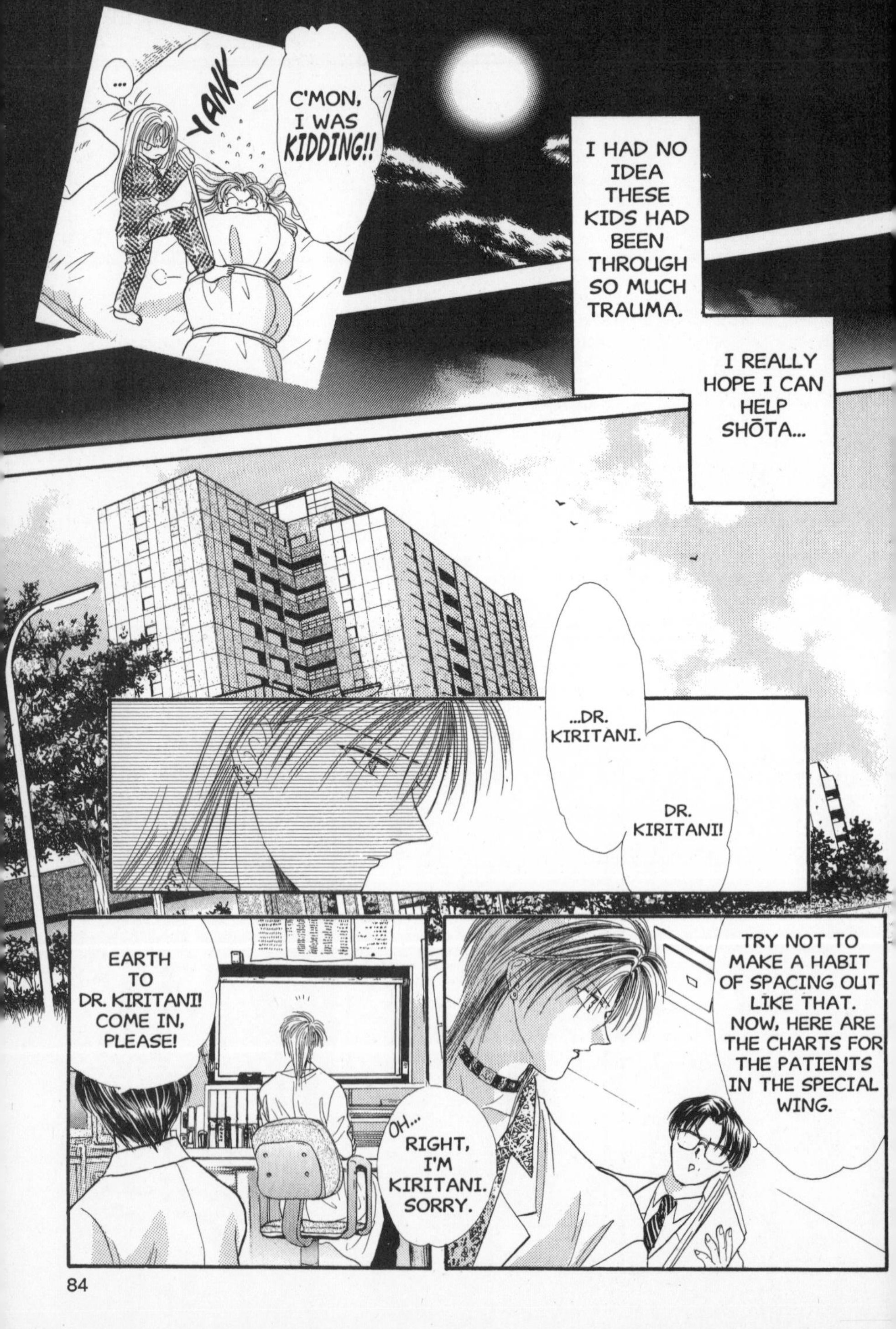
...
YANK
C'MON, I WAS KIDDING!!
I HAD NO IDEA THESE KIDS HAD BEEN THROUGH SO MUCH TRAUMA.
I REALLY HOPE I CAN HELP SHŌTA...
...DR. KIRITANI.
DR. KIRITANI!
EARTH TO DR. KIRITANI! COME IN, PLEASE!
OH... RIGHT, I'M KIRITANI. SORRY.
TRY NOT TO MAKE A HABIT OF SPACING OUT LIKE THAT. NOW, HERE ARE THE CHARTS FOR THE PATIENTS IN THE SPECIAL WING.

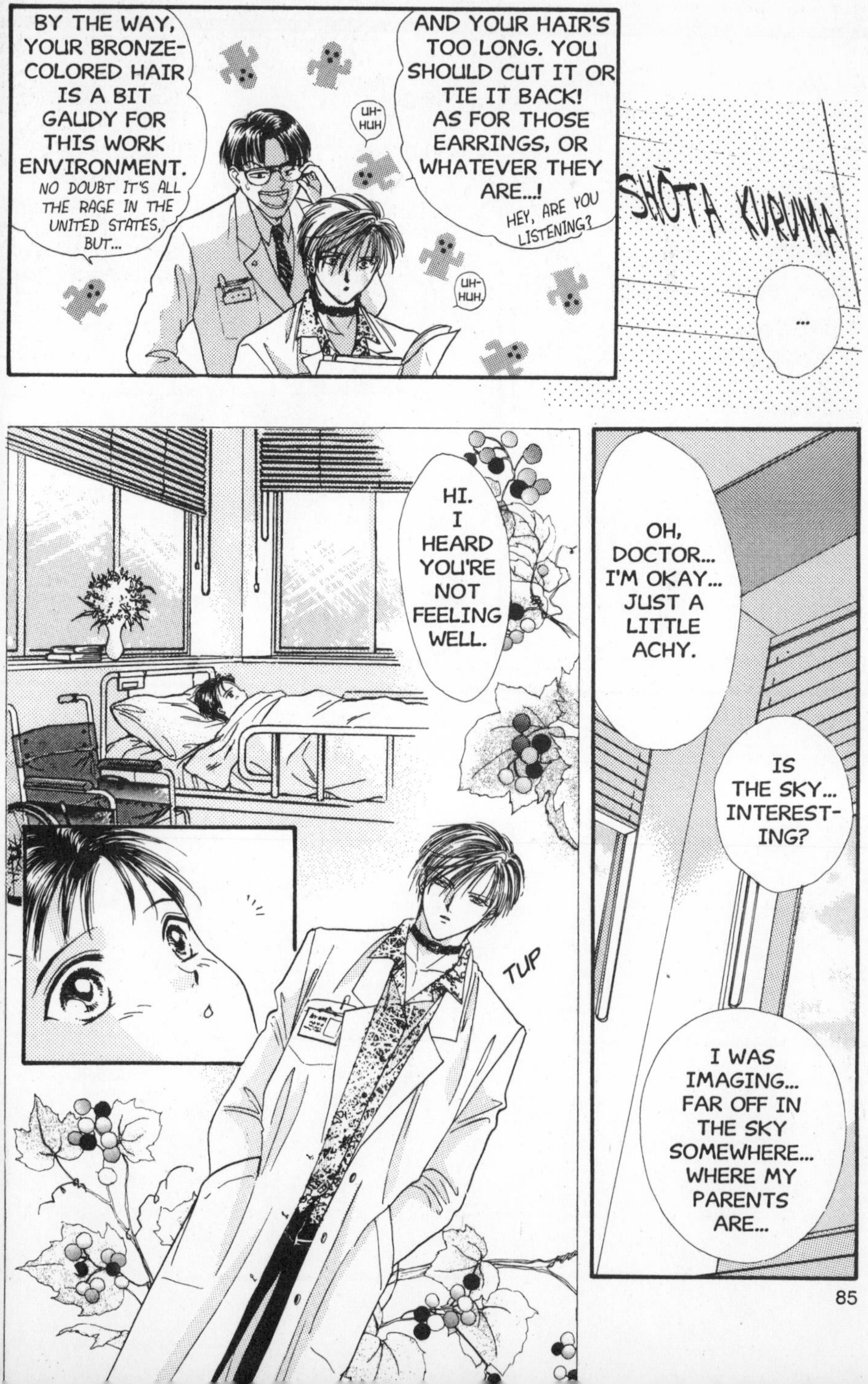
BY THE WAY, YOUR BRONZE-COLORED HAIR IS A BIT GAUDY FOR THIS WORK ENVIRONMENT.
NO DOUBT IT'S ALL THE RAGE IN THE UNITED STATES, BUT...
UH-HUH
AND YOUR HAIR'S TOO LONG. YOU SHOULD CUT IT OR TIE IT BACK! AS FOR THOSE EARRINGS, OR WHATEVER THEY ARE...!
HEY, ARE YOU LISTENING?
UH-HUH.
SHŌTA KURUMA
...
HI. I HEARD YOU'RE NOT FEELING WELL.
TUP
OH, DOCTOR... I'M OKAY... JUST A LITTLE ACHY.
IS THE SKY... INTEREST-ING?
I WAS IMAGING... FAR OFF IN THE SKY SOMEWHERE... WHERE MY PARENTS ARE...

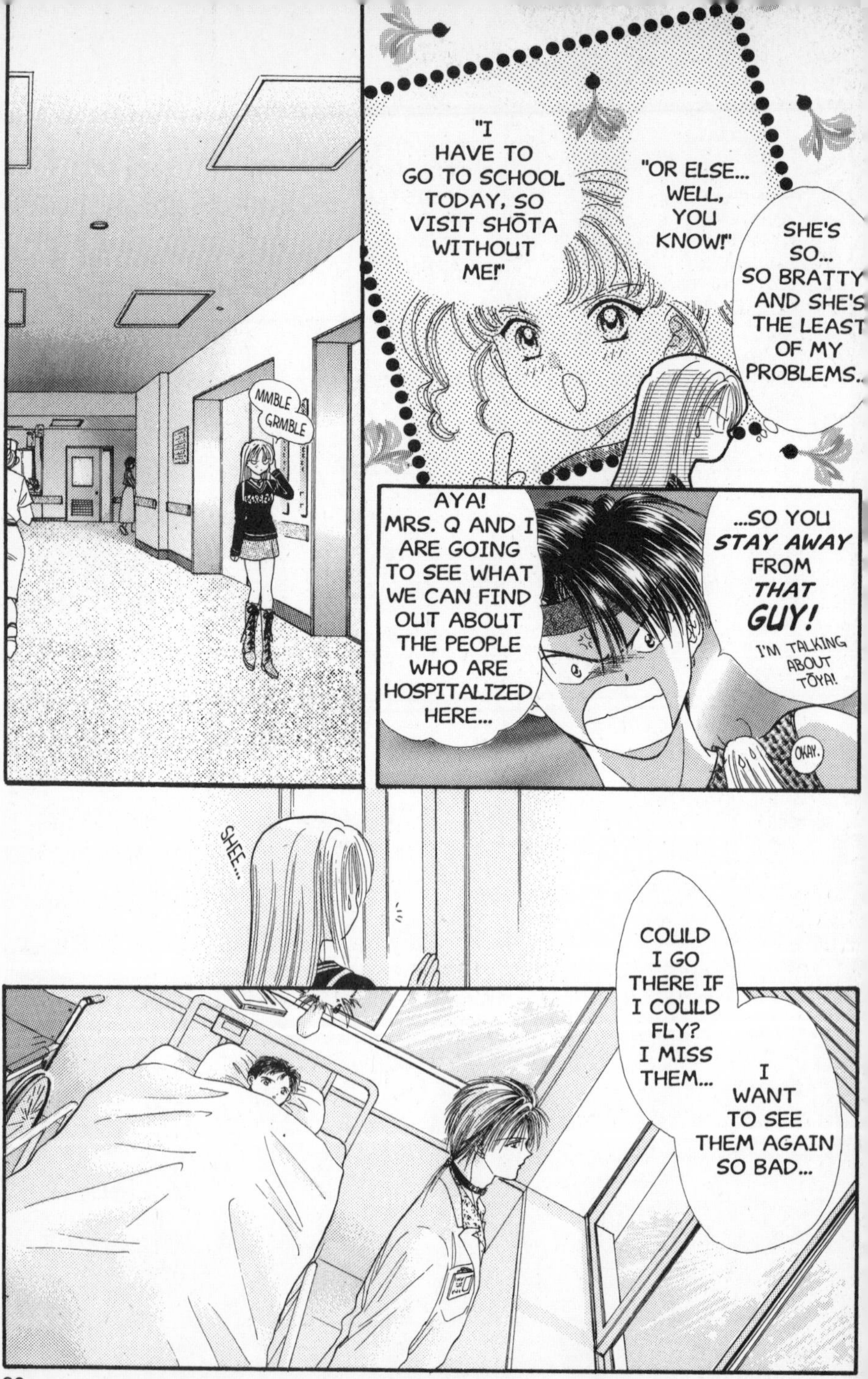
"I HAVE TO GO TO SCHOOL TODAY, SO VISIT SHŌTA WITHOUT ME!"
"OR ELSE... WELL, YOU KNOW!"
SHE'S SO... SO BRATTY AND SHE'S THE LEAST OF MY PROBLEMS...
AYA! MRS. Q AND I ARE GOING TO SEE WHAT WE CAN FIND OUT ABOUT THE PEOPLE WHO ARE HOSPITALIZED HERE...
...SO YOU STAY AWAY FROM THAT GUY!
I'M TALKING ABOUT TŌYA!
OKAY.
MMBLE GRMBLE
SHEE...
COULD I GO THERE IF I COULD FLY? I MISS THEM...
I WANT TO SEE THEM AGAIN SO BAD...

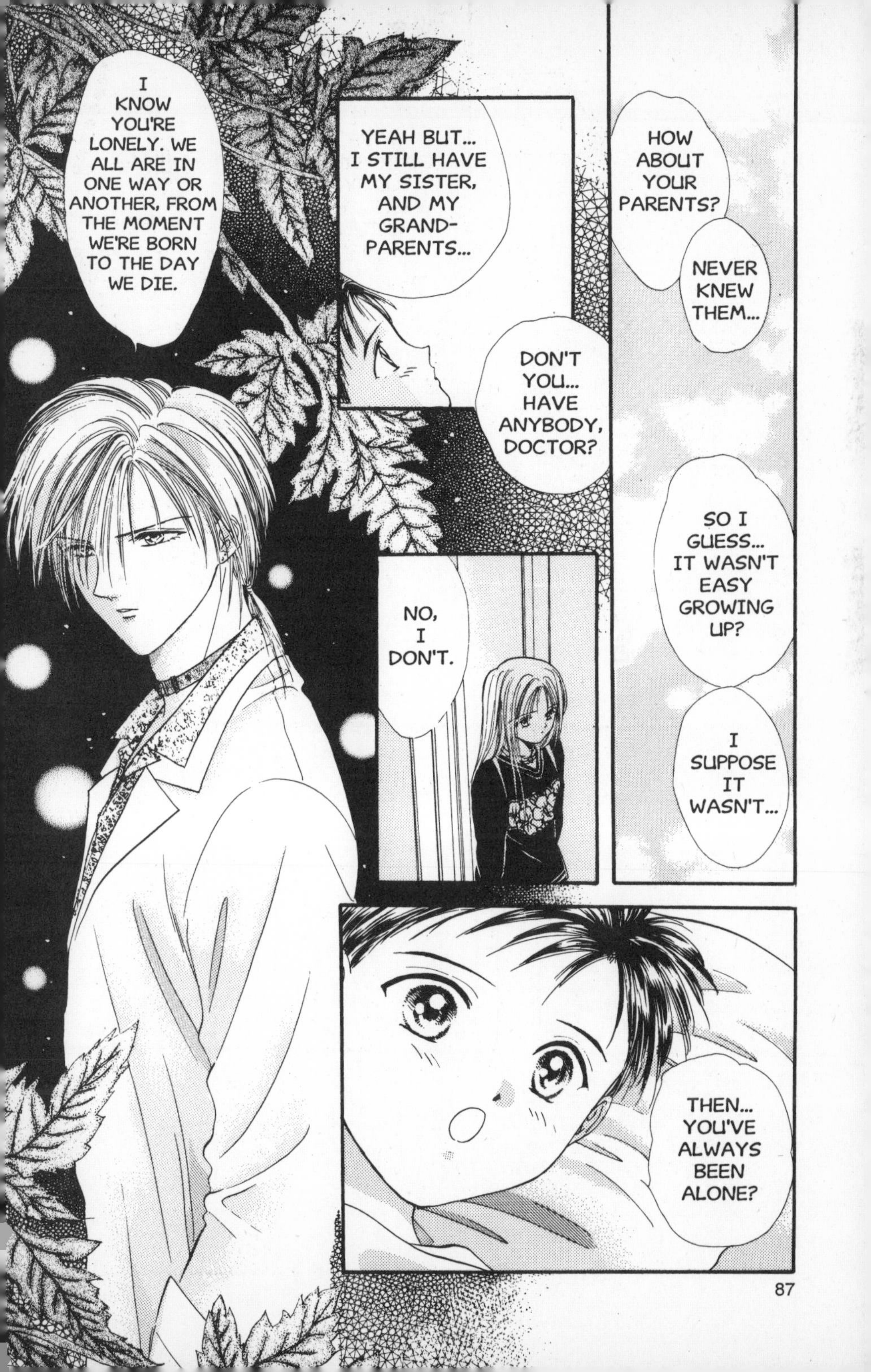
HOW ABOUT YOUR PARENTS?
NEVER KNEW THEM...
SO I GUESS... IT WASN'T EASY GROWING UP?
I SUPPOSE IT WASN'T...
YEAH BUT... I STILL HAVE MY SISTER, AND MY GRAND-PARENTS...
DON'T YOU... HAVE ANYBODY, DOCTOR?
NO, I DON'T.
THEN... YOU'VE ALWAYS BEEN ALONE?
I KNOW YOU'RE LONELY. WE ALL ARE IN ONE WAY OR ANOTHER, FROM THE MOMENT WE'RE BORN TO THE DAY WE DIE.

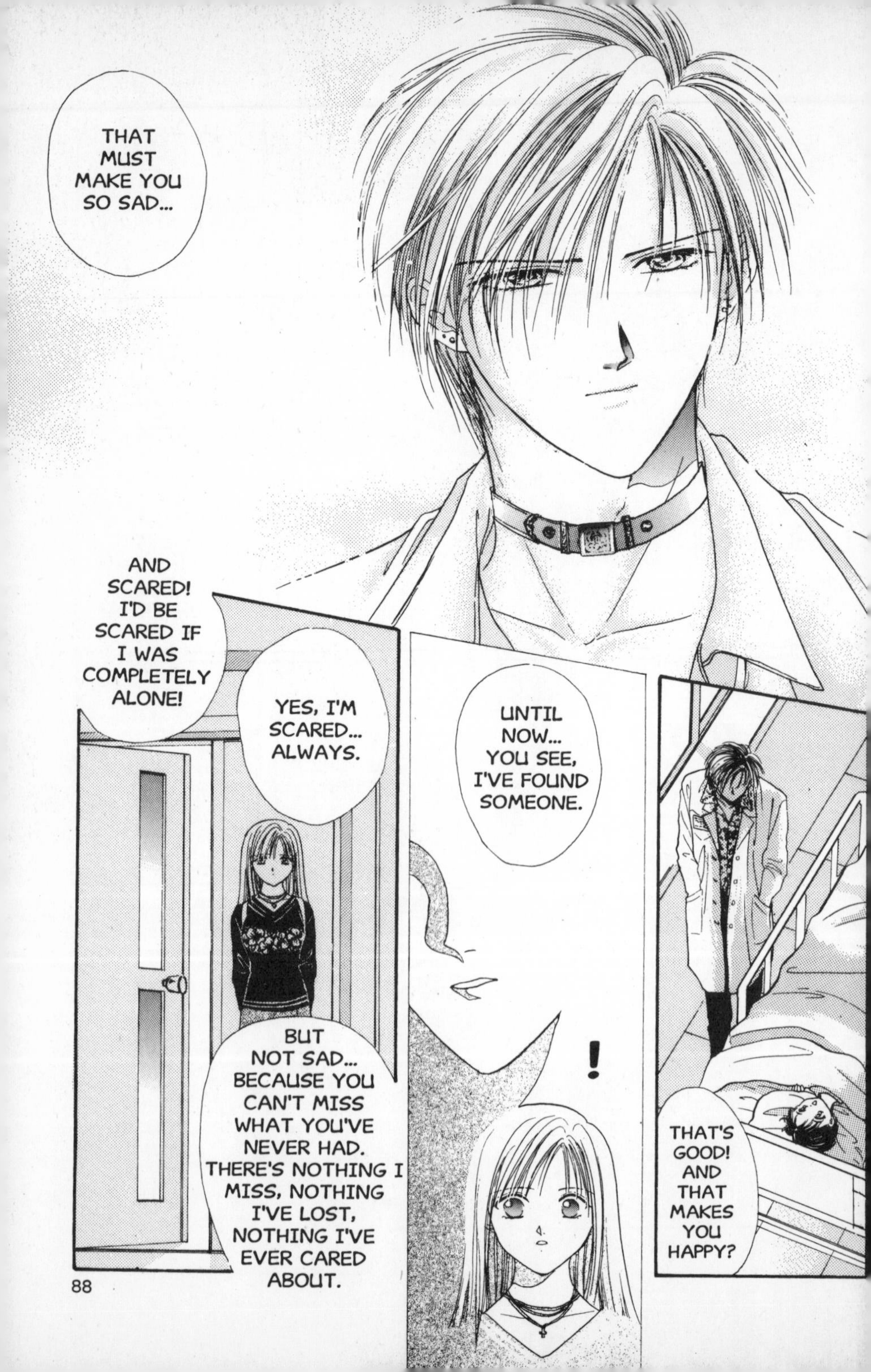
THAT MUST MAKE YOU SO SAD...
AND SCARED! I'D BE SCARED IF I WAS COMPLETELY ALONE!
YES, I'M SCARED... ALWAYS.
BUT NOT SAD... BECAUSE YOU CAN'T MISS WHAT YOU'VE NEVER HAD. THERE'S NOTHING I MISS, NOTHING I'VE LOST, NOTHING I'VE EVER CARED ABOUT.
UNTIL NOW... YOU SEE, I'VE FOUND SOMEONE.
!
THAT'S GOOD! AND THAT MAKES YOU HAPPY?

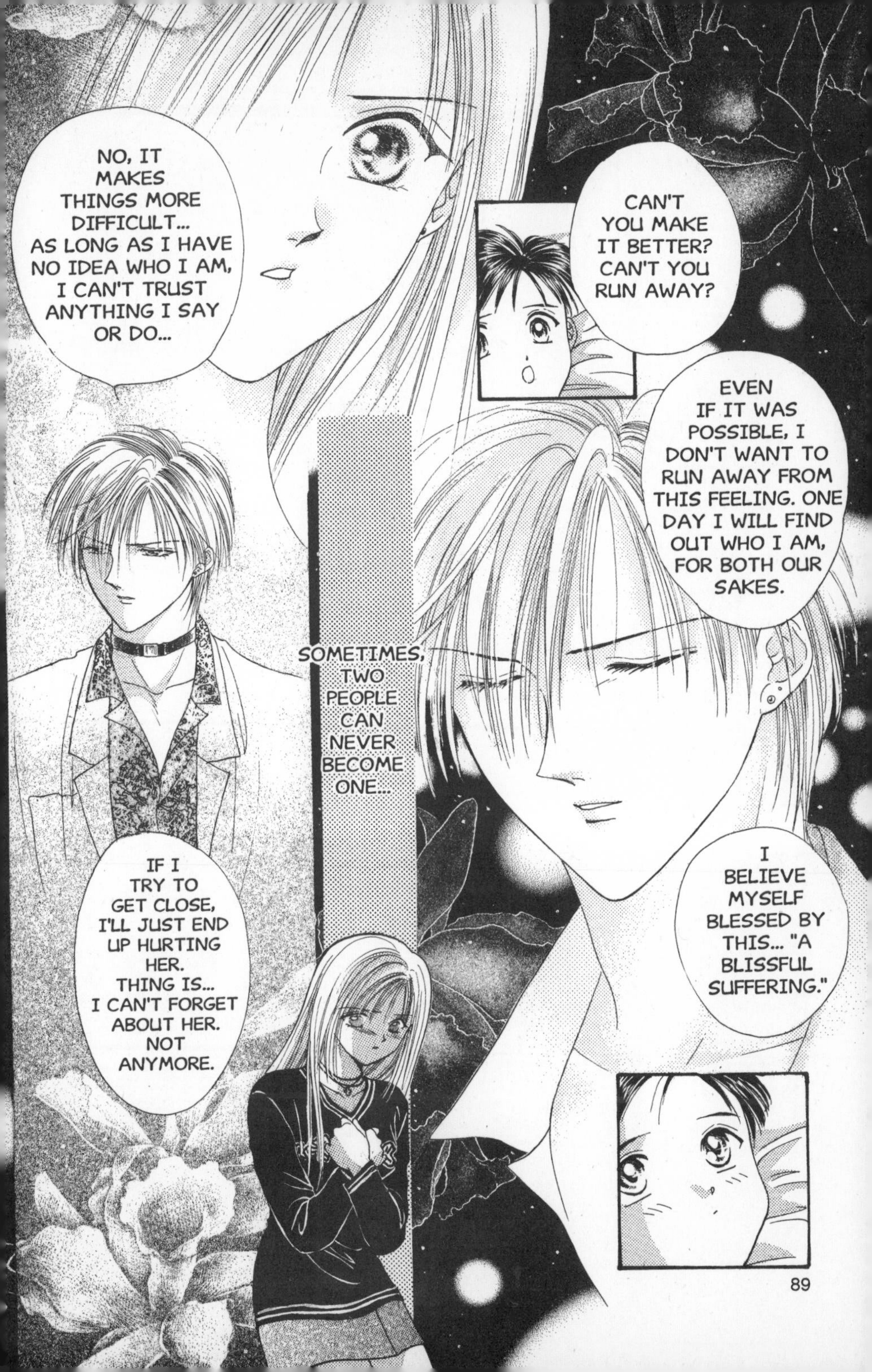
CAN'T YOU MAKE IT BETTER? CAN'T YOU RUN AWAY?
EVEN IF IT WAS POSSIBLE, I DON'T WANT TO RUN AWAY FROM THIS FEELING. ONE DAY I WILL FIND OUT WHO I AM, FOR BOTH OUR SAKES.
NO, IT MAKES THINGS MORE DIFFICULT... AS LONG AS I HAVE NO IDEA WHO I AM, I CAN'T TRUST ANYTHING I SAY OR DO...
SOMETIMES, TWO PEOPLE CAN NEVER BECOME ONE...
I BELIEVE MYSELF BLESSED BY THIS... "A BLISSFUL SUFFERING."
IF I TRY TO GET CLOSE, I'LL JUST END UP HURTING HER. THING IS... I CAN'T FORGET ABOUT HER. NOT ANYMORE.

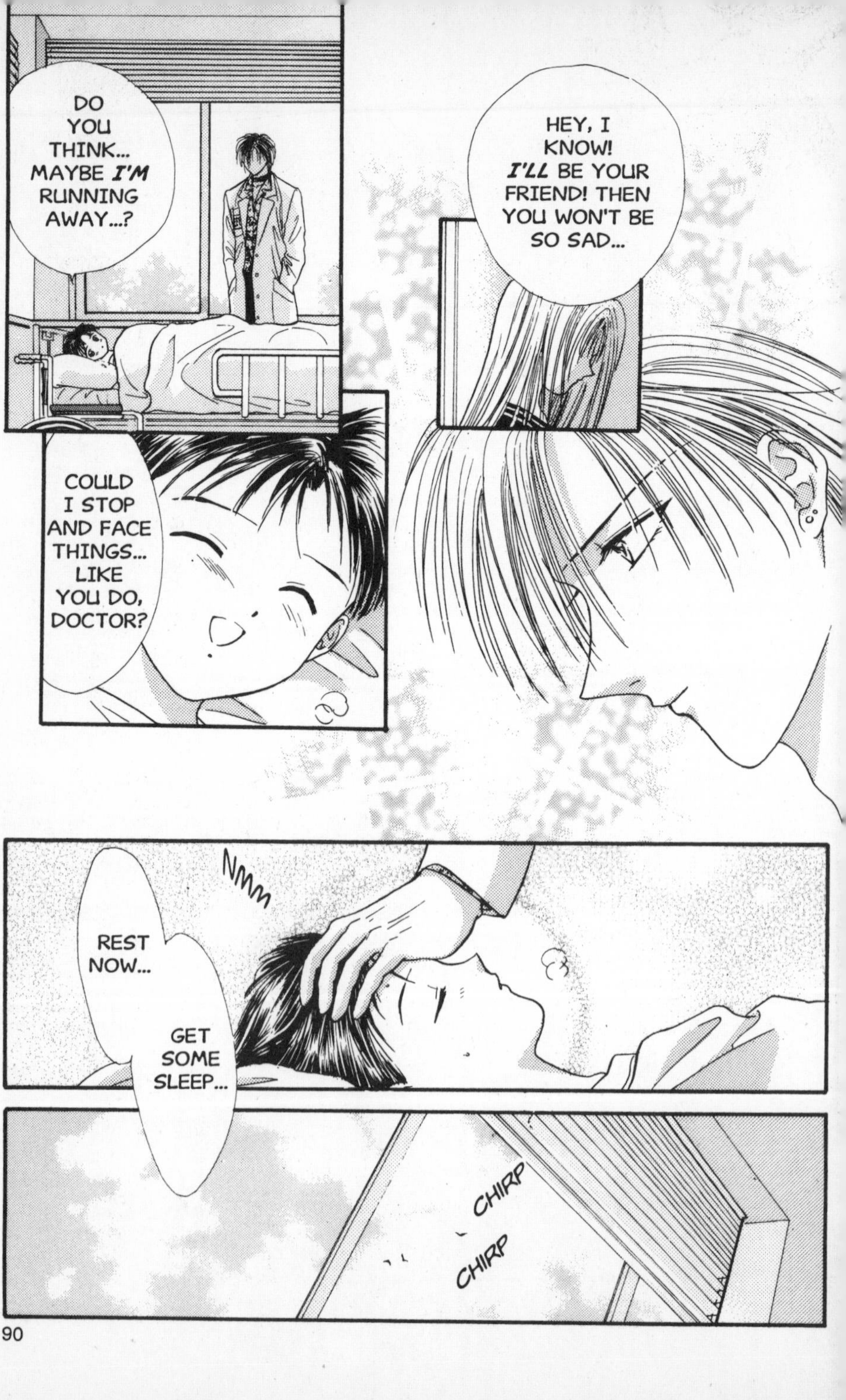
DO YOU THINK... MAYBE I'M RUNNING AWAY...?
COULD I STOP AND FACE THINGS... LIKE YOU DO, DOCTOR?
HEY, I KNOW! I'LL BE YOUR FRIEND! THEN YOU WON'T BE SO SAD...
NMMM
REST NOW...
GET SOME SLEEP...
CHIRP
CHIRP

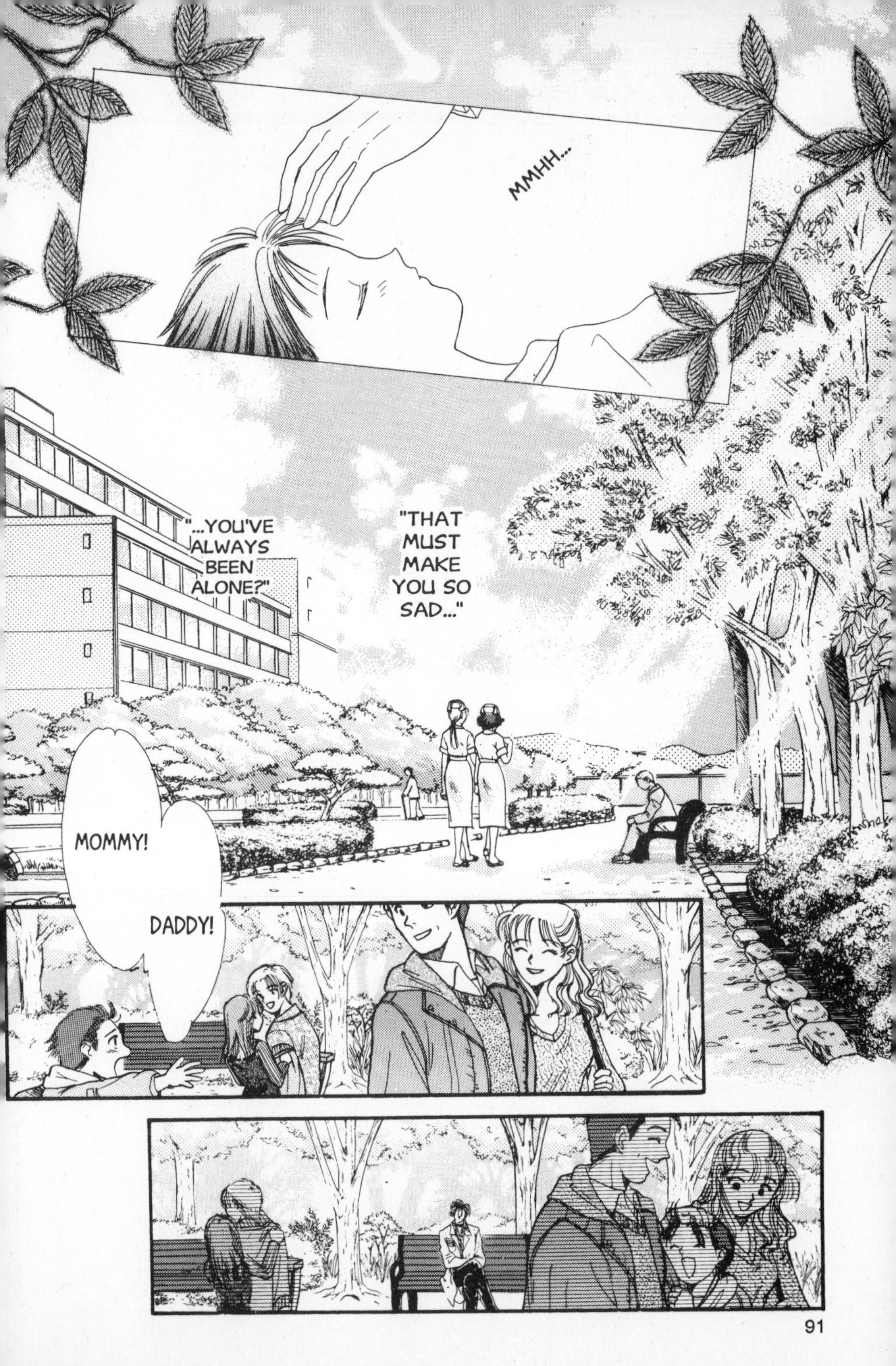
MMHH...
"...YOU'VE ALWAYS BEEN ALONE?"
"THAT MUST MAKE YOU SO SAD..."
MOMMY!
DADDY!

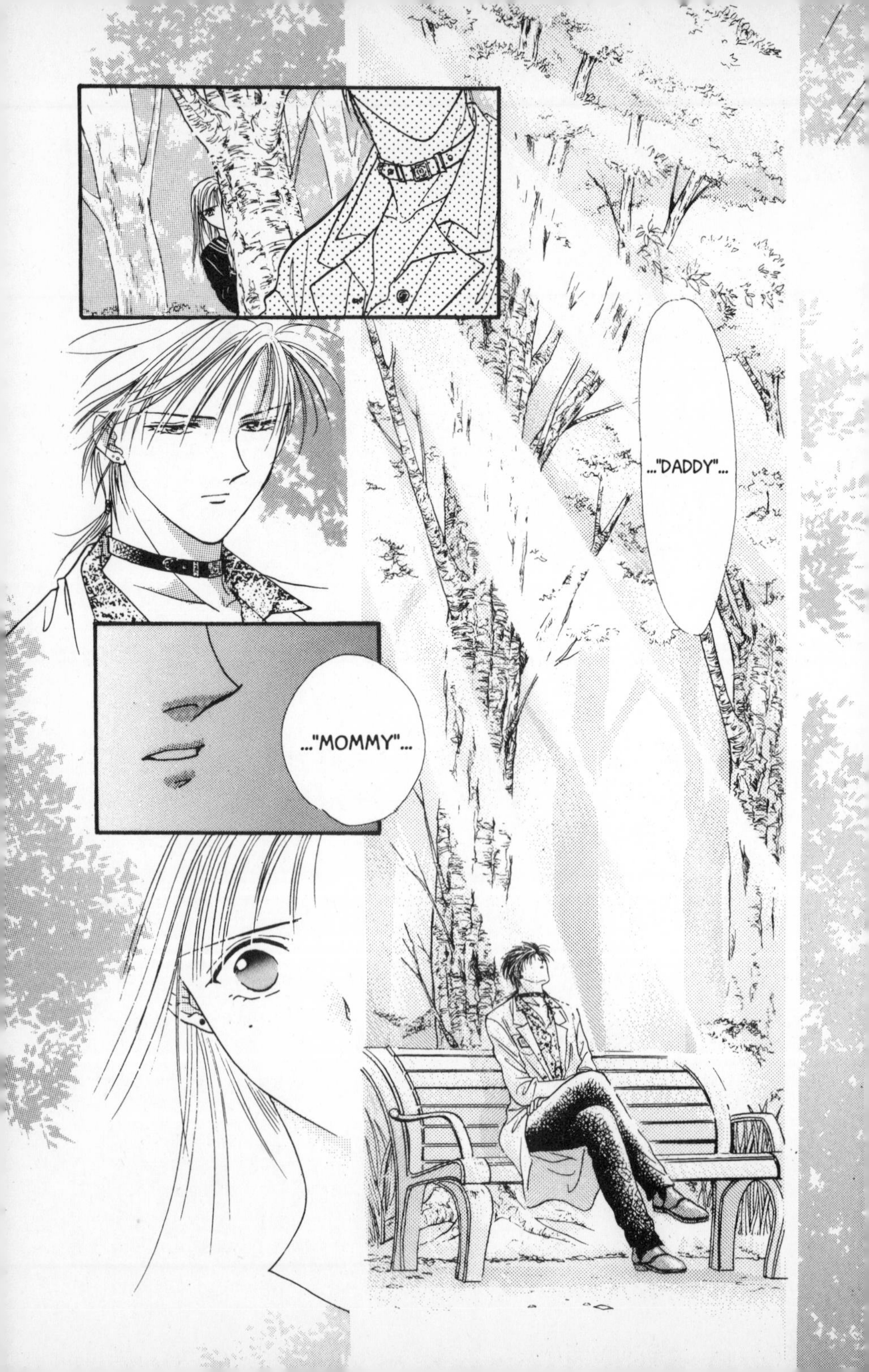
..."DADDY"...
..."MOMMY"...

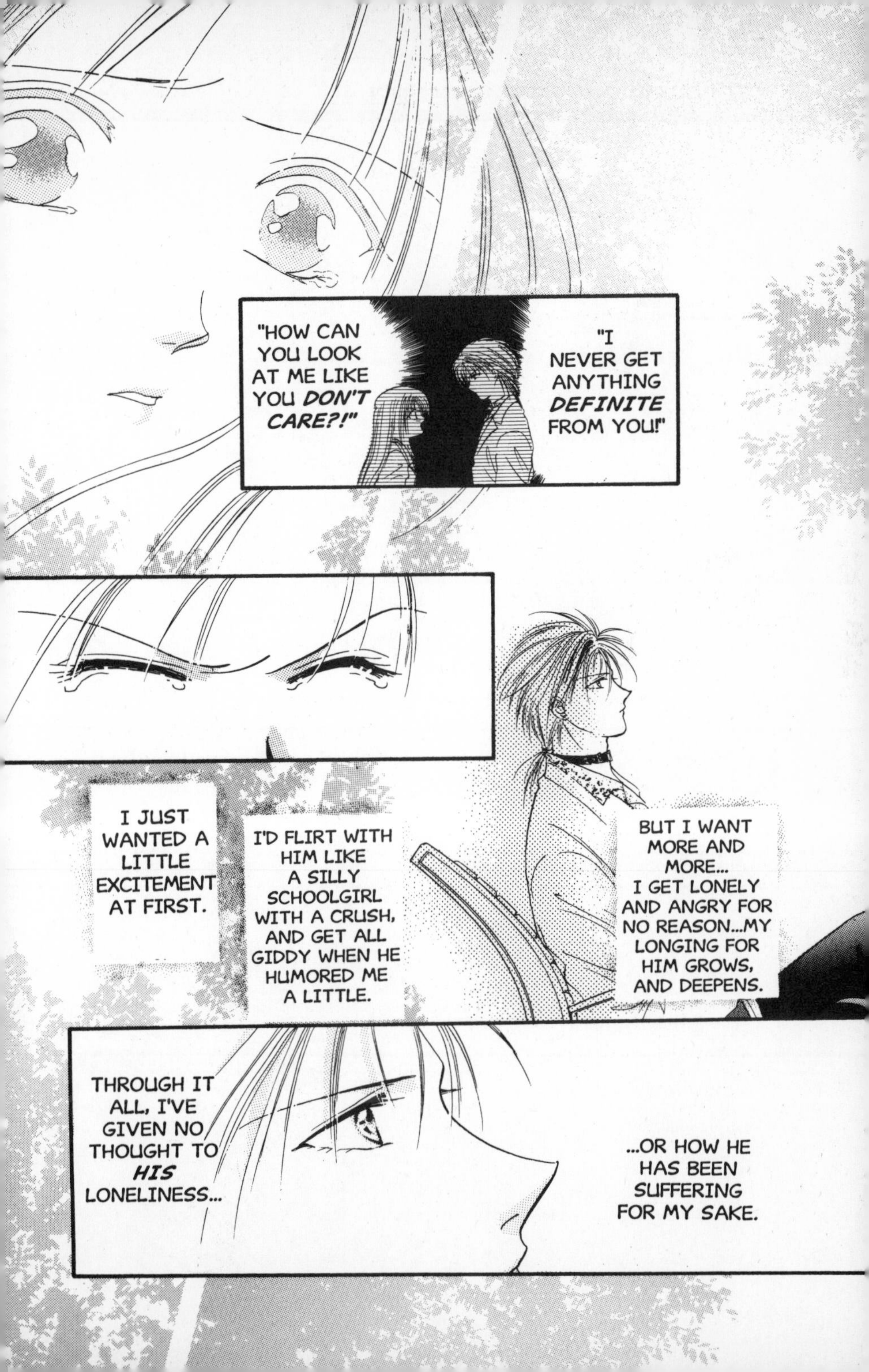
"HOW CAN YOU LOOK AT ME LIKE YOU *DON'T CARE?!*"
"I NEVER GET ANYTHING *DEFINITE* FROM YOU!"
I JUST WANTED A LITTLE EXCITEMENT AT FIRST.
I'D FLIRT WITH HIM LIKE A SILLY SCHOOLGIRL WITH A CRUSH, AND GET ALL GIDDY WHEN HE HUMORED ME A LITTLE.
BUT I WANT MORE AND MORE... I GET LONELY AND ANGRY FOR NO REASON...MY LONGING FOR HIM GROWS, AND DEEPENS.
THROUGH IT ALL, I'VE GIVEN NO THOUGHT TO *HIS* LONELINESS...
...OR HOW HE HAS BEEN SUFFERING FOR MY SAKE.

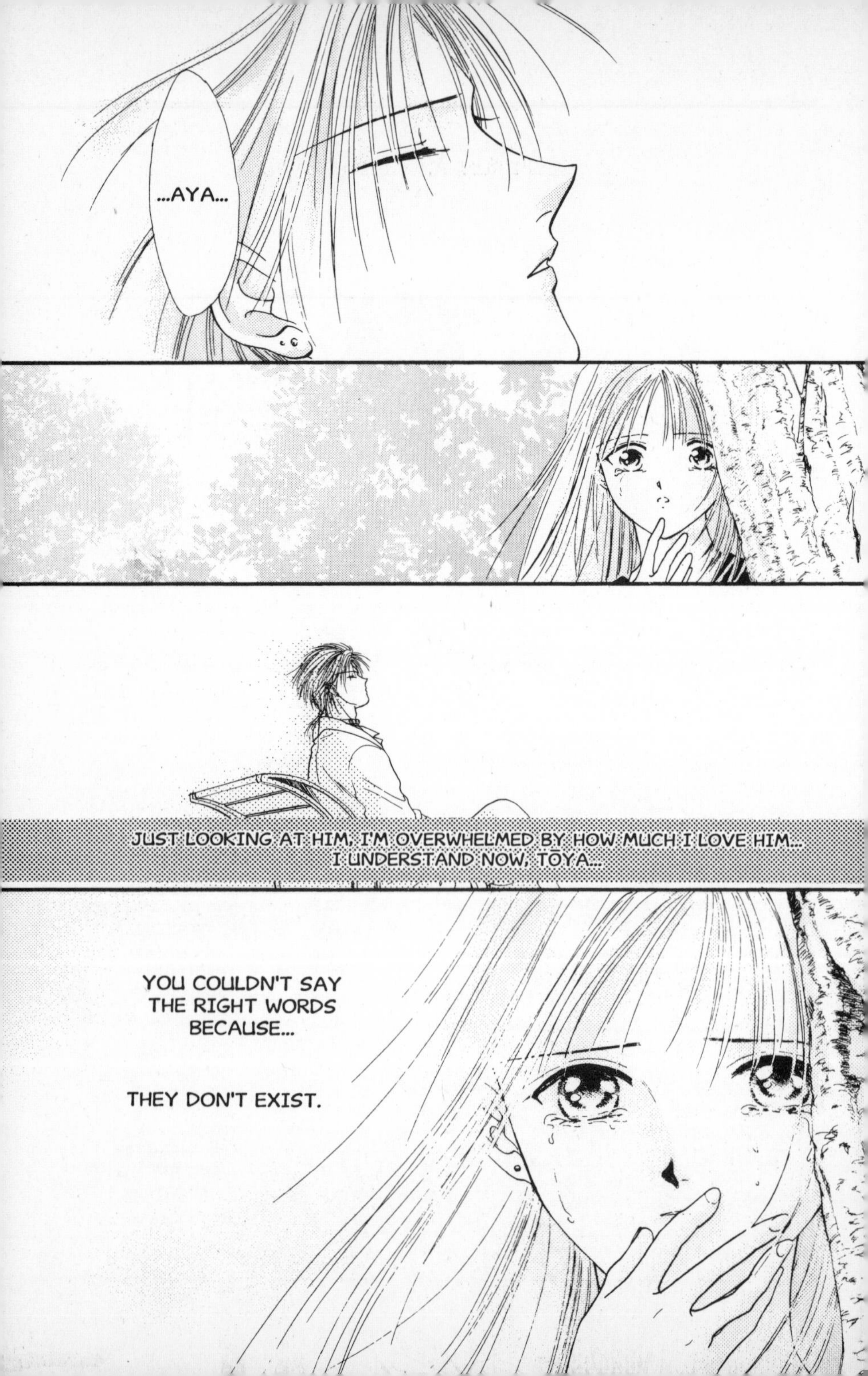
...AYA...
JUST LOOKING AT HIM, I'M OVERWHELMED BY HOW MUCH I LOVE HIM...
I UNDERSTAND NOW, TŌYA...
YOU COULDN'T SAY THE RIGHT WORDS BECAUSE...
THEY DON'T EXIST.

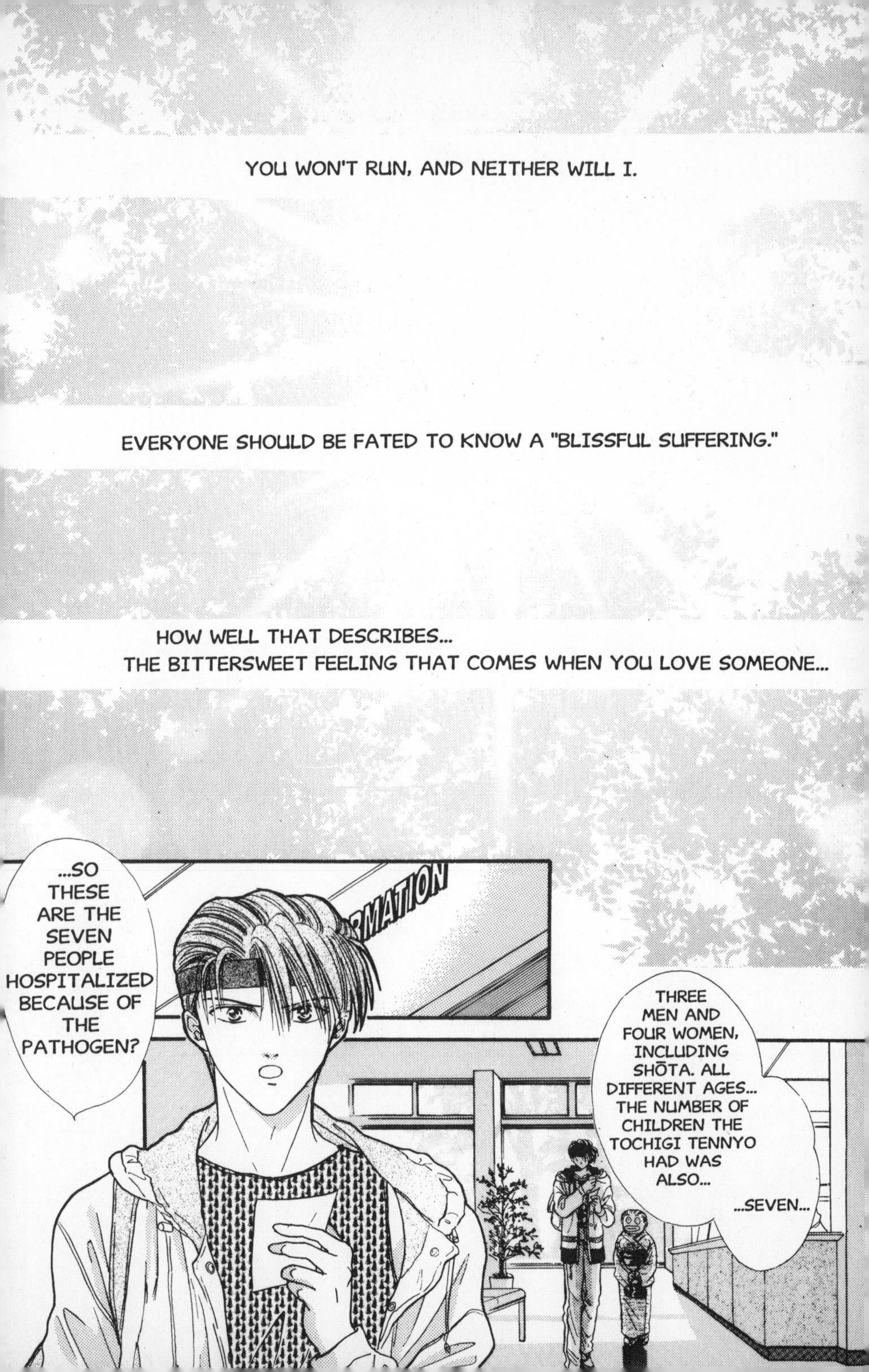
YOU WON'T RUN, AND NEITHER WILL I.
EVERYONE SHOULD BE FATED TO KNOW A "BLISSFUL SUFFERING."
HOW WELL THAT DESCRIBES... THE BITTERSWEET FEELING THAT COMES WHEN YOU LOVE SOMEONE...
...SO THESE ARE THE SEVEN PEOPLE HOSPITALIZED BECAUSE OF THE PATHOGEN?
THREE MEN AND FOUR WOMEN, INCLUDING SHŌTA. ALL DIFFERENT AGES... THE NUMBER OF CHILDREN THE TOCHIGI TENNYO HAD WAS ALSO...
...SEVEN...

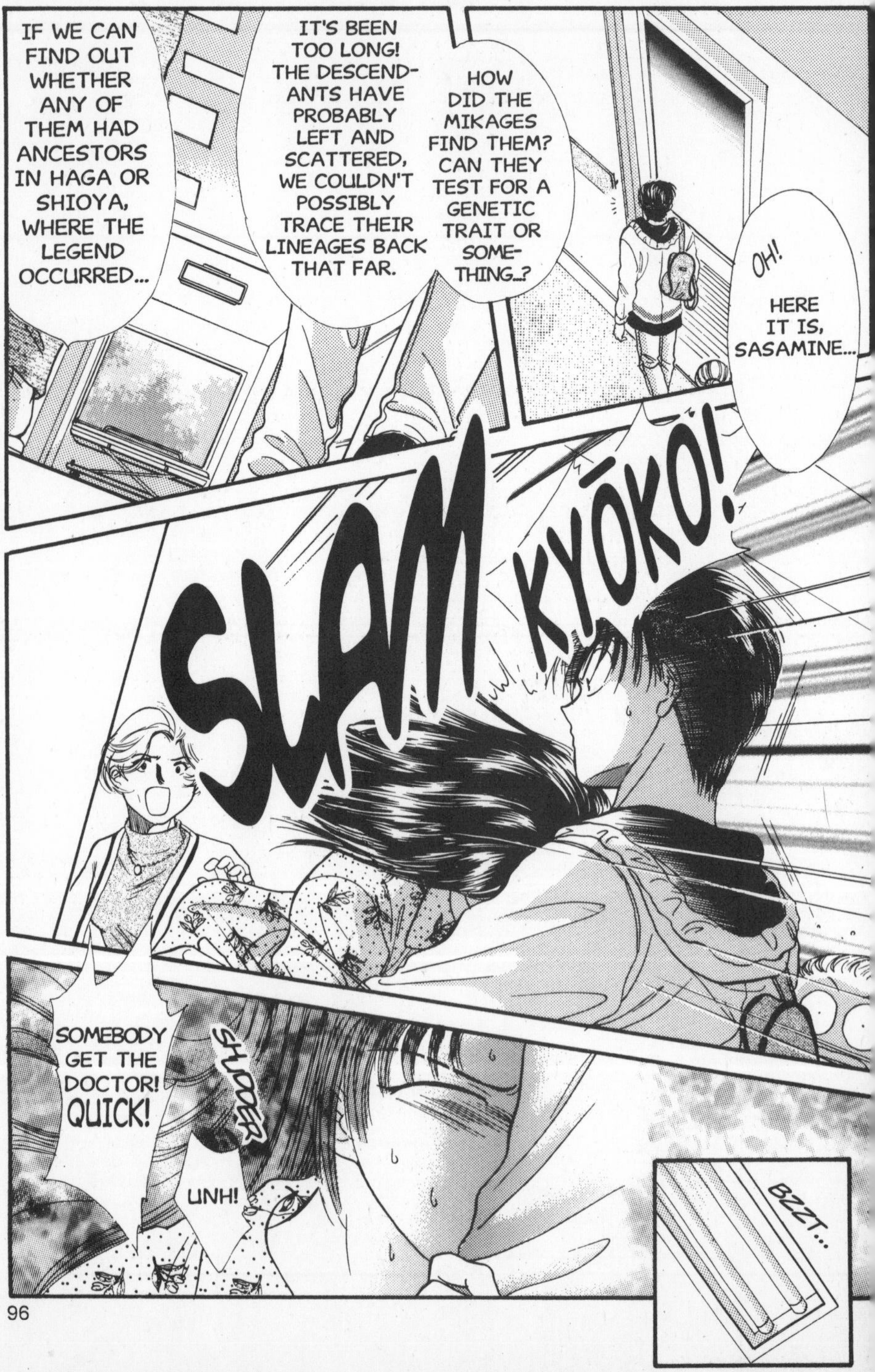
IF WE CAN FIND OUT WHETHER ANY OF THEM HAD ANCESTORS IN HAGA OR SHIOYA, WHERE THE LEGEND OCCURRED...
IT'S BEEN TOO LONG! THE DESCEND-ANTS HAVE PROBABLY LEFT AND SCATTERED, WE COULDN'T POSSIBLY TRACE THEIR LINEAGES BACK THAT FAR.
HOW DID THE MIKAGES FIND THEM? CAN THEY TEST FOR A GENETIC TRAIT OR SOME-THING..?
OH!
HERE IT IS, SASAMINE...
SLAM
KYŌKO!
SOMEBODY GET THE DOCTOR! QUICK!
SHUDDER
UNH!
BZZT...

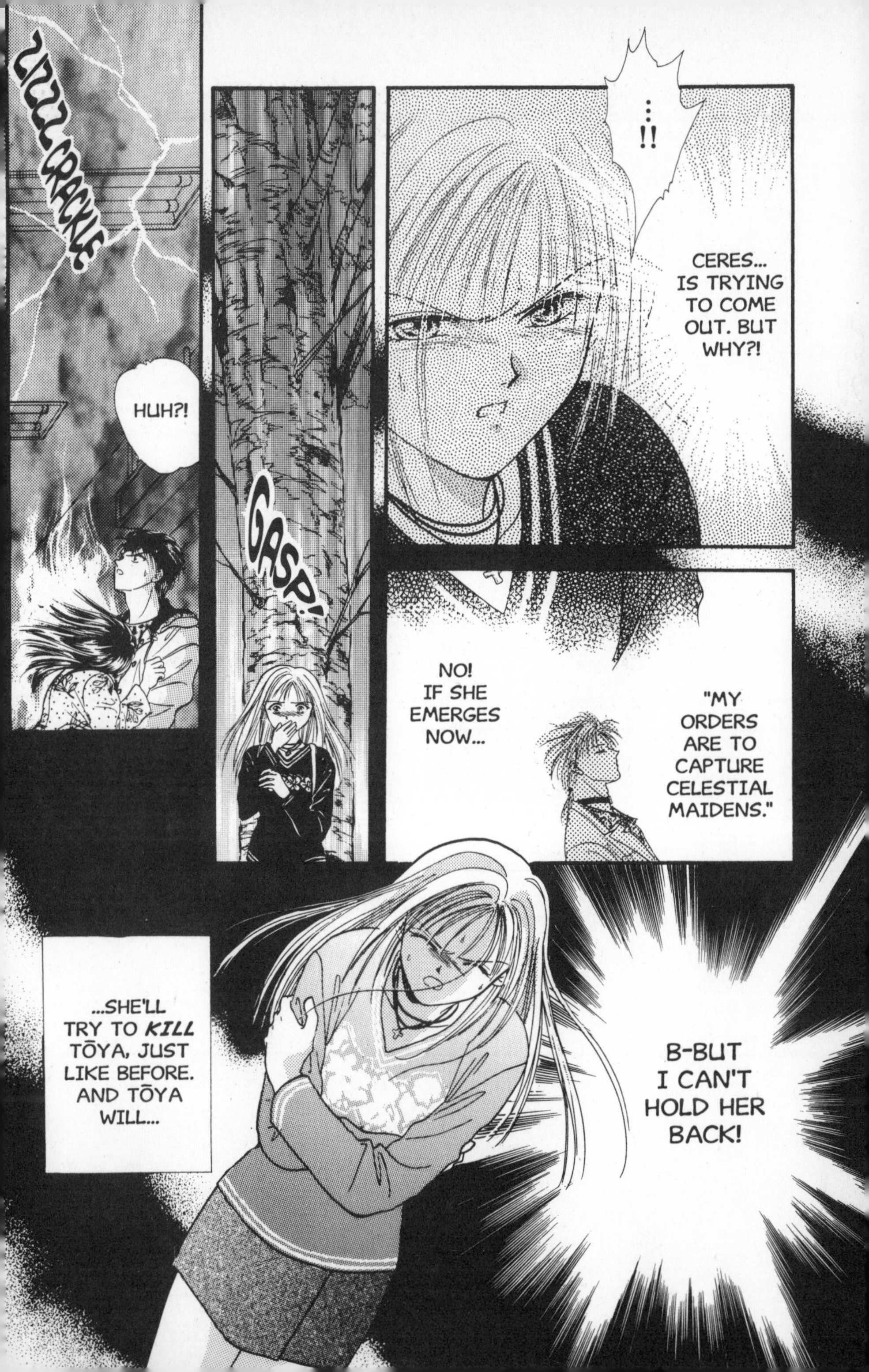

...!!
CERES... IS TRYING TO COME OUT. BUT WHY?!
"MY ORDERS ARE TO CAPTURE CELESTIAL MAIDENS."
NO! IF SHE EMERGES NOW...
GASP!
ZIZZZ CRACKLE
HUH?!
B-BUT I CAN'T HOLD HER BACK!
...SHE'LL TRY TO *KILL* TŌYA, JUST LIKE BEFORE. AND TŌYA WILL...

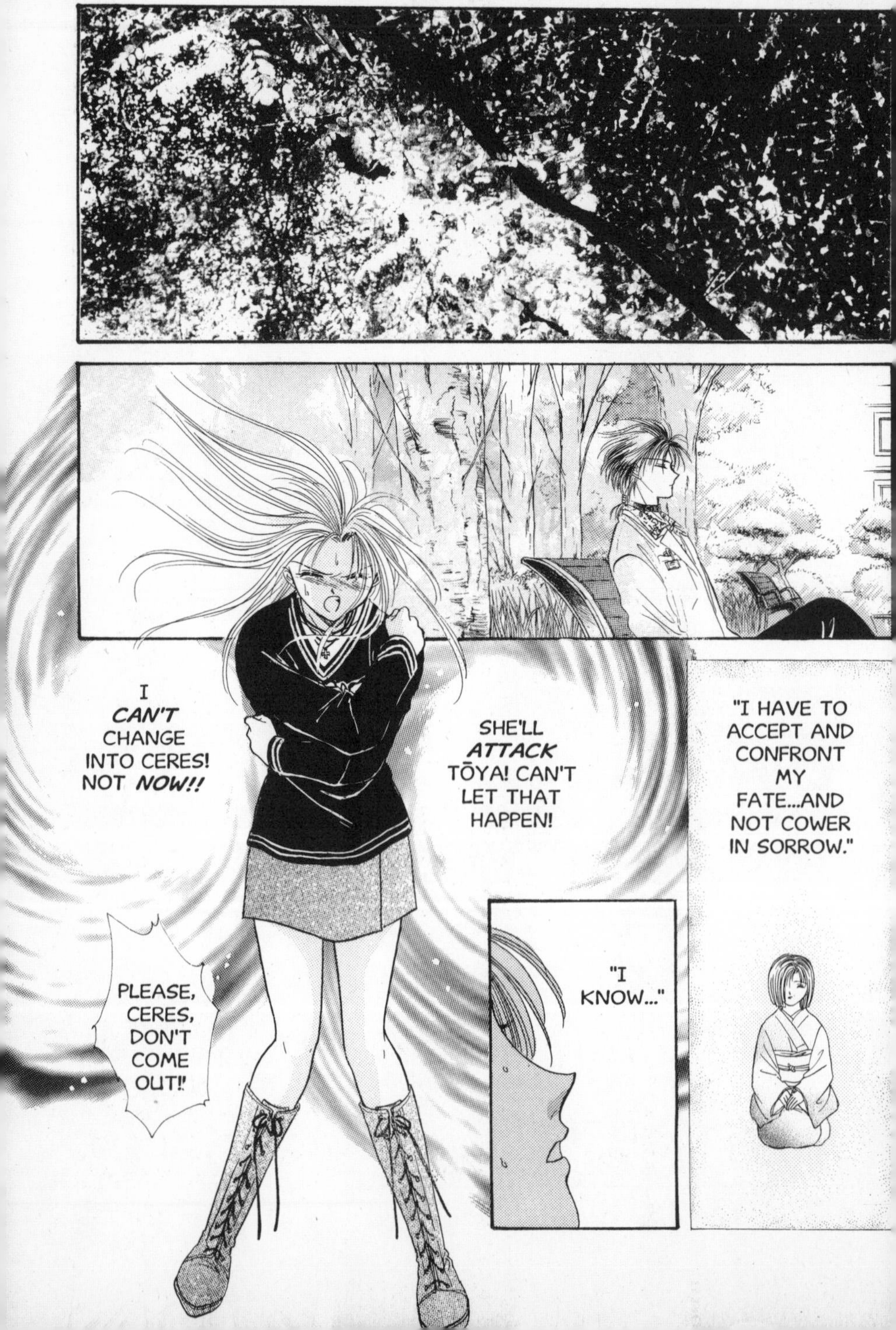

"I HAVE TO ACCEPT AND CONFRONT MY FATE...AND NOT COWER IN SORROW."
"I KNOW..."
SHE'LL ATTACK TŌYA! CAN'T LET THAT HAPPEN!
I CAN'T CHANGE INTO CERES! NOT NOW!!
PLEASE, CERES, DON'T COME OUT!!

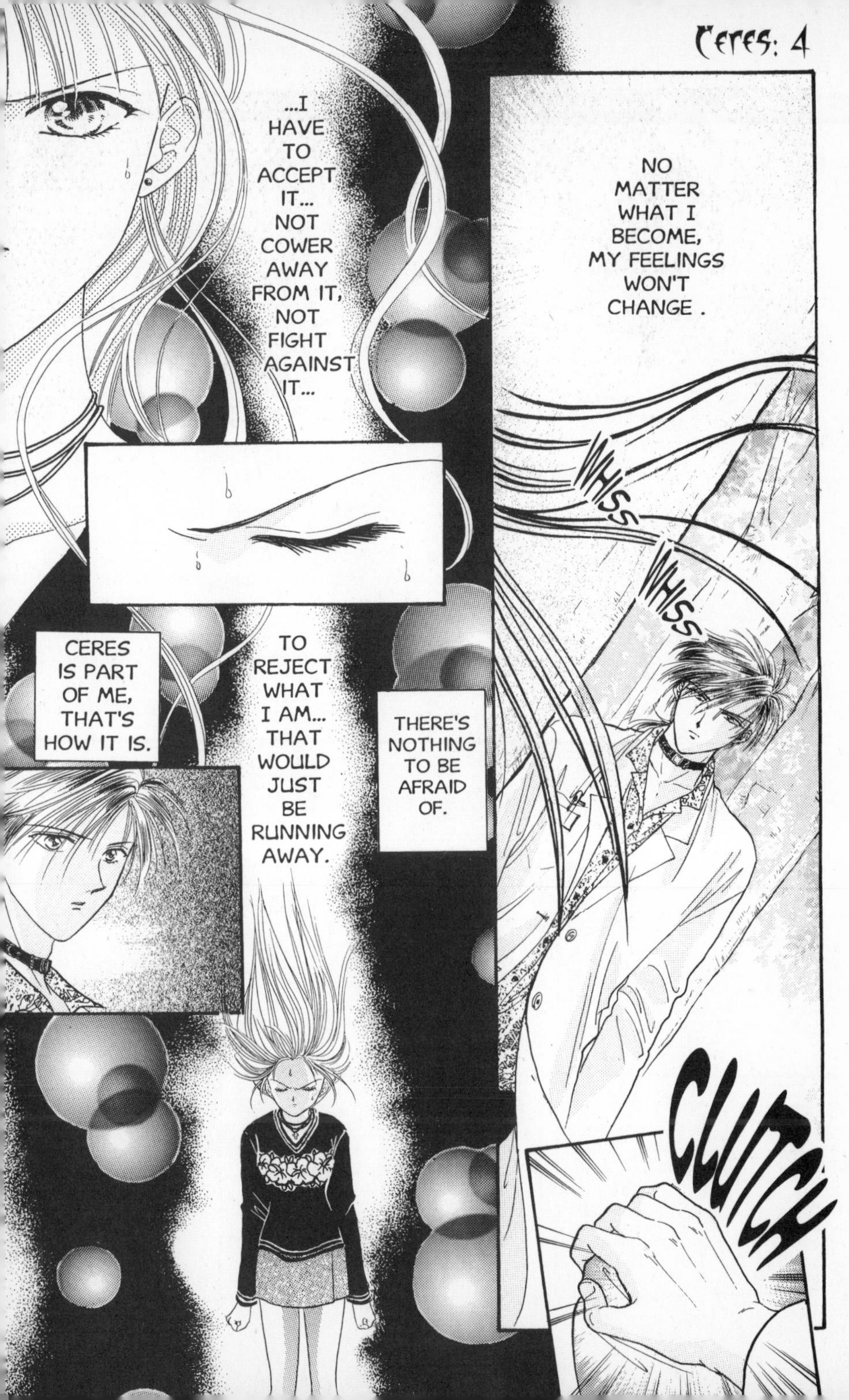
NO MATTER WHAT I BECOME, MY FEELINGS WON'T CHANGE.
WHISS
WHISS
CLUTCH
...I HAVE TO ACCEPT IT... NOT COWER AWAY FROM IT, NOT FIGHT AGAINST IT...
THERE'S NOTHING TO BE AFRAID OF.
TO REJECT WHAT I AM... THAT WOULD JUST BE RUNNING AWAY.
CERES IS PART OF ME, THAT'S HOW IT IS.

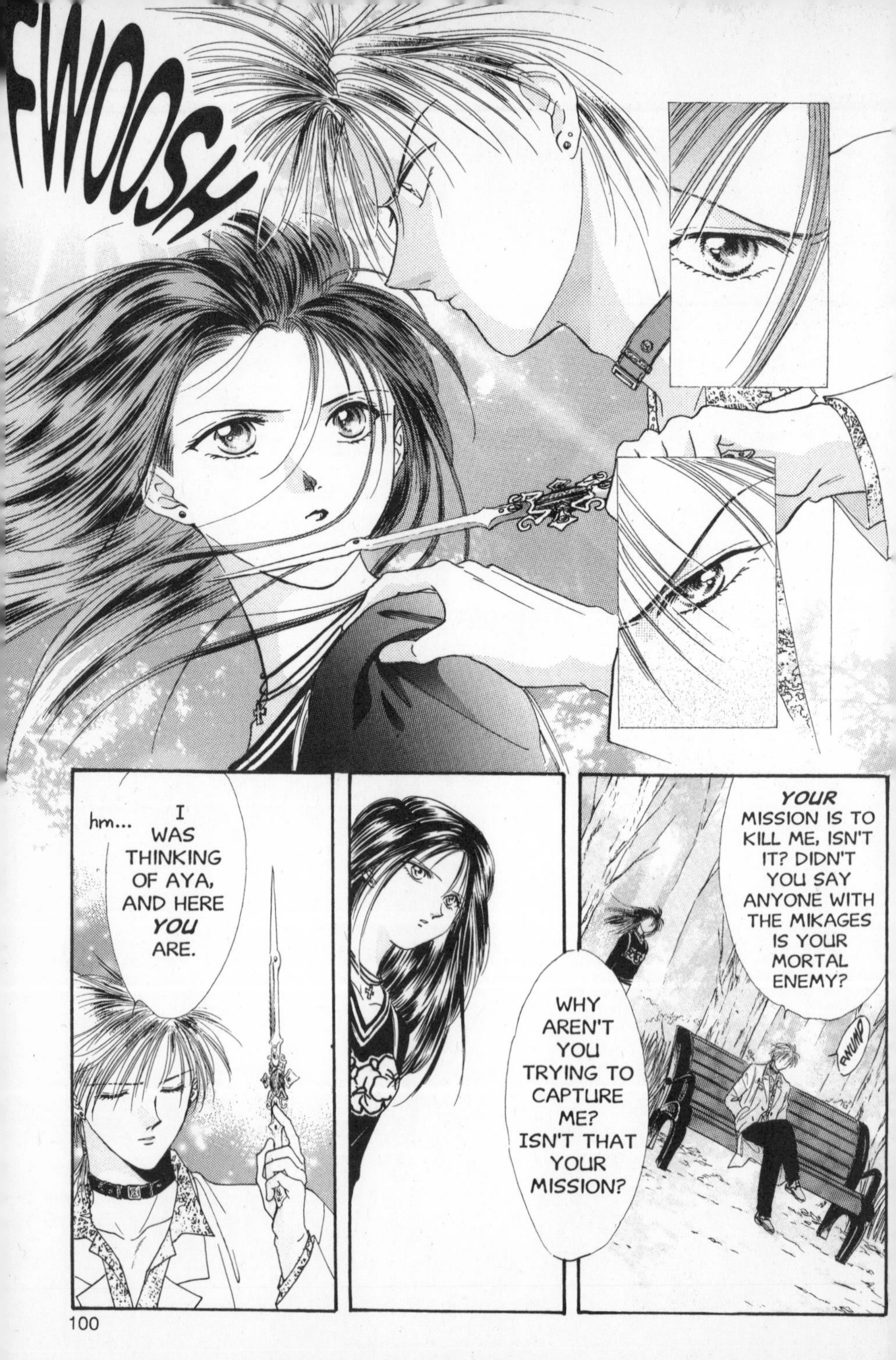
FWOOSH
hm...
I WAS THINKING OF AYA, AND HERE *YOU* ARE.
WHY AREN'T YOU TRYING TO CAPTURE ME? ISN'T THAT YOUR MISSION?
YOUR MISSION IS TO KILL ME, ISN'T IT? DIDN'T YOU SAY ANYONE WITH THE MIKAGES IS YOUR MORTAL ENEMY?
FWUMP

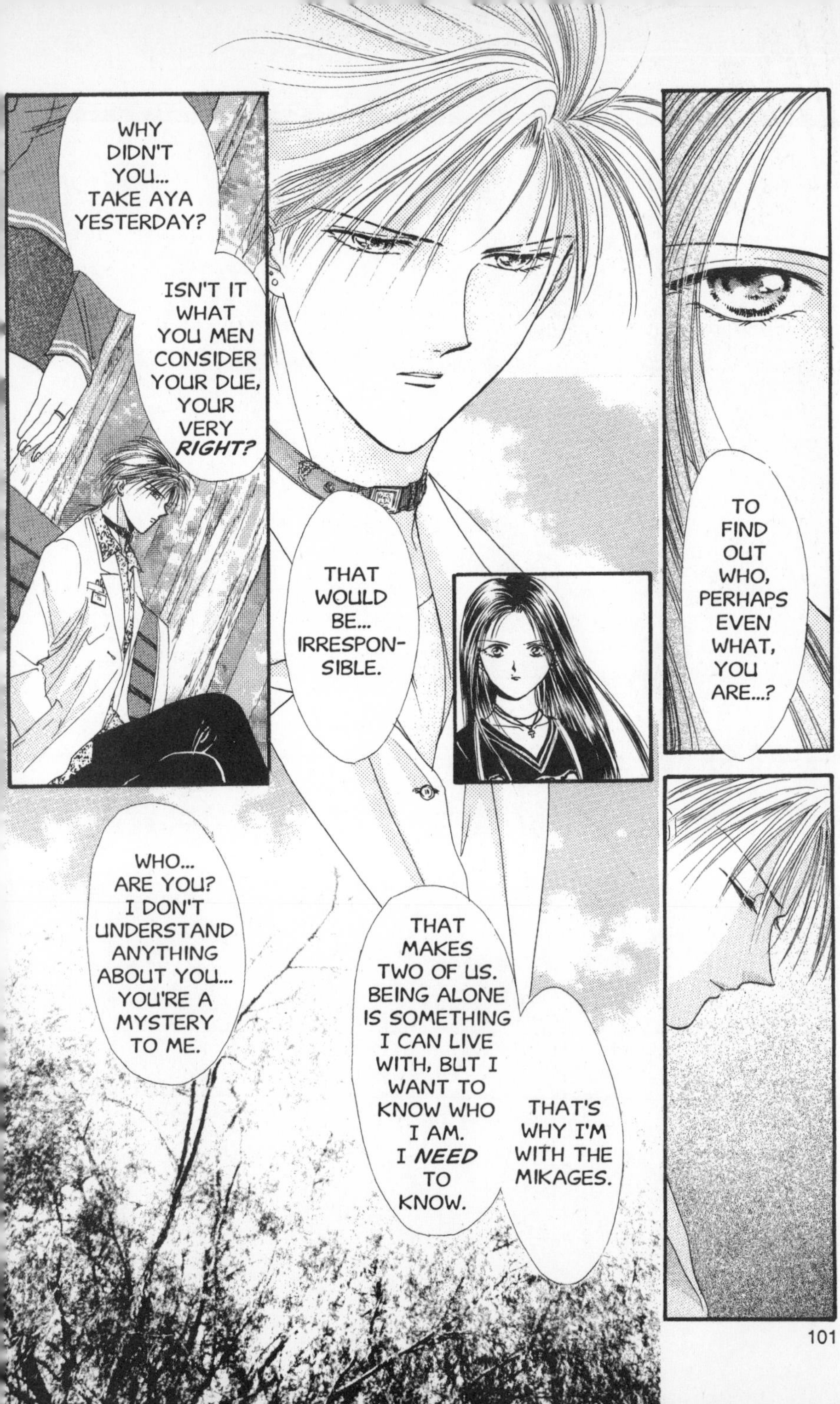
WHY DIDN'T YOU... TAKE AYA YESTERDAY?
ISN'T IT WHAT YOU MEN CONSIDER YOUR DUE, YOUR VERY ***RIGHT?***
THAT WOULD BE... IRRESPON-SIBLE.
WHO... ARE YOU? I DON'T UNDERSTAND ANYTHING ABOUT YOU... YOU'RE A MYSTERY TO ME.
THAT MAKES TWO OF US. BEING ALONE IS SOMETHING I CAN LIVE WITH, BUT I WANT TO KNOW WHO I AM. I ***NEED*** TO KNOW.
THAT'S WHY I'M WITH THE MIKAGES.
TO FIND OUT WHO, PERHAPS EVEN WHAT, YOU ARE...?

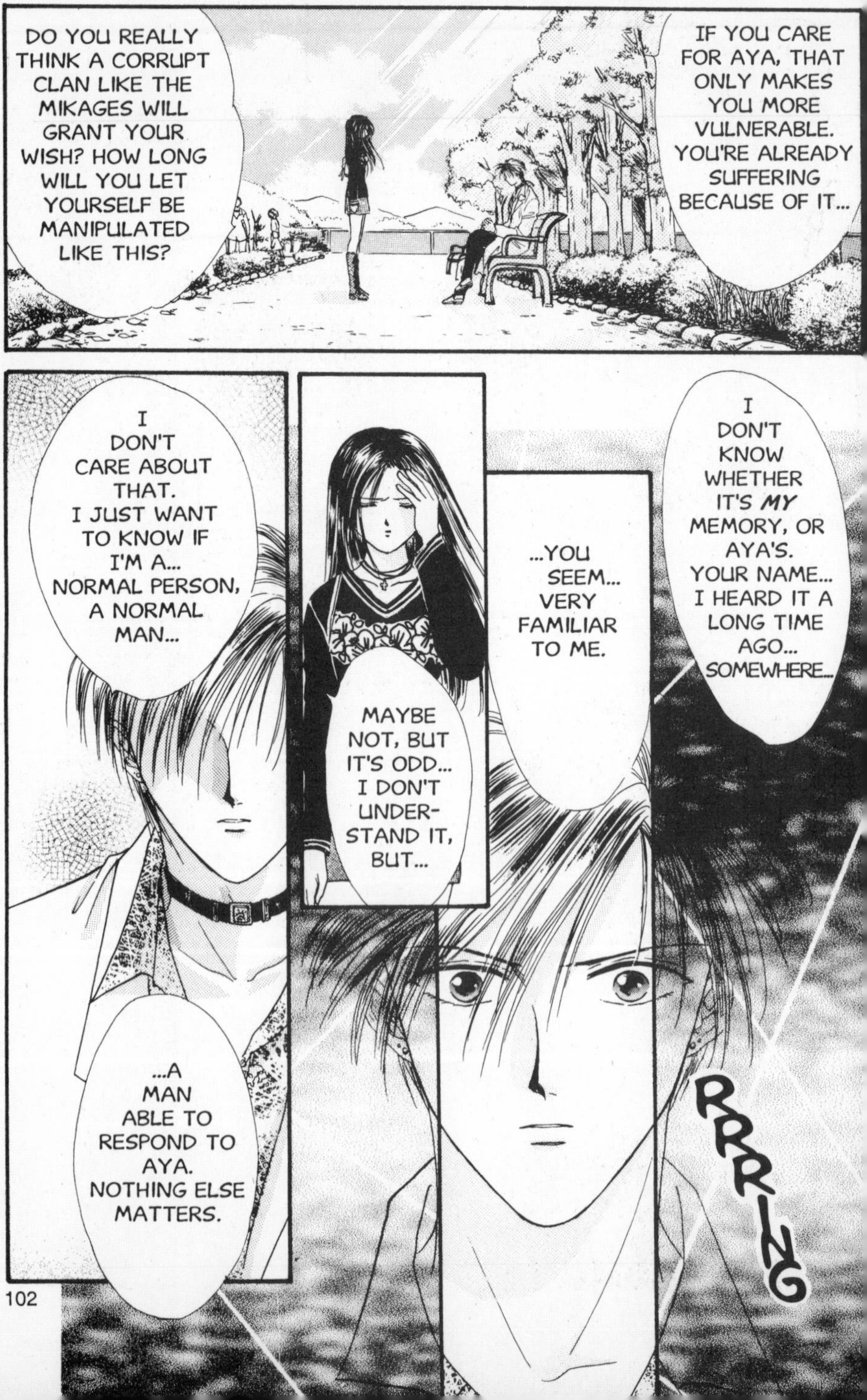
DO YOU REALLY THINK A CORRUPT CLAN LIKE THE MIKAGES WILL GRANT YOUR WISH? HOW LONG WILL YOU LET YOURSELF BE MANIPULATED LIKE THIS?
IF YOU CARE FOR AYA, THAT ONLY MAKES YOU MORE VULNERABLE. YOU'RE ALREADY SUFFERING BECAUSE OF IT...
I DON'T CARE ABOUT THAT. I JUST WANT TO KNOW IF I'M A... NORMAL PERSON, A NORMAL MAN...
...A MAN ABLE TO RESPOND TO AYA. NOTHING ELSE MATTERS.
MAYBE NOT, BUT IT'S ODD... I DON'T UNDER-STAND IT, BUT...
...YOU SEEM... VERY FAMILIAR TO ME.
I DON'T KNOW WHETHER IT'S *MY* MEMORY, OR AYA'S. YOUR NAME... I HEARD IT A LONG TIME AGO... SOMEWHERE...
RRRING

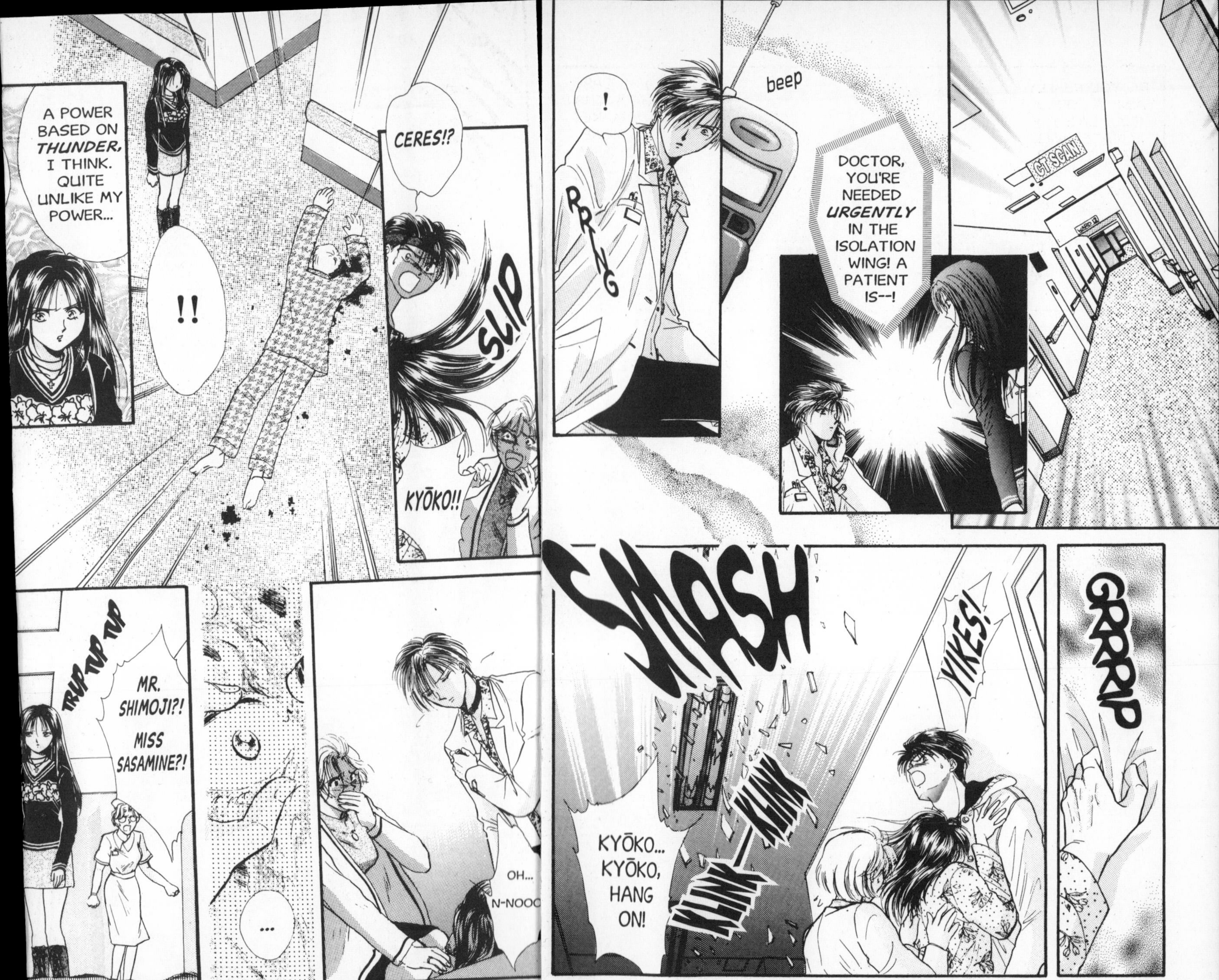
A POWER BASED ON THUNDER, I THINK. QUITE UNLIKE MY POWER...
!!
CERES!?
SLIP
KYŌKO!!
TRUP TUP TUP
MR. SHIMOJI?!
MISS SASAMINE?!
...
OH...
N-NOOO
!
RRRING
beep
DOCTOR, YOU'RE NEEDED URGENTLY IN THE ISOLATION WING! A PATIENT IS--!
CT SCAN
SMASH
KYŌKO... KYŌKO, HANG ON!
KLINK KLINK KLINK
YIKES!
GRRRIP

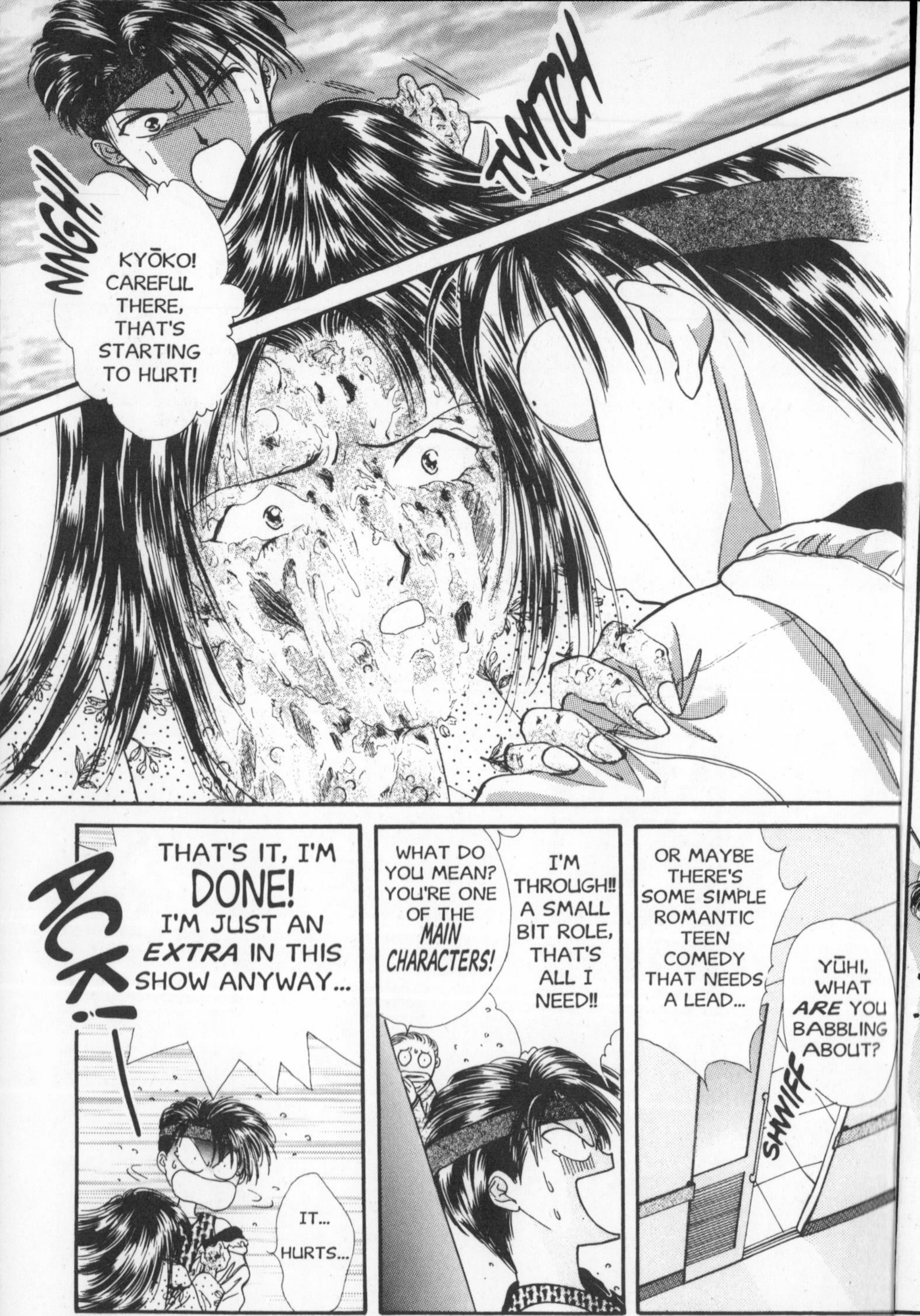
NNGH!
TWITCH
KYŌKO! CAREFUL THERE, THAT'S STARTING TO HURT!
THAT'S IT, I'M DONE! I'M JUST AN EXTRA IN THIS SHOW ANYWAY...
ACK!!
IT... HURTS...
WHAT DO YOU MEAN? YOU'RE ONE OF THE MAIN CHARACTERS!
I'M THROUGH!! A SMALL BIT ROLE, THAT'S ALL I NEED!!
OR MAYBE THERE'S SOME SIMPLE ROMANTIC TEEN COMEDY THAT NEEDS A LEAD...
YŪHI, WHAT ARE YOU BABBLING ABOUT?
SHNIFF

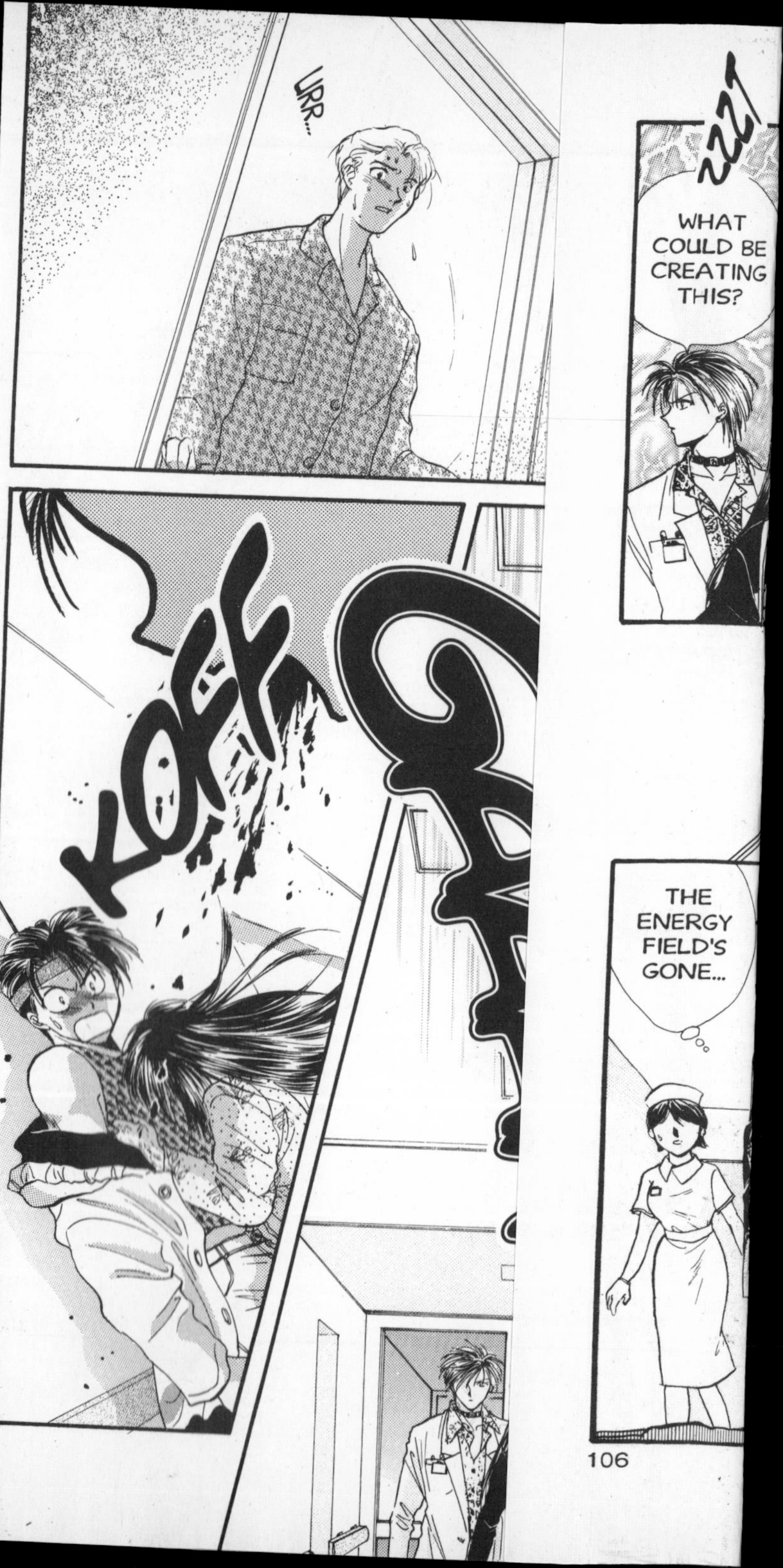
URR...
KOFF
ZZZT
WHAT COULD BE CREATING THIS?
THE ENERGY FIELD'S GONE...

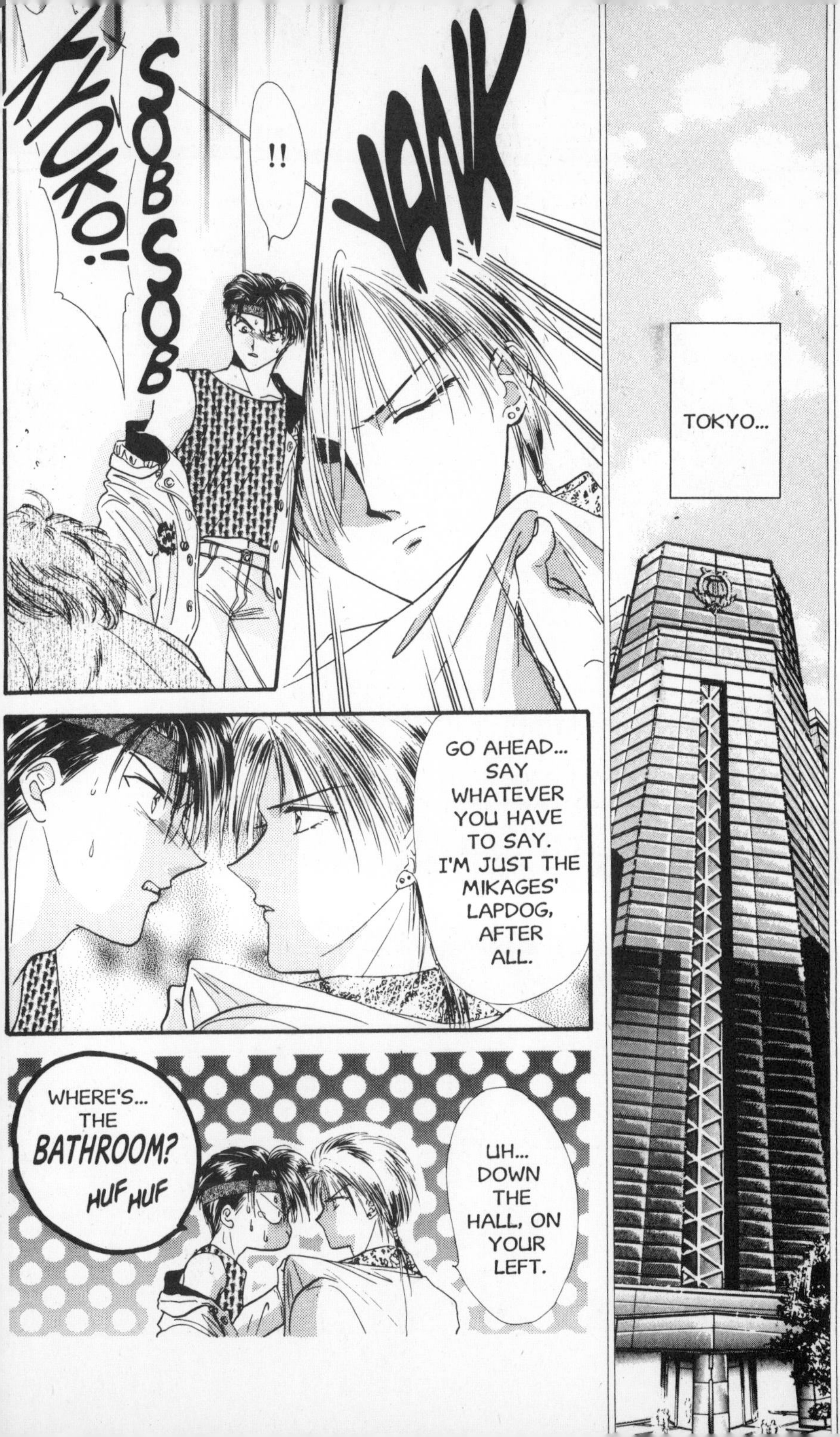
KYOKO!
SOB SOB
!!
YANK
GO AHEAD... SAY WHATEVER YOU HAVE TO SAY. I'M JUST THE MIKAGES' LAPDOG, AFTER ALL.
WHERE'S... THE BATHROOM?
HUF HUF
UH... DOWN THE HALL, ON YOUR LEFT.
TOKYO...

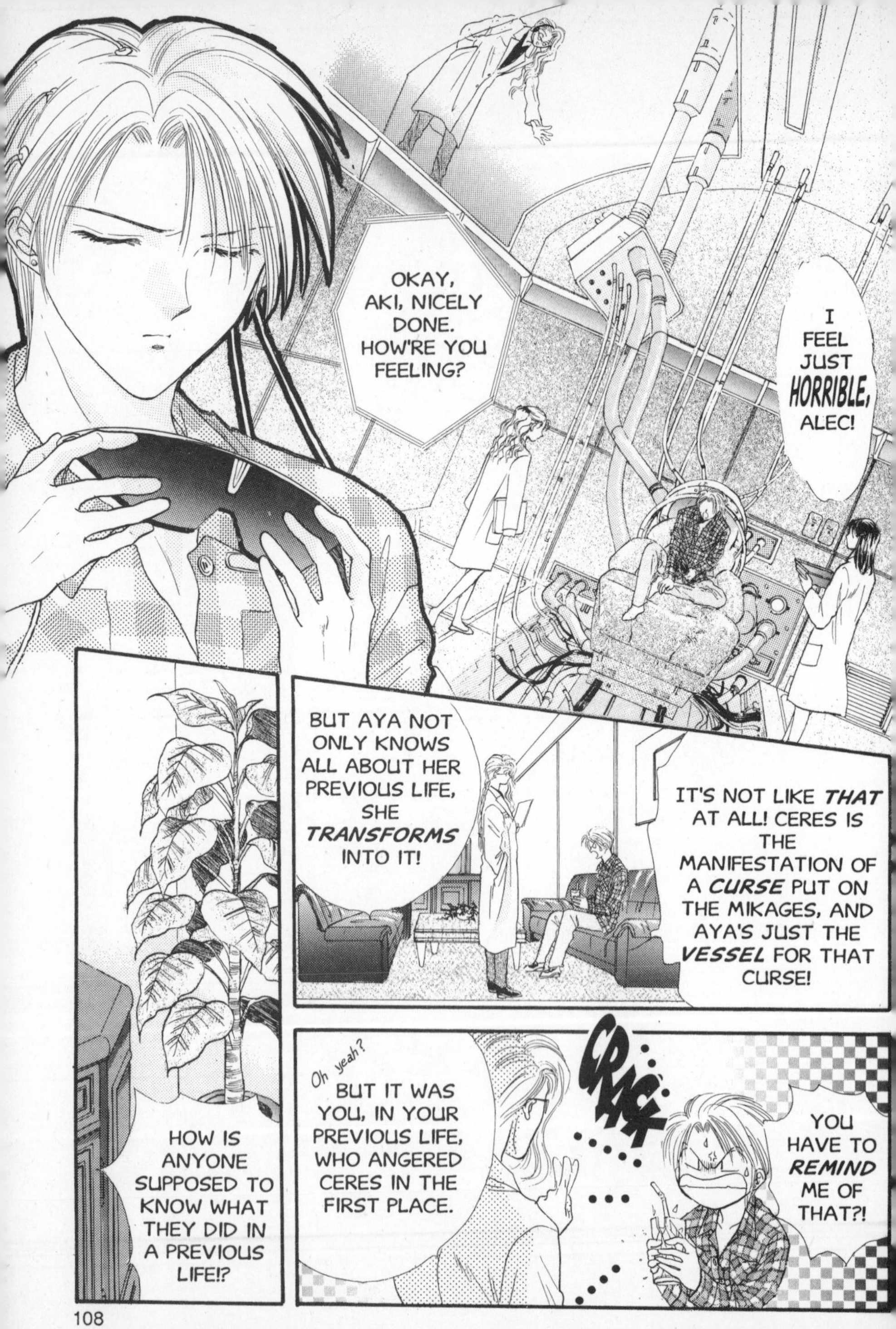
OKAY, AKI, NICELY DONE. HOW'RE YOU FEELING?
I FEEL JUST HORRIBLE, ALEC!
BUT AYA NOT ONLY KNOWS ALL ABOUT HER PREVIOUS LIFE, SHE *TRANSFORMS* INTO IT!
IT'S NOT LIKE *THAT* AT ALL! CERES IS THE MANIFESTATION OF A *CURSE* PUT ON THE MIKAGES, AND AYA'S JUST THE *VESSEL* FOR THAT CURSE!
Oh yeah?
BUT IT WAS YOU, IN YOUR PREVIOUS LIFE, WHO ANGERED CERES IN THE FIRST PLACE.
CRACK
...
...
...
YOU HAVE TO *REMIND* ME OF THAT?!
HOW IS ANYONE SUPPOSED TO KNOW WHAT THEY DID IN A PREVIOUS LIFE!?

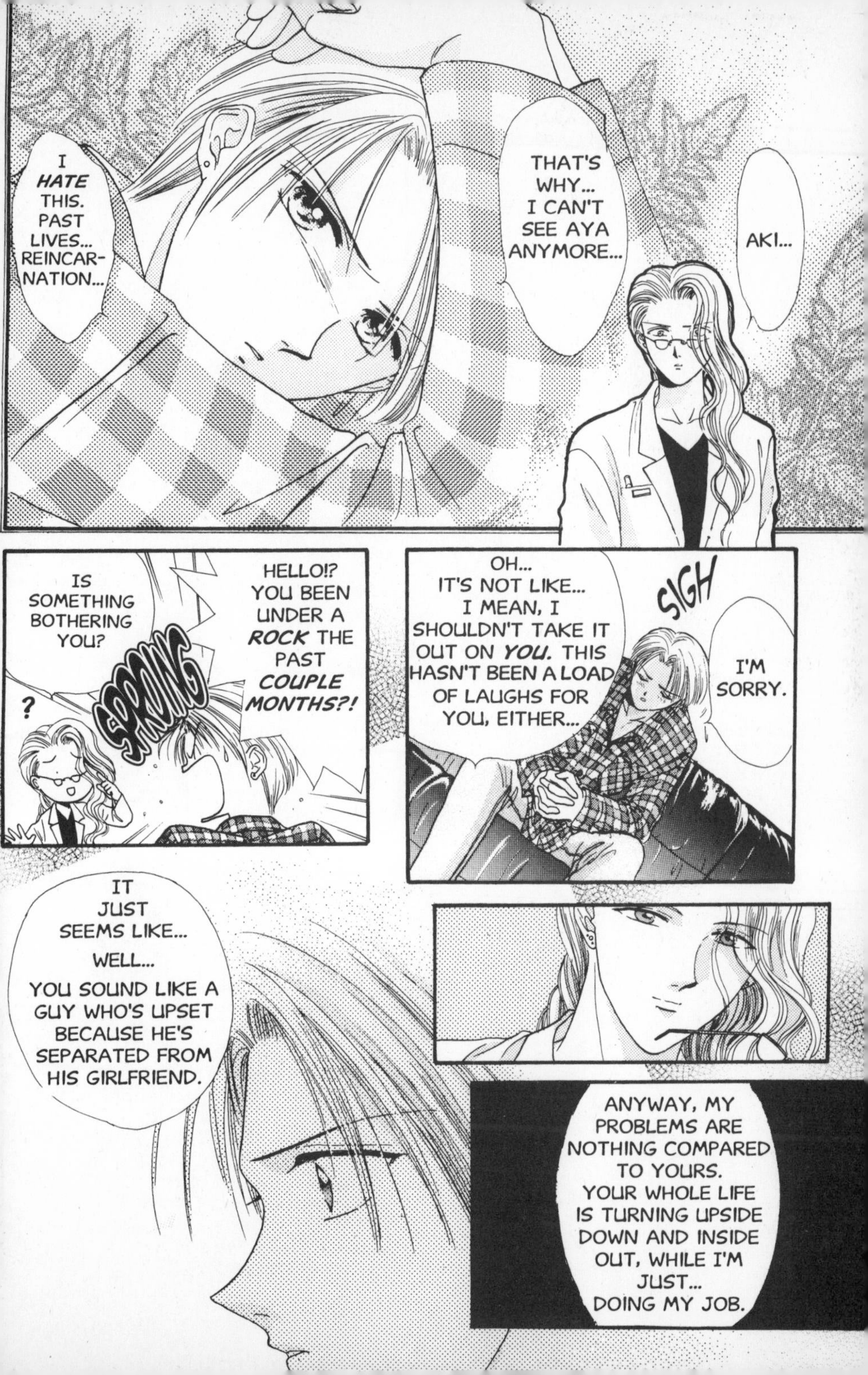

I *HATE* THIS. PAST LIVES... REINCARNATION...
THAT'S WHY... I CAN'T SEE AYA ANYMORE...
AKI...
IS SOMETHING BOTHERING YOU?
?
SPROING
HELLO!? YOU BEEN UNDER A *ROCK* THE PAST *COUPLE MONTHS?!*
OH... IT'S NOT LIKE... I MEAN, I SHOULDN'T TAKE IT OUT ON *YOU.* THIS HASN'T BEEN A LOAD OF LAUGHS FOR YOU, EITHER...
SIGH
I'M SORRY.
IT JUST SEEMS LIKE... WELL... YOU SOUND LIKE A GUY WHO'S UPSET BECAUSE HE'S SEPARATED FROM HIS GIRLFRIEND.
ANYWAY, MY PROBLEMS ARE NOTHING COMPARED TO YOURS. YOUR WHOLE LIFE IS TURNING UPSIDE DOWN AND INSIDE OUT, WHILE I'M JUST... DOING MY JOB.

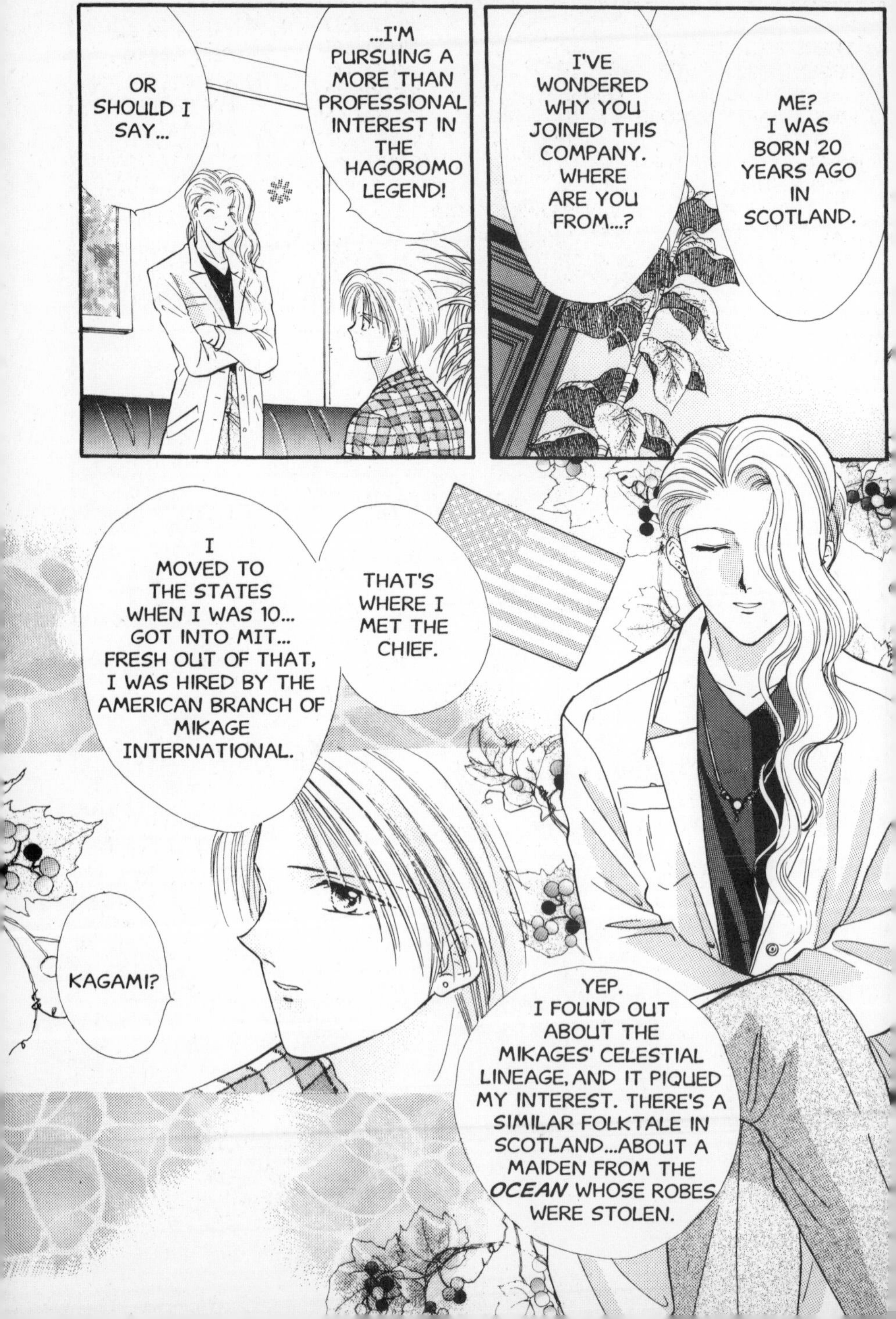
OR SHOULD I SAY...
...I'M PURSUING A MORE THAN PROFESSIONAL INTEREST IN THE HAGOROMO LEGEND!
I'VE WONDERED WHY YOU JOINED THIS COMPANY. WHERE ARE YOU FROM...?
ME? I WAS BORN 20 YEARS AGO IN SCOTLAND.
I MOVED TO THE STATES WHEN I WAS 10... GOT INTO MIT... FRESH OUT OF THAT, I WAS HIRED BY THE AMERICAN BRANCH OF MIKAGE INTERNATIONAL.
THAT'S WHERE I MET THE CHIEF.
KAGAMI?
YEP. I FOUND OUT ABOUT THE MIKAGES' CELESTIAL LINEAGE, AND IT PIQUED MY INTEREST. THERE'S A SIMILAR FOLKTALE IN SCOTLAND...ABOUT A MAIDEN FROM THE *OCEAN* WHOSE ROBES WERE STOLEN.

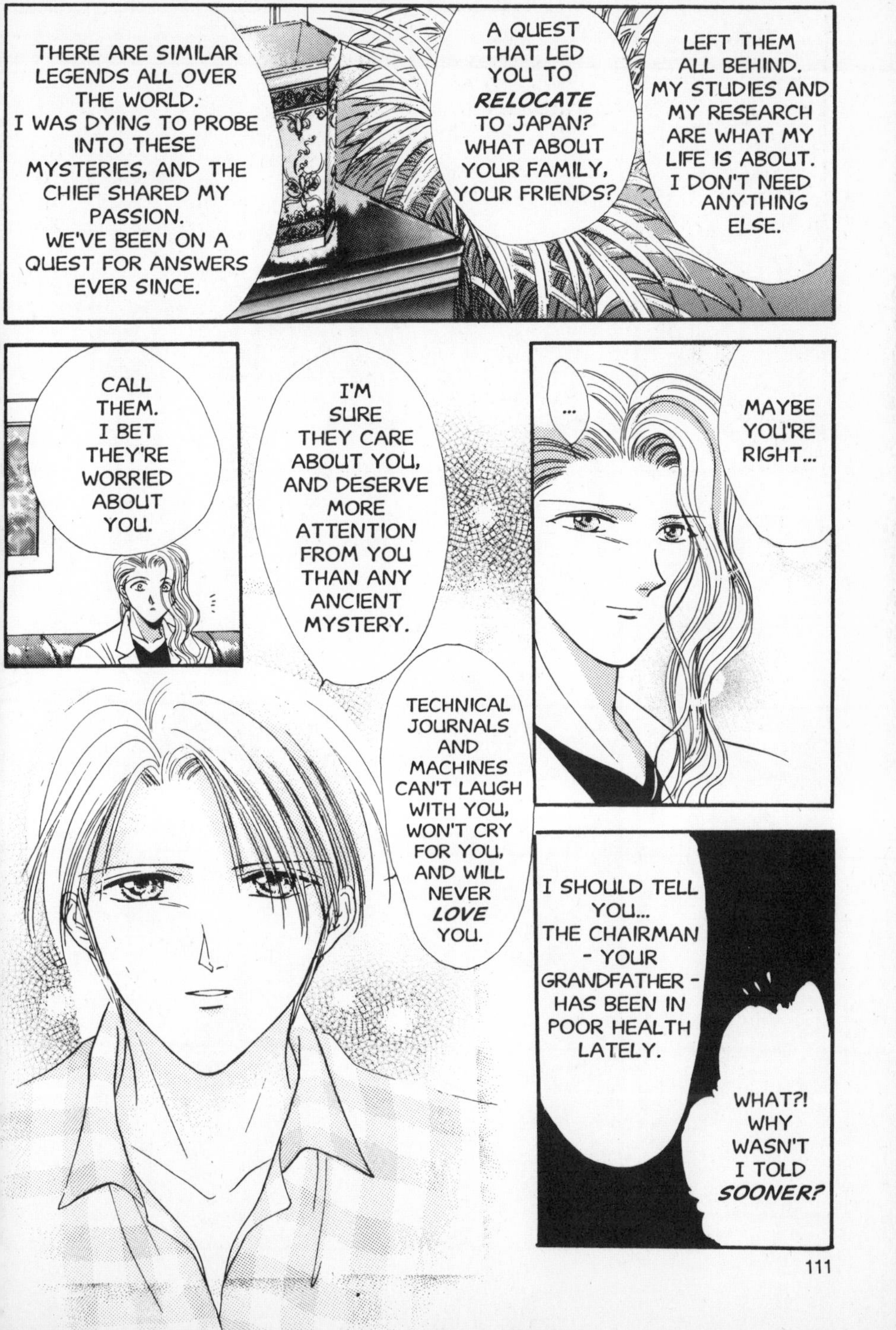
THERE ARE SIMILAR LEGENDS ALL OVER THE WORLD. I WAS DYING TO PROBE INTO THESE MYSTERIES, AND THE CHIEF SHARED MY PASSION. WE'VE BEEN ON A QUEST FOR ANSWERS EVER SINCE.
A QUEST THAT LED YOU TO *RELOCATE* TO JAPAN? WHAT ABOUT YOUR FAMILY, YOUR FRIENDS?
LEFT THEM ALL BEHIND. MY STUDIES AND MY RESEARCH ARE WHAT MY LIFE IS ABOUT. I DON'T NEED ANYTHING ELSE.
CALL THEM. I BET THEY'RE WORRIED ABOUT YOU.
I'M SURE THEY CARE ABOUT YOU, AND DESERVE MORE ATTENTION FROM YOU THAN ANY ANCIENT MYSTERY.
TECHNICAL JOURNALS AND MACHINES CAN'T LAUGH WITH YOU, WON'T CRY FOR YOU, AND WILL NEVER *LOVE* YOU.
...
MAYBE YOU'RE RIGHT...
I SHOULD TELL YOU... THE CHAIRMAN - YOUR GRANDFATHER - HAS BEEN IN POOR HEALTH LATELY.
WHAT?! WHY WASN'T I TOLD *SOONER?*

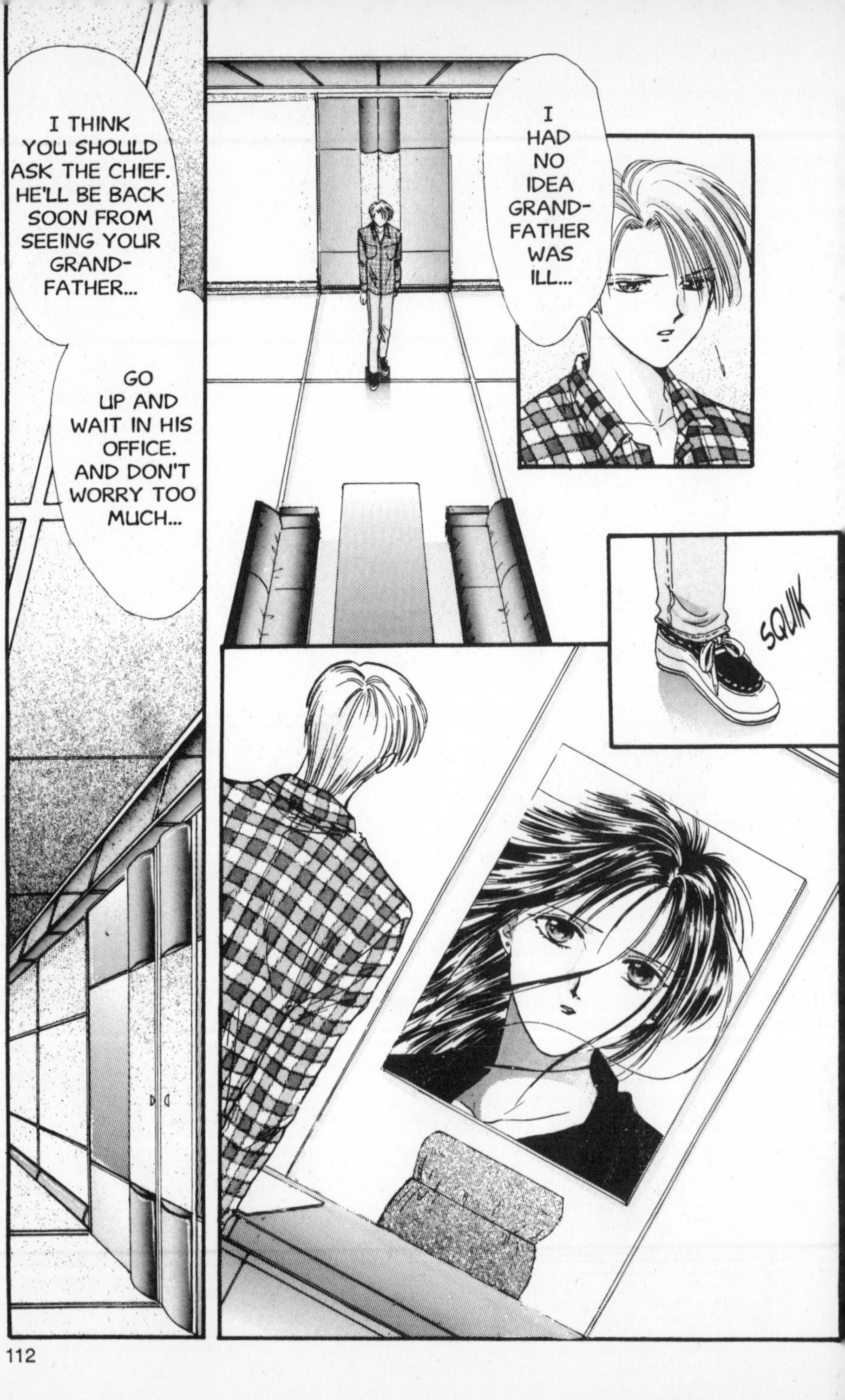
I HAD NO IDEA GRAND-FATHER WAS ILL...
I THINK YOU SHOULD ASK THE CHIEF. HE'LL BE BACK SOON FROM SEEING YOUR GRAND-FATHER...
GO UP AND WAIT IN HIS OFFICE. AND DON'T WORRY TOO MUCH...
SQUIK

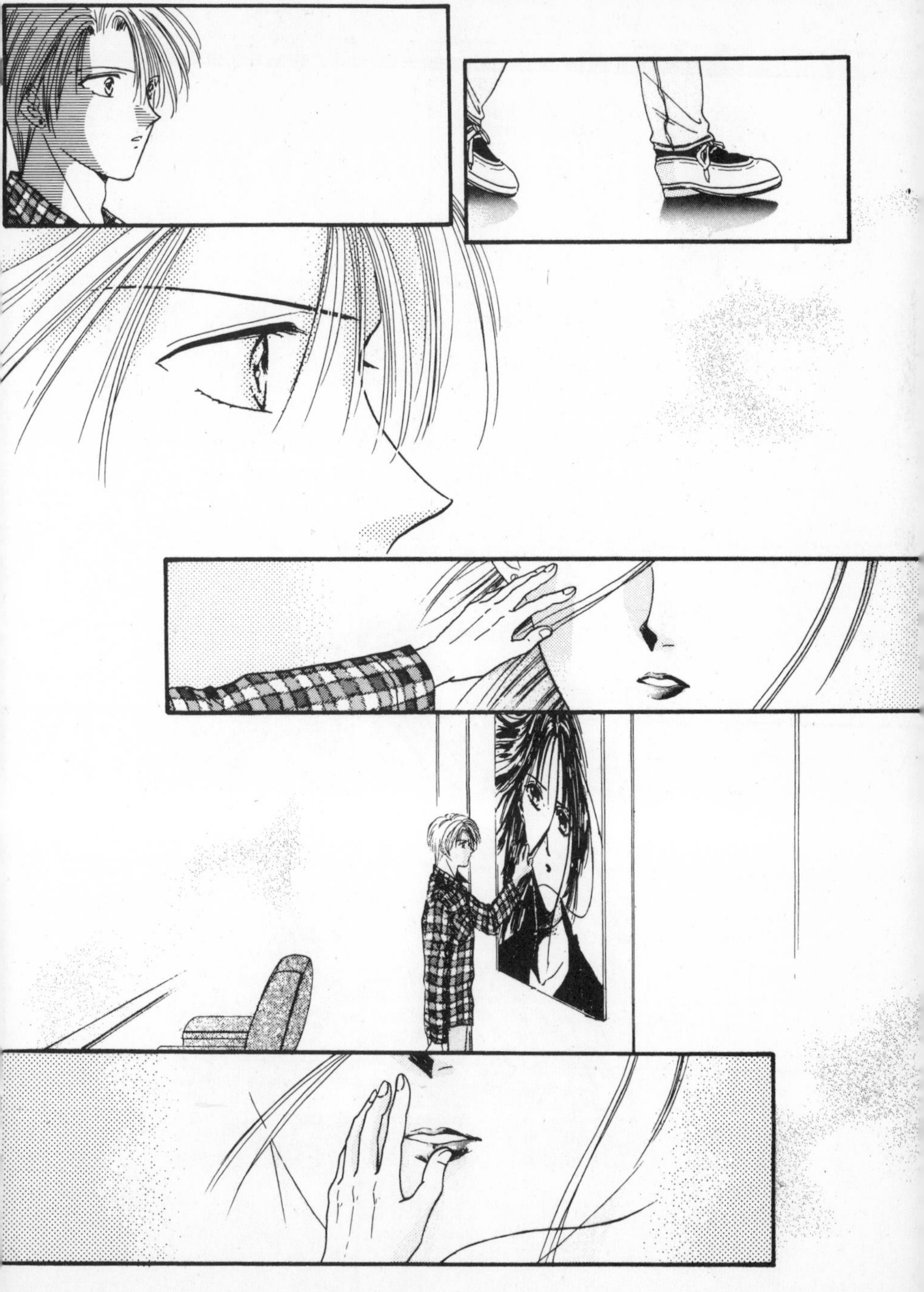

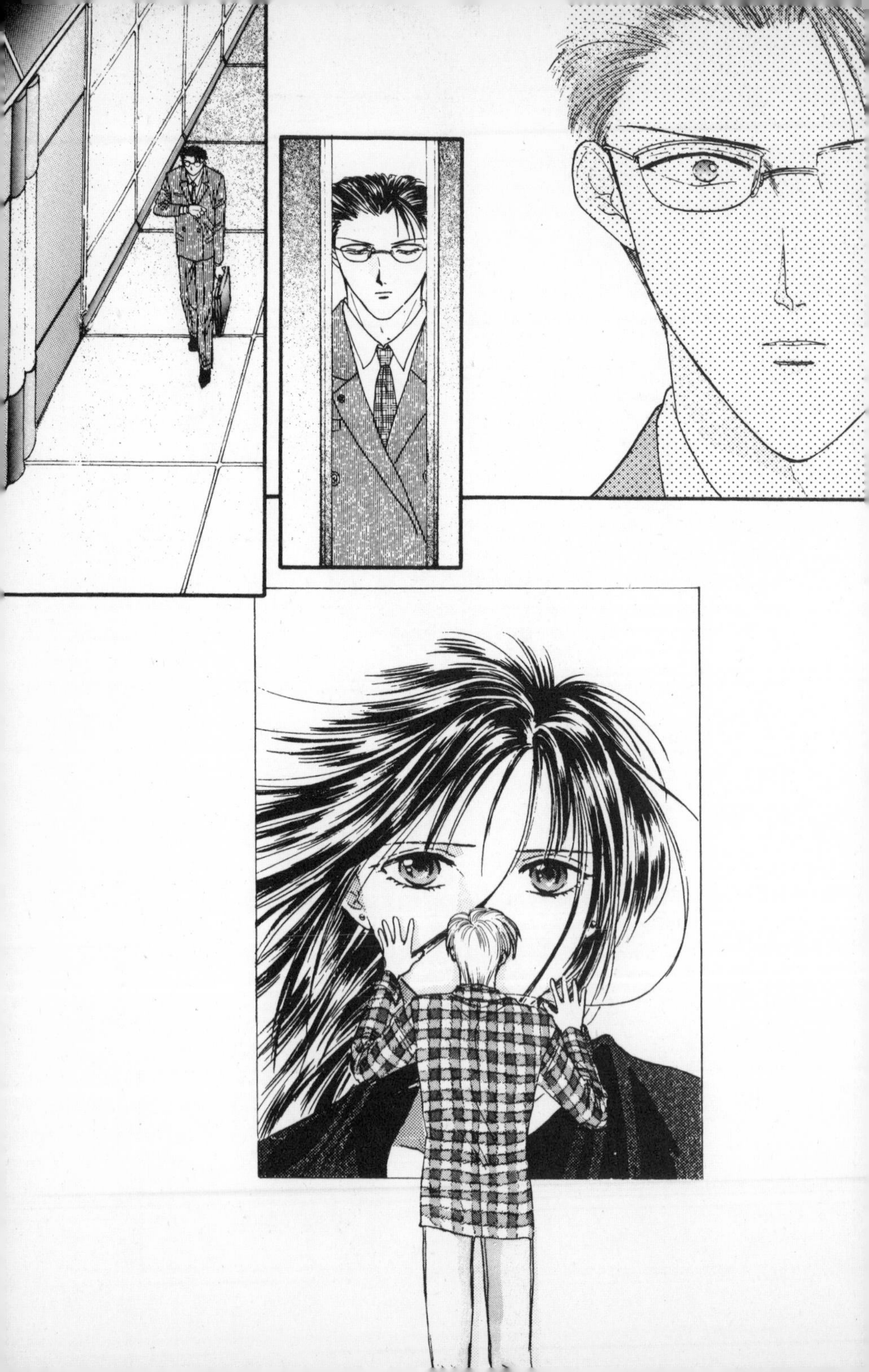

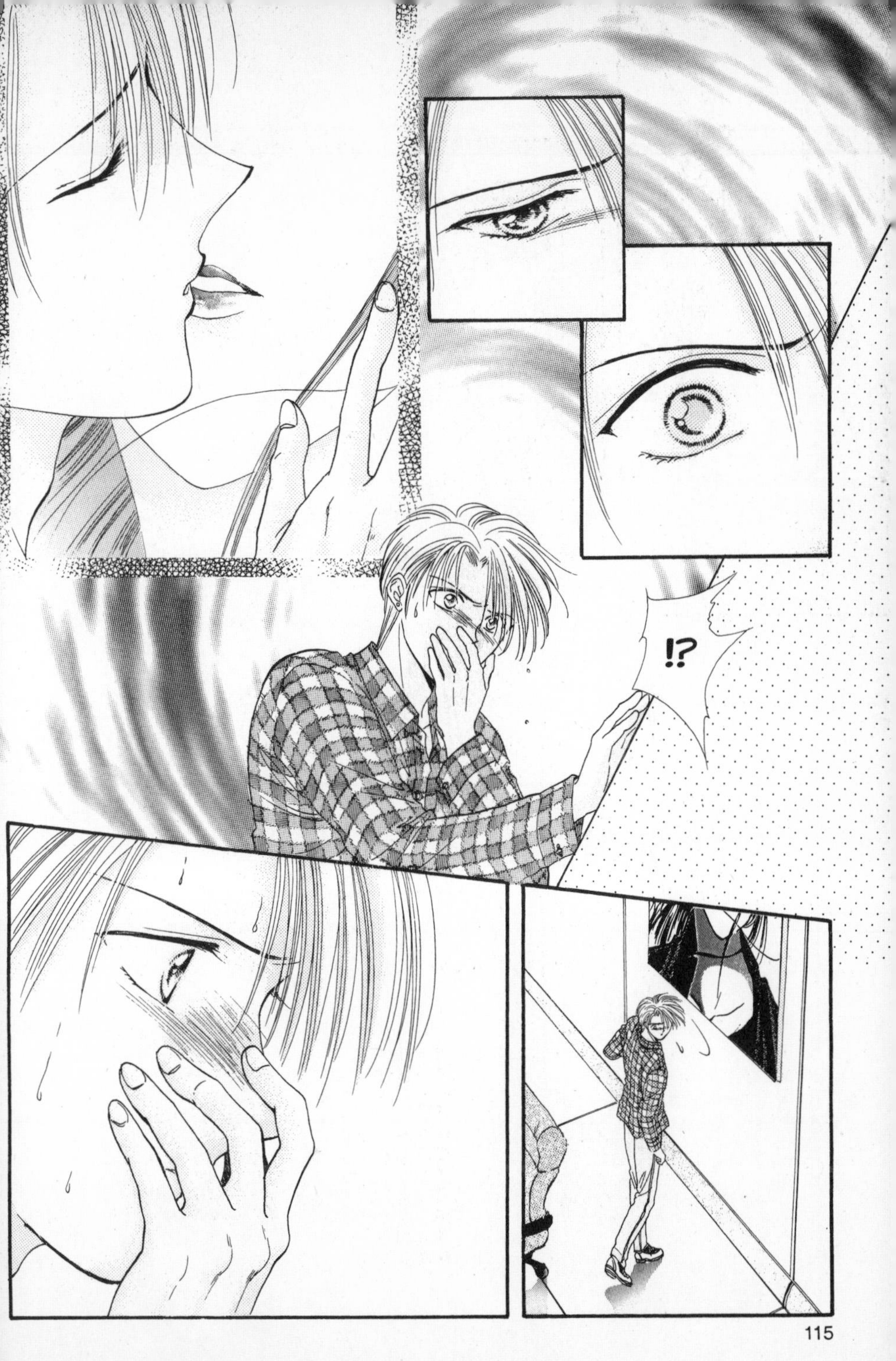
!?

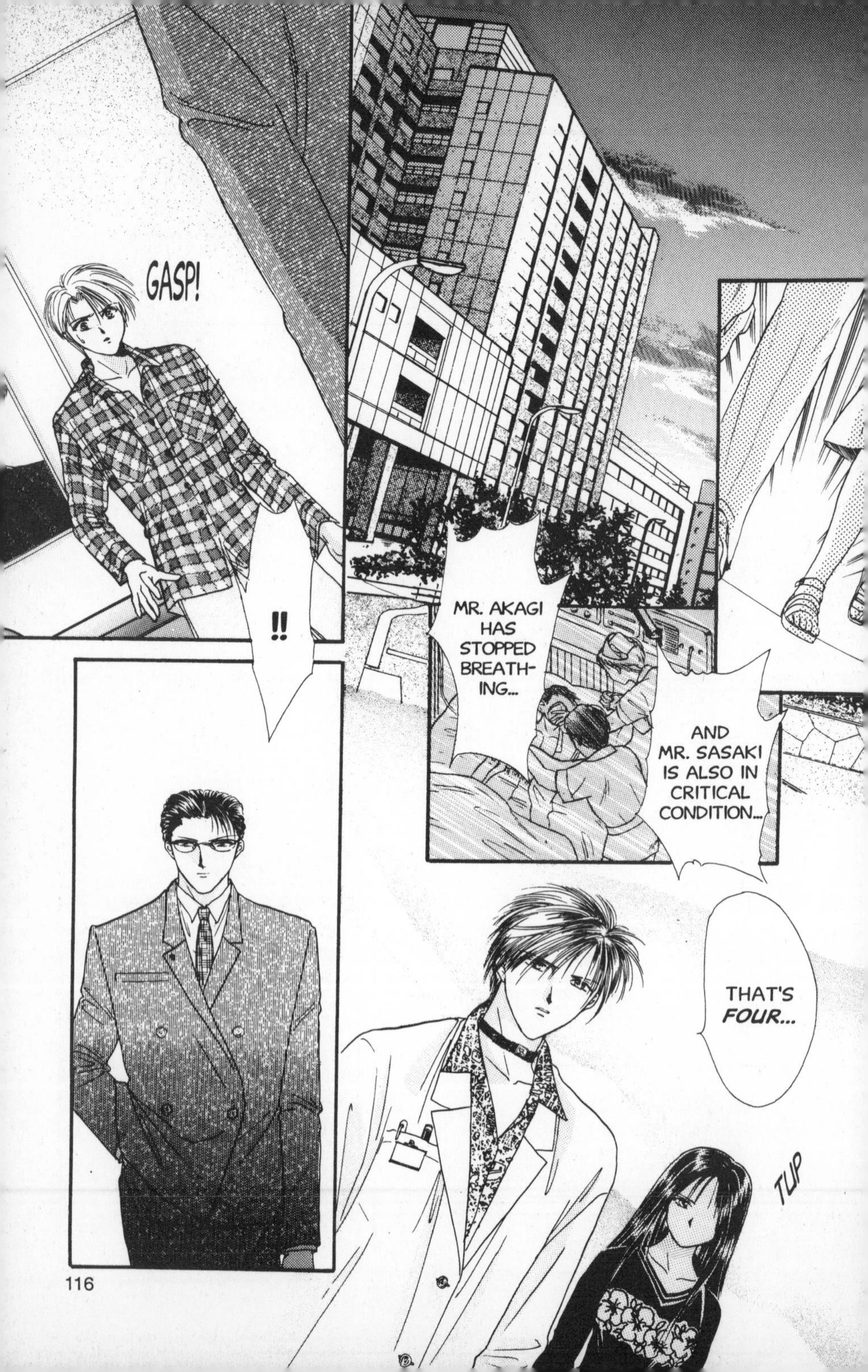
MR. AKAGI HAS STOPPED BREATH-ING...
AND MR. SASAKI IS ALSO IN CRITICAL CONDITION...
GASP!
!!
THAT'S *FOUR*...
TUP

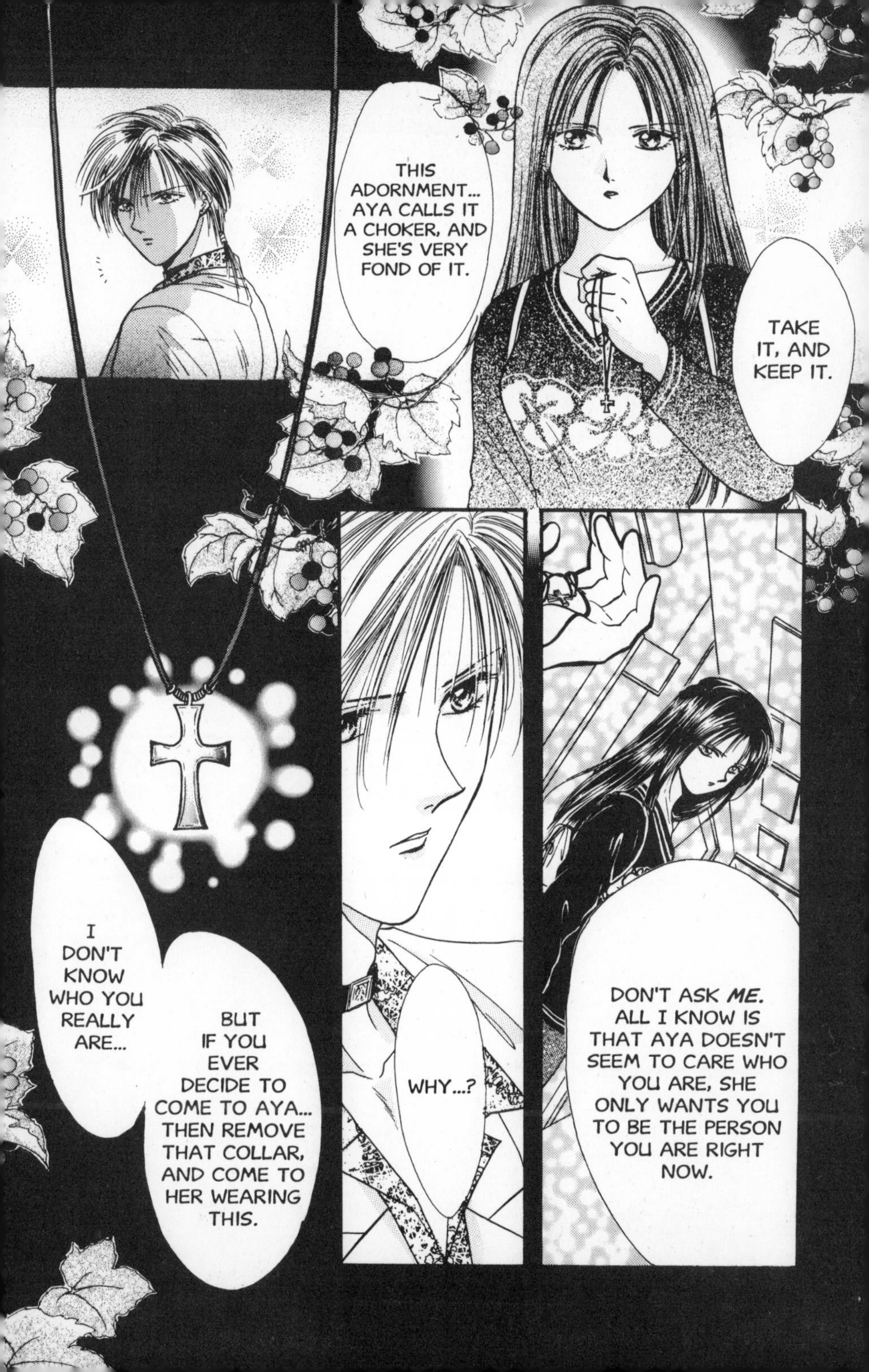
THIS ADORNMENT... AYA CALLS IT A CHOKER, AND SHE'S VERY FOND OF IT.
TAKE IT, AND KEEP IT.
I DON'T KNOW WHO YOU REALLY ARE...
BUT IF YOU EVER DECIDE TO COME TO AYA... THEN REMOVE THAT COLLAR, AND COME TO HER WEARING THIS.
WHY...?
DON'T ASK *ME.* ALL I KNOW IS THAT AYA DOESN'T SEEM TO CARE WHO YOU ARE, SHE ONLY WANTS YOU TO BE THE PERSON YOU ARE RIGHT NOW.

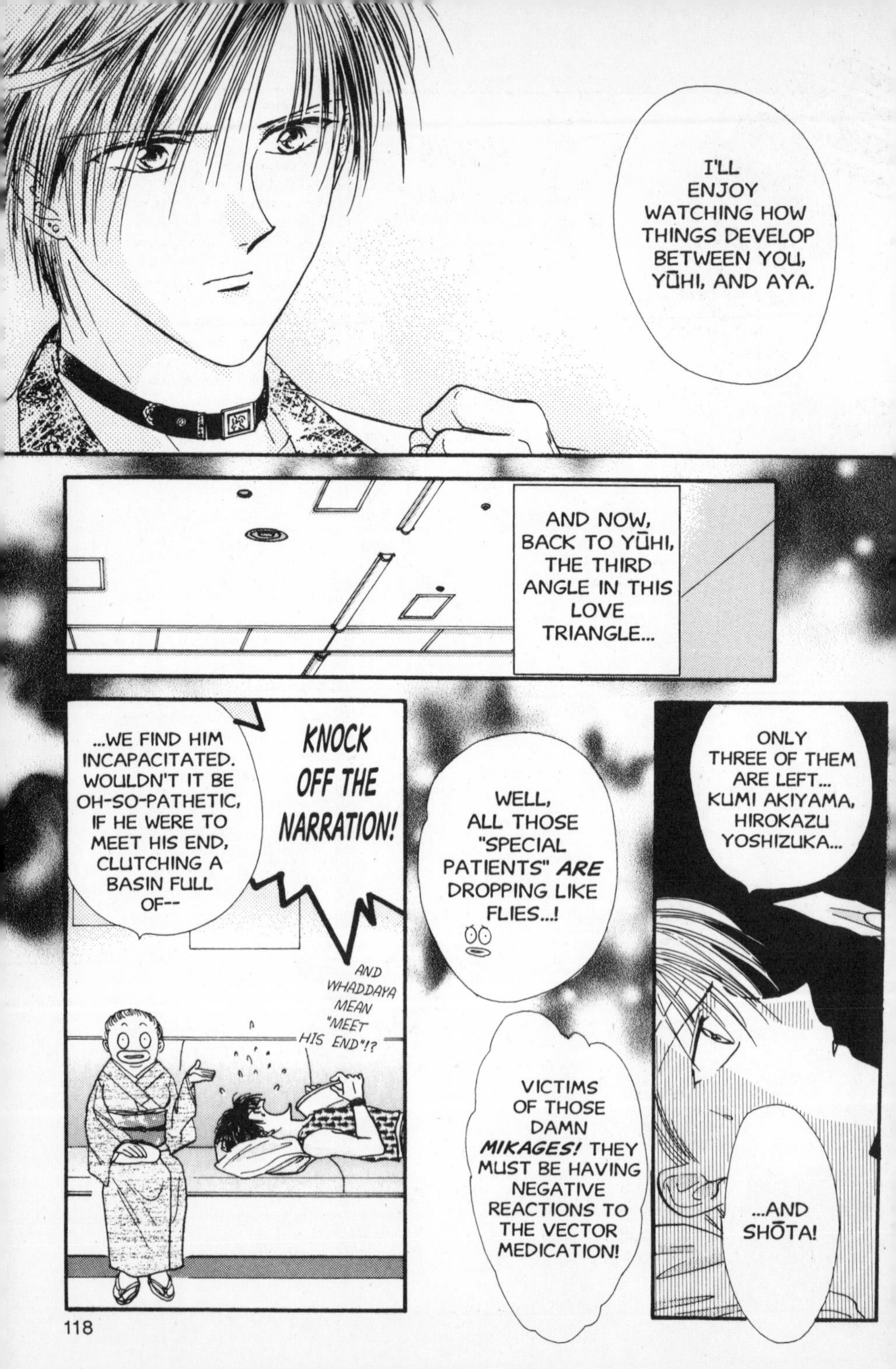

I'LL ENJOY WATCHING HOW THINGS DEVELOP BETWEEN YOU, YŪHI, AND AYA.
AND NOW, BACK TO YŪHI, THE THIRD ANGLE IN THIS LOVE TRIANGLE...
ONLY THREE OF THEM ARE LEFT... KUMI AKIYAMA, HIROKAZU YOSHIZUKA...
...AND SHŌTA!
WELL, ALL THOSE "SPECIAL PATIENTS" ARE DROPPING LIKE FLIES...!
VICTIMS OF THOSE DAMN MIKAGES! THEY MUST BE HAVING NEGATIVE REACTIONS TO THE VECTOR MEDICATION!
...WE FIND HIM INCAPACITATED. WOULDN'T IT BE OH-SO-PATHETIC, IF HE WERE TO MEET HIS END, CLUTCHING A BASIN FULL OF--
KNOCK OFF THE NARRATION!
AND WHADDAYA MEAN "MEET HIS END"!?

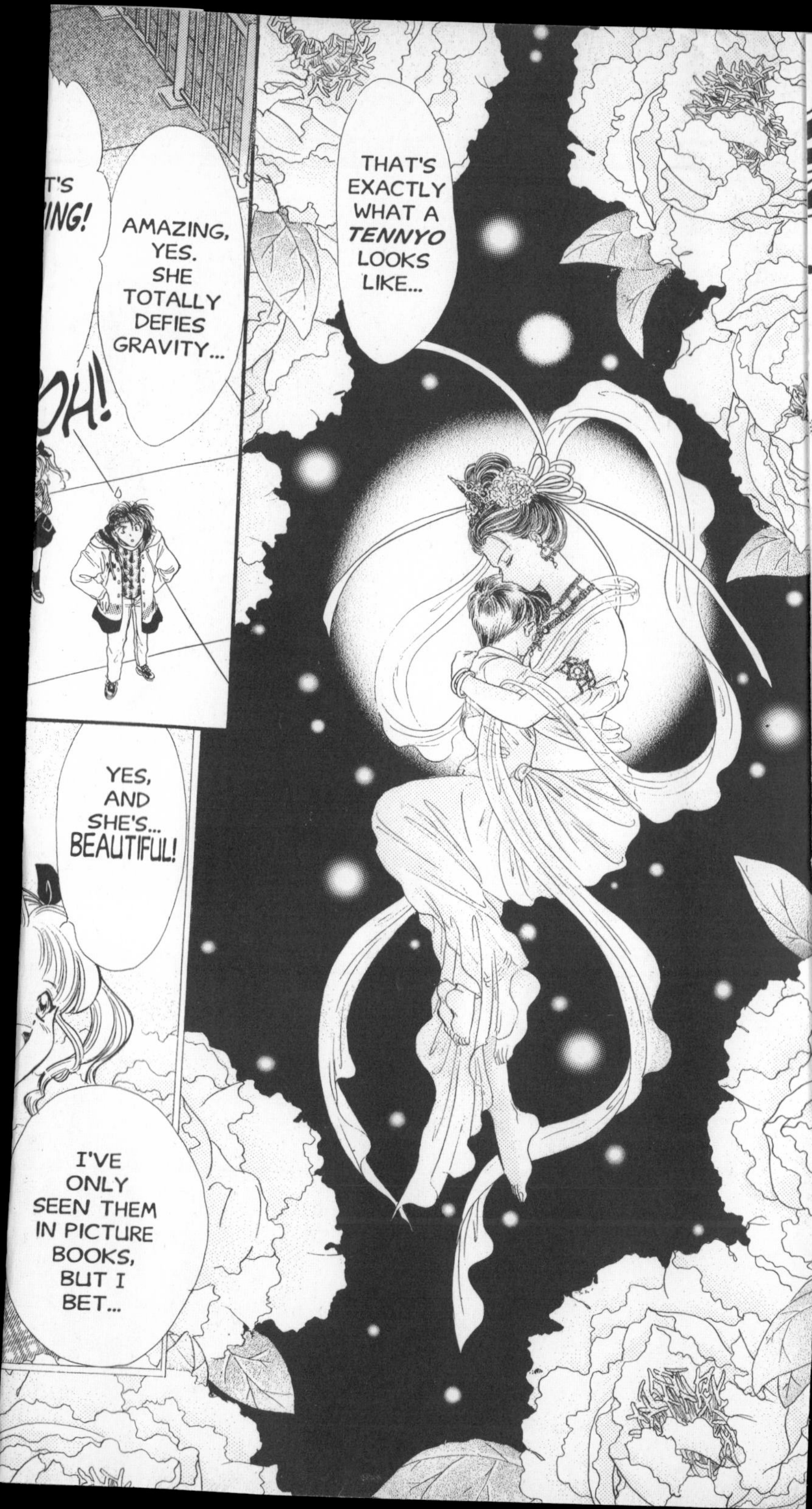
AMAZING, YES. SHE TOTALLY DEFIES GRAVITY...
YES, AND SHE'S... BEAUTIFUL!
I'VE ONLY SEEN THEM IN PICTURE BOOKS, BUT I BET...
THAT'S EXACTLY WHAT A *TENNYO* LOOKS LIKE...

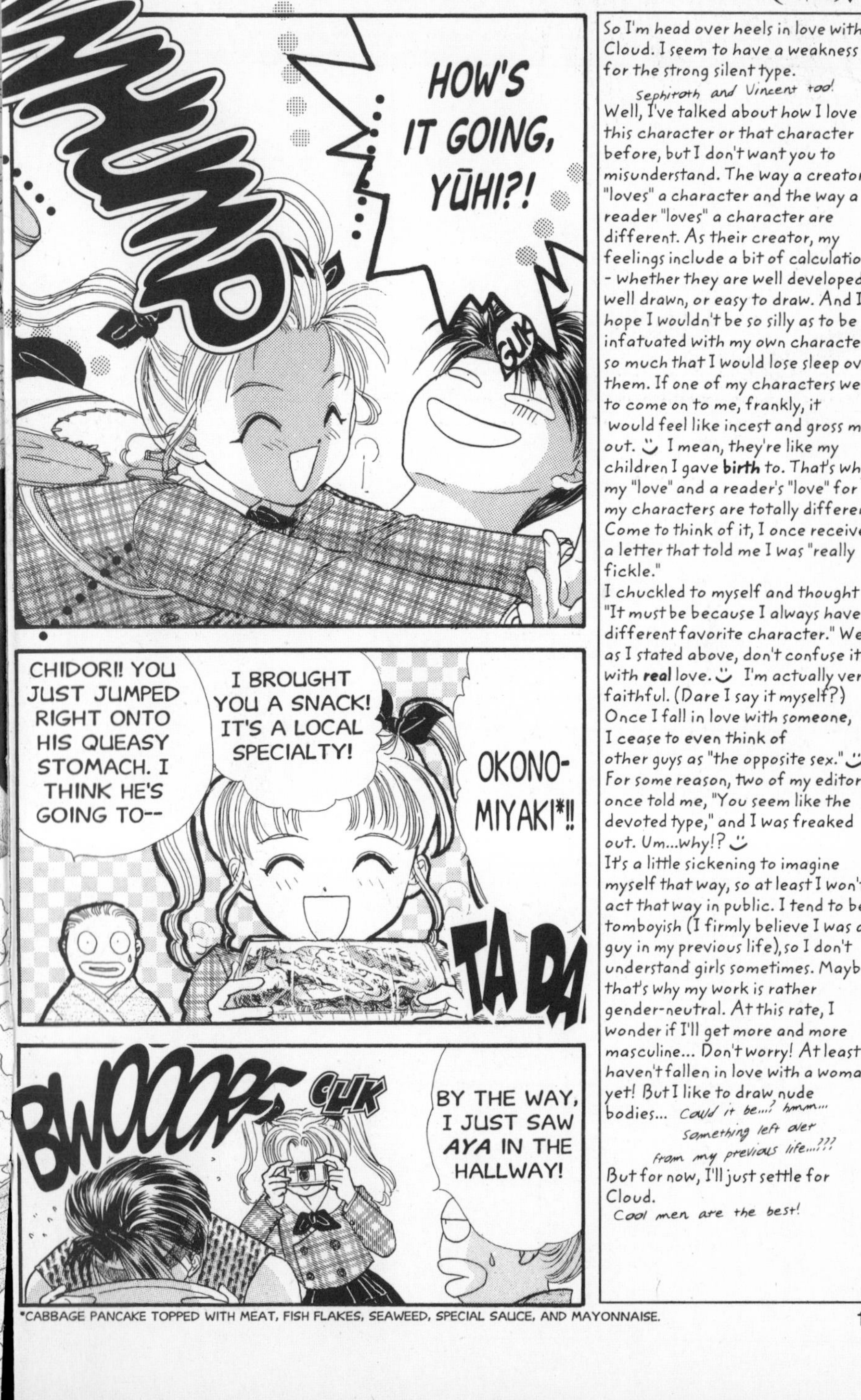
WHUMP
HOW'S IT GOING, YŪHI?!
GUK
I BROUGHT YOU A SNACK! IT'S A LOCAL SPECIALTY!
OKONO-MIYAKI*!!
TA DA
CHIDORI!! YOU JUST JUMPED RIGHT ONTO HIS QUEASY STOMACH. I THINK HE'S GOING TO--
BWOOORP
CLIK
BY THE WAY, I JUST SAW *AYA* IN THE HALLWAY!

So I'm head over heels in love with Cloud. I seem to have a weakness for the strong silent type.
Sephiroth and Vincent too!
Well, I've talked about how I love this character or that character before, but I don't want you to misunderstand. The way a creator "loves" a character and the way a reader "loves" a character are different. As their creator, my feelings include a bit of calculation - whether they are well developed, well drawn, or easy to draw. And I hope I wouldn't be so silly as to be infatuated with my own characters so much that I would lose sleep over them. If one of my characters were to come on to me, frankly, it would feel like incest and gross me out. ☺ I mean, they're like my children I gave **birth** to. That's why my "love" and a reader's "love" for my characters are totally different. Come to think of it, I once received a letter that told me I was "really fickle."
I chuckled to myself and thought "It must be because I always have a different favorite character." Well, as I stated above, don't confuse it with **real** love. ☺ I'm actually very faithful. (Dare I say it myself?) Once I fall in love with someone, I cease to even think of other guys as "the opposite sex." ☺ For some reason, two of my editors once told me, "You seem like the devoted type," and I was freaked out. Um...why!? ☺
It's a little sickening to imagine myself that way, so at least I won't act that way in public. I tend to be tomboyish (I firmly believe I was a guy in my previous life), so I don't understand girls sometimes. Maybe that's why my work is rather gender-neutral. At this rate, I wonder if I'll get more and more masculine... Don't worry! At least I haven't fallen in love with a woman yet! But I like to draw nude bodies... *Could it be...? hmm... Something left over from my previous life...???*
But for now, I'll just settle for Cloud.
Cool men are the best!

*CABBAGE PANCAKE TOPPED WITH MEAT, FISH FLAKES, SEAWEED, SPECIAL SAUCE, AND MAYONNAISE.

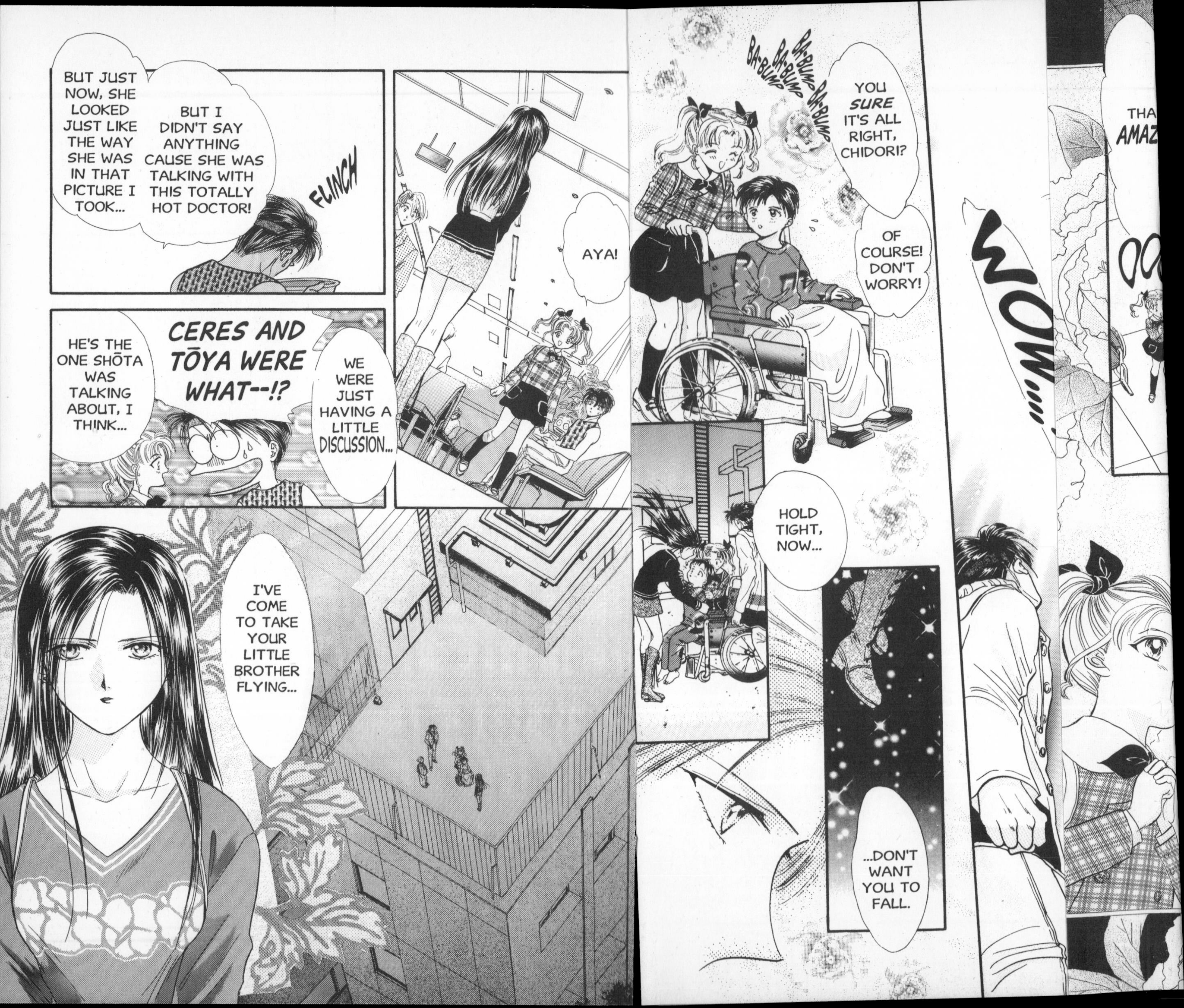
WOW...!
BA-BUMP BA-BUMP BA-BUMP BA-BUMP
YOU SURE IT'S ALL RIGHT, CHIDORI?
OF COURSE! DON'T WORRY!
HOLD TIGHT, NOW...
...DON'T WANT YOU TO FALL.
AYA!
BUT I DIDN'T SAY ANYTHING CAUSE SHE WAS TALKING WITH THIS TOTALLY HOT DOCTOR!
BUT JUST NOW, SHE LOOKED JUST LIKE THE WAY SHE WAS IN THAT PICTURE I TOOK...
FLINCH
WE WERE JUST HAVING A LITTLE DISCUSSION...
CERES AND TŌYA WERE WHAT--!?
HE'S THE ONE SHŌTA WAS TALKING ABOUT, I THINK...
I'VE COME TO TAKE YOUR LITTLE BROTHER FLYING...

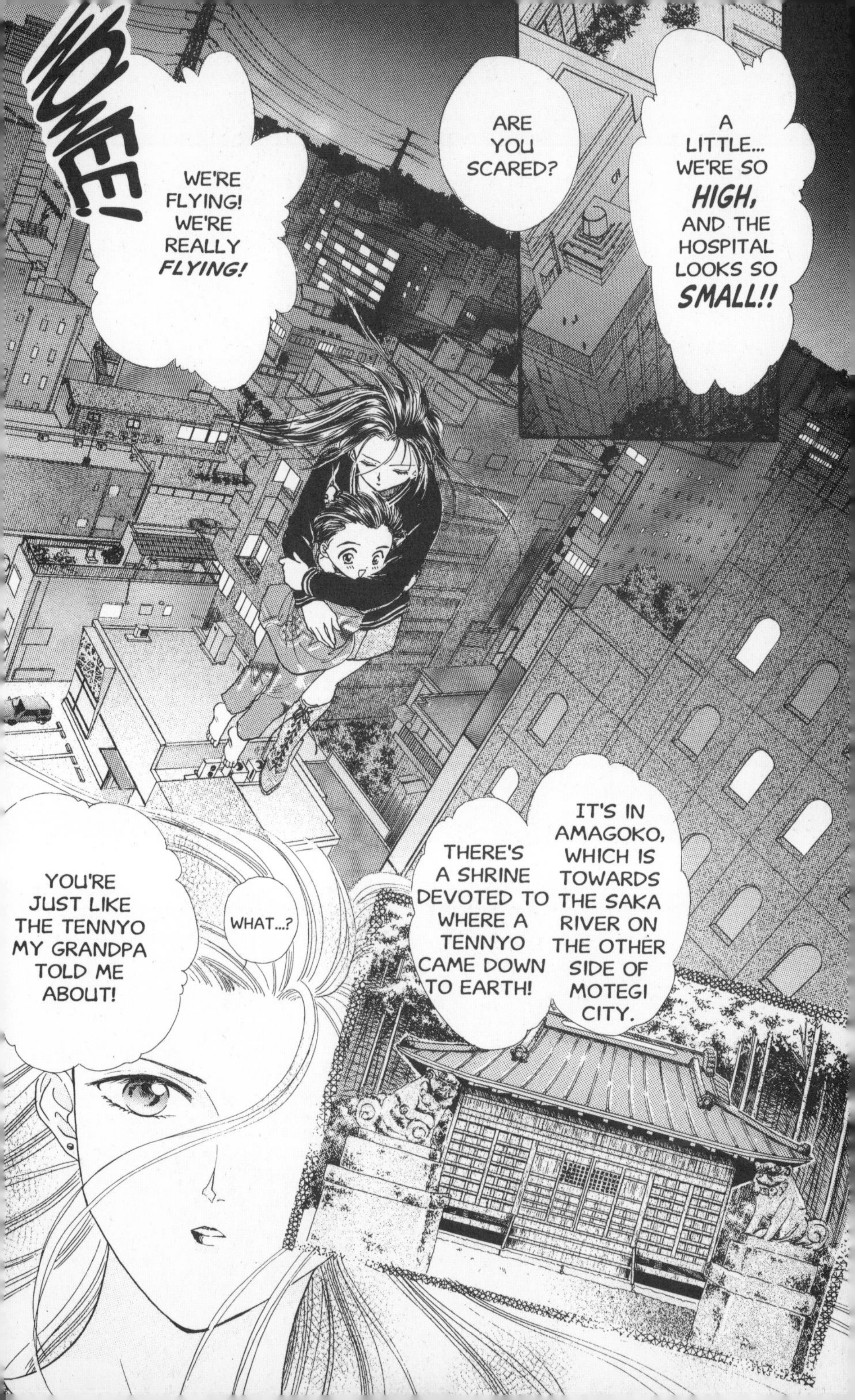
WOWEE!
WE'RE FLYING! WE'RE REALLY *FLYING!*
ARE YOU SCARED?
A LITTLE... WE'RE SO **HIGH,** AND THE HOSPITAL LOOKS SO **SMALL!!**
YOU'RE JUST LIKE THE TENNYO MY GRANDPA TOLD ME ABOUT!
WHAT...?
THERE'S A SHRINE DEVOTED TO WHERE A TENNYO CAME DOWN TO EARTH!
IT'S IN AMAGOKO, WHICH IS TOWARDS THE SAKA RIVER ON THE OTHER SIDE OF MOTEGI CITY.

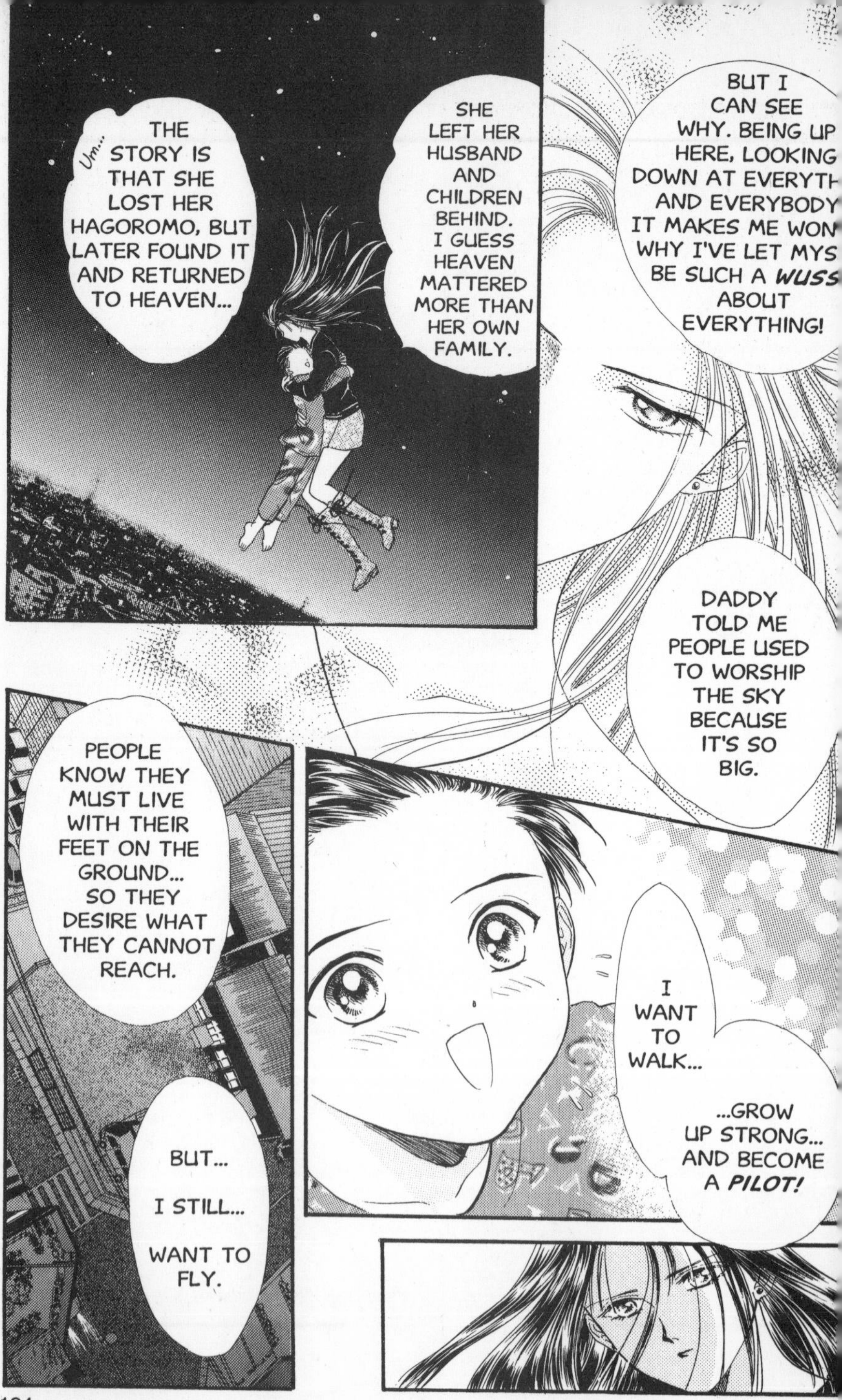
Um...
THE STORY IS THAT SHE LOST HER HAGOROMO, BUT LATER FOUND IT AND RETURNED TO HEAVEN...
SHE LEFT HER HUSBAND AND CHILDREN BEHIND. I GUESS HEAVEN MATTERED MORE THAN HER OWN FAMILY.
BUT I CAN SEE WHY. BEING UP HERE, LOOKING DOWN AT EVERYTH AND EVERYBODY IT MAKES ME WON WHY I'VE LET MYS BE SUCH A *WUSS* ABOUT EVERYTHING!
DADDY TOLD ME PEOPLE USED TO WORSHIP THE SKY BECAUSE IT'S SO BIG.
PEOPLE KNOW THEY MUST LIVE WITH THEIR FEET ON THE GROUND... SO THEY DESIRE WHAT THEY CANNOT REACH.
BUT... I STILL... WANT TO FLY.
I WANT TO WALK...
...GROW UP STRONG... AND BECOME A *PILOT!*

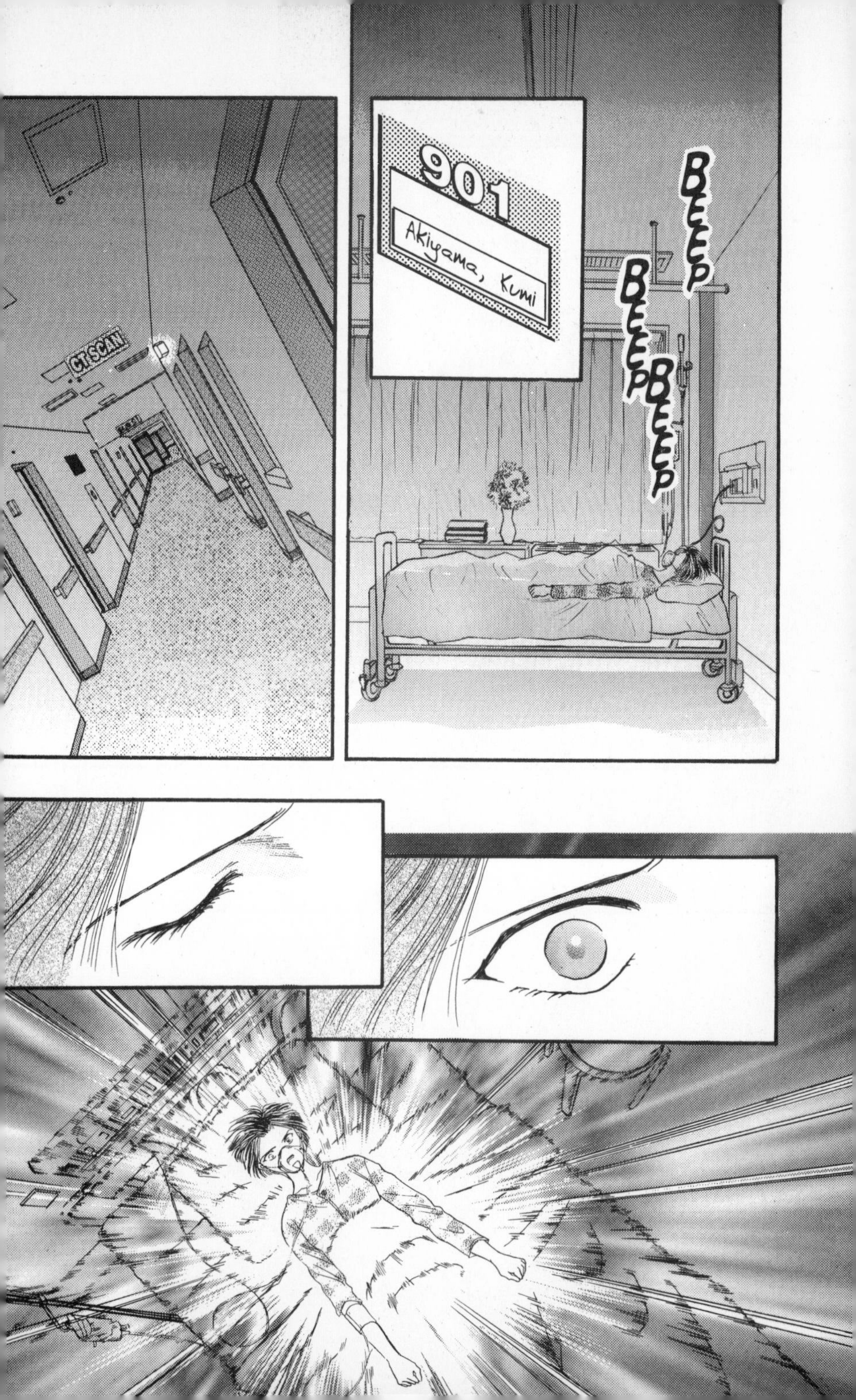
901
Akiyama, Kumi
BEEP
BEEP
BEEP
CT SCAN

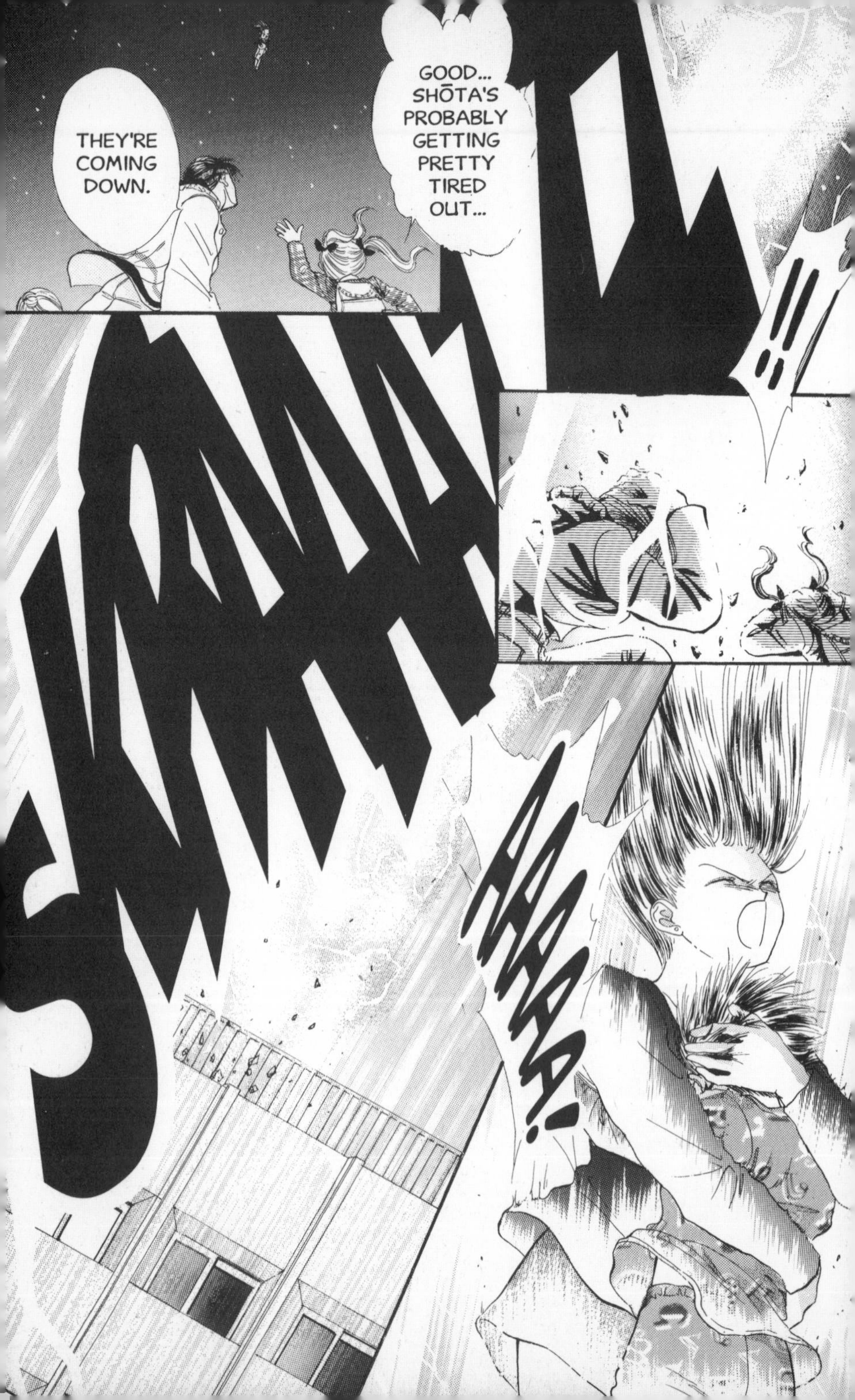
THEY'RE COMING DOWN.
GOOD... SHŌTA'S PROBABLY GETTING PRETTY TIRED OUT...

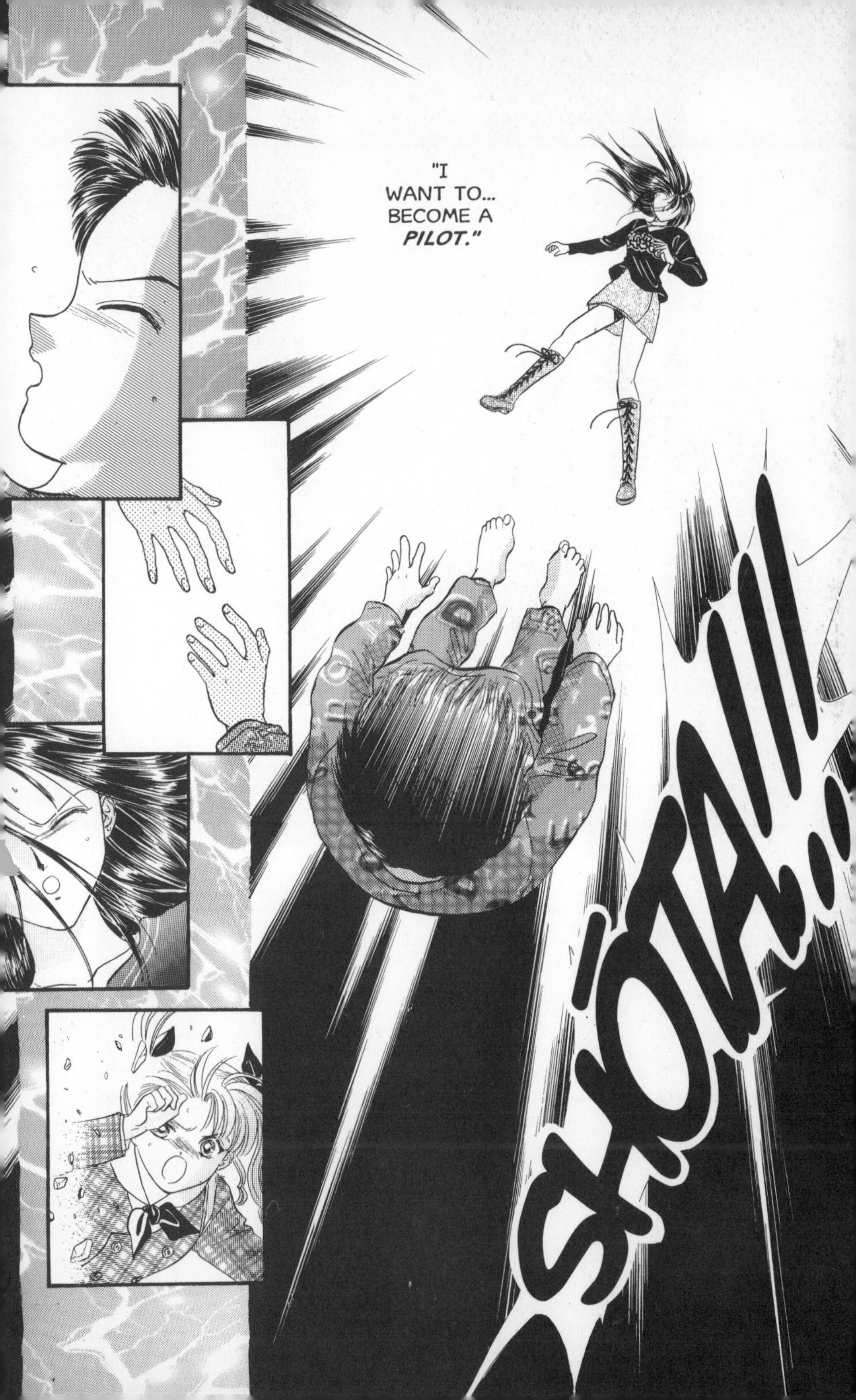
"I WANT TO... BECOME A *PILOT.*"
SHOTA!!...

BIRTHDAY: September 5 (Virgo) Currently 25 years old

BLOOD TYPE: O

HEIGHT: 5'4" BUST: 34" WAIST: 24" HIPS: 34"

HOBBIES: Shopping, swimming

TALENT: Japanese traditional dance

SUZUMI AOGIRI

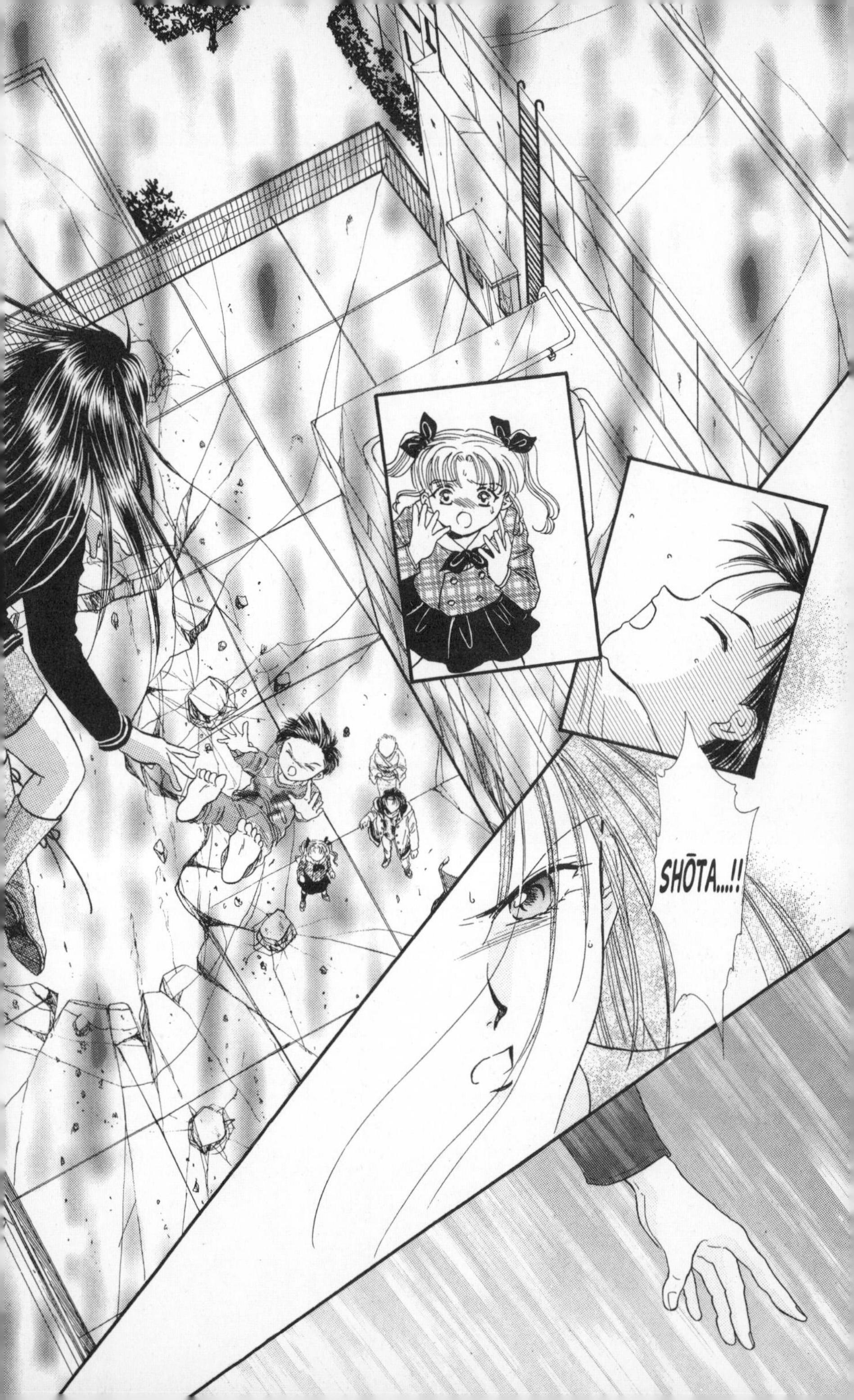
SHŌTA...!!

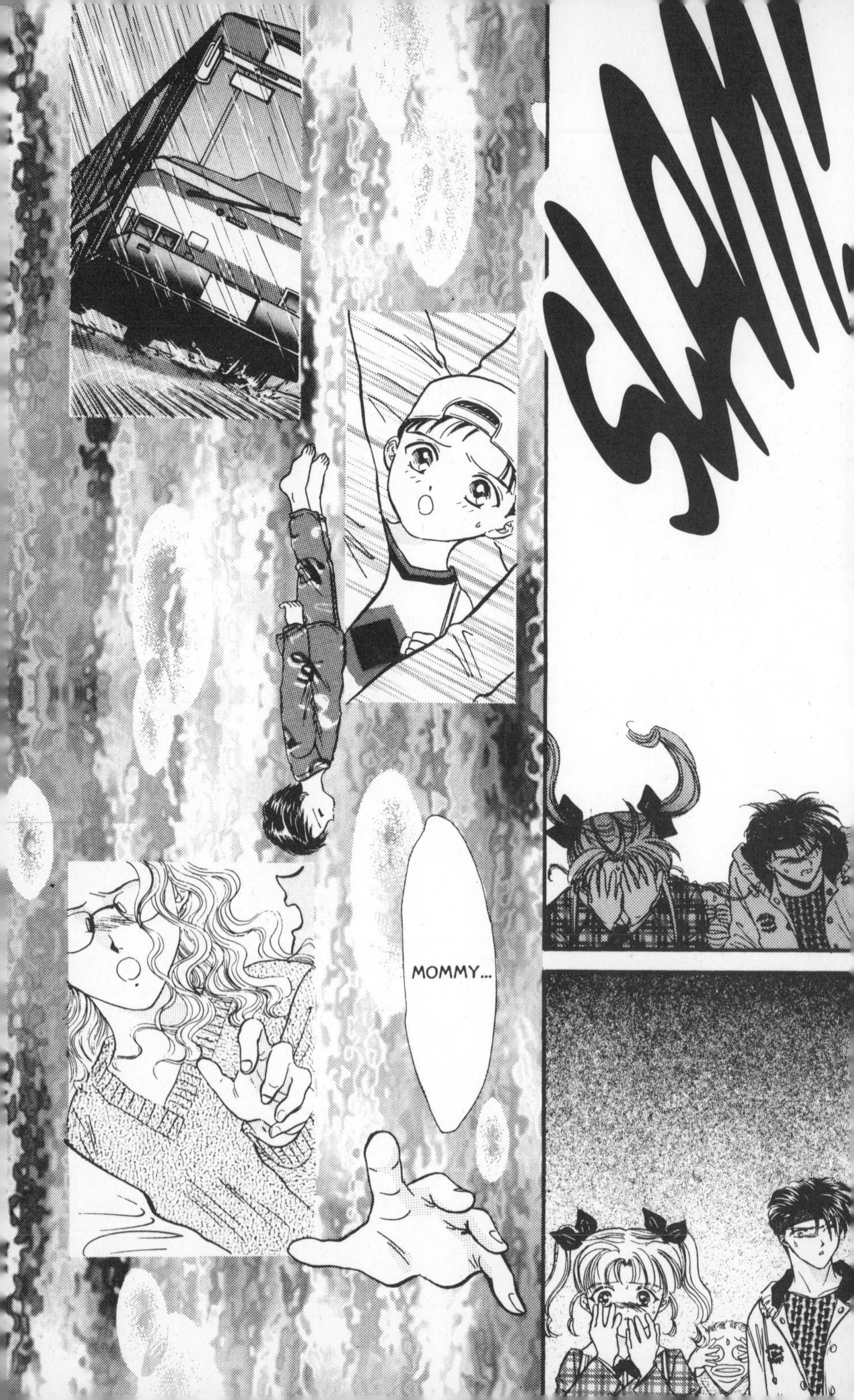
MOMMY...
SLAM!

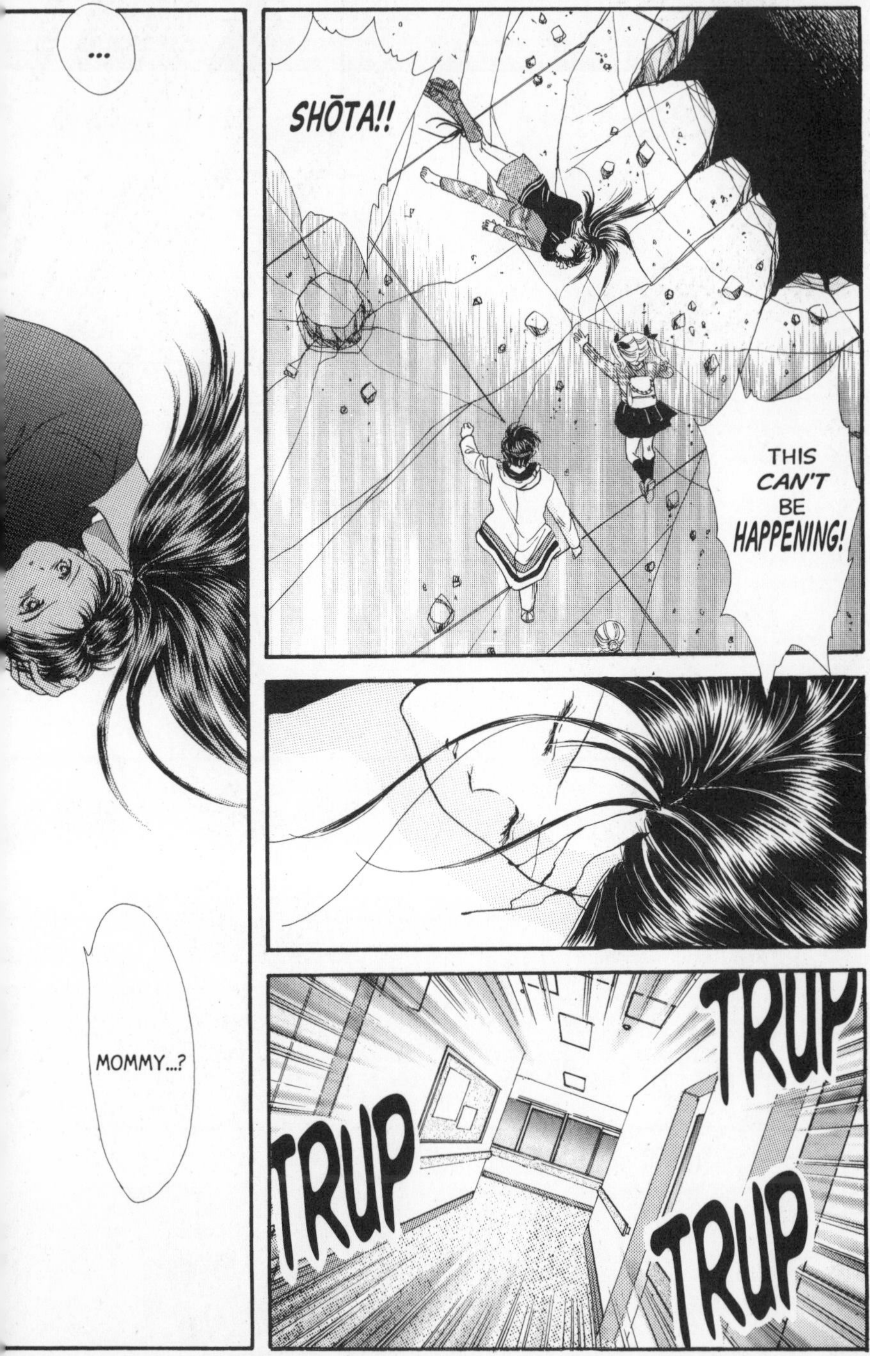
SHŌTA!!
THIS CAN'T BE HAPPENING!
TRUP
TRUP
TRUP
...
MOMMY...?

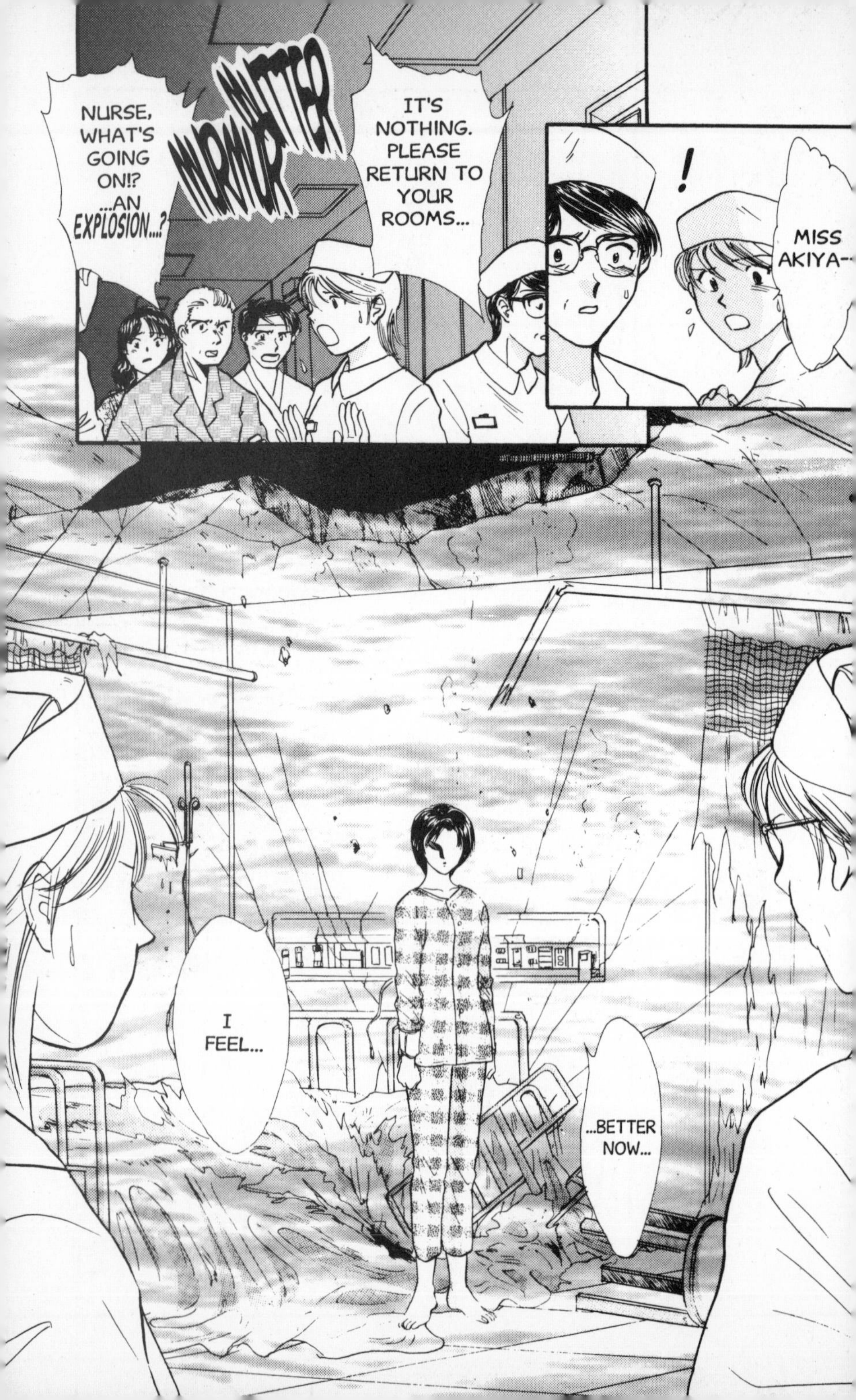
NURSE, WHAT'S GOING ON!? ...AN EXPLOSION...?
MURMUR CHATTER
IT'S NOTHING. PLEASE RETURN TO YOUR ROOMS...
!
MISS AKIYA--
I FEEL...
...BETTER NOW...

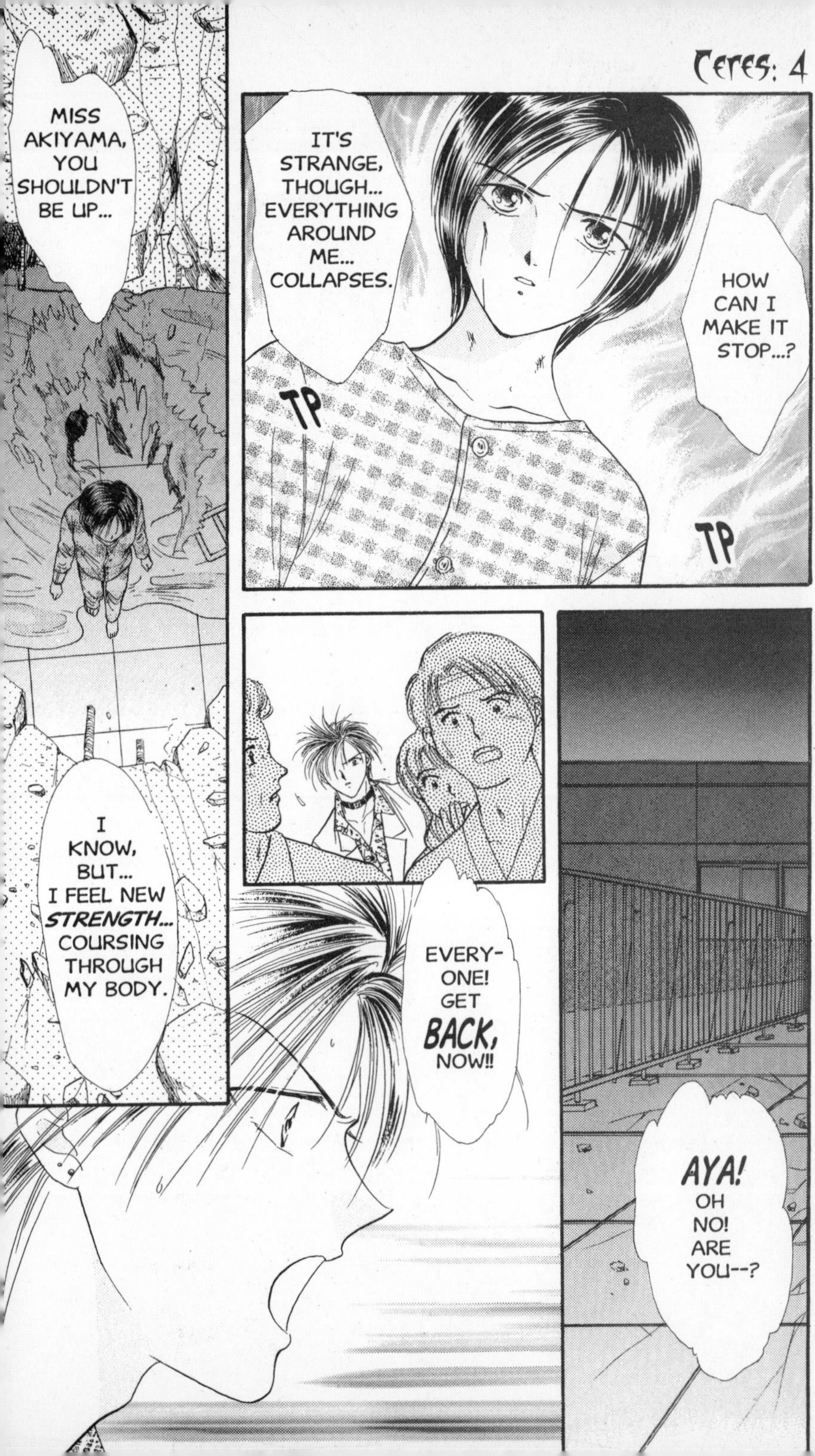
IT'S STRANGE, THOUGH... EVERYTHING AROUND ME... COLLAPSES.
TP
HOW CAN I MAKE IT STOP...?
TP
MISS AKIYAMA, YOU SHOULDN'T BE UP...
I KNOW, BUT... I FEEL NEW *STRENGTH...* COURSING THROUGH MY BODY.
AYA! OH NO! ARE YOU--?
EVERY-ONE! GET **BACK,** NOW!!

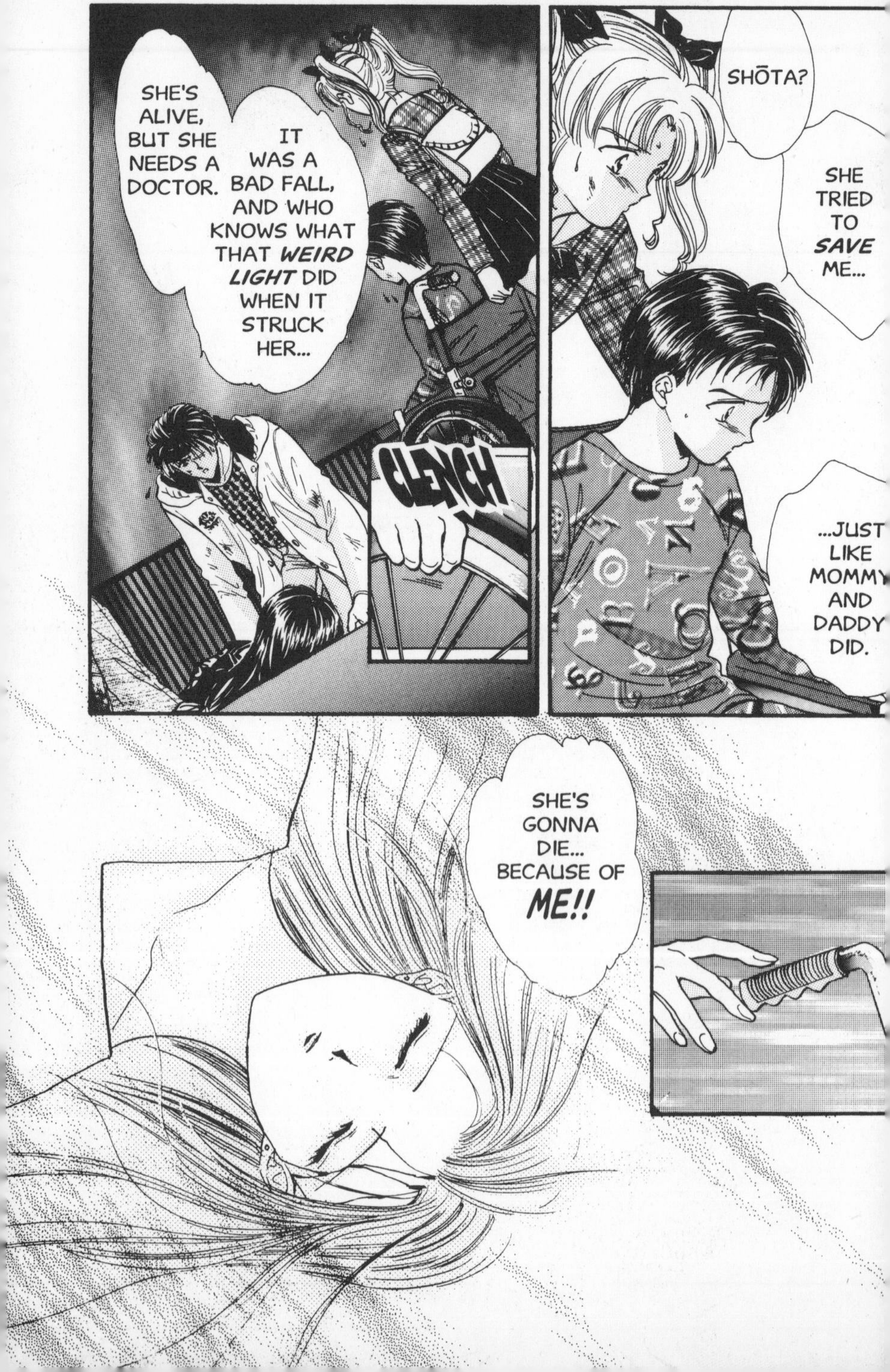
SHŌTA?
SHE TRIED TO *SAVE* ME...
...JUST LIKE MOMMY AND DADDY DID.
SHE'S ALIVE, BUT SHE NEEDS A DOCTOR.
IT WAS A BAD FALL, AND WHO KNOWS WHAT THAT *WEIRD LIGHT* DID WHEN IT STRUCK HER...
CLENCH
SHE'S GONNA DIE... BECAUSE OF *ME!!*

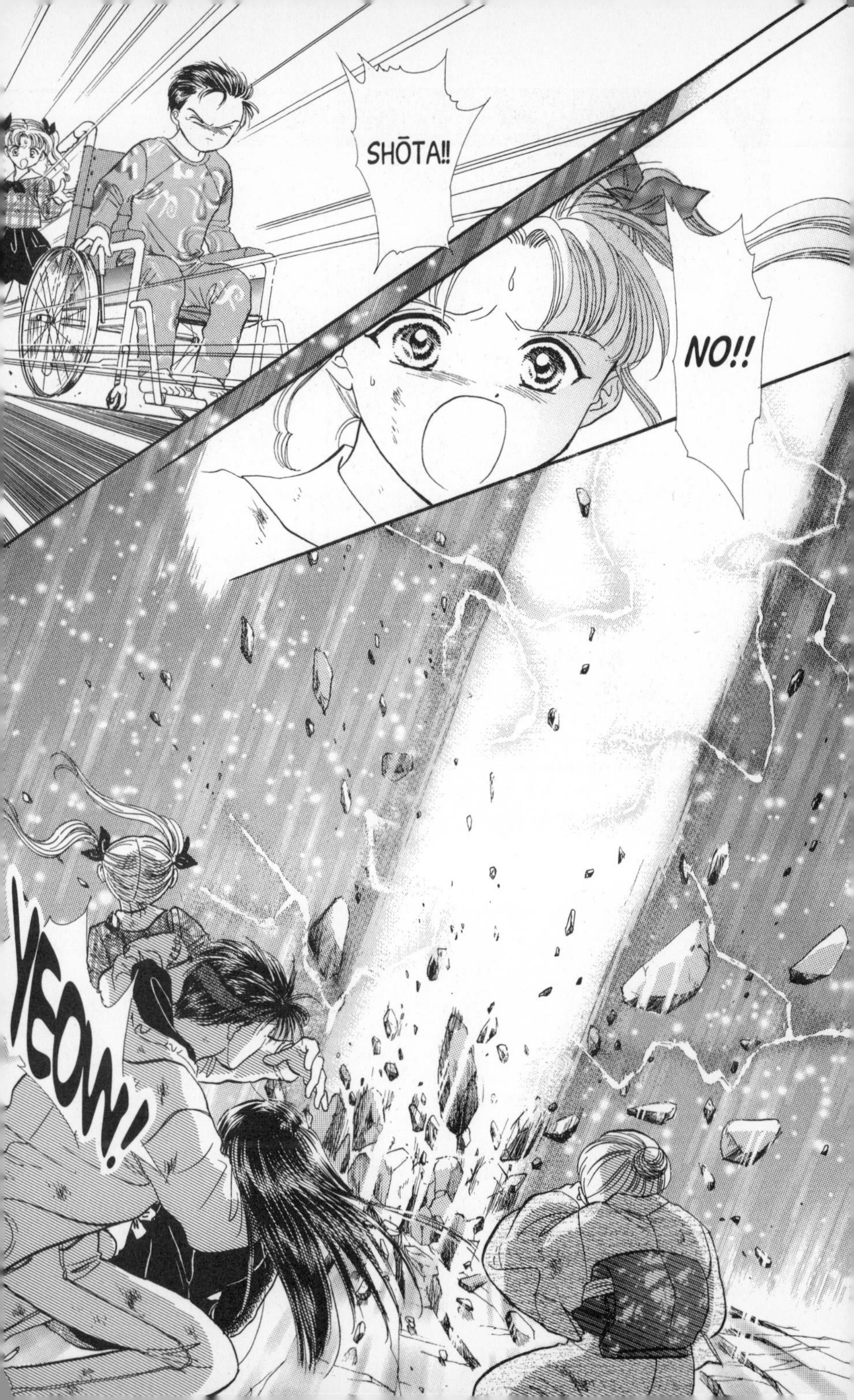
SHŌTA!!
NO!!
YEOW!!

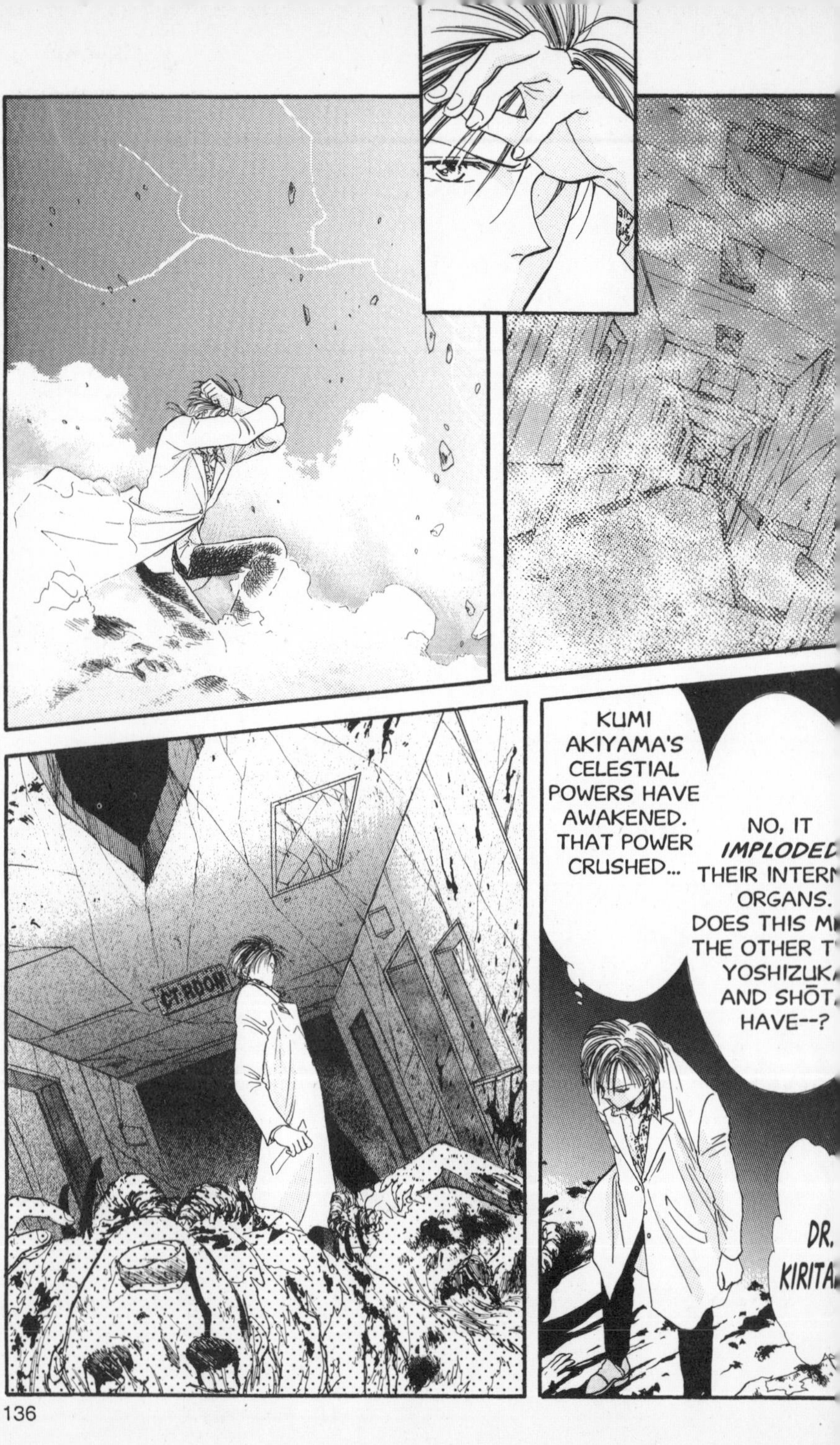
NO, IT *IMPLODED* THEIR INTERN ORGANS. DOES THIS M THE OTHER T YOSHIZUKA AND SHŌT HAVE--?
KUMI AKIYAMA'S CELESTIAL POWERS HAVE AWAKENED. THAT POWER CRUSHED...
DR. KIRITA
CT. ROOM

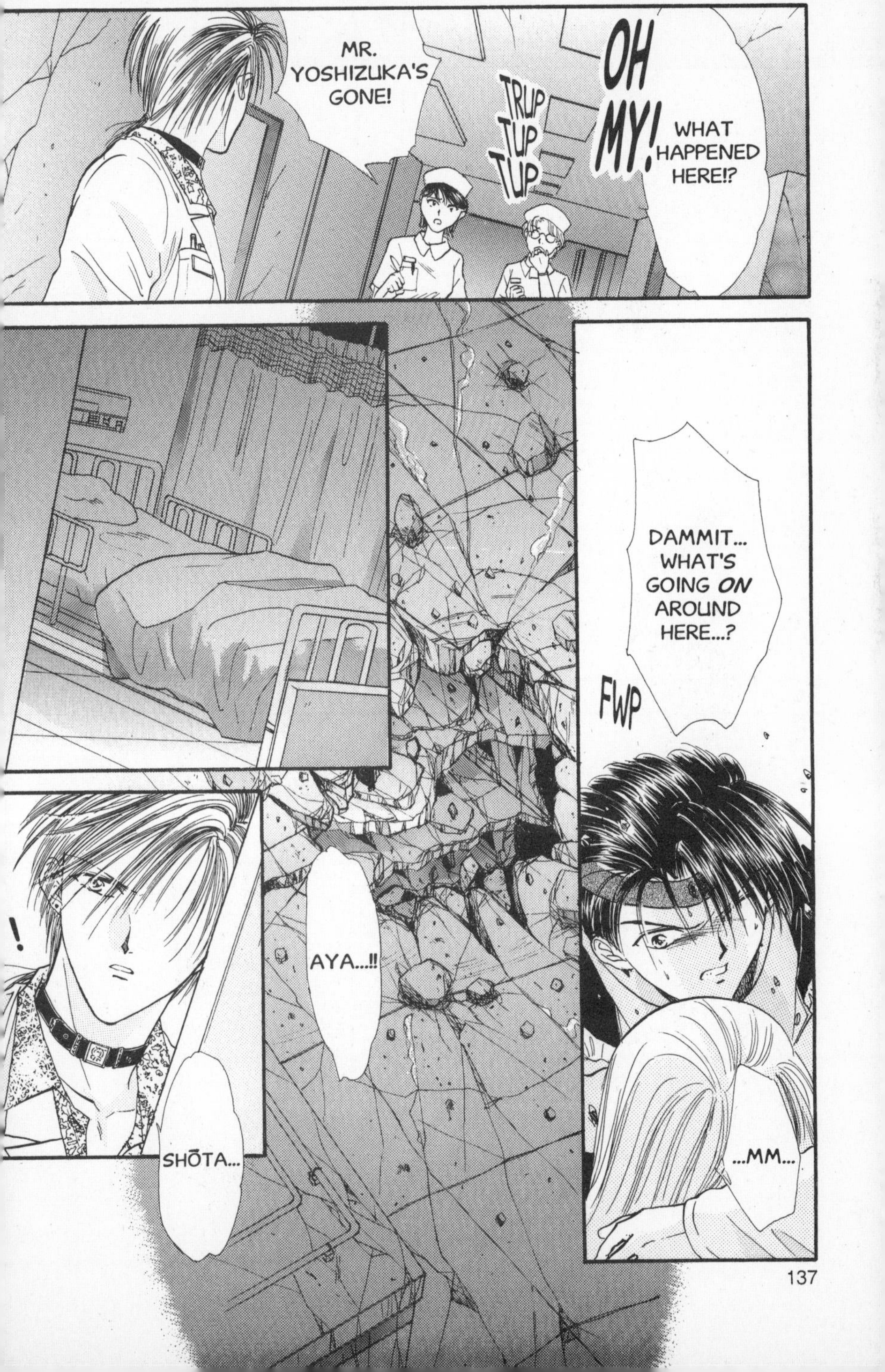
OH MY!
WHAT HAPPENED HERE!?
TRUP TUP TUP
MR. YOSHIZUKA'S GONE!
DAMMIT... WHAT'S GOING *ON* AROUND HERE...?
FWP
...MM...
AYA...!!
!
SHŌTA...

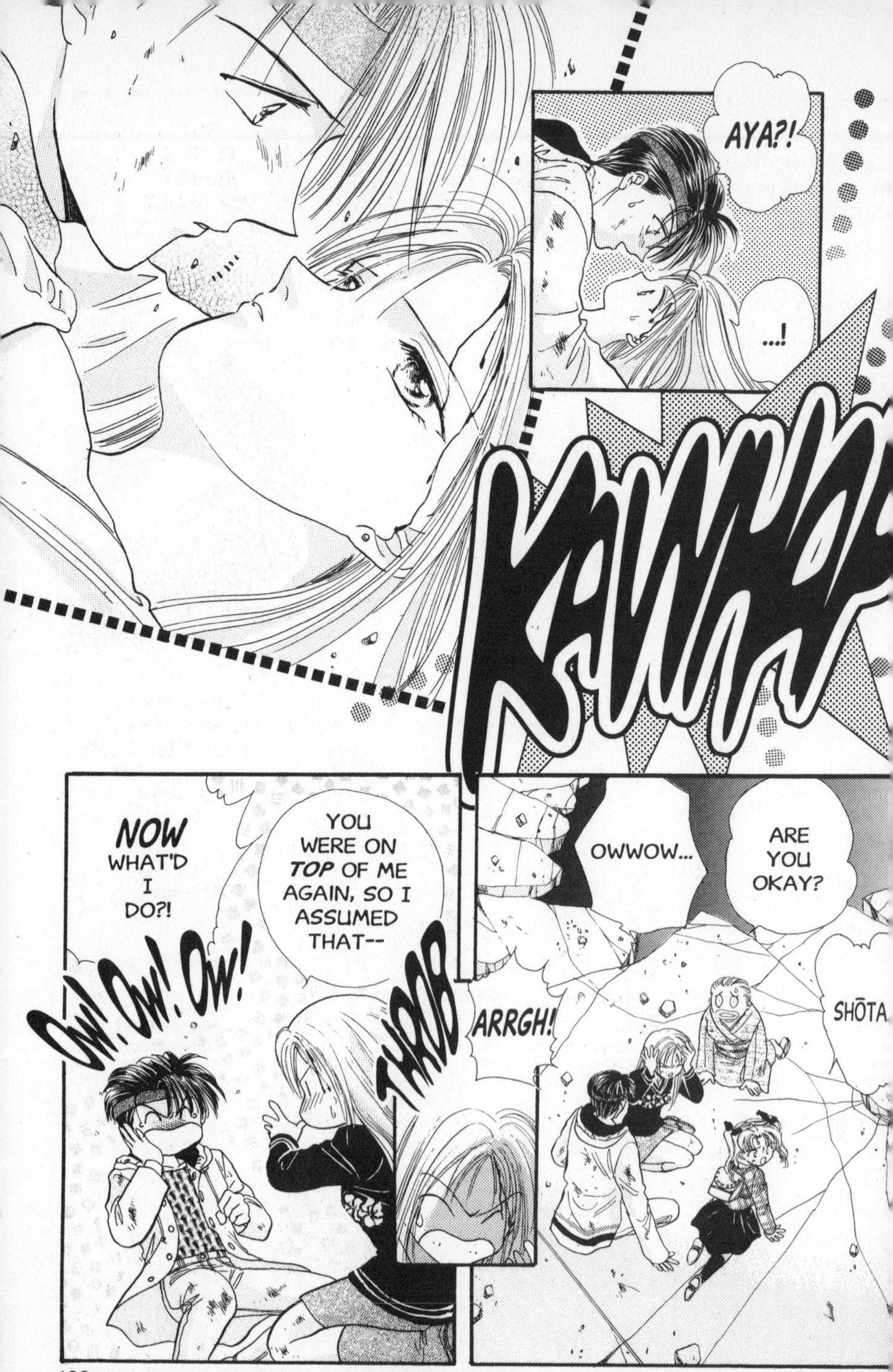
AYA?!
...!
ARE YOU OKAY?
OWWOW...
SHŌTA
ARRGH!
THROB
YOU WERE ON *TOP* OF ME AGAIN, SO I ASSUMED THAT--
NOW WHAT'D I DO?!
OW! OW! OW!

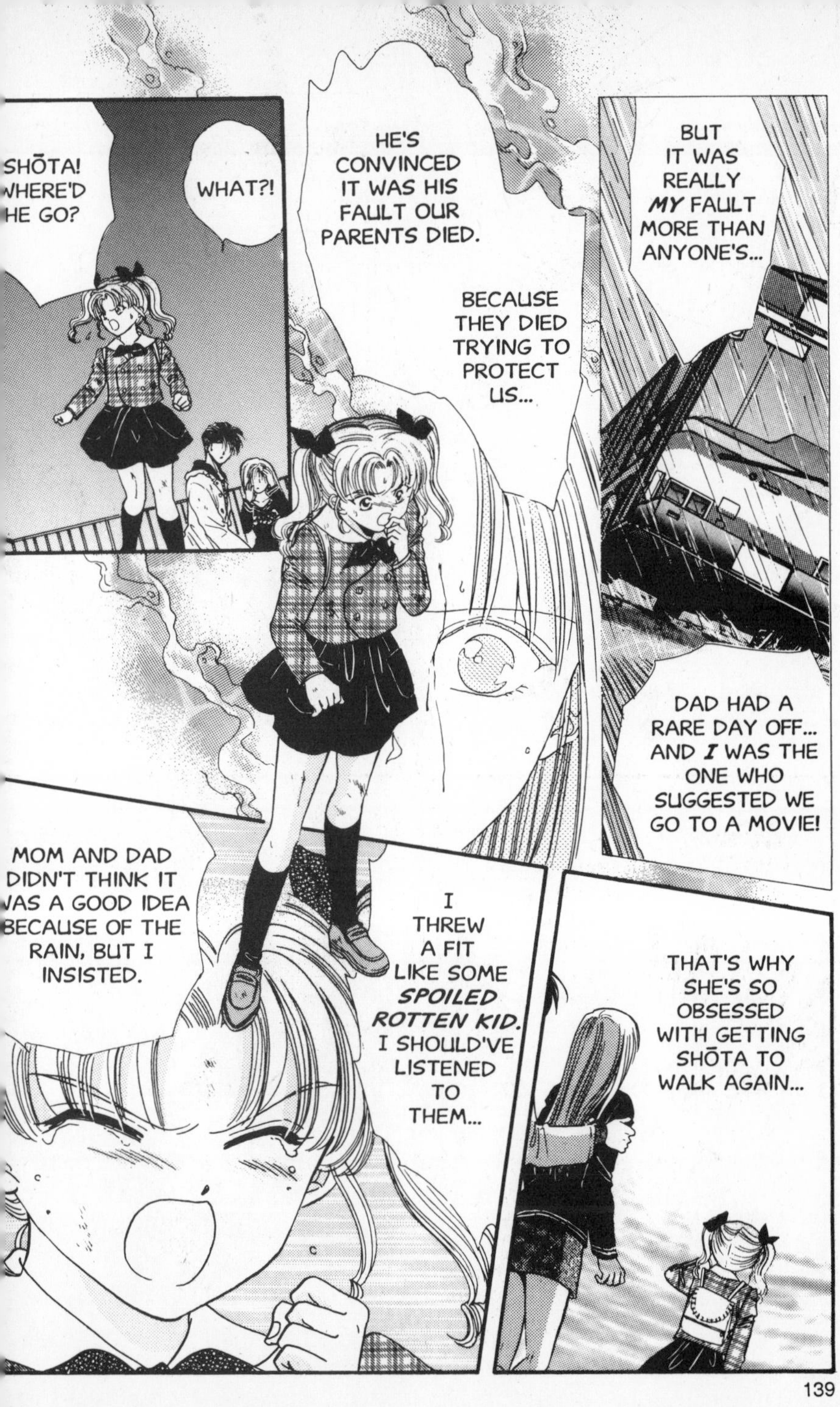
SHŌTA! WHERE'D HE GO?
WHAT?!
HE'S CONVINCED IT WAS HIS FAULT OUR PARENTS DIED.
BECAUSE THEY DIED TRYING TO PROTECT US...
BUT IT WAS REALLY *MY* FAULT MORE THAN ANYONE'S...
DAD HAD A RARE DAY OFF... AND *I* WAS THE ONE WHO SUGGESTED WE GO TO A MOVIE!
MOM AND DAD DIDN'T THINK IT WAS A GOOD IDEA BECAUSE OF THE RAIN, BUT I INSISTED.
I THREW A FIT LIKE SOME *SPOILED ROTTEN KID.* I SHOULD'VE LISTENED TO THEM...
THAT'S WHY SHE'S SO OBSESSED WITH GETTING SHŌTA TO WALK AGAIN...

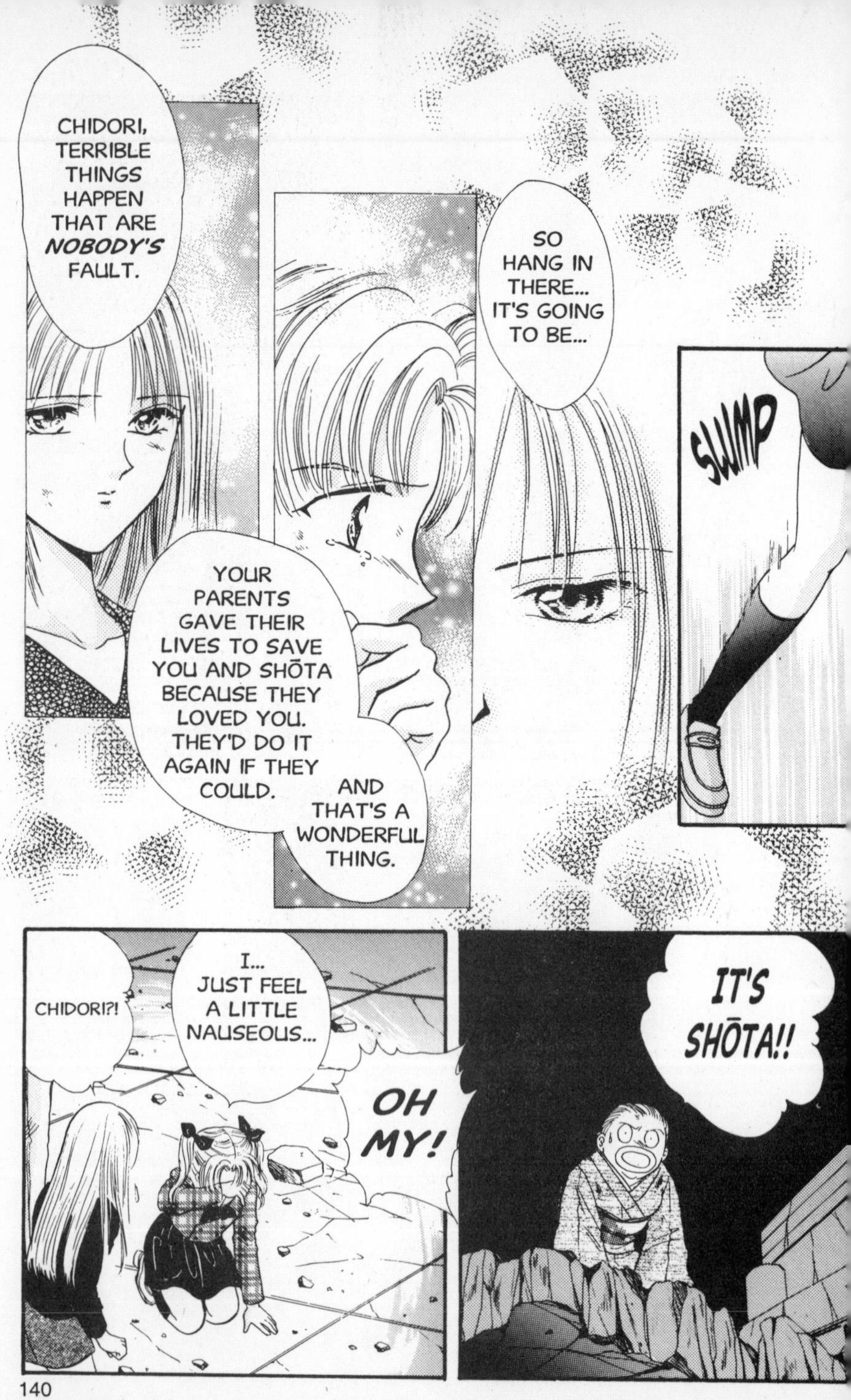
CHIDORI, TERRIBLE THINGS HAPPEN THAT ARE *NOBODY'S* FAULT.
YOUR PARENTS GAVE THEIR LIVES TO SAVE YOU AND SHŌTA BECAUSE THEY LOVED YOU. THEY'D DO IT AGAIN IF THEY COULD.
AND THAT'S A WONDERFUL THING.
SO HANG IN THERE... IT'S GOING TO BE...
SLUMP
CHIDORI?!
I... JUST FEEL A LITTLE NAUSEOUS...
OH MY!
IT'S SHŌTA!!

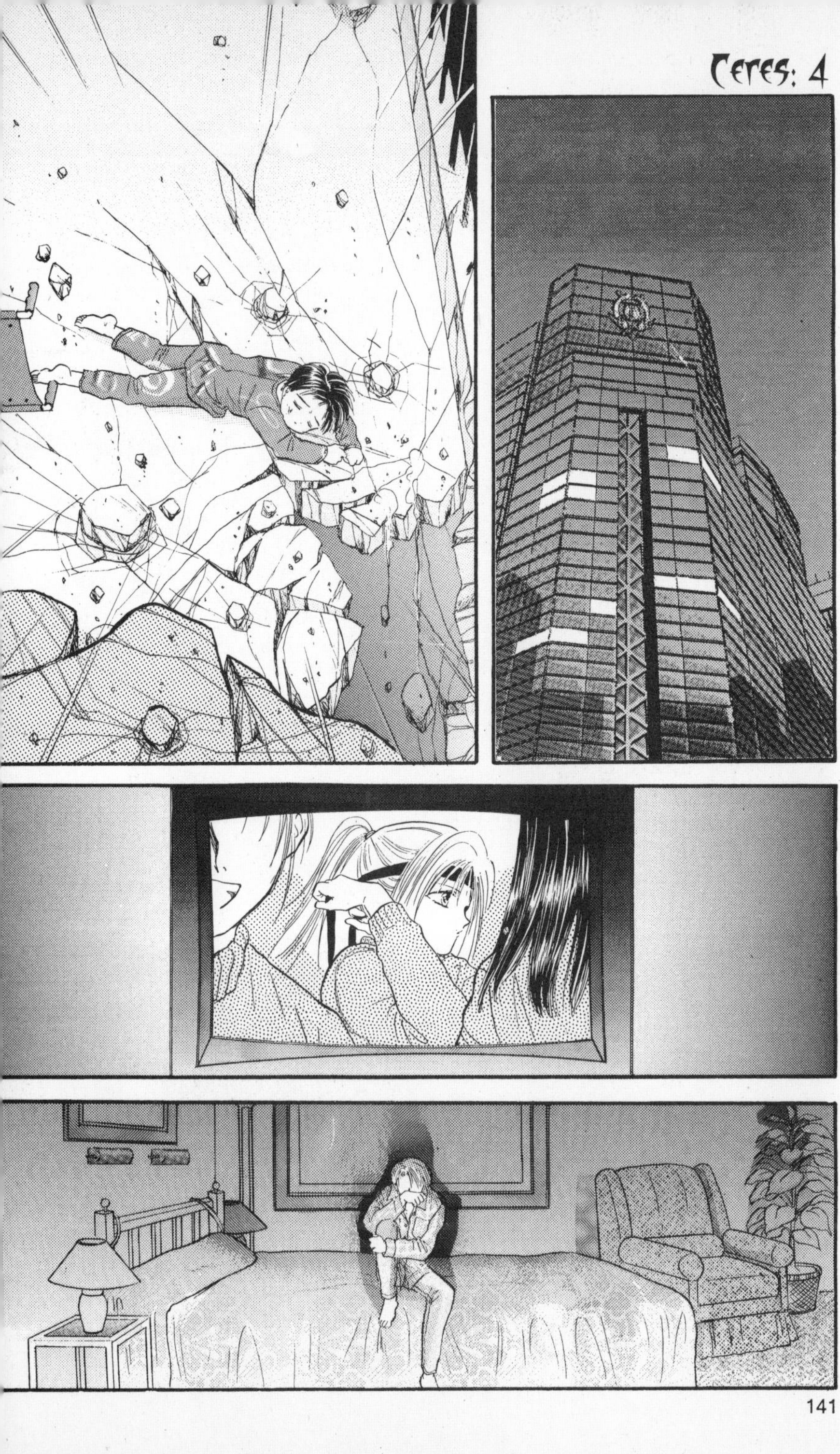

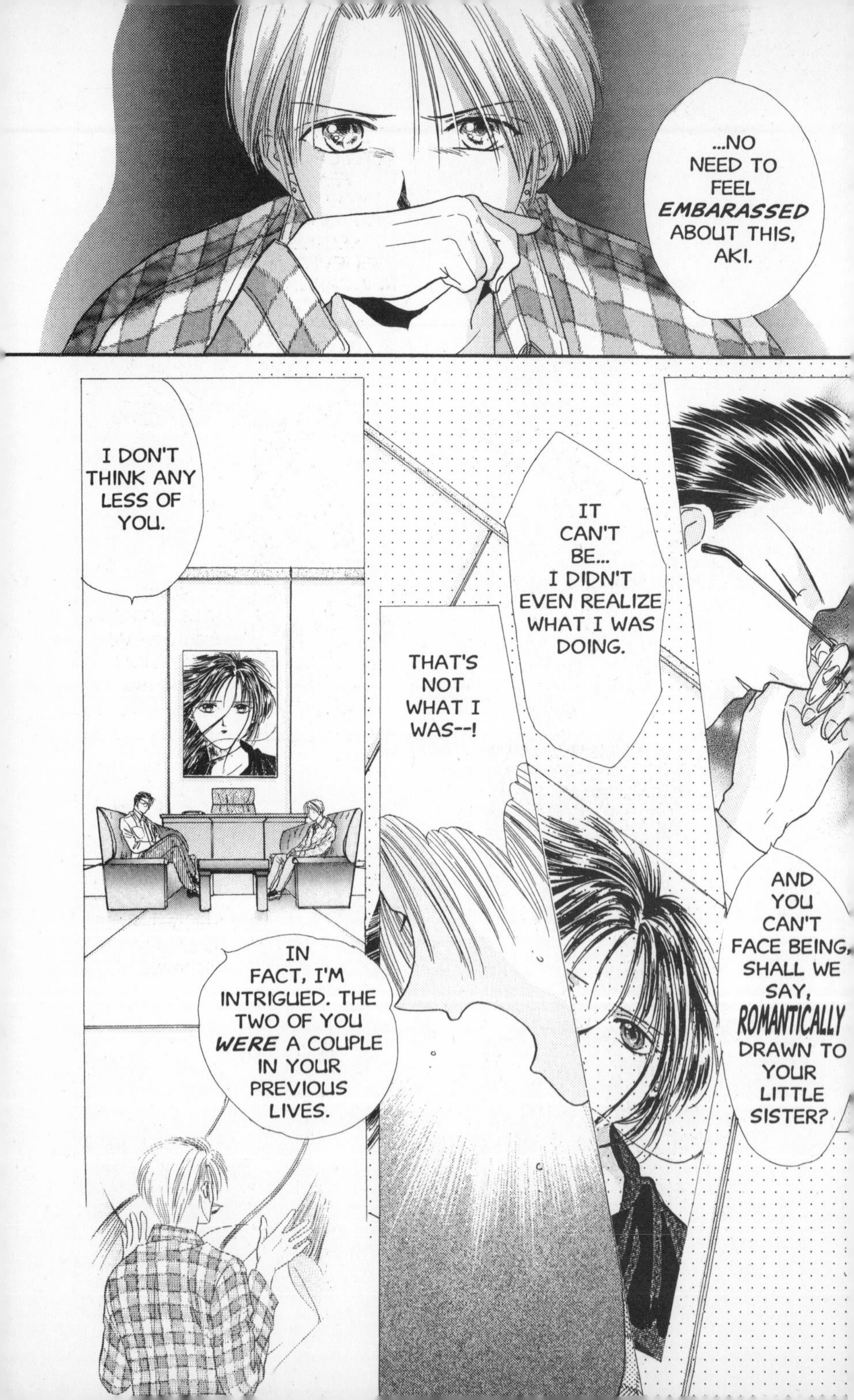
...NO NEED TO FEEL *EMBARASSED* ABOUT THIS, AKI.
AND YOU CAN'T FACE BEING, SHALL WE SAY, **ROMANTICALLY** DRAWN TO YOUR LITTLE SISTER?
IT CAN'T BE... I DIDN'T EVEN REALIZE WHAT I WAS DOING.
THAT'S NOT WHAT I WAS--!
I DON'T THINK ANY LESS OF YOU.
IN FACT, I'M INTRIGUED. THE TWO OF YOU *WERE* A COUPLE IN YOUR PREVIOUS LIVES.

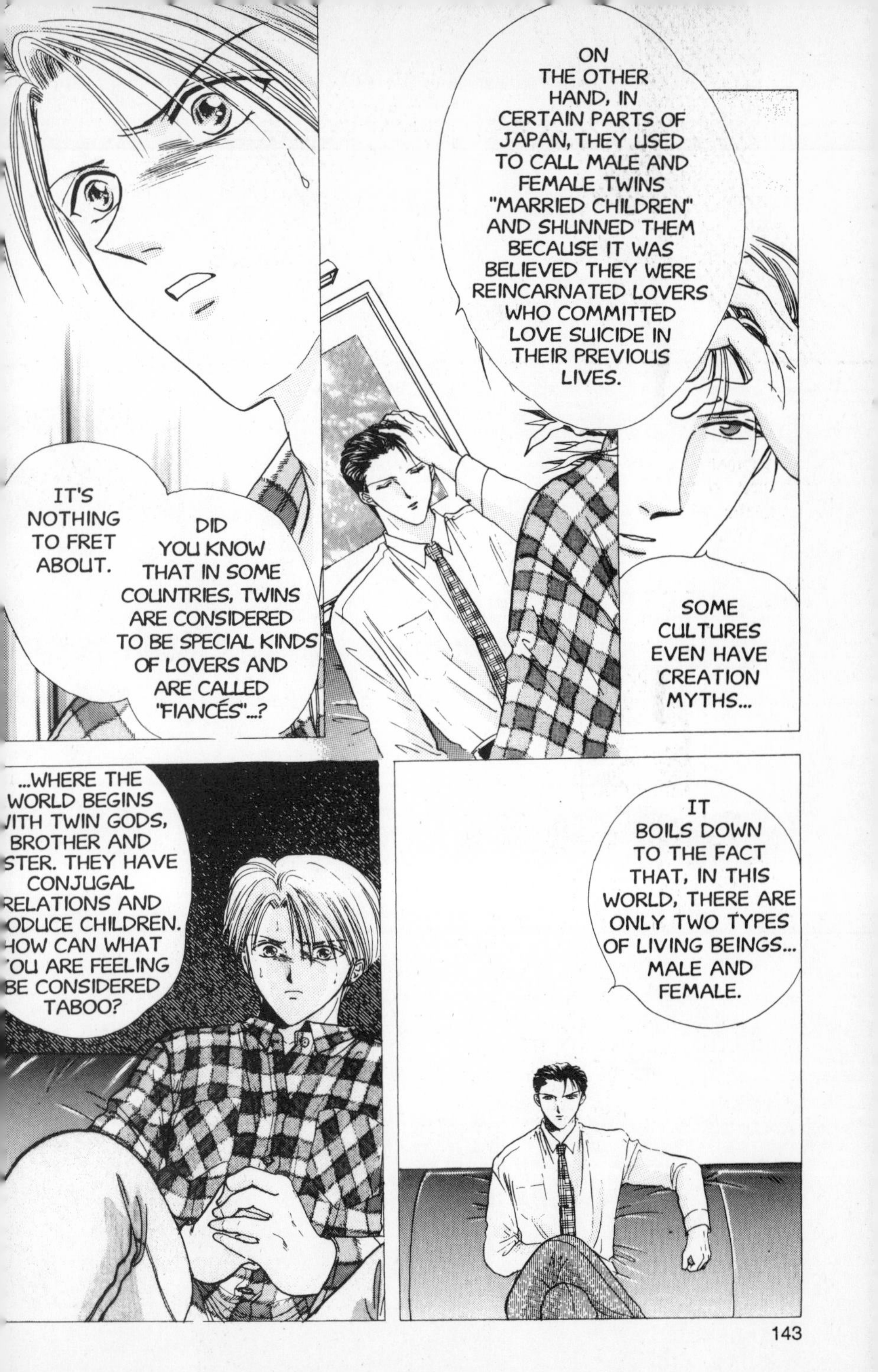
IT'S NOTHING TO FRET ABOUT.
DID YOU KNOW THAT IN SOME COUNTRIES, TWINS ARE CONSIDERED TO BE SPECIAL KINDS OF LOVERS AND ARE CALLED "FIANCÉS"...?
ON THE OTHER HAND, IN CERTAIN PARTS OF JAPAN, THEY USED TO CALL MALE AND FEMALE TWINS "MARRIED CHILDREN" AND SHUNNED THEM BECAUSE IT WAS BELIEVED THEY WERE REINCARNATED LOVERS WHO COMMITTED LOVE SUICIDE IN THEIR PREVIOUS LIVES.
SOME CULTURES EVEN HAVE CREATION MYTHS...
...WHERE THE WORLD BEGINS ITH TWIN GODS, BROTHER AND STER. THEY HAVE CONJUGAL RELATIONS AND ODUCE CHILDREN. HOW CAN WHAT OU ARE FEELING BE CONSIDERED TABOO?
IT BOILS DOWN TO THE FACT THAT, IN THIS WORLD, THERE ARE ONLY TWO TYPES OF LIVING BEINGS... MALE AND FEMALE.

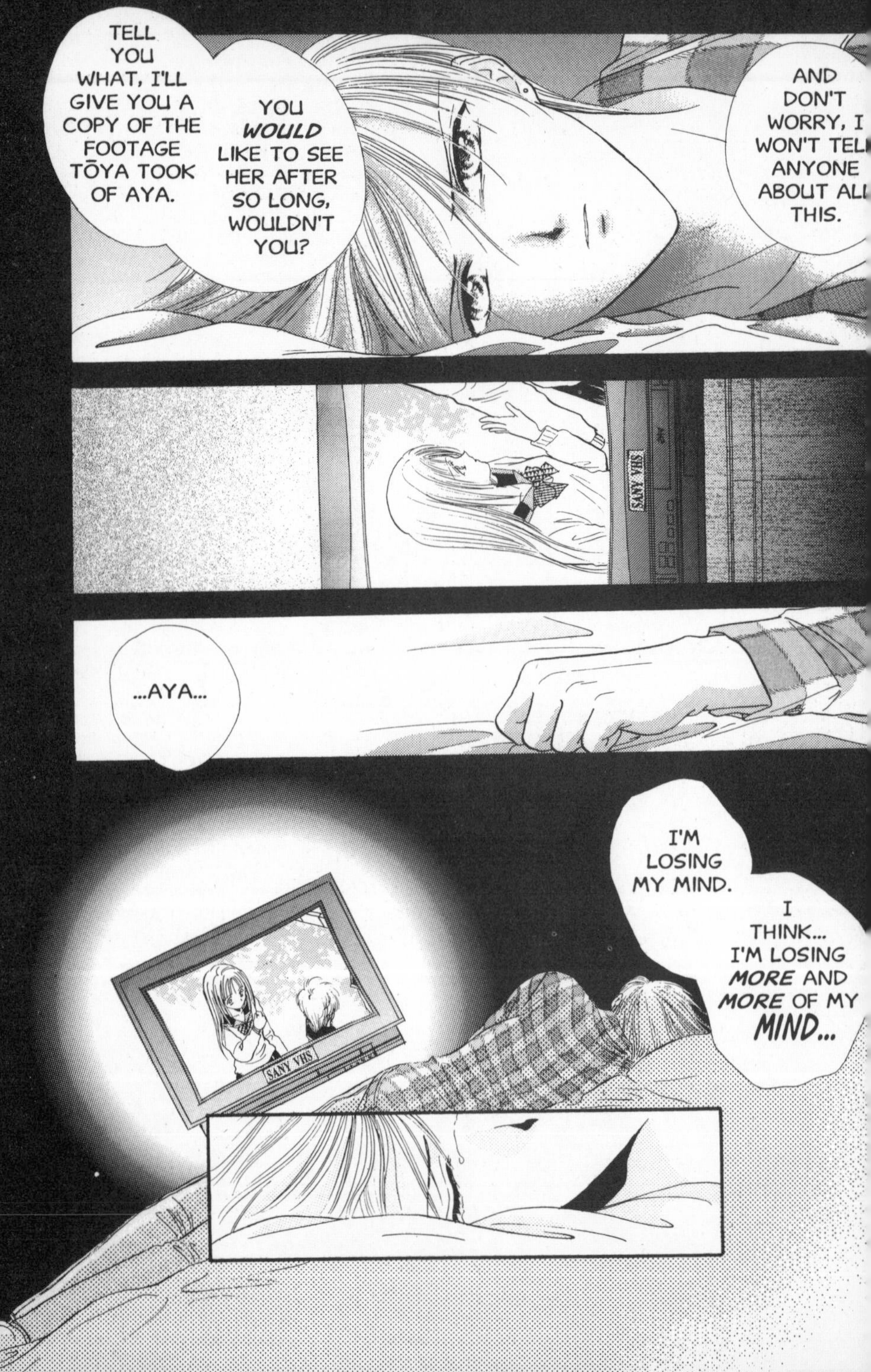
AND DON'T WORRY, I WON'T TELL ANYONE ABOUT ALL THIS.
YOU *WOULD* LIKE TO SEE HER AFTER SO LONG, WOULDN'T YOU?
TELL YOU WHAT, I'LL GIVE YOU A COPY OF THE FOOTAGE TŌYA TOOK OF AYA.
SANY VHS
...AYA...
I'M LOSING MY MIND.
I THINK... I'M LOSING *MORE* AND *MORE* OF MY ***MIND...***
SANY VHS

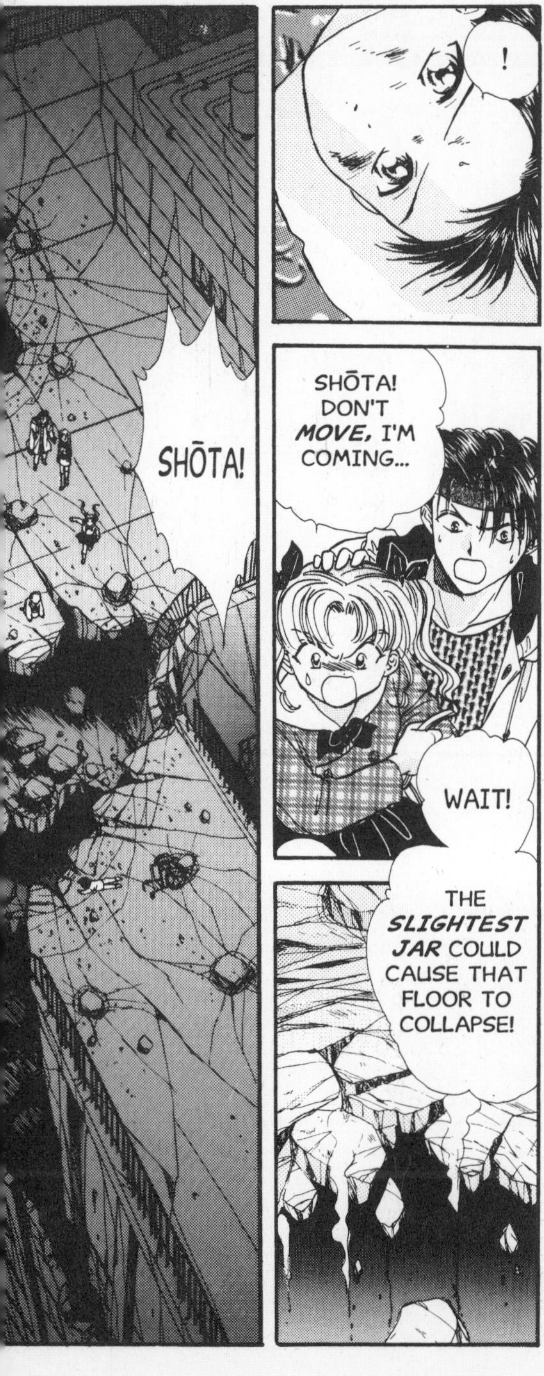
!
SHŌTA! DON'T *MOVE,* I'M COMING...
WAIT!
THE *SLIGHTEST JAR* COULD CAUSE THAT FLOOR TO COLLAPSE!
SHŌTA!

So... This story arc is set in Tochigi, but Amago Village actually does exist. My editor videotaped footage there for me because I was too busy with work and couldn't go myself. (I cause him a lot of trouble)
There was an old lady there who claimed she was descended from a celestial maiden! My editor interviewed her, and she talked about Amago Village and how it may or may not have existed since the Jōmon Period (approx. 13,000 - 300 B.C.). Wow, I guess tennyo really did exist. If we were to search all over Japan, I bet we'd find even more people of "celestial lineage." I mean, there's even a legend that Sugawara no Michizane (revered as the god of Academics) is descended from a tennyo. ...
W-Wait a minute...does this mean that little old lady is a C-Genome!?
Actually, I heard a story about a guy (outside of Japan) whom DNA testing found to be a direct descendant of some stone age man—Cro-Magnon Man or something like that.
These days, you can find out just about anything from DNA. But get this, his wife commented, "Now I know why my husband likes his meat rare." What a sense of humor...
"HA HA HA"—Yes, that's how Americans really laugh! How can I say this? Because I just got back from vacation in Florida! It was actually supposed to be a trip to Arizona, but I thought, I might as well have some fun so I went to Disney World & Universal Studios! But the work just piled up while I was away! I'm tired, but I sure had a great time! There were rides that they don't have in Tokyo Disneyland, and they were so great! There's an alien ride called "EX" and it was **so** freaky! Things explode and water sprays on you, and you feel this warm breath on your neck... and then its **right** behind you!! I was screaming my head off!
I wonder if it'll be coming to Japan anytime soon...

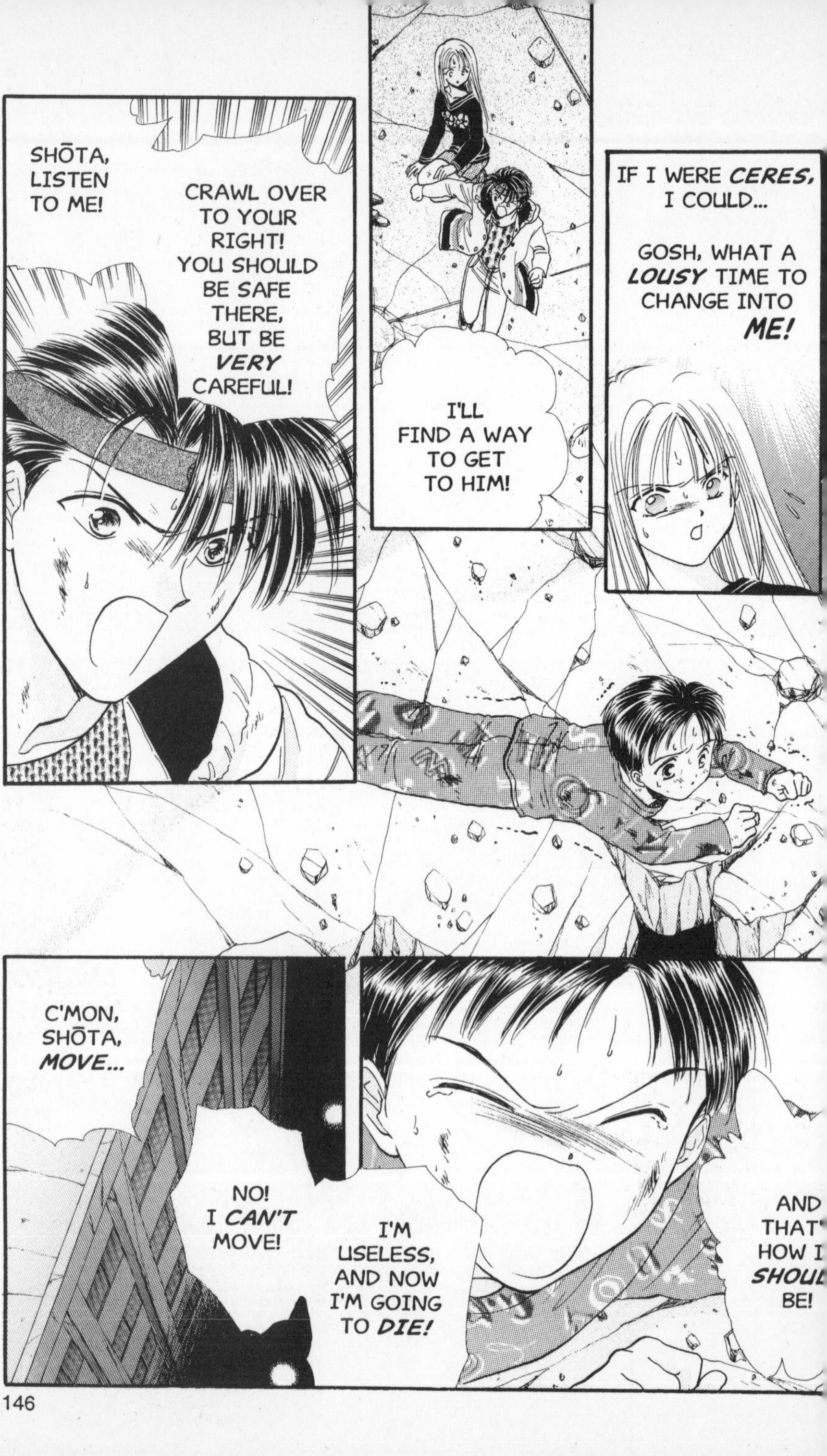
SHŌTA, LISTEN TO ME!
CRAWL OVER TO YOUR RIGHT! YOU SHOULD BE SAFE THERE, BUT BE *VERY* CAREFUL!
I'LL FIND A WAY TO GET TO HIM!
IF I WERE *CERES,* I COULD...
GOSH, WHAT A *LOUSY* TIME TO CHANGE INTO *ME!*
C'MON, SHŌTA, *MOVE...*
NO! I *CAN'T* MOVE!
I'M USELESS, AND NOW I'M GOING TO *DIE!*
AND THAT' HOW I *SHOUL* BE!

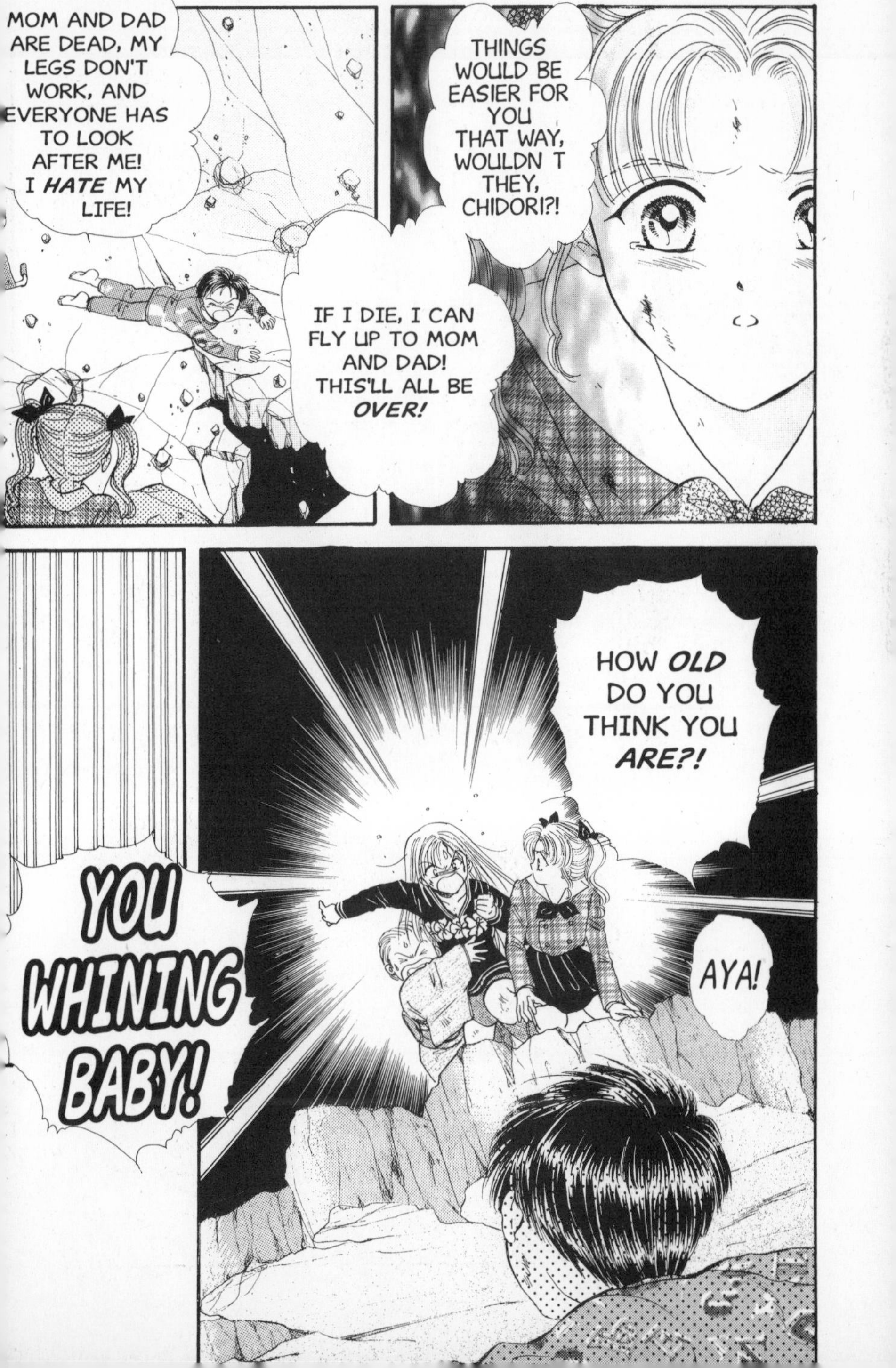
MOM AND DAD ARE DEAD, MY LEGS DON'T WORK, AND EVERYONE HAS TO LOOK AFTER ME! I *HATE* MY LIFE!
IF I DIE, I CAN FLY UP TO MOM AND DAD! THIS'LL ALL BE *OVER!*
THINGS WOULD BE EASIER FOR YOU THAT WAY, WOULDN T THEY, CHIDORI?!
HOW *OLD* DO YOU THINK YOU *ARE?!*
YOU WHINING BABY!
AYA!

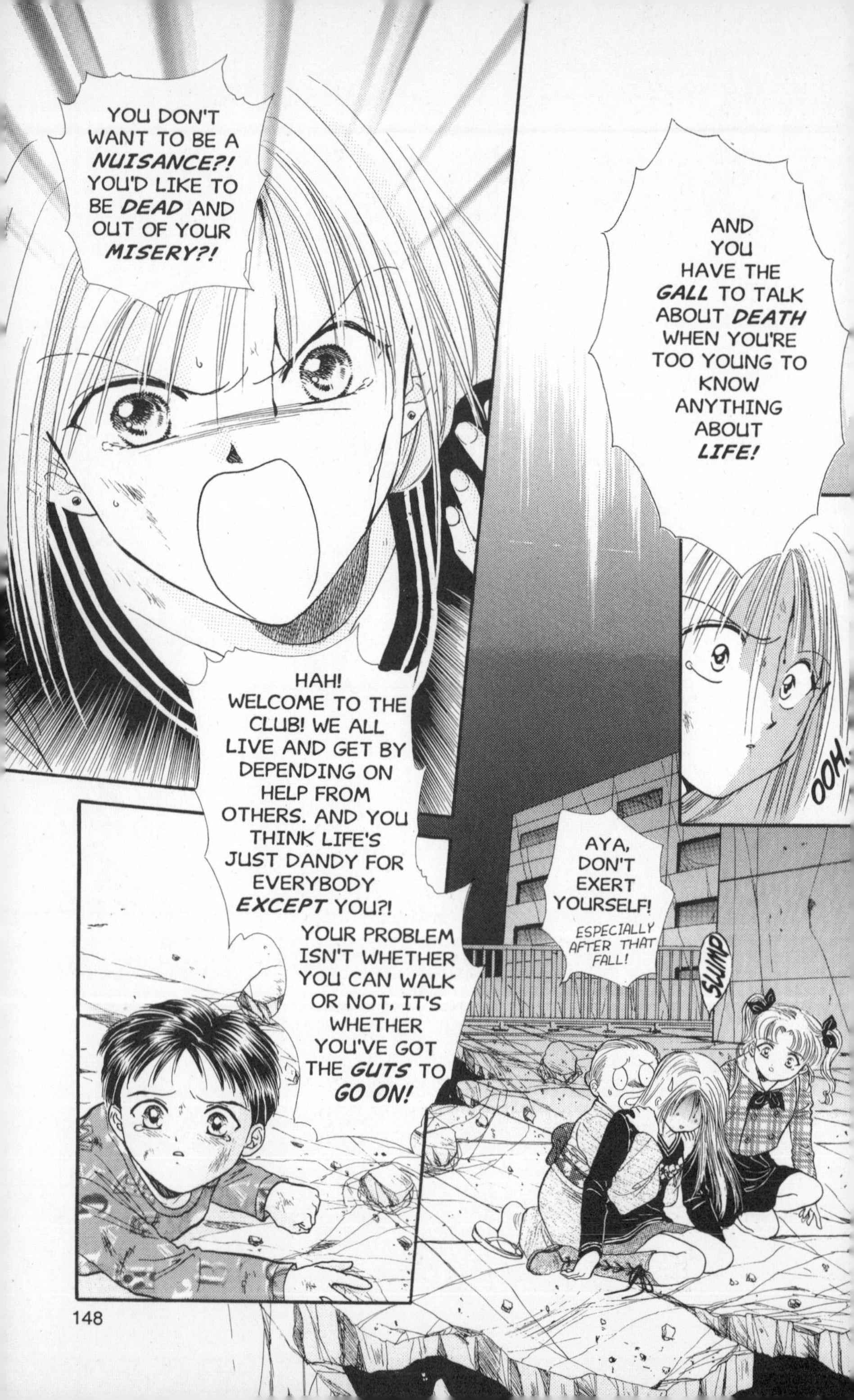
YOU DON'T WANT TO BE A NUISANCE?! YOU'D LIKE TO BE DEAD AND OUT OF YOUR MISERY?!
AND YOU HAVE THE GALL TO TALK ABOUT DEATH WHEN YOU'RE TOO YOUNG TO KNOW ANYTHING ABOUT LIFE!
OOH.
HAH! WELCOME TO THE CLUB! WE ALL LIVE AND GET BY DEPENDING ON HELP FROM OTHERS. AND YOU THINK LIFE'S JUST DANDY FOR EVERYBODY EXCEPT YOU?!
YOUR PROBLEM ISN'T WHETHER YOU CAN WALK OR NOT, IT'S WHETHER YOU'VE GOT THE GUTS TO GO ON!
AYA, DON'T EXERT YOURSELF!
ESPECIALLY AFTER THAT FALL!
SLUMP

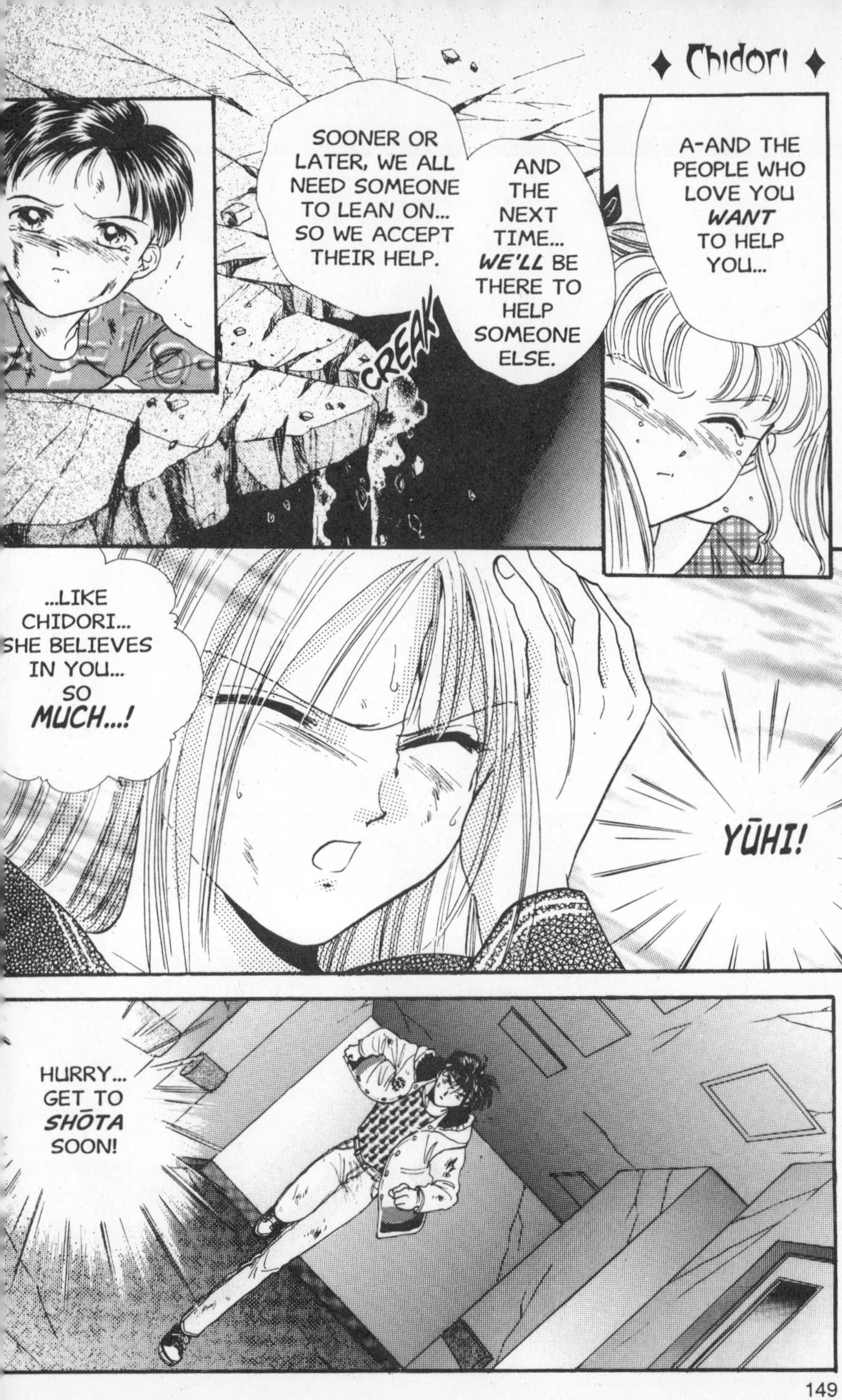
A-AND THE PEOPLE WHO LOVE YOU *WANT* TO HELP YOU...
SOONER OR LATER, WE ALL NEED SOMEONE TO LEAN ON... SO WE ACCEPT THEIR HELP.
AND THE NEXT TIME... *WE'LL* BE THERE TO HELP SOMEONE ELSE.
CREAK
...LIKE CHIDORI... SHE BELIEVES IN YOU... SO *MUCH...!*
YŪHI!
HURRY... GET TO *SHŌTA* SOON!

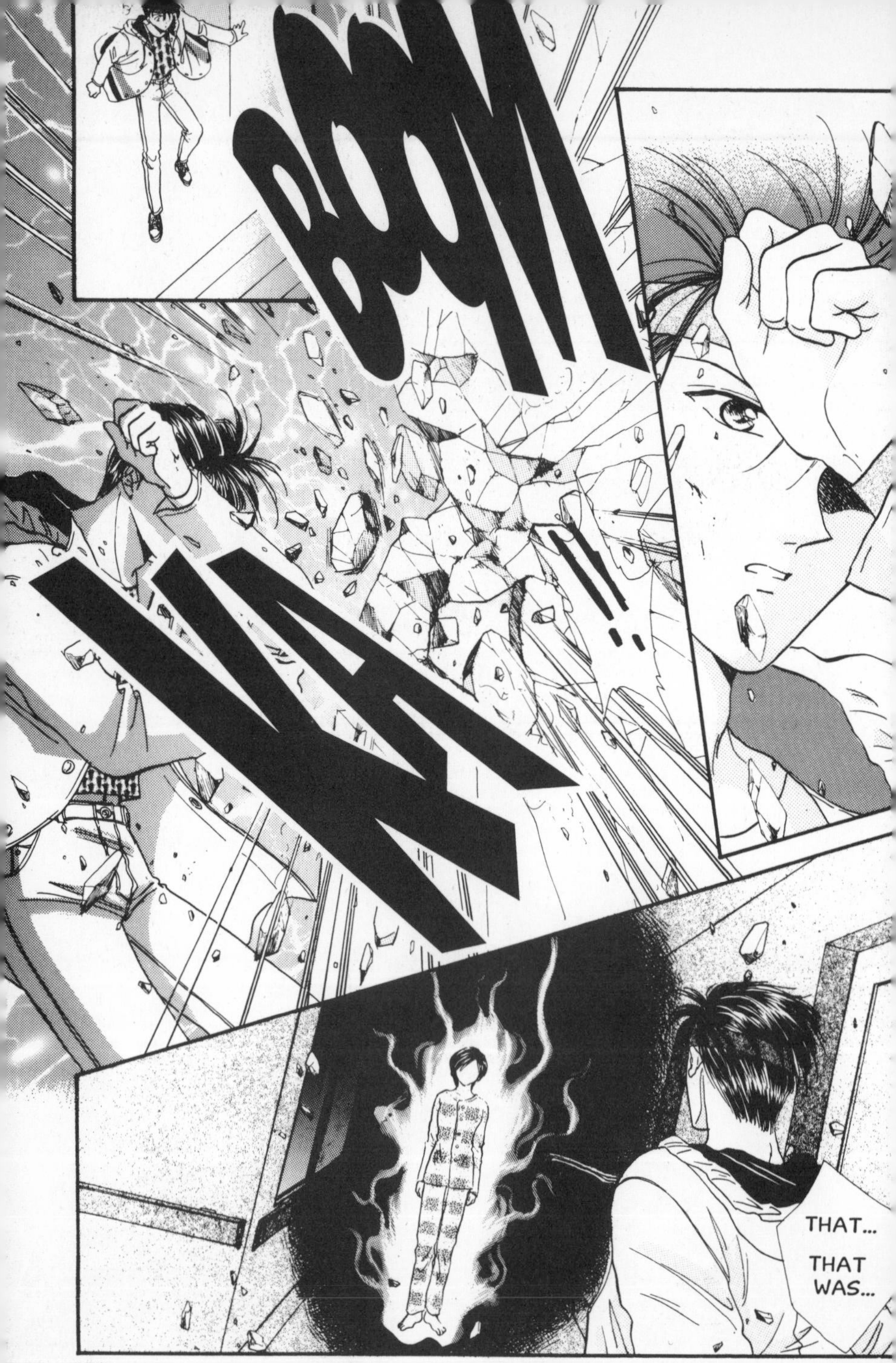
BOOM
WAH!!
THAT...
THAT WAS...

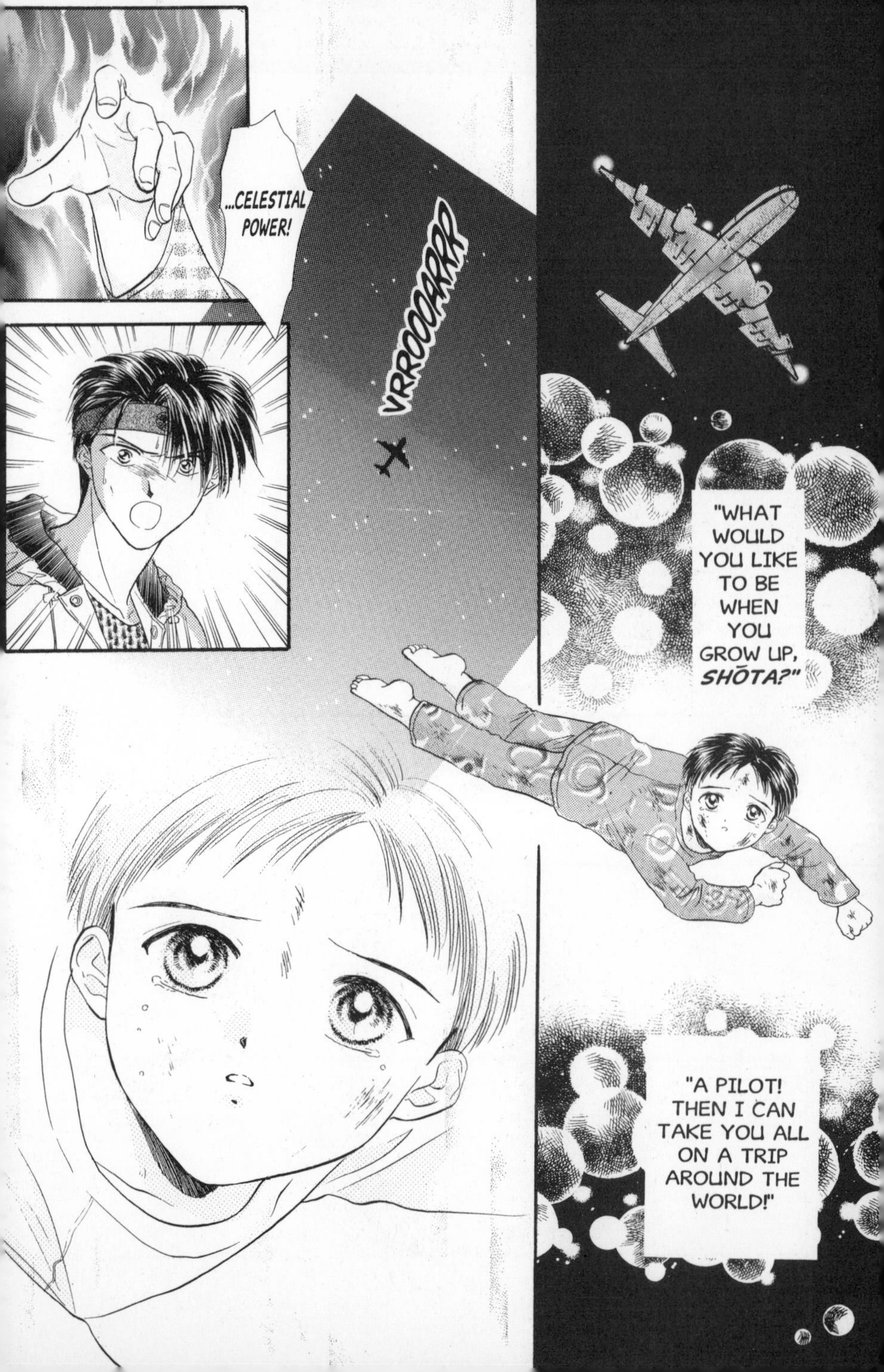
...CELESTIAL POWER!
VRROOOARRR
"WHAT WOULD YOU LIKE TO BE WHEN YOU GROW UP, *SHŌTA?"*
"A PILOT! THEN I CAN TAKE YOU ALL ON A TRIP AROUND THE WORLD!"

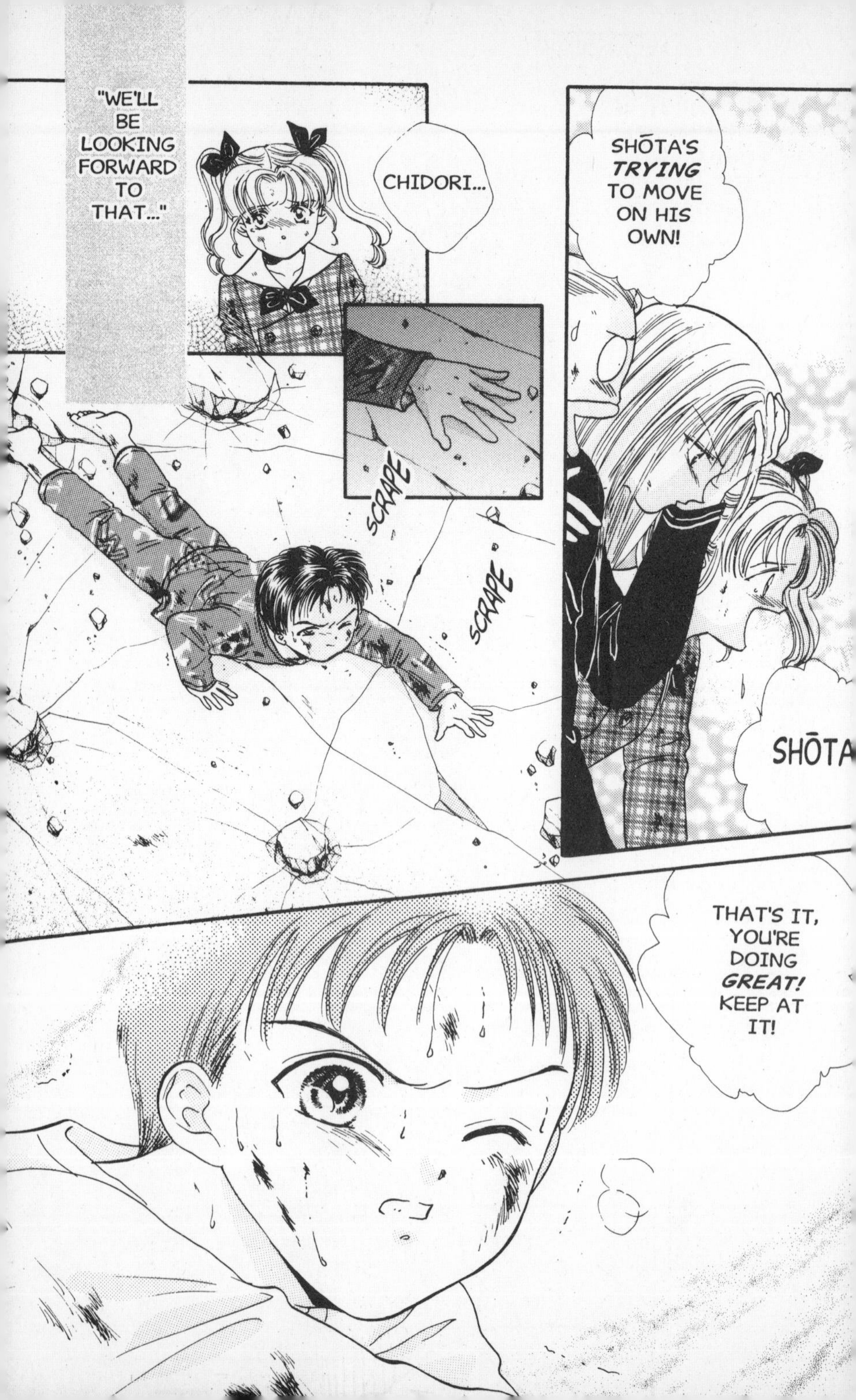
"WE'LL BE LOOKING FORWARD TO THAT..."
CHIDORI...
SCRAPE
SCRAPE
SHŌTA'S *TRYING* TO MOVE ON HIS OWN!
SHŌTA
THAT'S IT, YOU'RE DOING *GREAT!* KEEP AT IT!

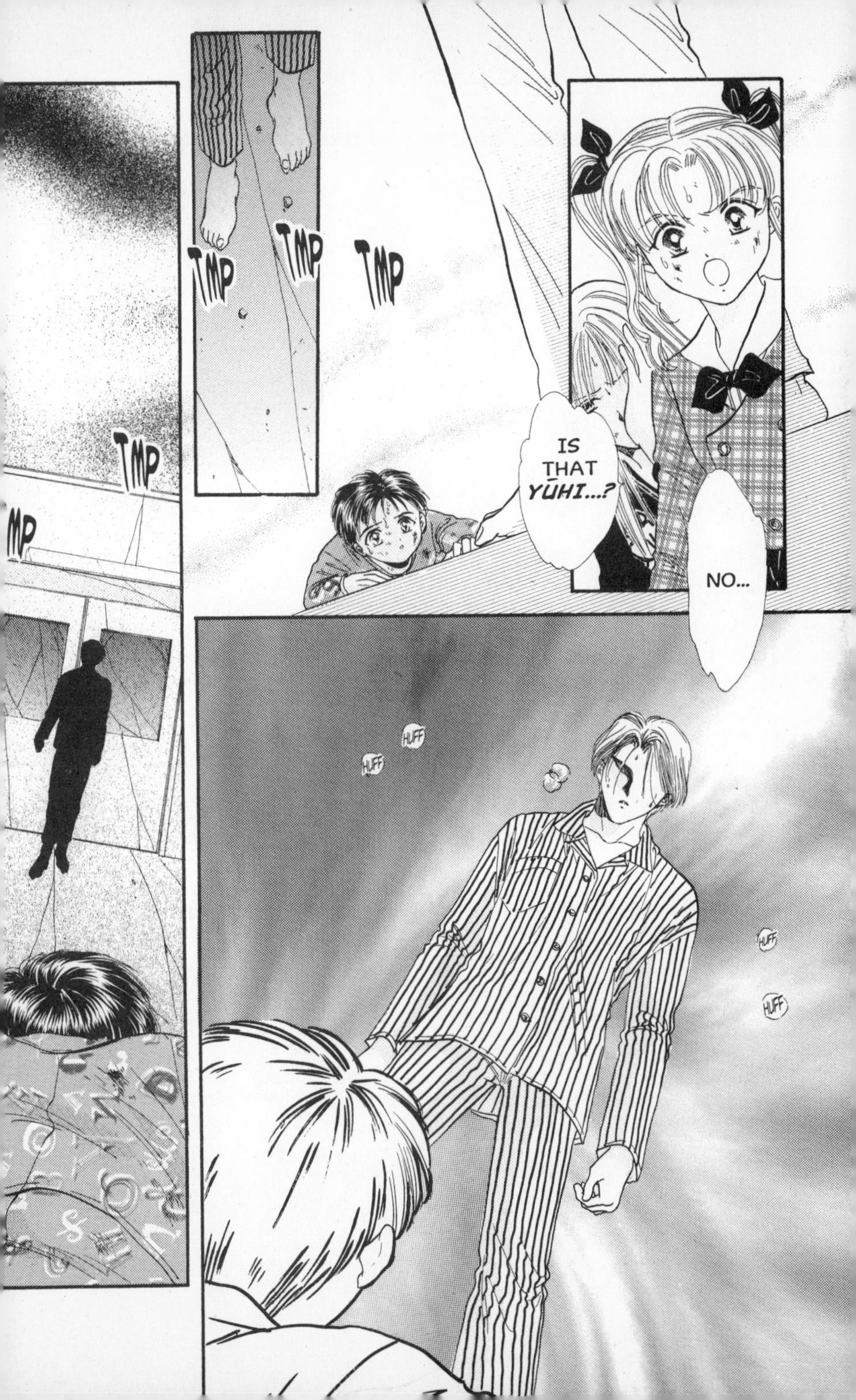
IS THAT YŪHI...?
NO...
TMP
TMP
TMP
TMP
MP
HUFF
HUFF
HUFF
HUFF

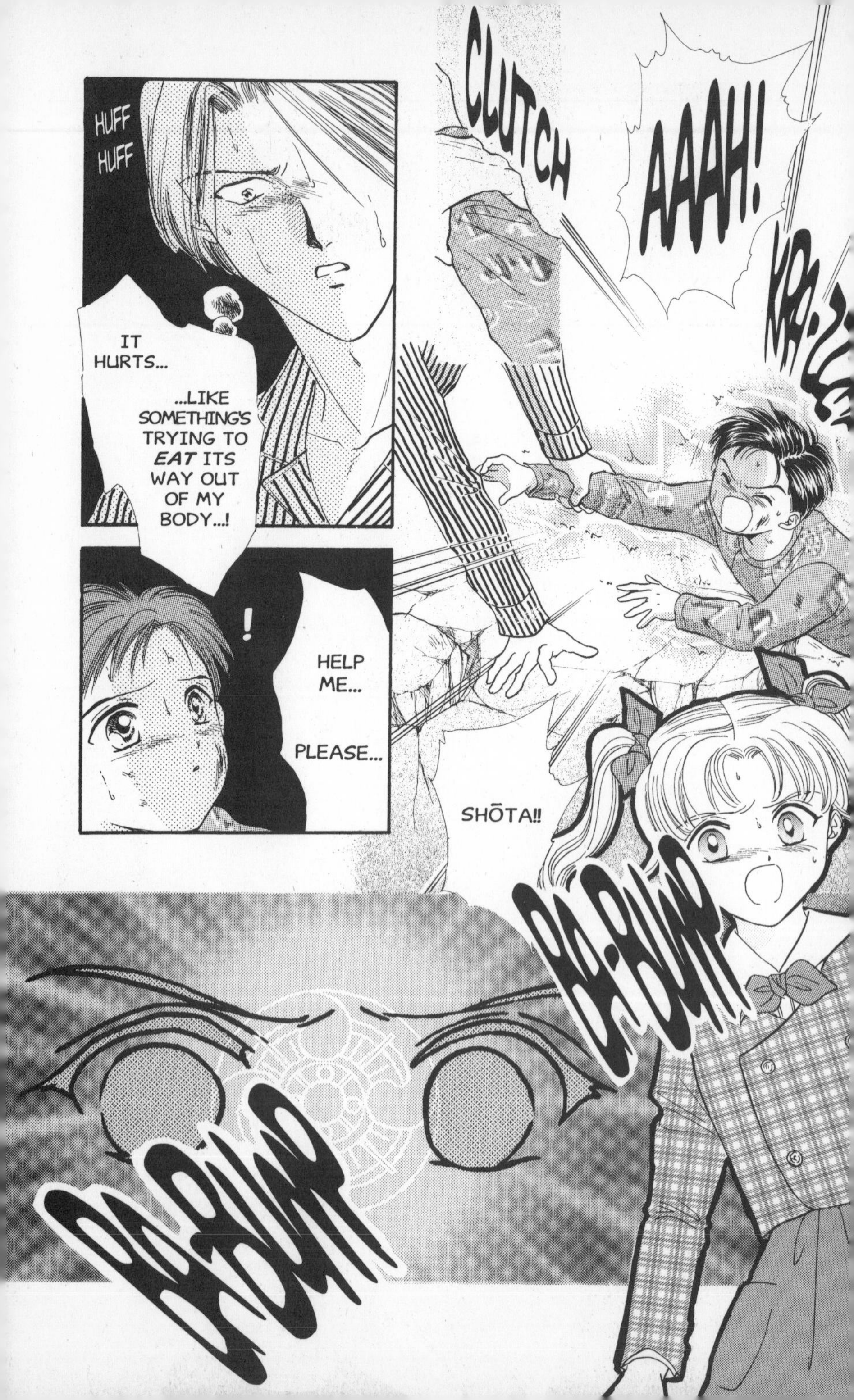
CLUTCH
AAAH!
HUFF
HUFF
IT HURTS...
...LIKE SOMETHING'S TRYING TO *EAT* ITS WAY OUT OF MY BODY...!
!
HELP ME...
PLEASE...
SHŌTA!!
BA-BUMP
BA-BUMP

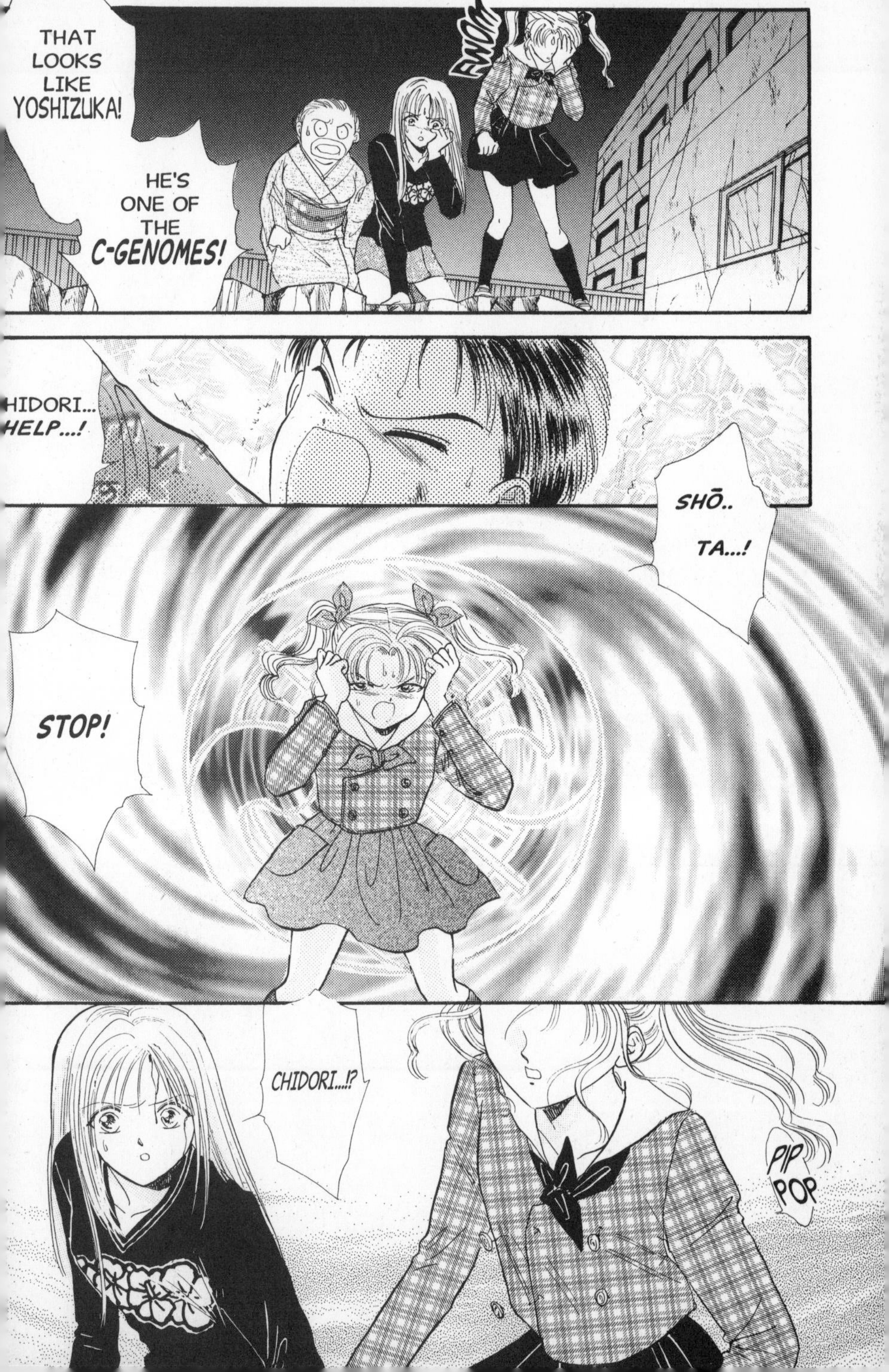
FWOOM
THAT LOOKS LIKE YOSHIZUKA!
HE'S ONE OF THE C-GENOMES!
SHŌ.. TA...!
HIDORI... HELP...!
STOP!
PIP POP
CHIDORI...!?

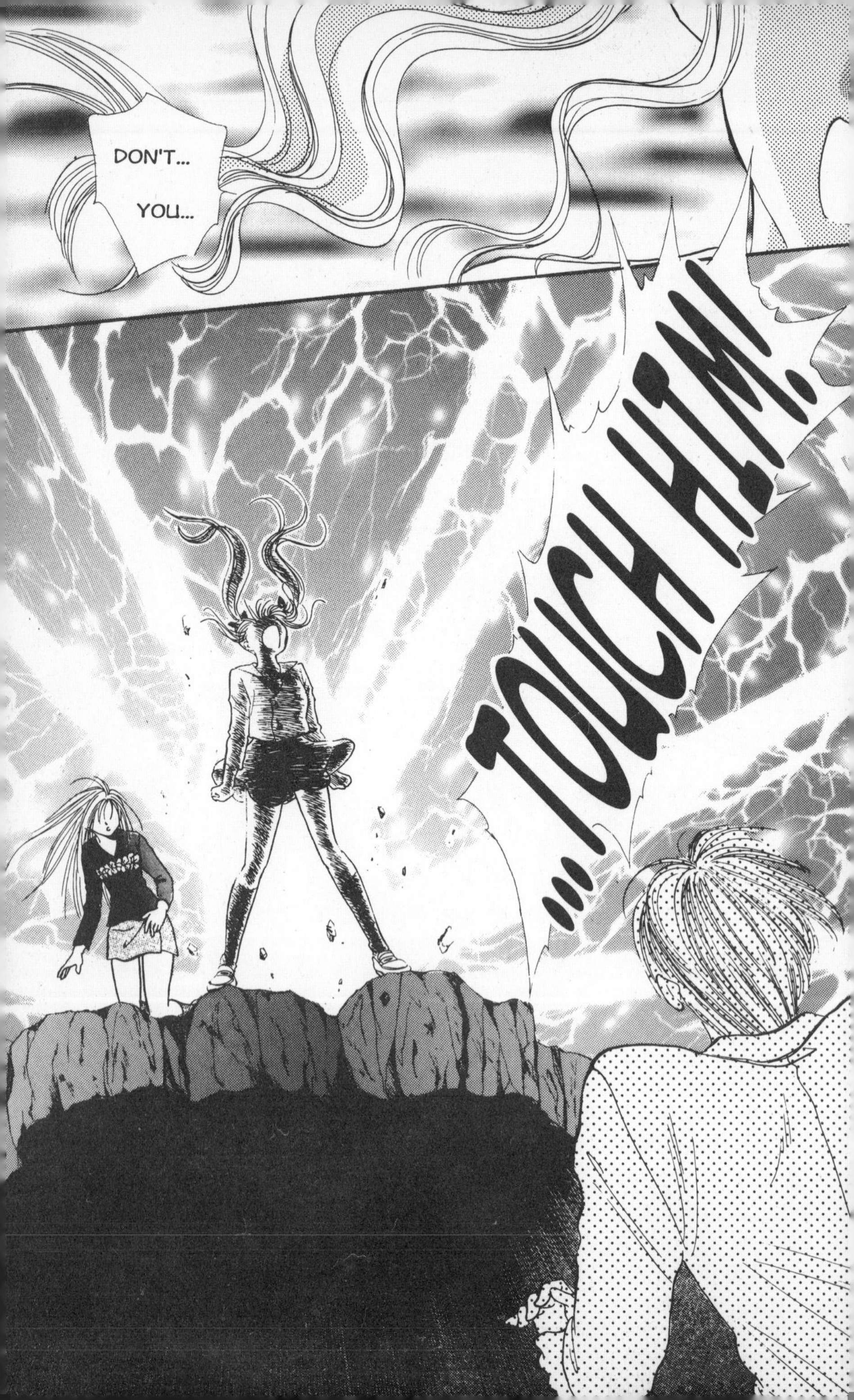
DON'T... YOU...
...TOUCH HIM.

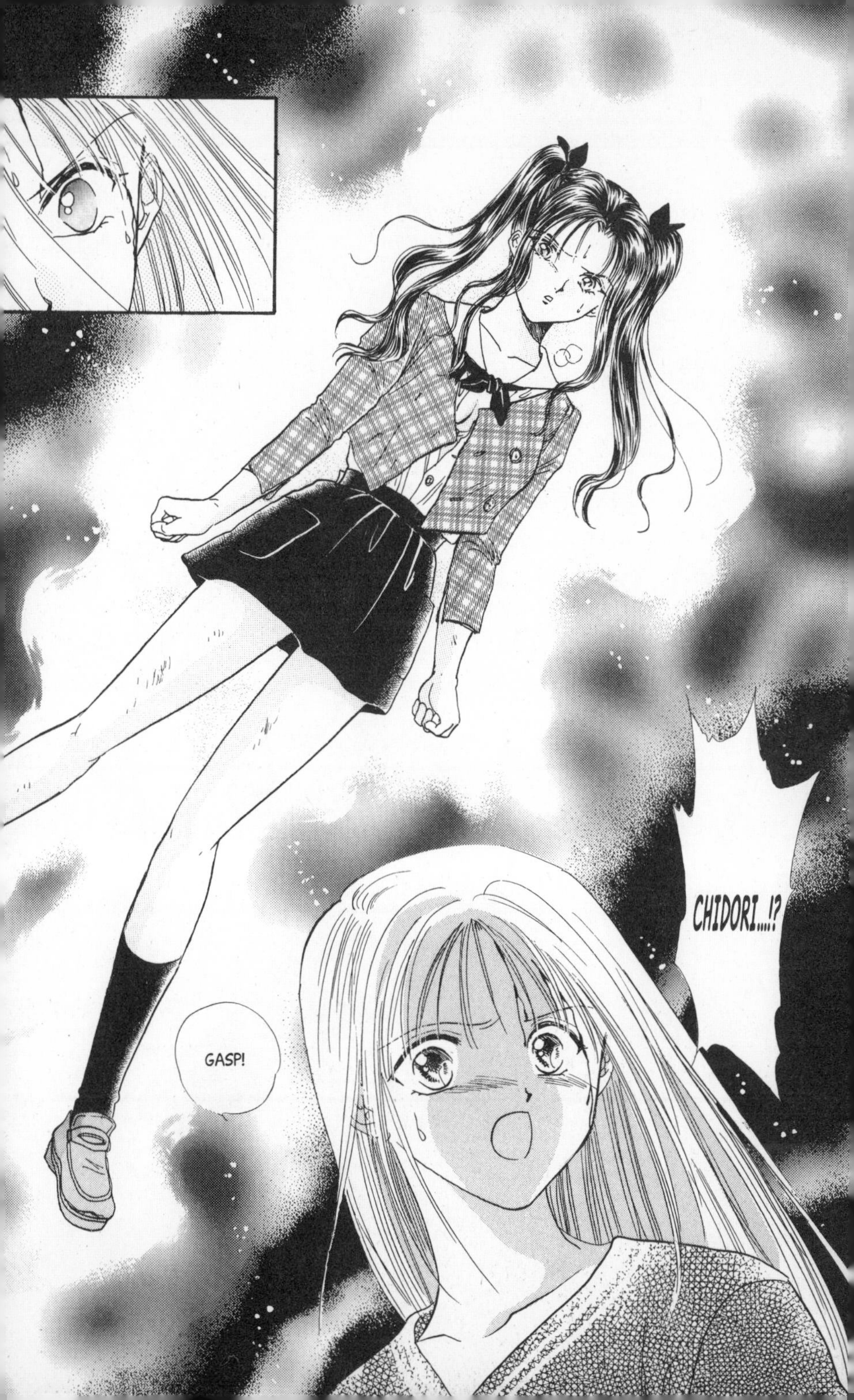
CHIDORI...!?
GASP!

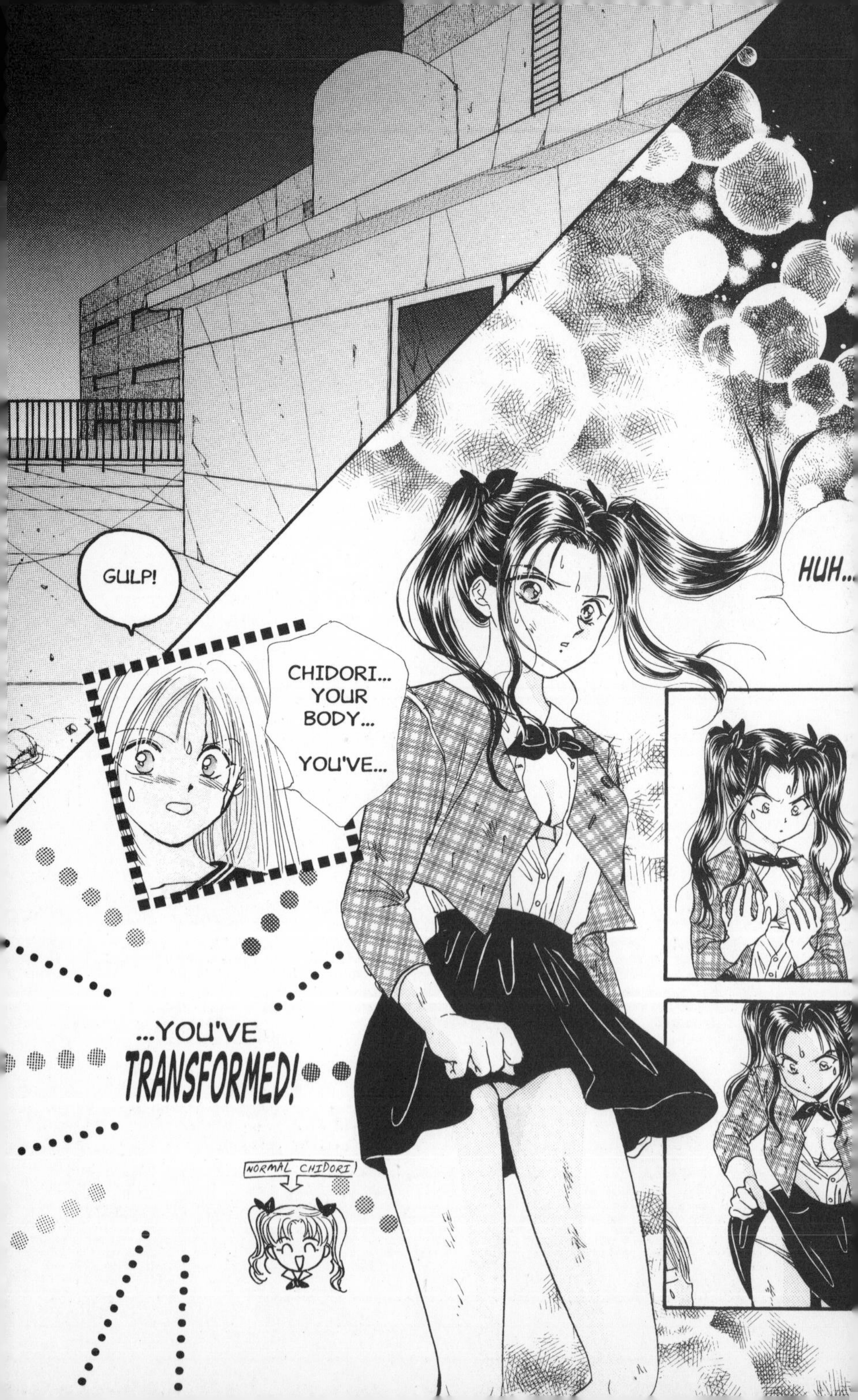
HUH...
GULP!
CHIDORI... YOUR BODY... YOU'VE...
...YOU'VE TRANSFORMED!
NORMAL CHIDORI

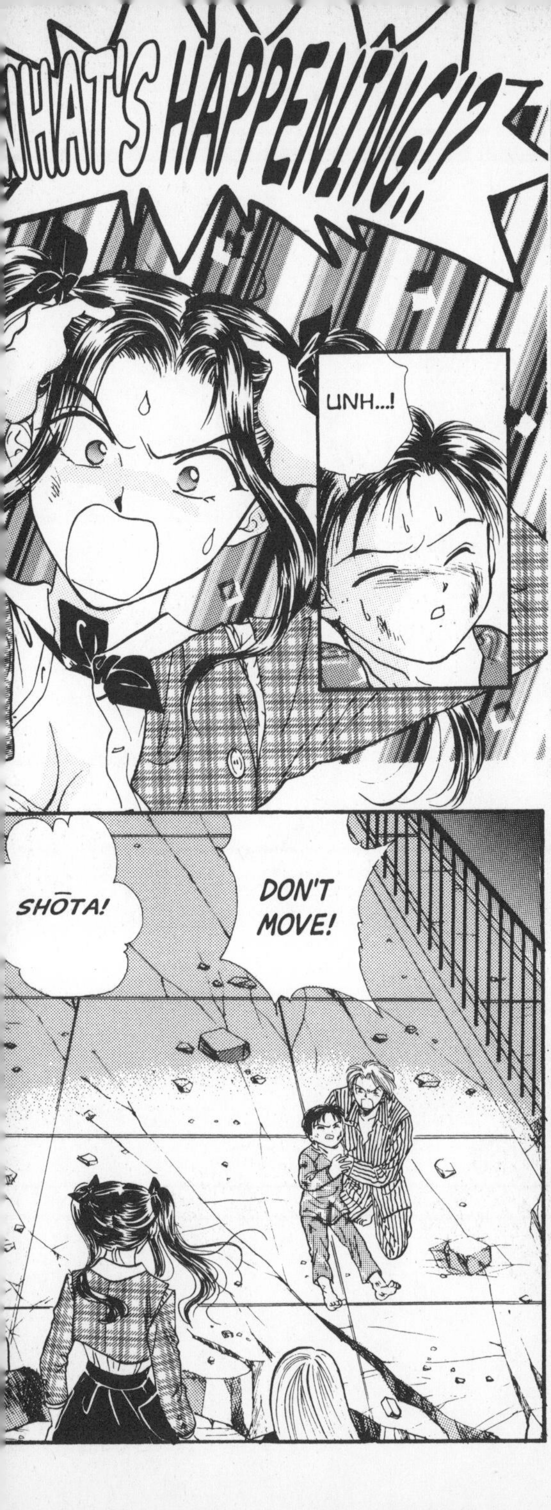
WHAT'S HAPPENING!?
UNH...!
DON'T MOVE!
SHŌTA!

♦ Chidori ♦

In Disney World, I went to Magic Kingdom, MGM, and Epcot, and they were all great in different ways. But at Universal Studios, the big attraction was "Terminator 2 - 3D"!!!! It was incredible! We thought all the other rides were great, but they just paled in comparison. If you ever go, it's definitely a must-see! You'll get goose bumps (I did!). When it was all over, everyone cheered and clapped! It was awesome. They built a Universal Studios in Osaka, and I wanted T2 to come to Japan, but the feature ride here is "Back to the Future"... For certain reasons, I couldn't go on this ride, but my friend who **did** ride it said that after T2, it was "kinda lame." Well, I'll talk about that more next time...

Hmm, I talked about some serious stuff in the beginning of this volume, but it did relate to the manga. I had Chidori's character created even before serialization of **Ceres** started, and I have a lot of other characters lined up too. I've visualized the story up to the end, but it continues to change a little bit all the time, so I don't really know what'll happen. And regarding Chidori, my assistant says Chidori is "yummy"...(?) There are a lot of girl characters, unlike my previous title. But actually, the Mikages' side is mostly men. The structure of the story is men vs. women. There'll be a lot of significant developments in the next volume. Maybe you'll even be shocked and surprised. (Although it's already been printed in serialized format.) We'll be getting into the crux of the story, so please don't miss it. ...But Tōya will still remain as mysterious as ever.

See you next time!

"Princess Mononoke" soundtrack playing in the background... 8/19/'97

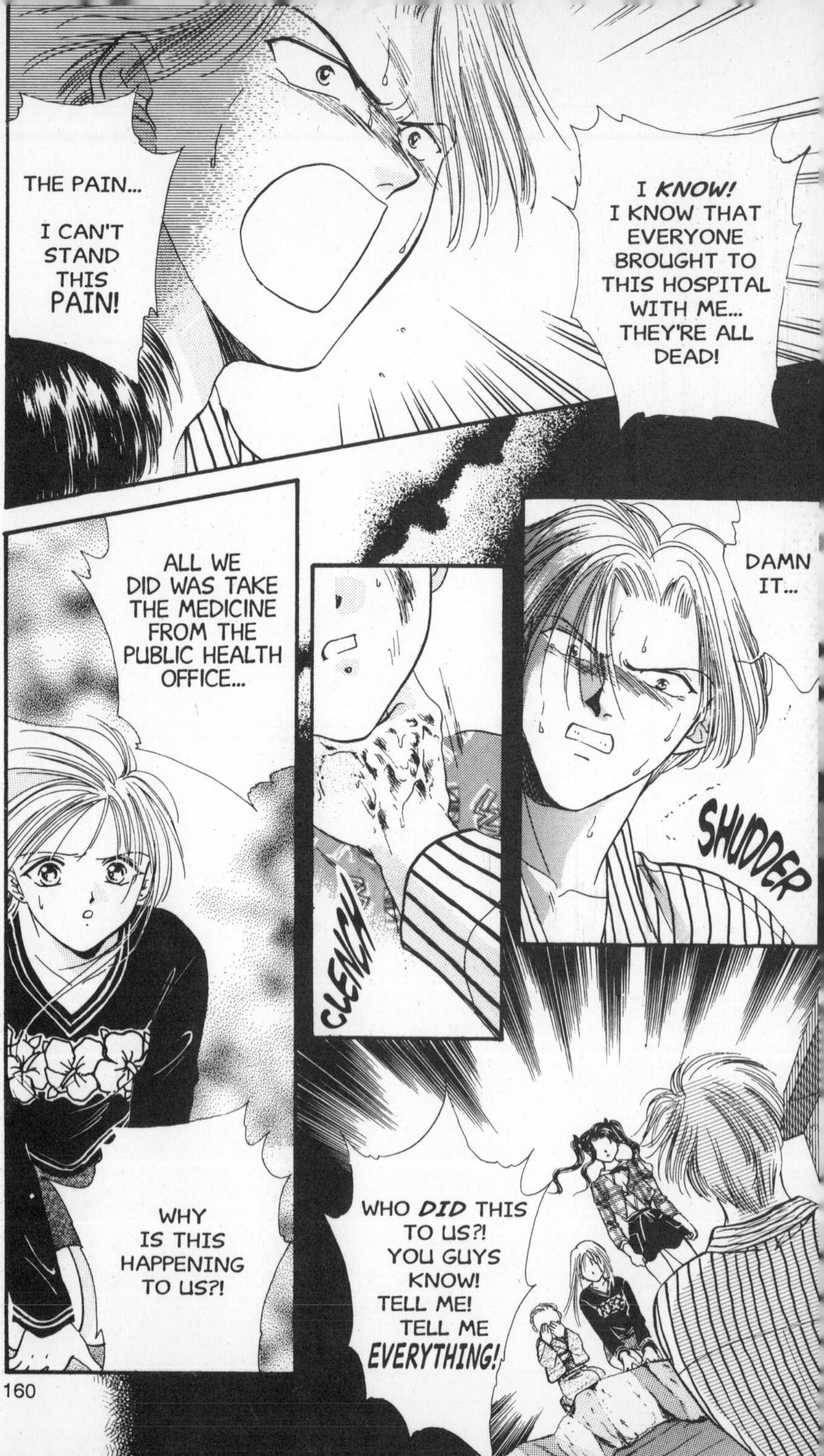
I KNOW! I KNOW THAT EVERYONE BROUGHT TO THIS HOSPITAL WITH ME... THEY'RE ALL DEAD!
THE PAIN...
I CAN'T STAND THIS PAIN!
DAMN IT...
SHUDDER
CLENCH
WHO DID THIS TO US?! YOU GUYS KNOW! TELL ME! TELL ME EVERYTHING!
ALL WE DID WAS TAKE THE MEDICINE FROM THE PUBLIC HEALTH OFFICE...
WHY IS THIS HAPPENING TO US?!

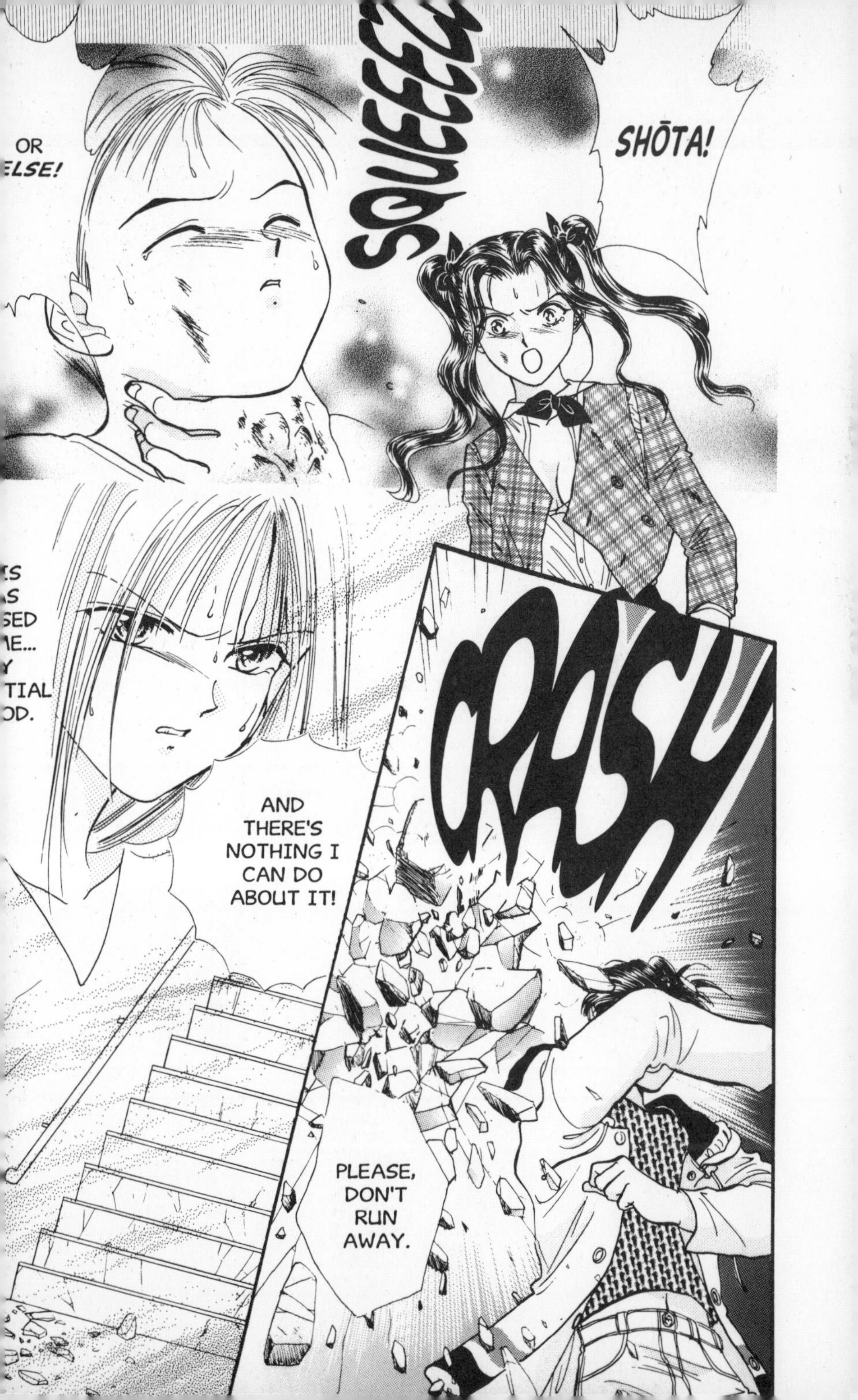
SHŌTA!
SQUEEEE
OR ELSE!
CRASH
AND THERE'S NOTHING I CAN DO ABOUT IT!
PLEASE, DON'T RUN AWAY.

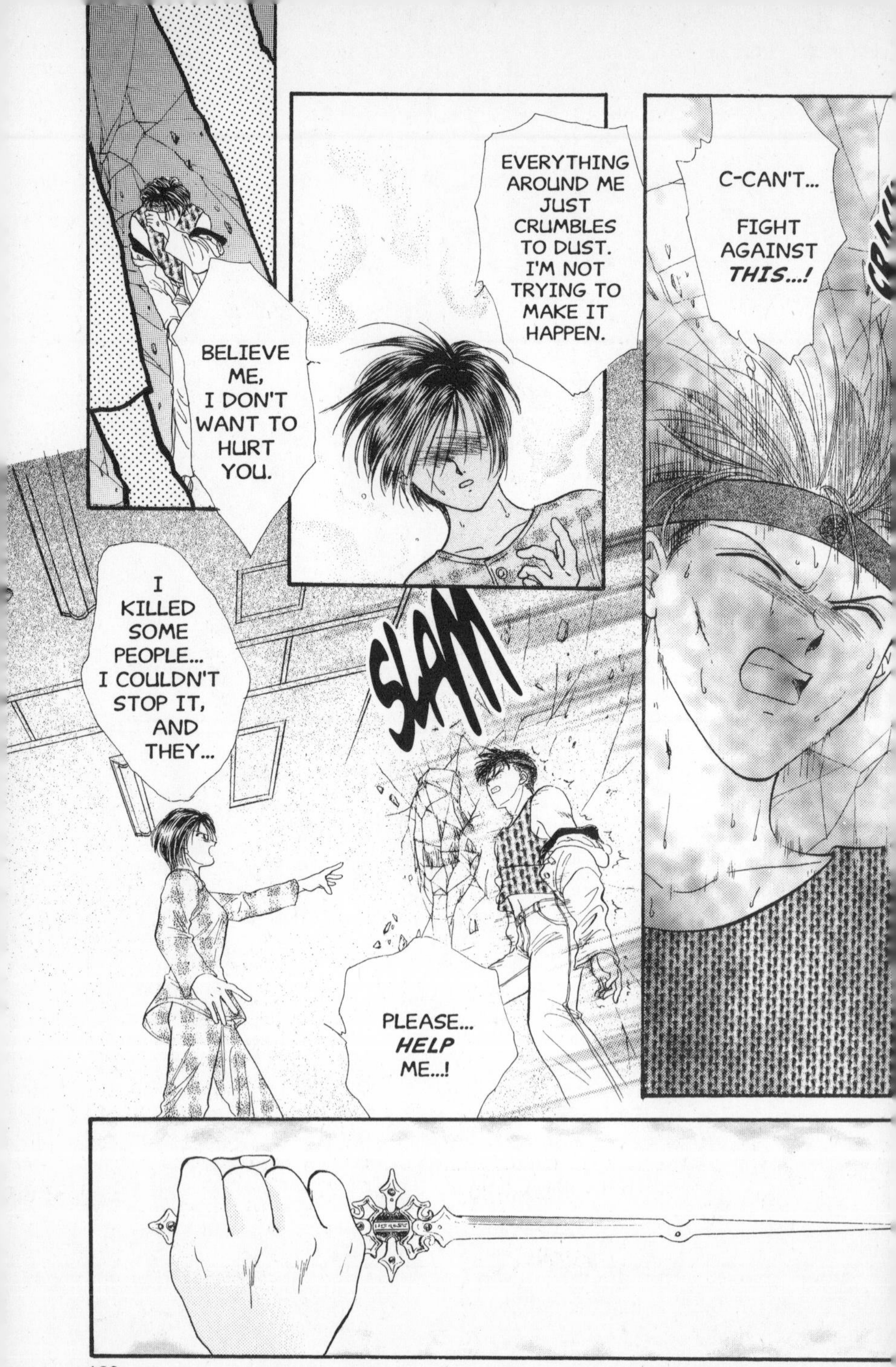
C-CAN'T... FIGHT AGAINST *THIS...!*
EVERYTHING AROUND ME JUST CRUMBLES TO DUST. I'M NOT TRYING TO MAKE IT HAPPEN.
BELIEVE ME, I DON'T WANT TO HURT YOU.
I KILLED SOME PEOPLE... I COULDN'T STOP IT, AND THEY...
SLAM
PLEASE... *HELP* ME...!

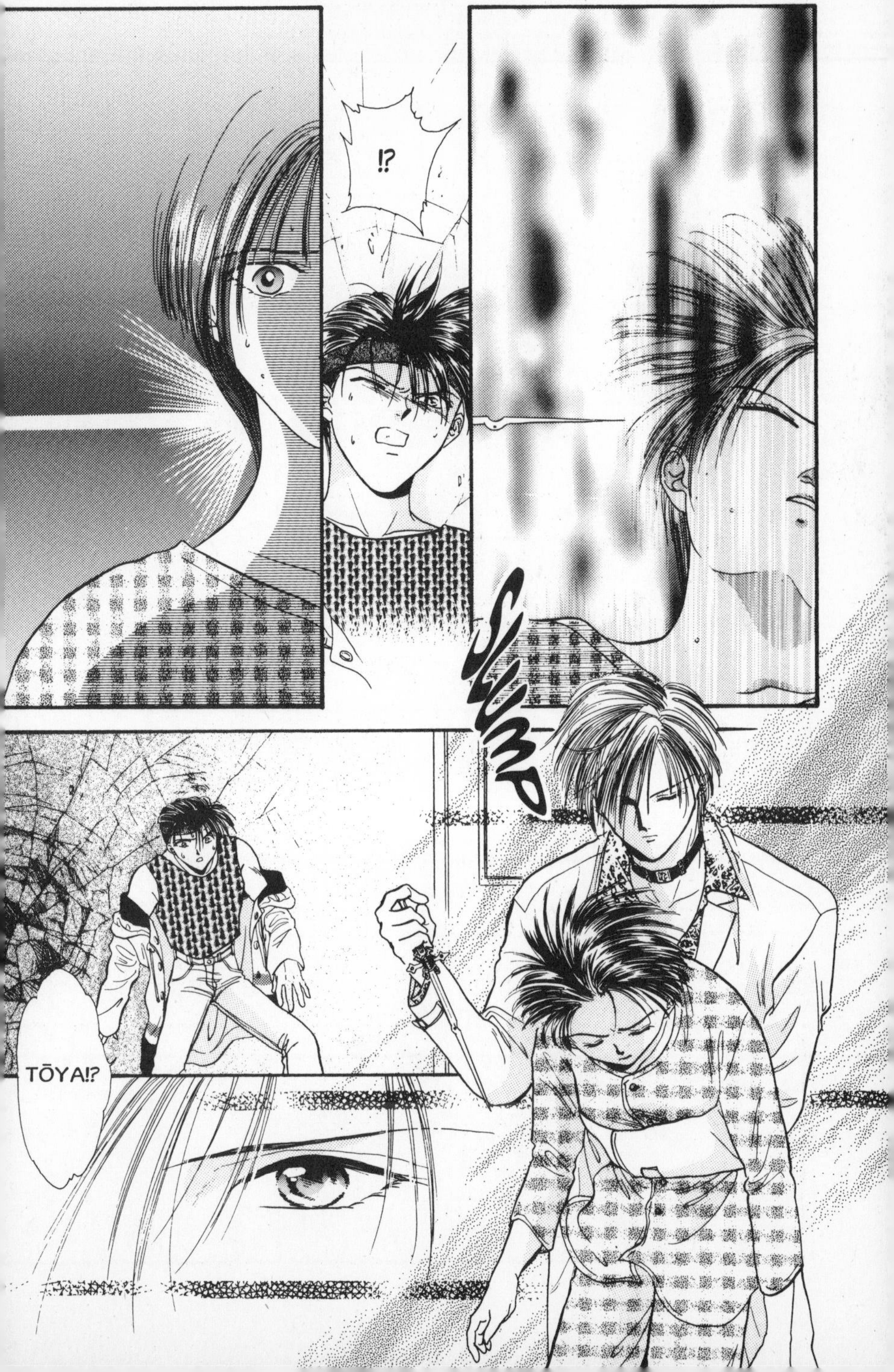
!?
SLUMP
TŌYA!?

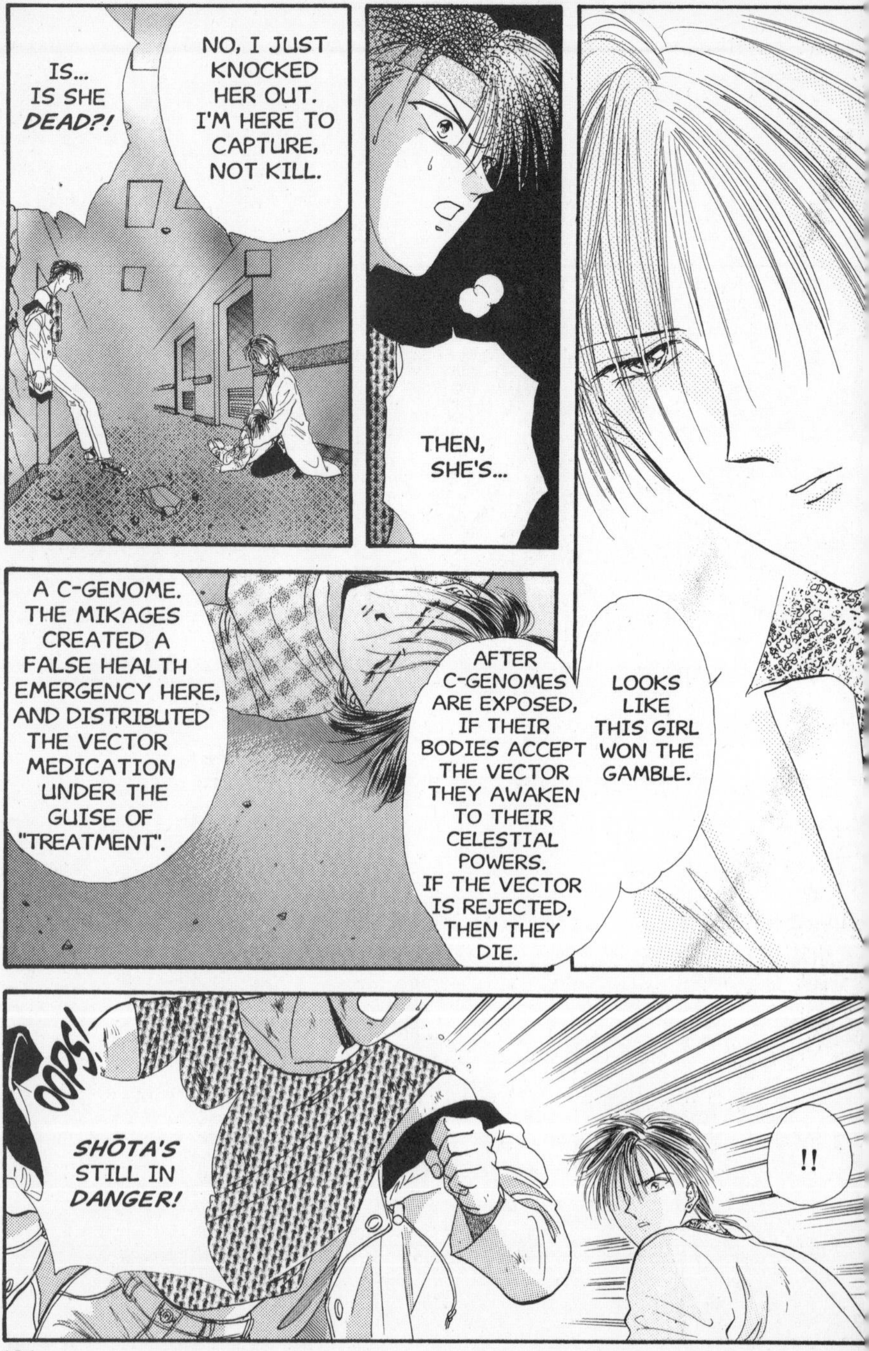
IS... IS SHE *DEAD?!*
NO, I JUST KNOCKED HER OUT. I'M HERE TO CAPTURE, NOT KILL.
THEN, SHE'S...
A C-GENOME. THE MIKAGES CREATED A FALSE HEALTH EMERGENCY HERE, AND DISTRIBUTED THE VECTOR MEDICATION UNDER THE GUISE OF "TREATMENT".
AFTER C-GENOMES ARE EXPOSED, IF THEIR BODIES ACCEPT THE VECTOR THEY AWAKEN TO THEIR CELESTIAL POWERS. IF THE VECTOR IS REJECTED, THEN THEY DIE.
LOOKS LIKE THIS GIRL WON THE GAMBLE.
OOPS!
SHŌTA'S STILL IN *DANGER!*
!!

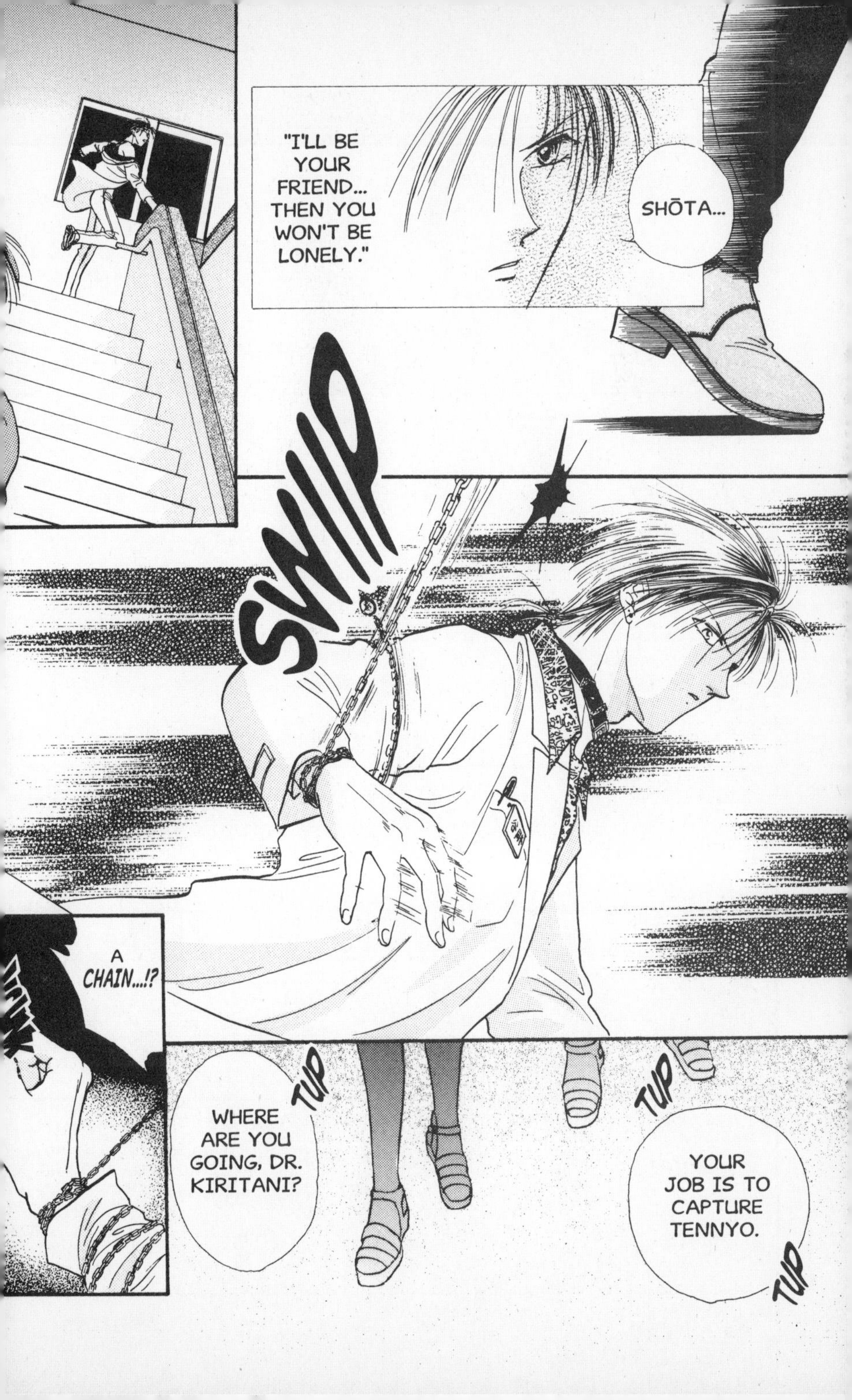
SHŌTA...
"I'LL BE YOUR FRIEND... THEN YOU WON'T BE LONELY."
SWIP
TUP
WHERE ARE YOU GOING, DR. KIRITANI?
TUP
YOUR JOB IS TO CAPTURE TENNYO.
TUP
A CHAIN...!?

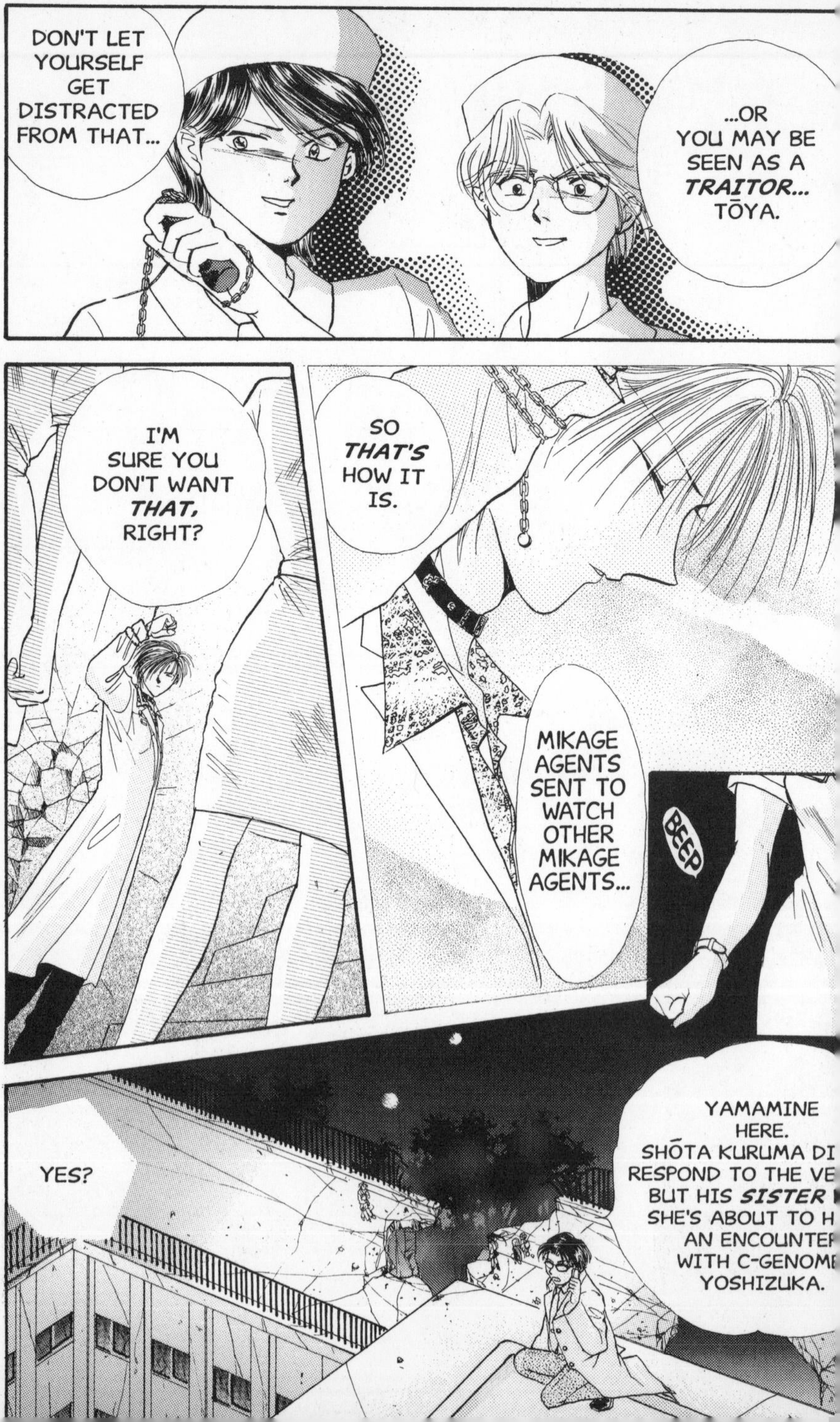
DON'T LET YOURSELF GET DISTRACTED FROM THAT...
...OR YOU MAY BE SEEN AS A *TRAITOR...* TŌYA.
I'M SURE YOU DON'T WANT *THAT,* RIGHT?
SO *THAT'S* HOW IT IS.
MIKAGE AGENTS SENT TO WATCH OTHER MIKAGE AGENTS...
BEEP
YES?
YAMAMINE HERE.
SHŌTA KURUMA DI
RESPOND TO THE VE
BUT HIS *SISTER*
SHE'S ABOUT TO H
AN ENCOUNTER
WITH C-GENOM
YOSHIZUKA.

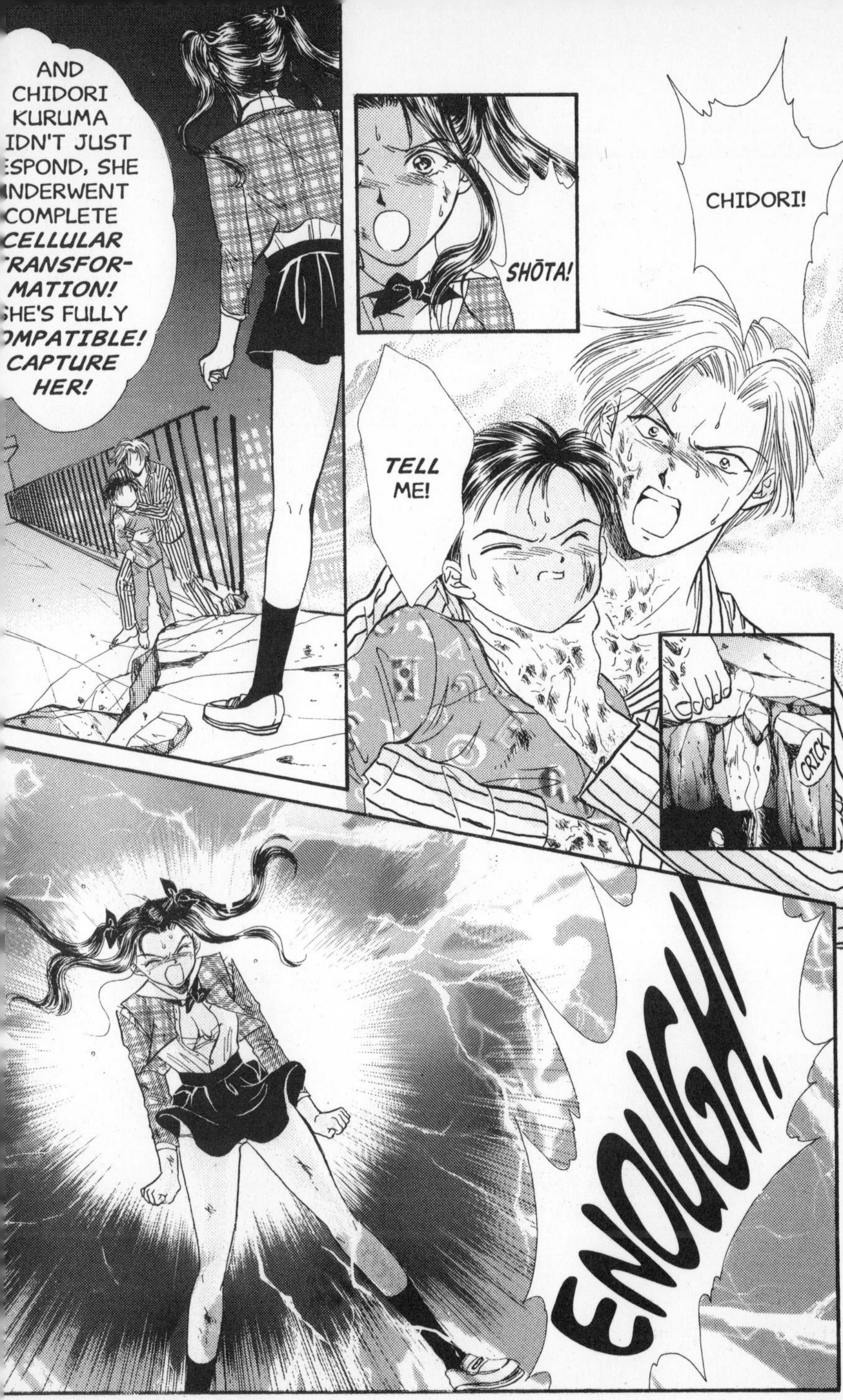
CHIDORI!
SHŌTA!
TELL ME!
CRICK
AND CHIDORI KURUMA IDN'T JUST ESPOND, SHE NDERWENT COMPLETE CELLULAR TRANSFOR-MATION! HE'S FULLY OMPATIBLE! CAPTURE HER!
ENOUGH!

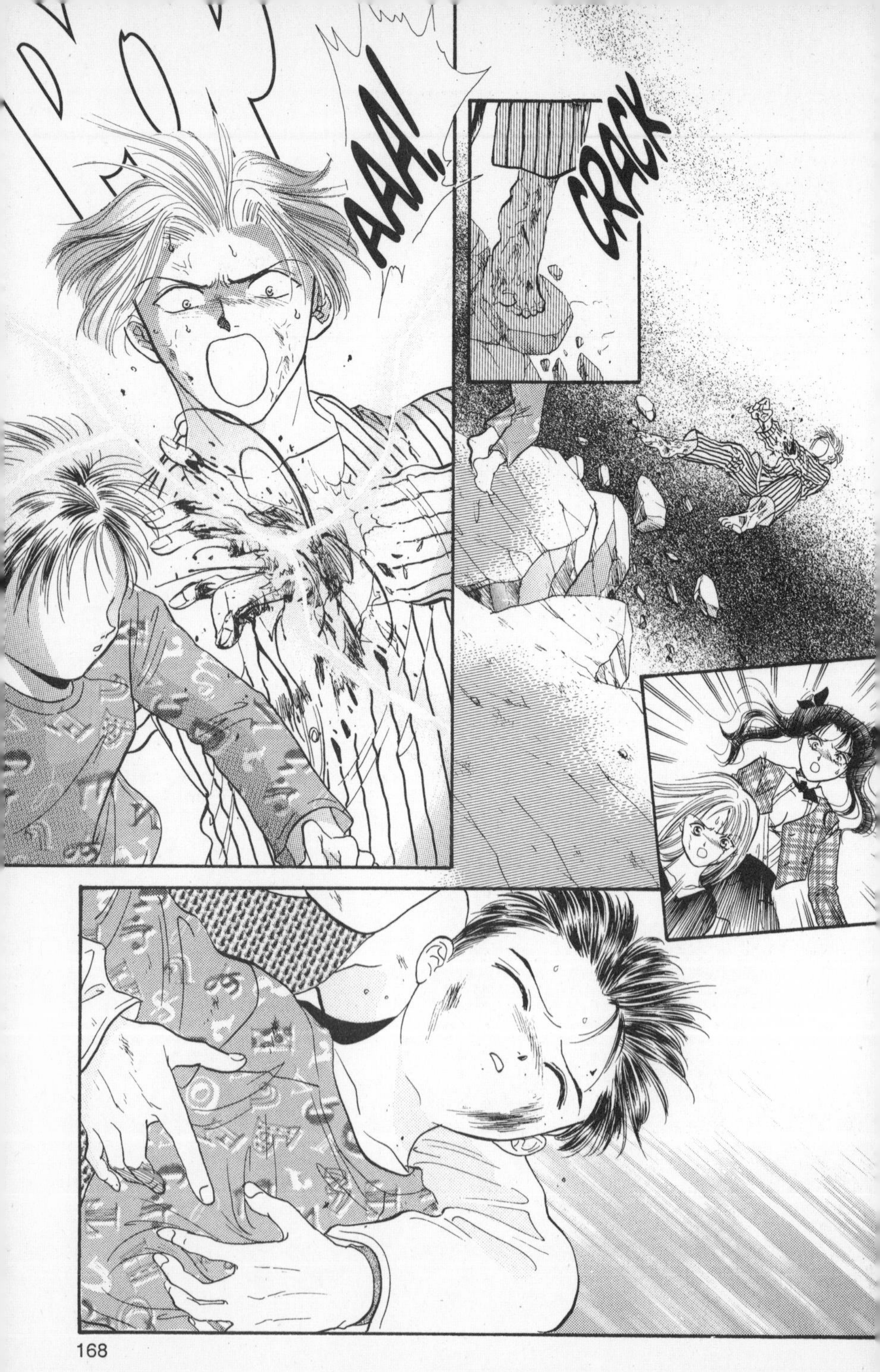
CRACK
AAA!

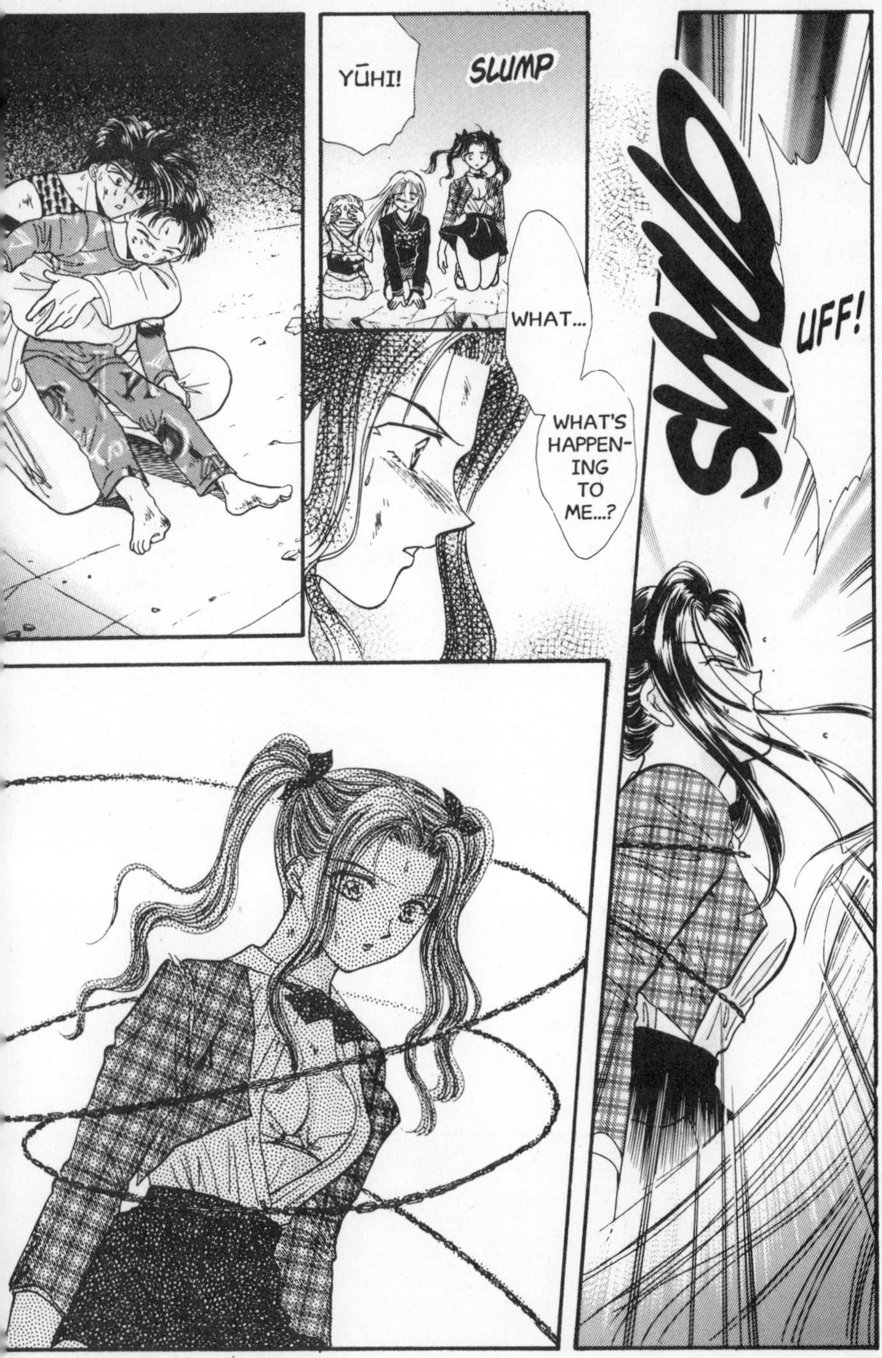
UFF!
YŪHI!
SLUMP
WHAT...
WHAT'S HAPPEN-ING TO ME...?

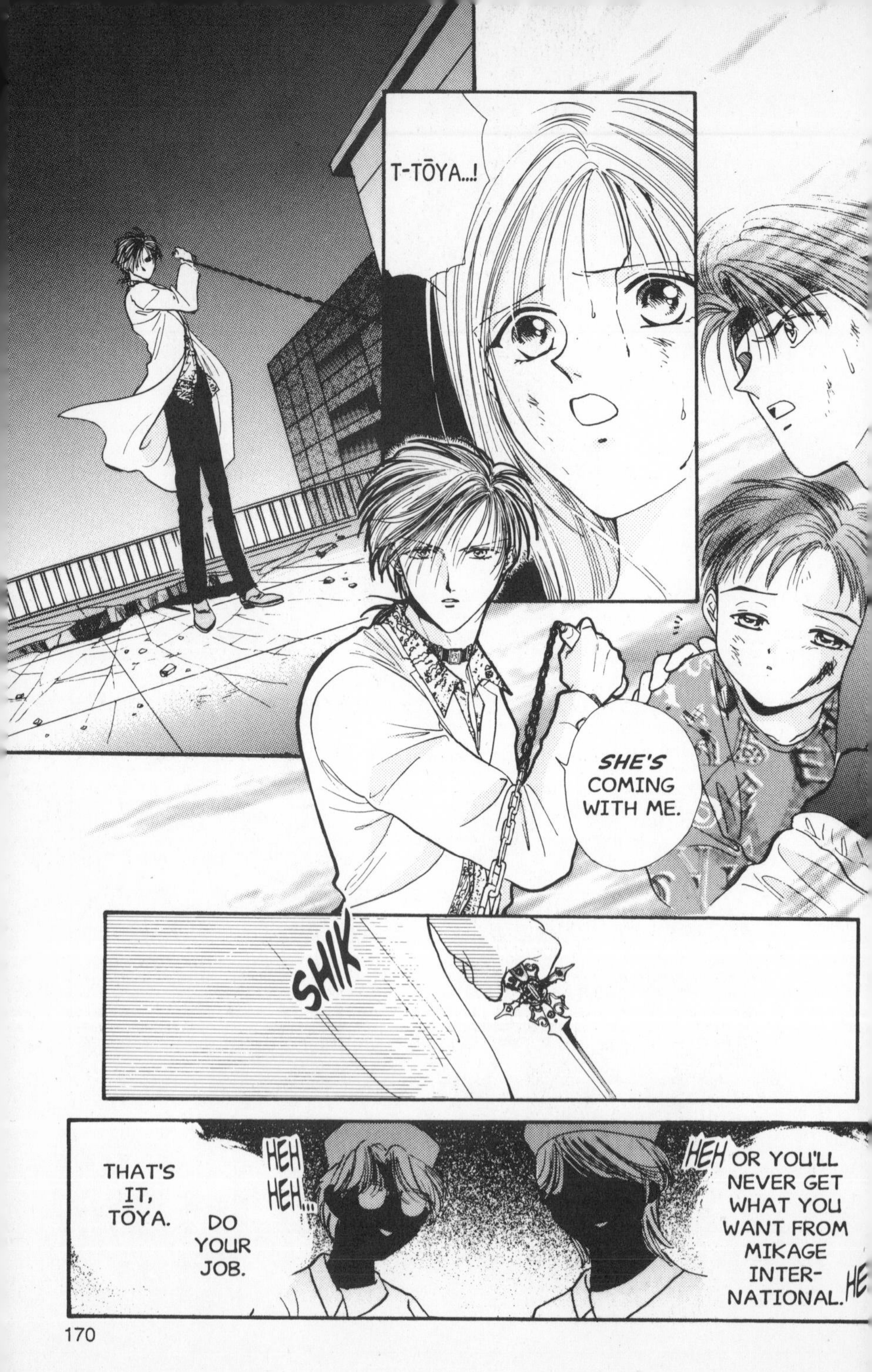
T-TŌYA...!
SHE'S COMING WITH ME.
SHIK
THAT'S IT, TŌYA.
DO YOUR JOB.
HEH HEH...
HEH
OR YOU'LL NEVER GET WHAT YOU WANT FROM MIKAGE INTER-NATIONAL.
HE

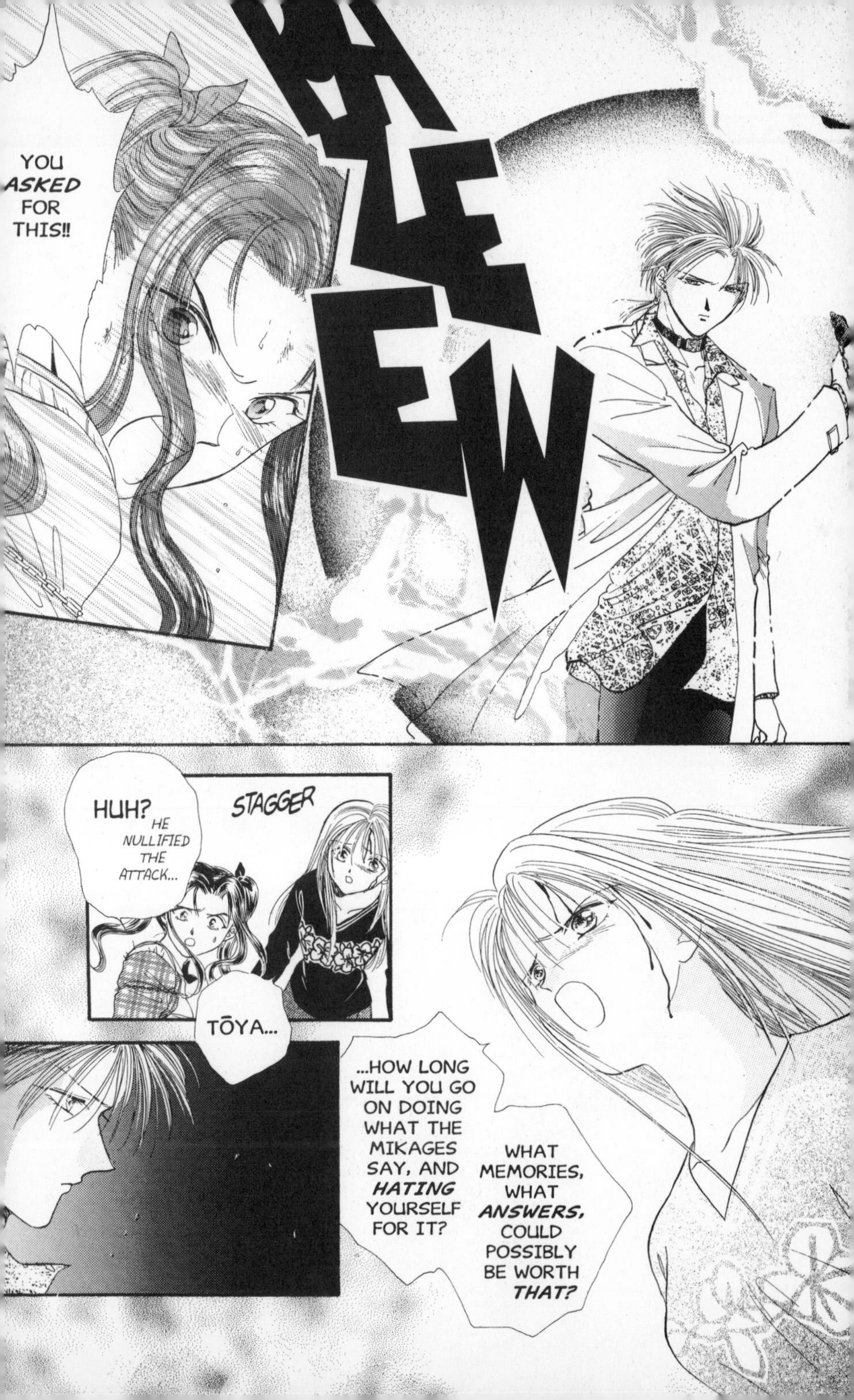
YOU ASKED FOR THIS!!
STAGGER
HUH? HE NULLIFIED THE ATTACK...
TŌYA...
...HOW LONG WILL YOU GO ON DOING WHAT THE MIKAGES SAY, AND HATING YOURSELF FOR IT?
WHAT MEMORIES, WHAT ANSWERS, COULD POSSIBLY BE WORTH THAT?

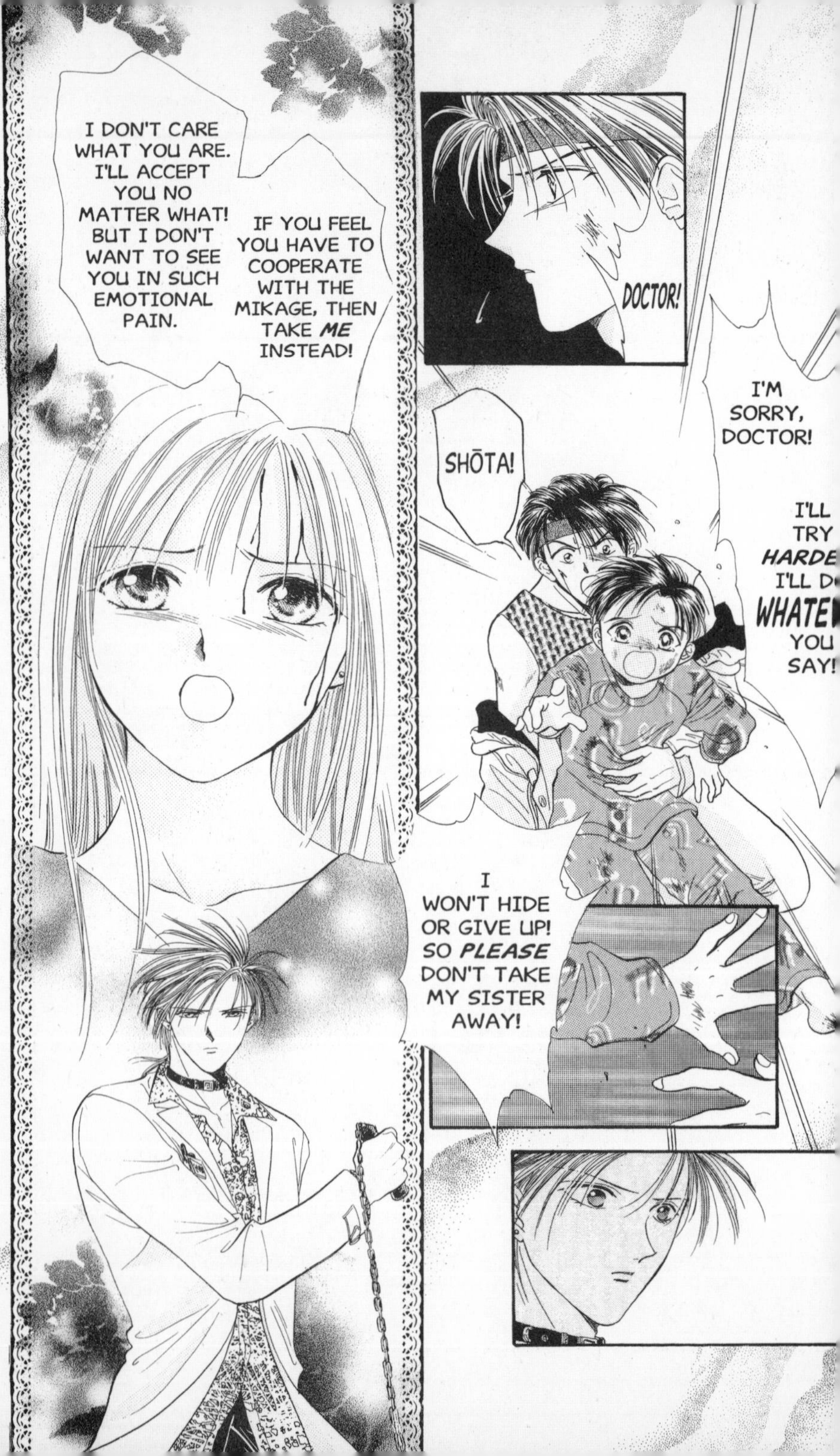
DOCTOR!
I'M SORRY, DOCTOR!
I'LL TRY HARDE I'LL D WHATE YOU SAY!
SHŌTA!
I WON'T HIDE OR GIVE UP! SO *PLEASE* DON'T TAKE MY SISTER AWAY!
I DON'T CARE WHAT YOU ARE. I'LL ACCEPT YOU NO MATTER WHAT! BUT I DON'T WANT TO SEE YOU IN SUCH EMOTIONAL PAIN.
IF YOU FEEL YOU HAVE TO COOPERATE WITH THE MIKAGE, THEN TAKE *ME* INSTEAD!

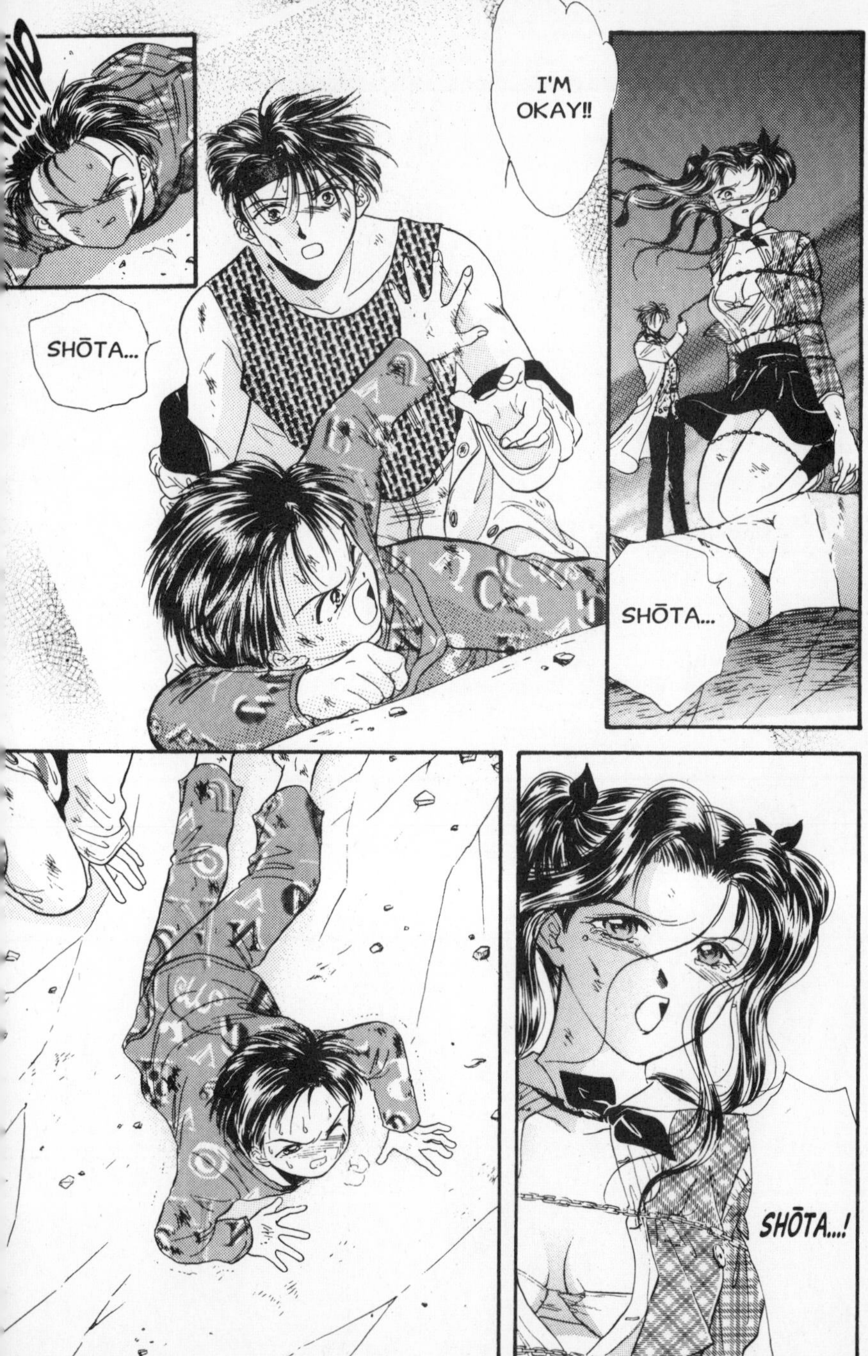
SHŌTA...
I'M OKAY!!
SHŌTA...
SHŌTA...!

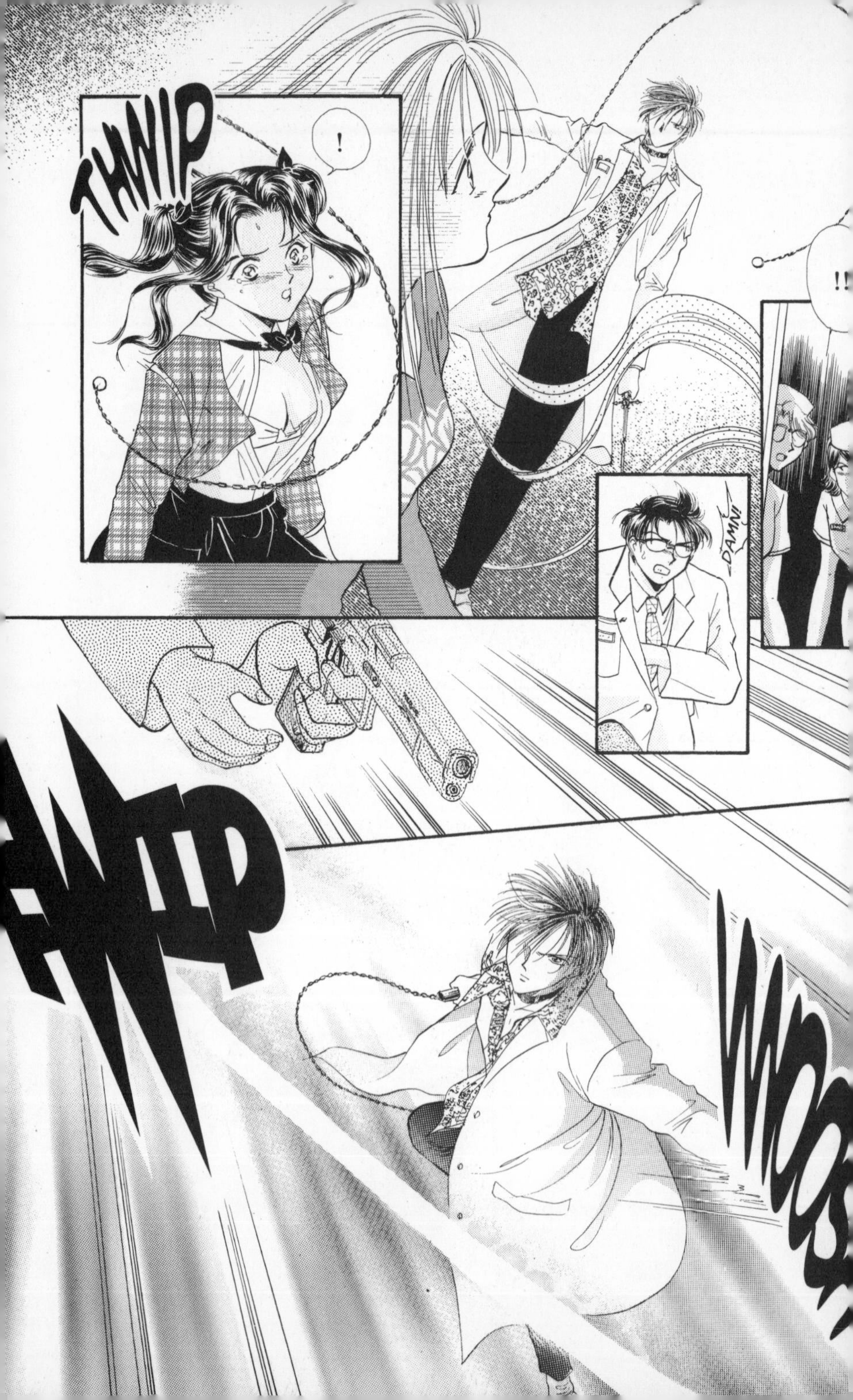

!!
DAMN!
THWIP
!
WHOOSH

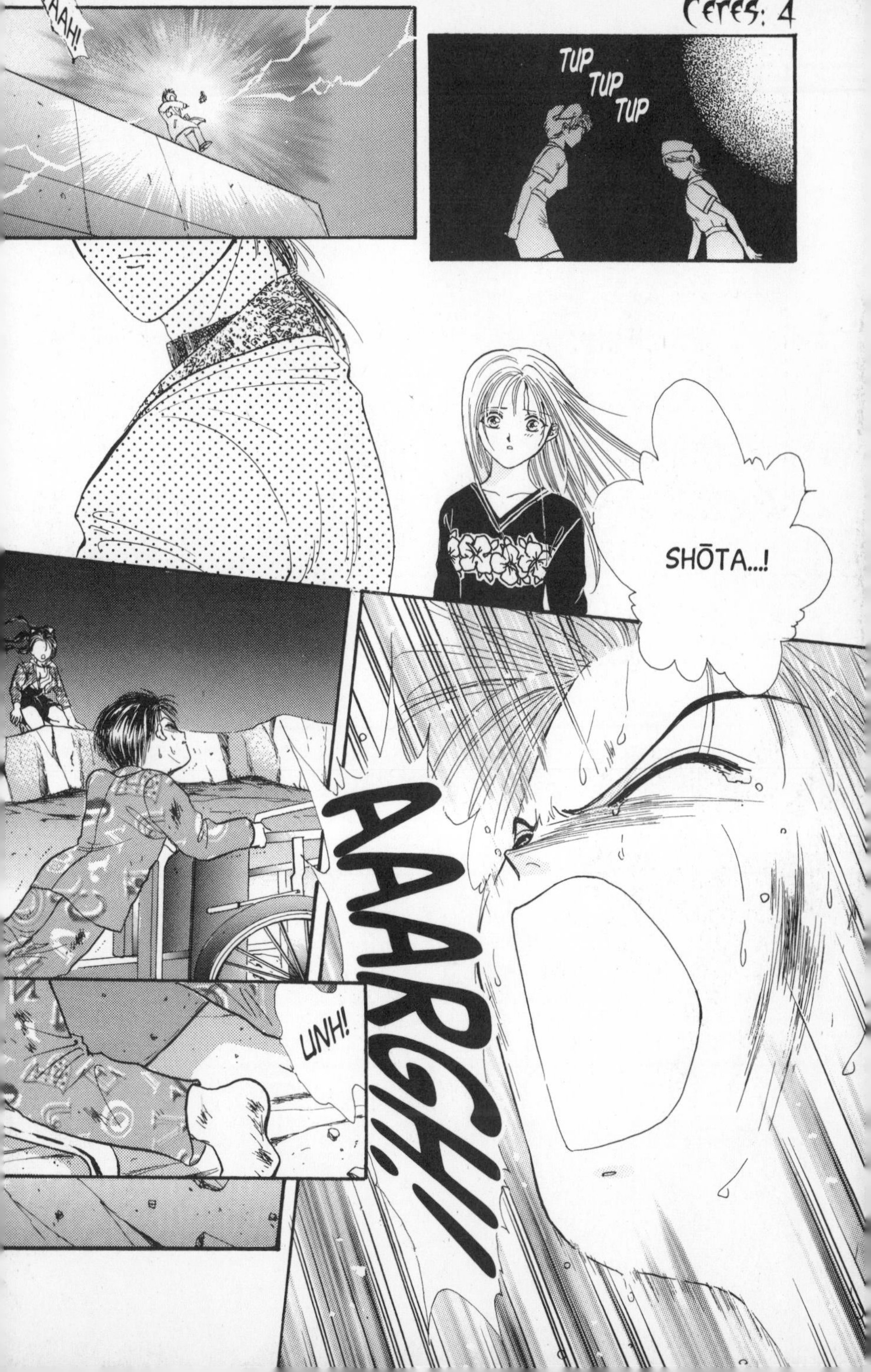
TUP
TUP
TUP
YAAAH!
SHŌTA...!
AAARGH!!
UNH!

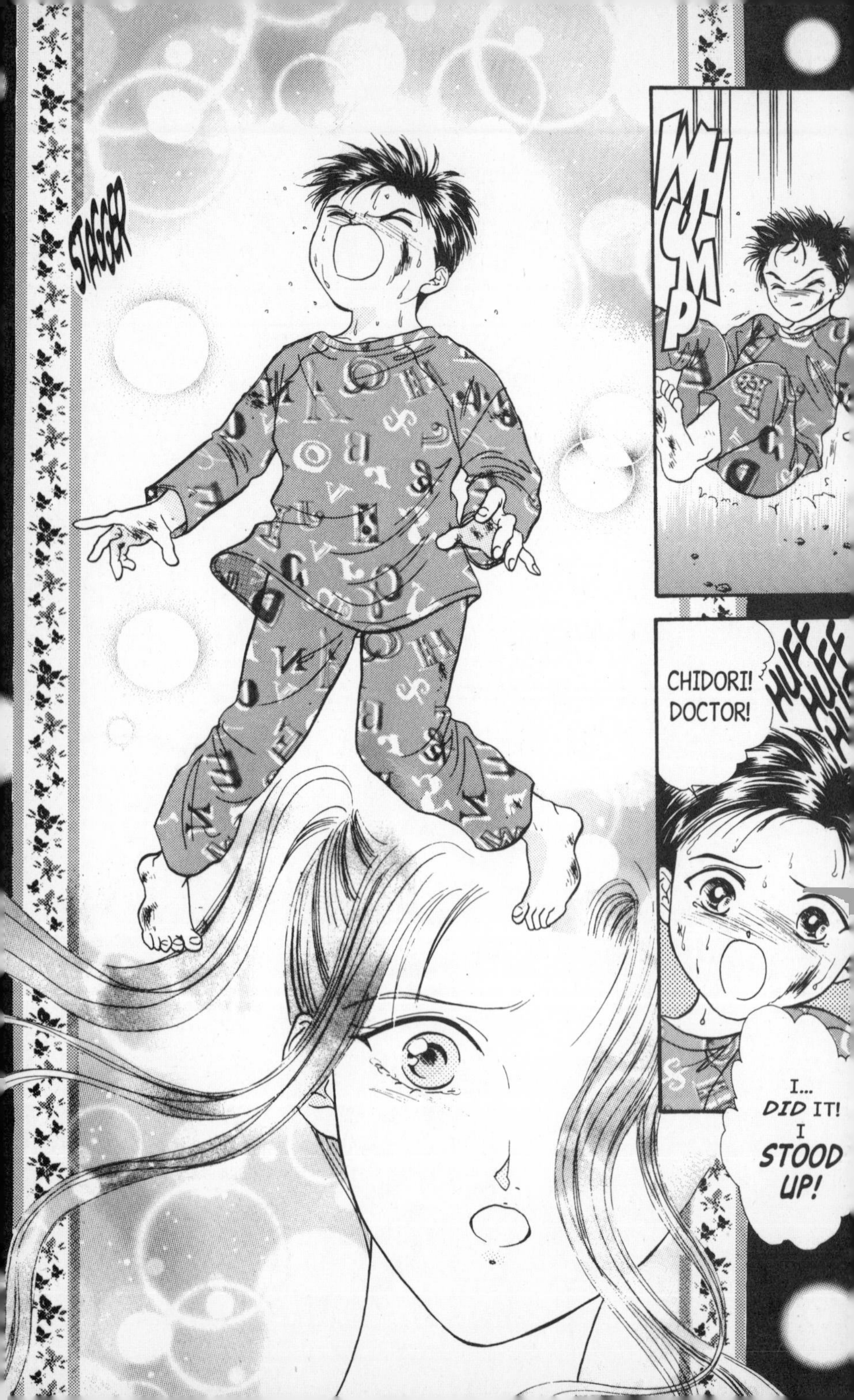
WHUMP
CHIDORI! DOCTOR!
HUFF HUFF
I... DID IT! I STOOD UP!
STAGGER

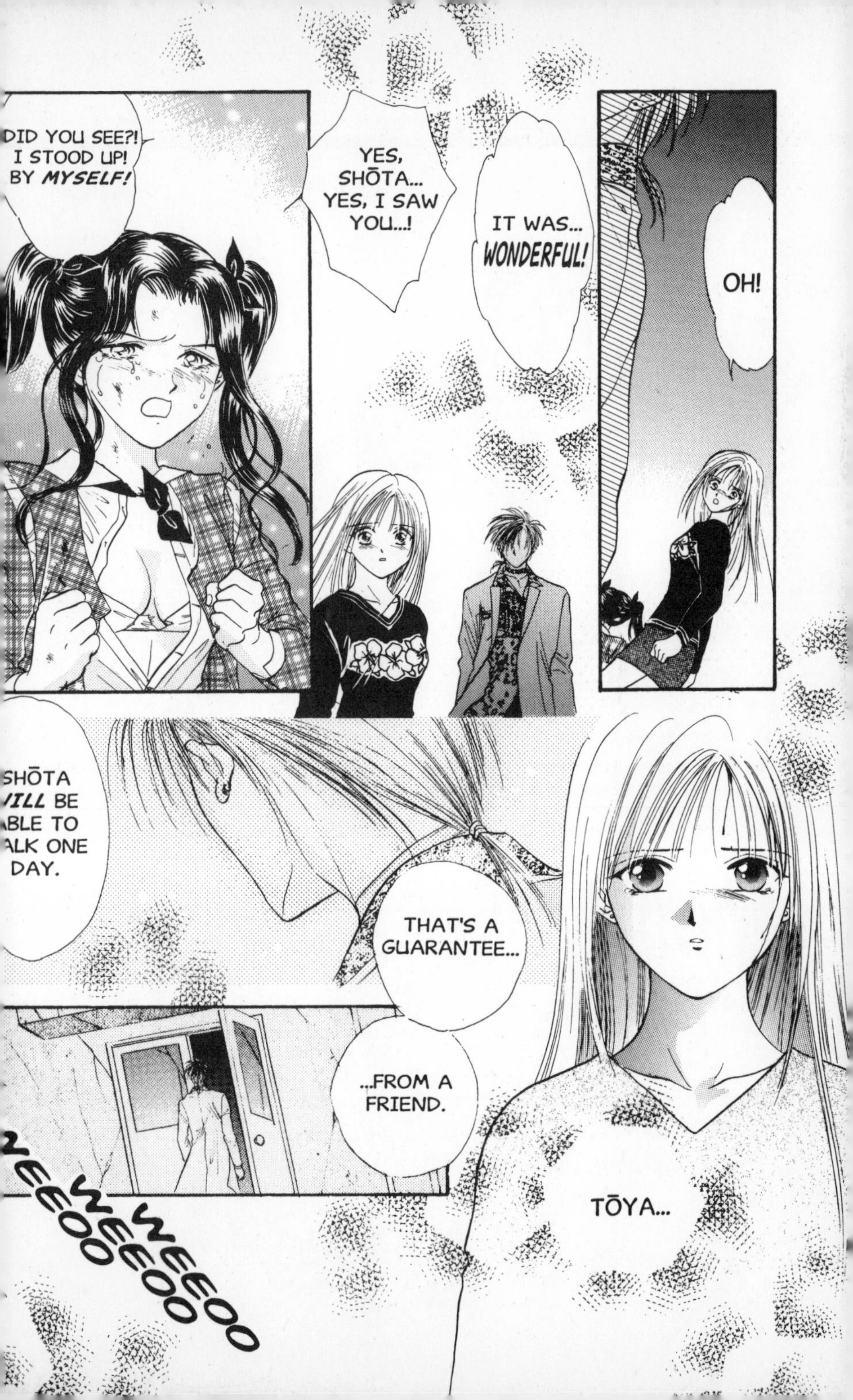
DID YOU SEE?! I STOOD UP! BY *MYSELF!*
YES, SHŌTA... YES, I SAW YOU...!
IT WAS... **WONDERFUL!**
OH!
SHŌTA *VILL* BE BLE TO ALK ONE DAY.
THAT'S A GUARANTEE...
...FROM A FRIEND.
WEEEOO WEEEOO
TŌYA...

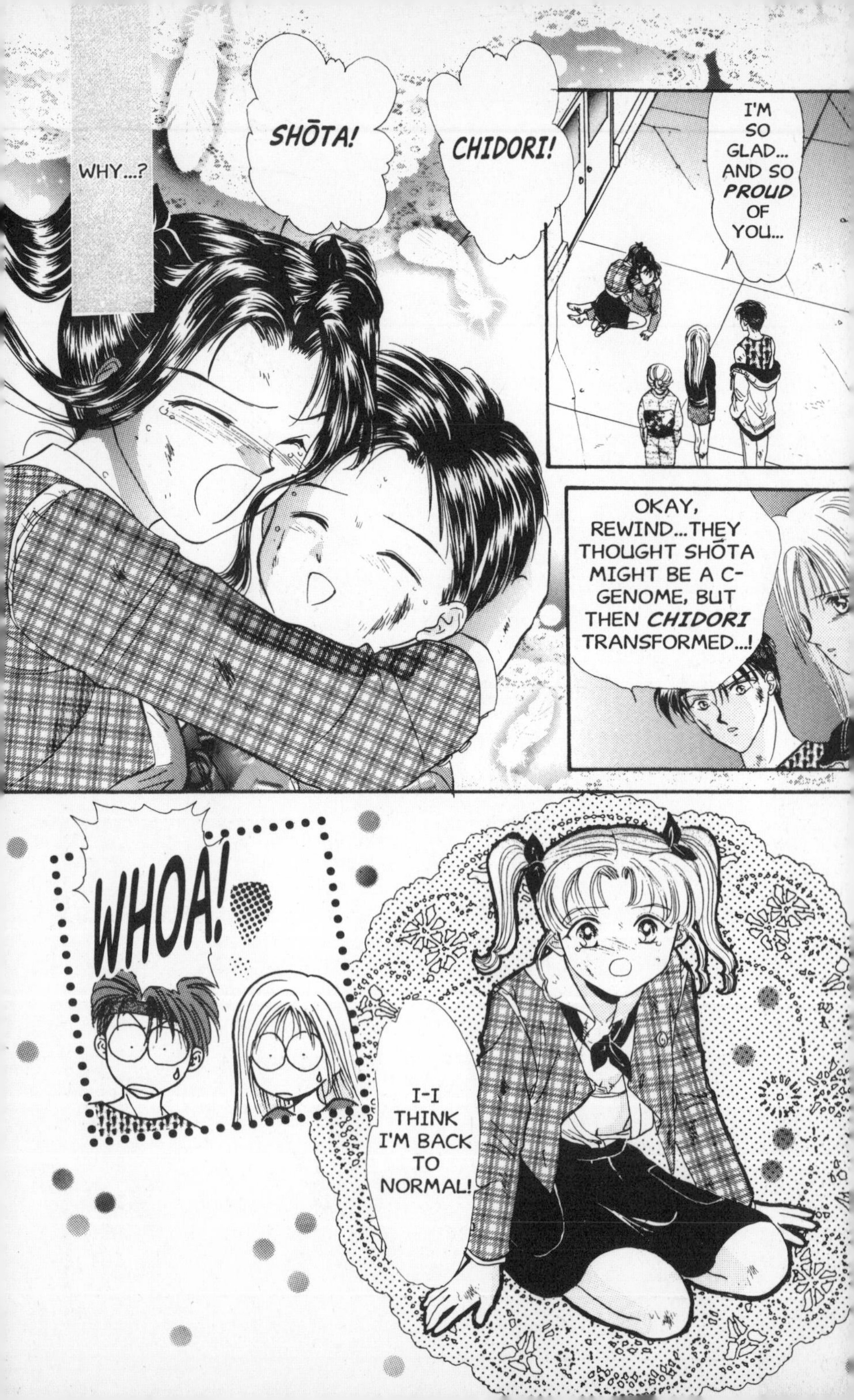
I'M SO GLAD... AND SO PROUD OF YOU...
OKAY, REWIND...THEY THOUGHT SHŌTA MIGHT BE A C-GENOME, BUT THEN CHIDORI TRANSFORMED...!
CHIDORI!
SHŌTA!
WHY...?
I-I THINK I'M BACK TO NORMAL!
WHOA!

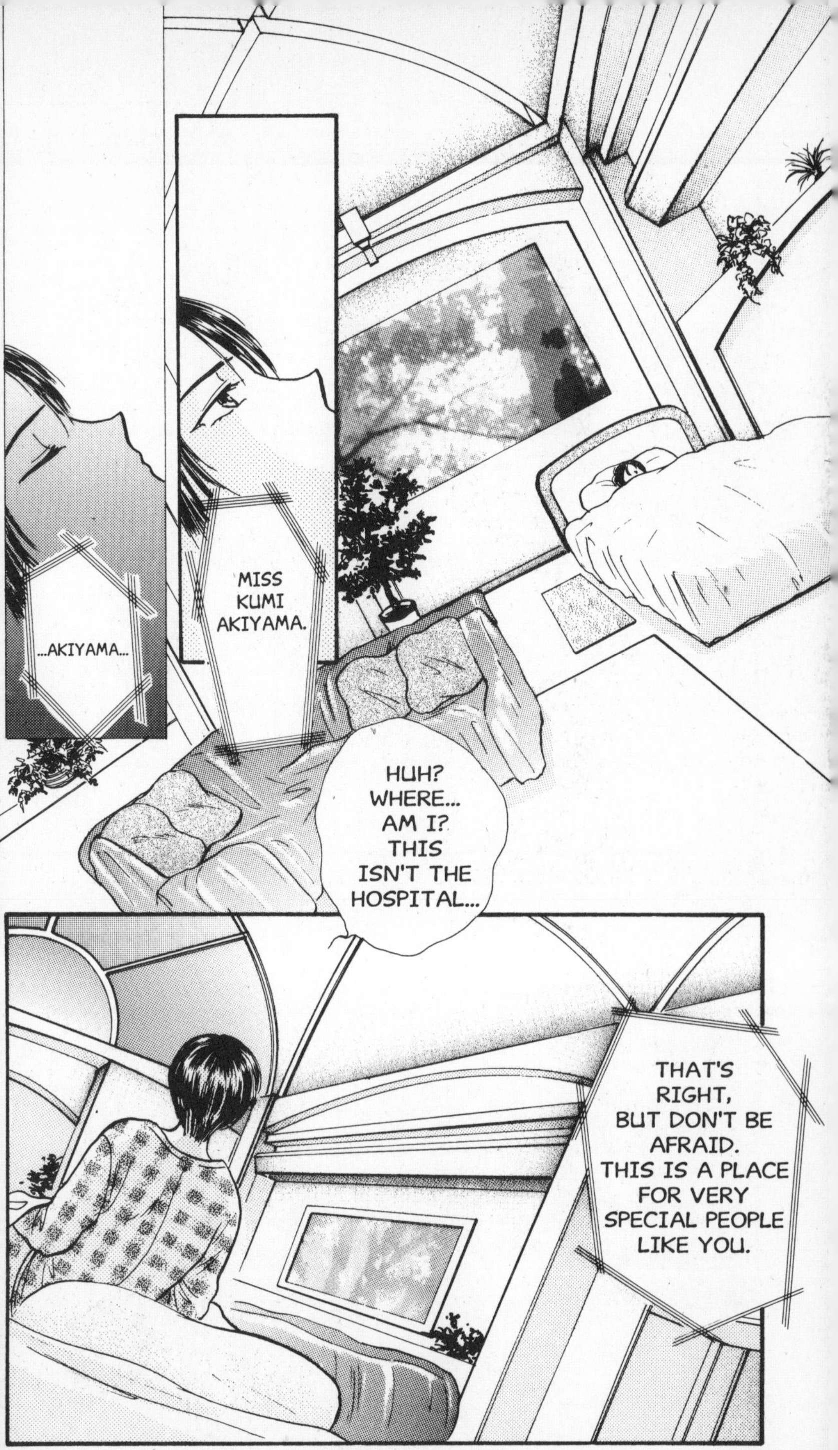
MISS KUMI AKIYAMA.
...AKIYAMA...
HUH? WHERE... AM I? THIS ISN'T THE HOSPITAL...
THAT'S RIGHT, BUT DON'T BE AFRAID. THIS IS A PLACE FOR VERY SPECIAL PEOPLE LIKE YOU.

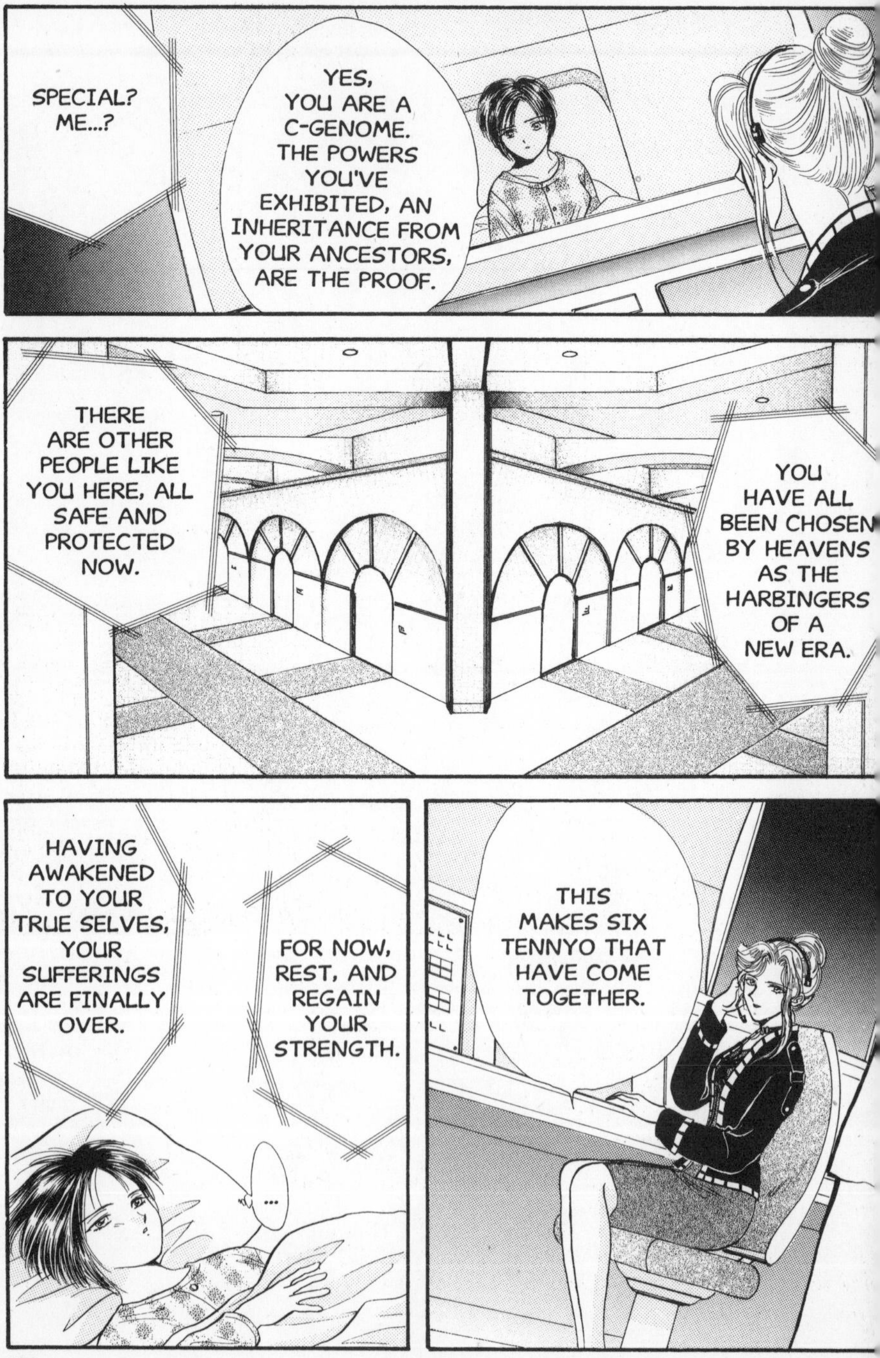
SPECIAL? ME...?
YES, YOU ARE A C-GENOME. THE POWERS YOU'VE EXHIBITED, AN INHERITANCE FROM YOUR ANCESTORS, ARE THE PROOF.
THERE ARE OTHER PEOPLE LIKE YOU HERE, ALL SAFE AND PROTECTED NOW.
YOU HAVE ALL BEEN CHOSEN BY HEAVENS AS THE HARBINGERS OF A NEW ERA.
HAVING AWAKENED TO YOUR TRUE SELVES, YOUR SUFFERINGS ARE FINALLY OVER.
FOR NOW, REST, AND REGAIN YOUR STRENGTH.
...
THIS MAKES SIX TENNYO THAT HAVE COME TOGETHER.

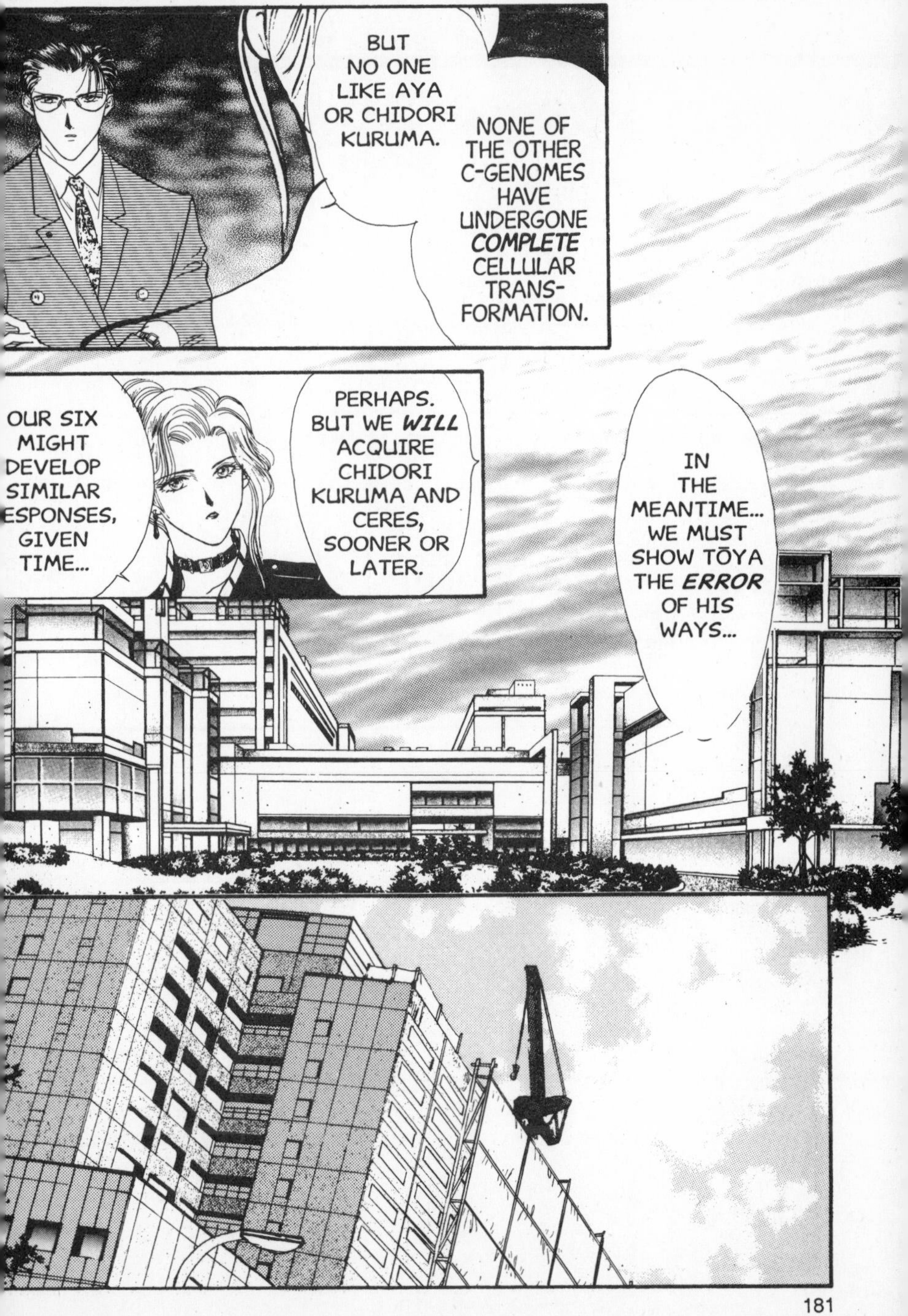
BUT NO ONE LIKE AYA OR CHIDORI KURUMA.
NONE OF THE OTHER C-GENOMES HAVE UNDERGONE ***COMPLETE*** CELLULAR TRANS-FORMATION.
OUR SIX MIGHT DEVELOP SIMILAR ESPONSES, GIVEN TIME...
PERHAPS. BUT WE ***WILL*** ACQUIRE CHIDORI KURUMA AND CERES, SOONER OR LATER.
IN THE MEANTIME... WE MUST SHOW TŌYA THE ***ERROR*** OF HIS WAYS...

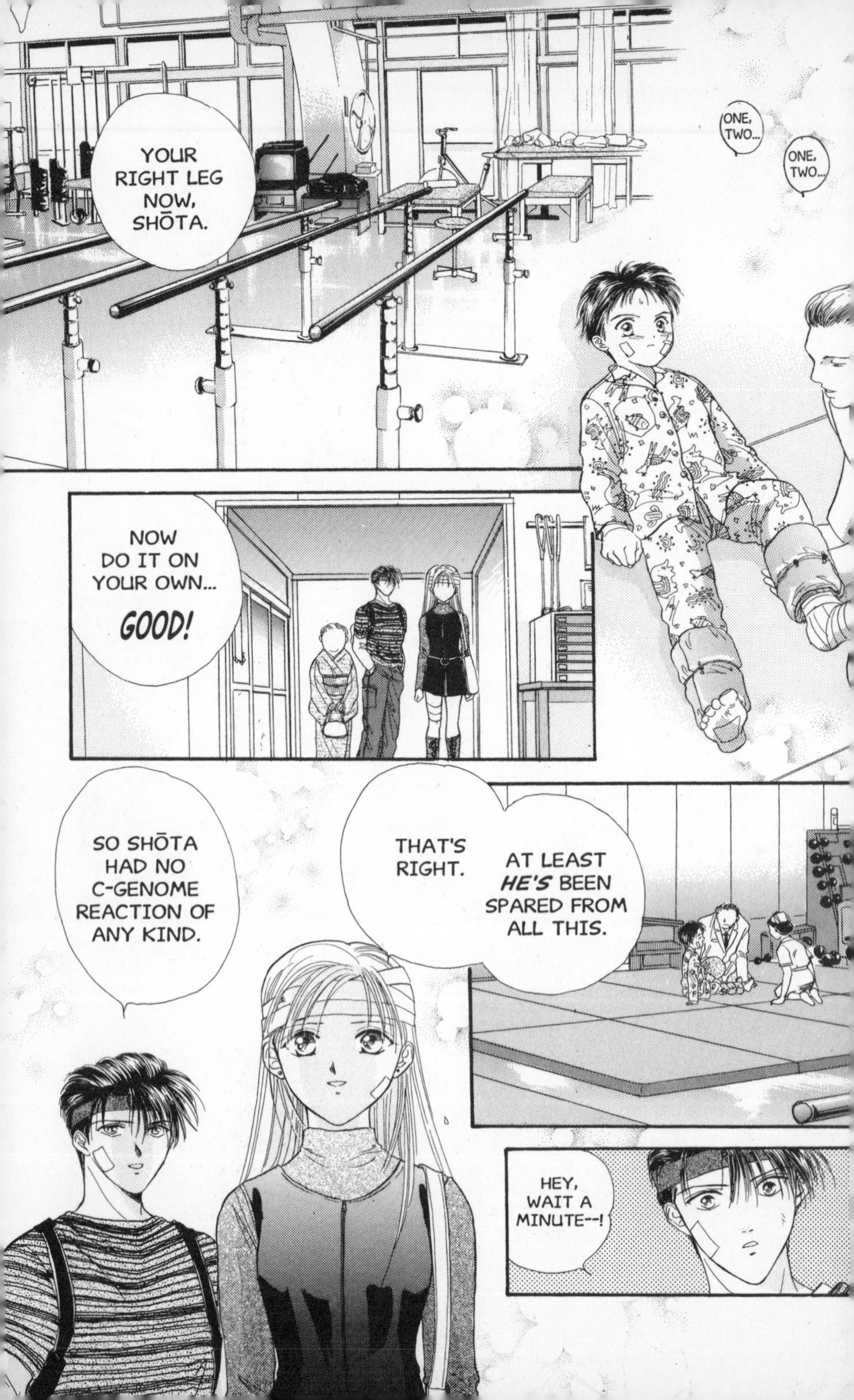
ONE, TWO...
ONE, TWO...
YOUR RIGHT LEG NOW, SHŌTA.
NOW DO IT ON YOUR OWN... GOOD!
SO SHŌTA HAD NO C-GENOME REACTION OF ANY KIND.
THAT'S RIGHT.
AT LEAST HE'S BEEN SPARED FROM ALL THIS.
HEY, WAIT A MINUTE--!

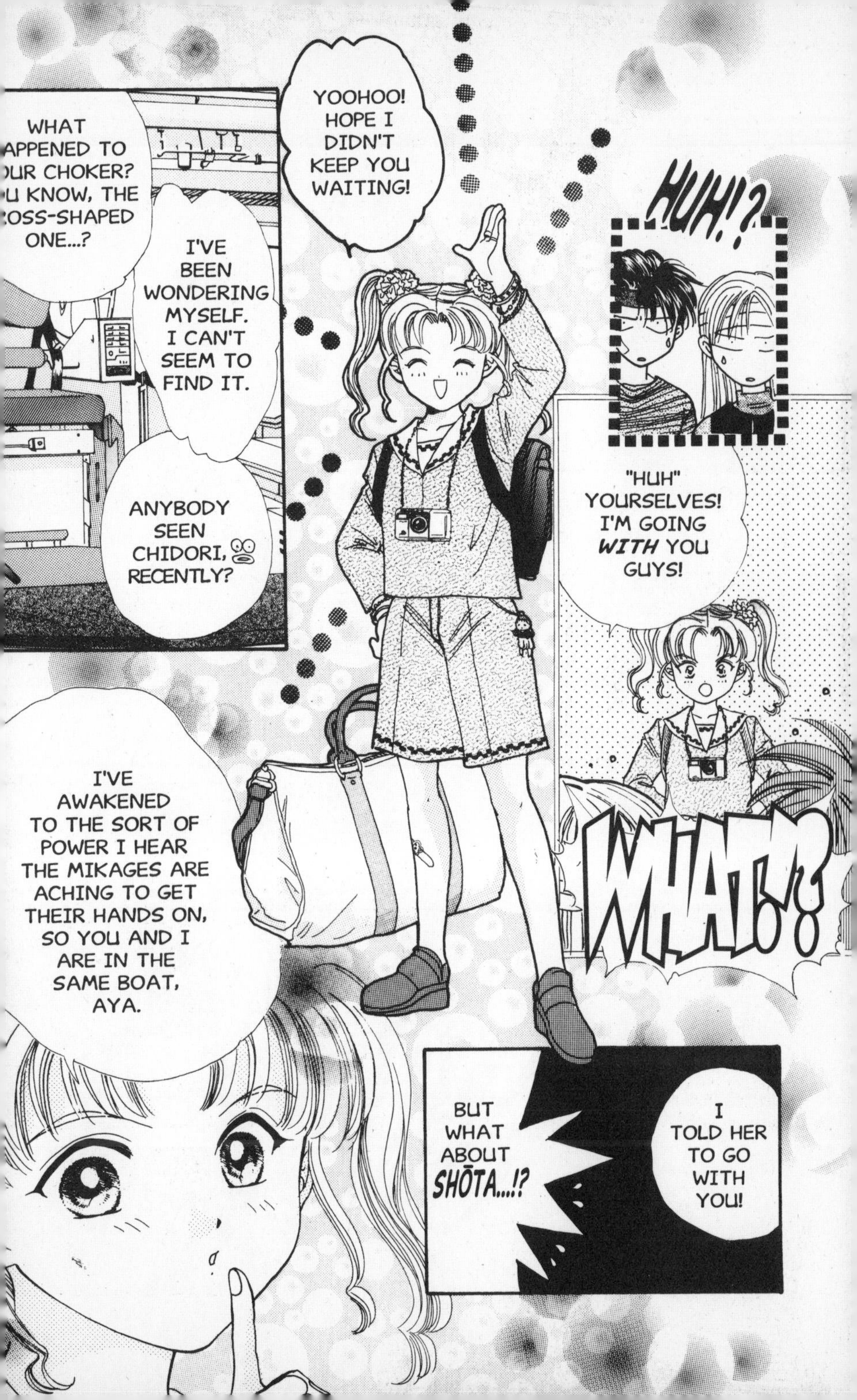
YOOHOO! HOPE I DIDN'T KEEP YOU WAITING!
HUH!?
"HUH" YOURSELVES! I'M GOING *WITH* YOU GUYS!
WHAT!?
WHAT APPENED TO UR CHOKER? U KNOW, THE OSS-SHAPED ONE...?
I'VE BEEN WONDERING MYSELF. I CAN'T SEEM TO FIND IT.
ANYBODY SEEN CHIDORI, RECENTLY?
BUT WHAT ABOUT SHŌTA...!?
I TOLD HER TO GO WITH YOU!
I'VE AWAKENED TO THE SORT OF POWER I HEAR THE MIKAGES ARE ACHING TO GET THEIR HANDS ON, SO YOU AND I ARE IN THE SAME BOAT, AYA.

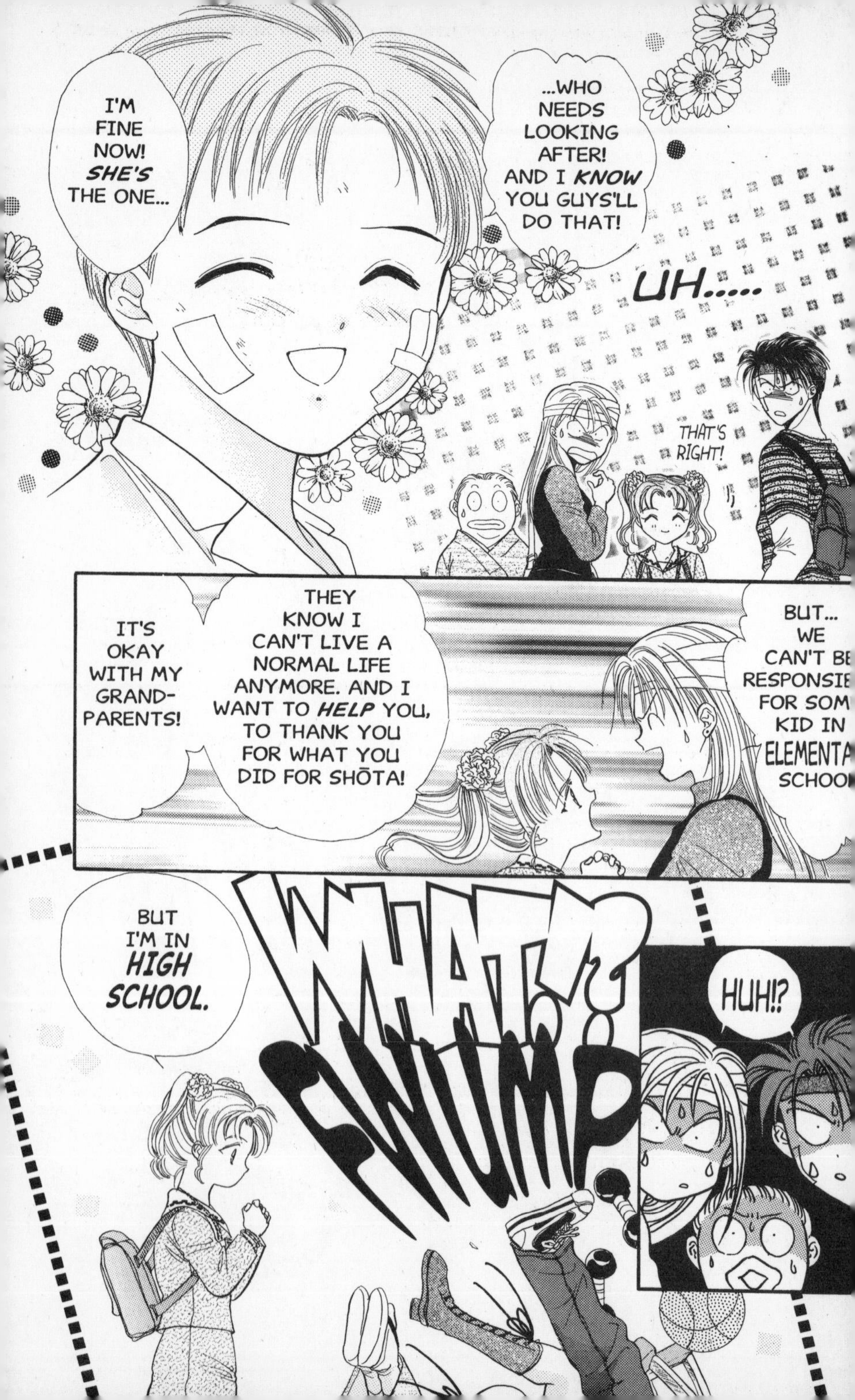
I'M FINE NOW! *SHE'S* THE ONE...
...WHO NEEDS LOOKING AFTER! AND I *KNOW* YOU GUYS'LL DO THAT!
UH.....
THAT'S RIGHT!
IT'S OKAY WITH MY GRAND-PARENTS!
THEY KNOW I CAN'T LIVE A NORMAL LIFE ANYMORE. AND I WANT TO *HELP* YOU, TO THANK YOU FOR WHAT YOU DID FOR SHŌTA!
BUT... WE CAN'T BE RESPONSIB FOR SOM KID IN ELEMENTA SCHOO
BUT I'M IN *HIGH SCHOOL.*
WHAT!?
WHUMP
HUH!?

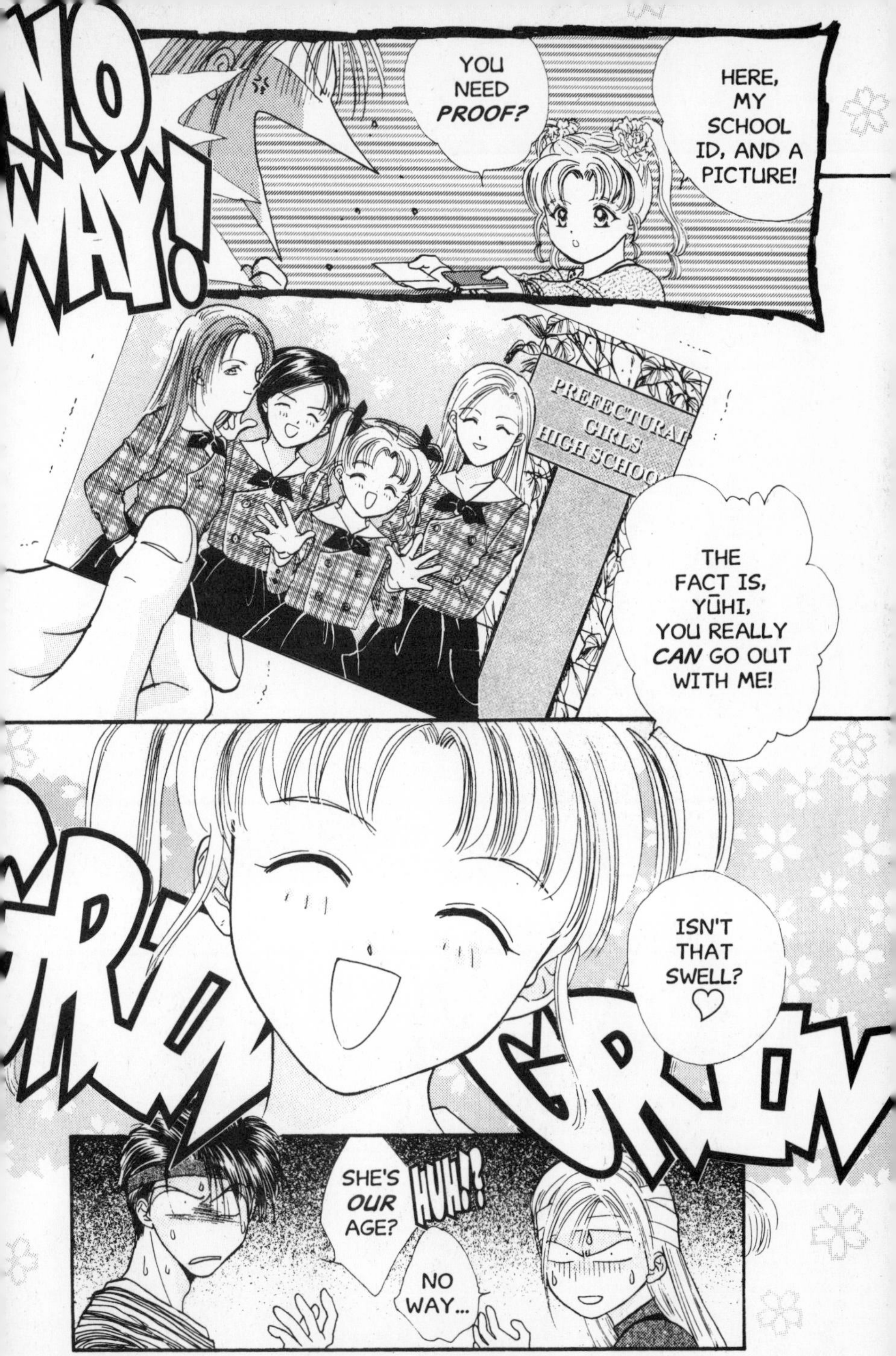
NO WAY!
YOU NEED PROOF?
HERE, MY SCHOOL ID, AND A PICTURE!
PREFECTURAL GIRLS HIGH SCHOOL
THE FACT IS, YŪHI, YOU REALLY CAN GO OUT WITH ME!
GRIN
ISN'T THAT SWELL? ♡
SHE'S OUR AGE?
HUH!?
NO WAY...

TO BE CONTINUED...

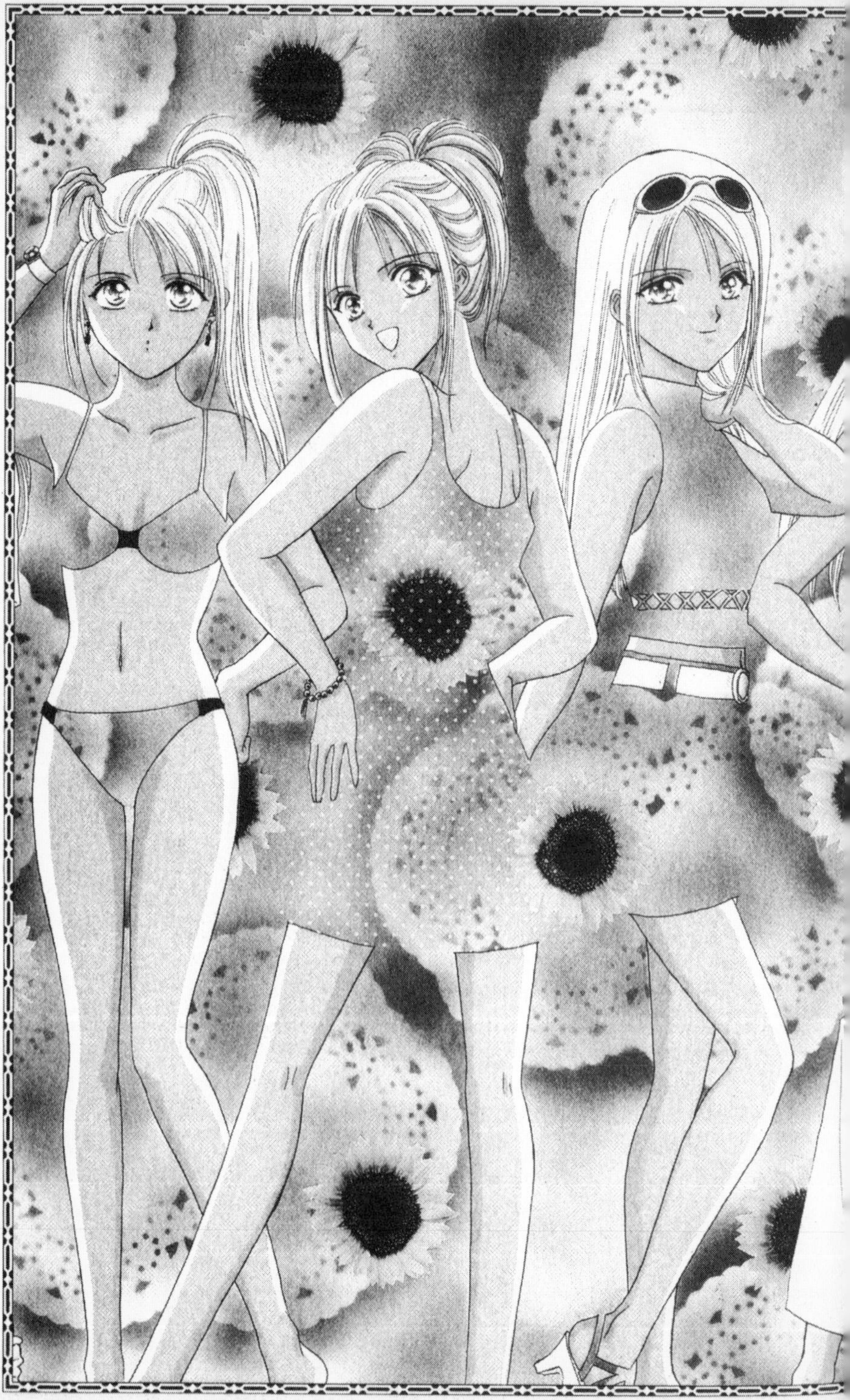

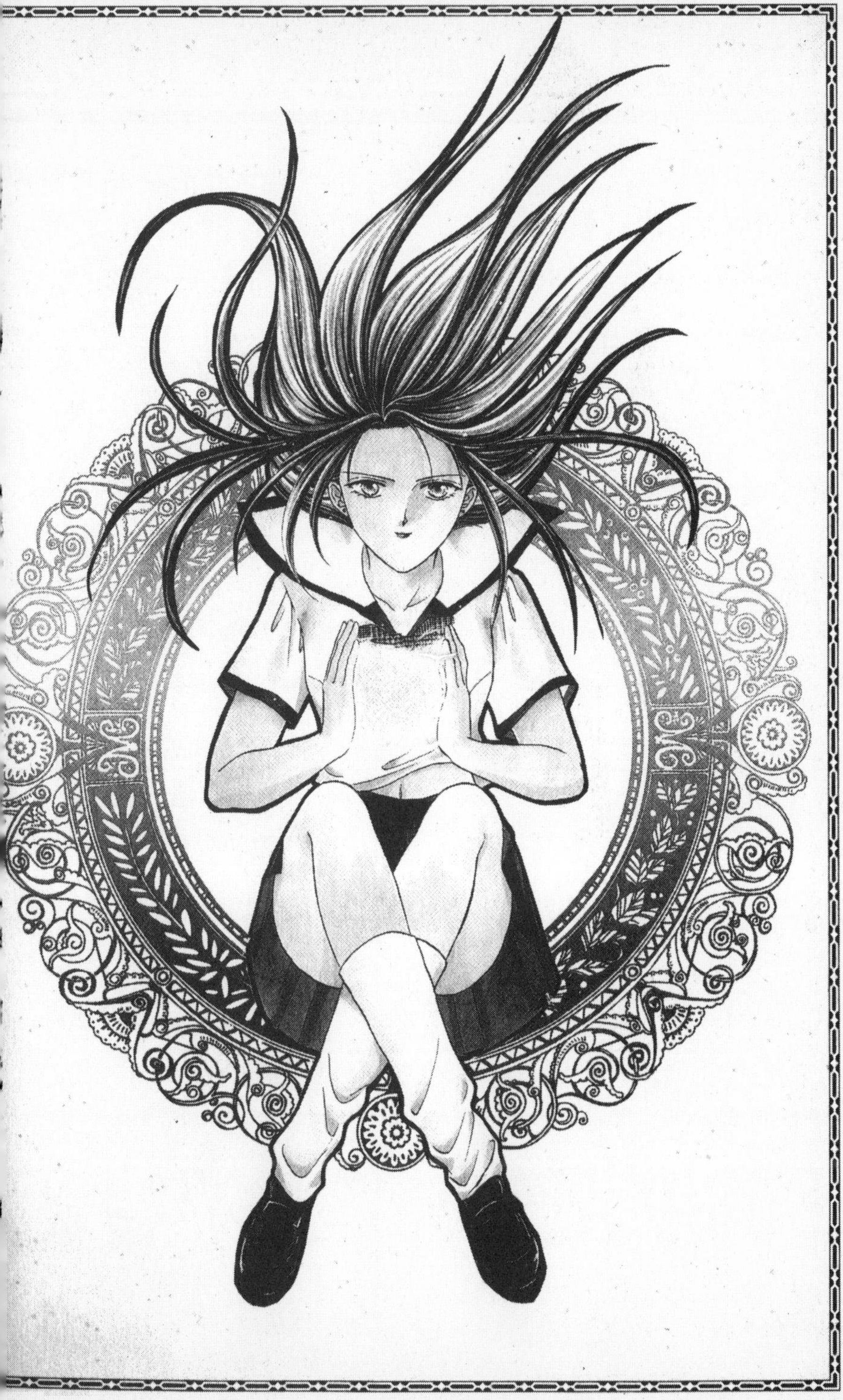

More Manga! More Mang

Did you notice? New logo, new lower price, and you'll be pleased to discover that Ceres graphic novels are going to start coming out four times a year! For those of you who may have already seen all the episodes of the Ceres anime series through to the end, rest assured that Yû Watase's manga provides greater depth of characterization and also includes several story arcs that weren't included in the anime. Stick with us and you'll find that Aya and Tôya's romance gets even steamier, that Yûhi is even more of an endearing "nice guy" than he is in the anime, that Mrs. Q is even wackier, and that the manga volumes to come are going to provide exciting spills and chills and take you through an emotional roller coaster ride in a way that only Yû Watase knows how to do. Watch out for the next volume of Ceres because Aki is about to go on a rampage!

IF YOU LIKE *CERES* HERE A SOME OTHER MANGA Y MIGHT BE INTERESTED IN:

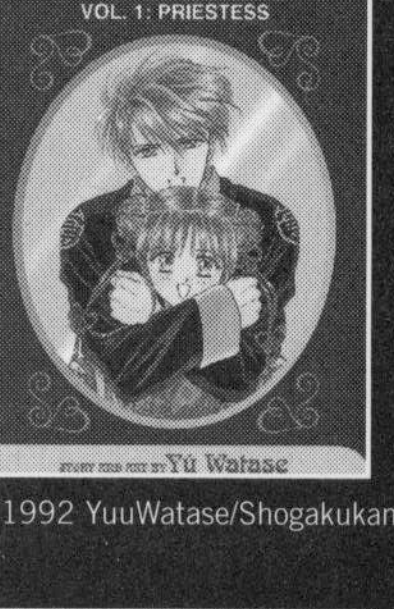
fushigi yûgi
The Mysterious Play
VOL. 1: PRIESTESS
Yû Watase

FUSHIGI YU

Another fantasy lo triangle extravagan brought to you by Watase! More hur male characters, mc of Yû Watse's gre artwork, and anoth intense storyline!

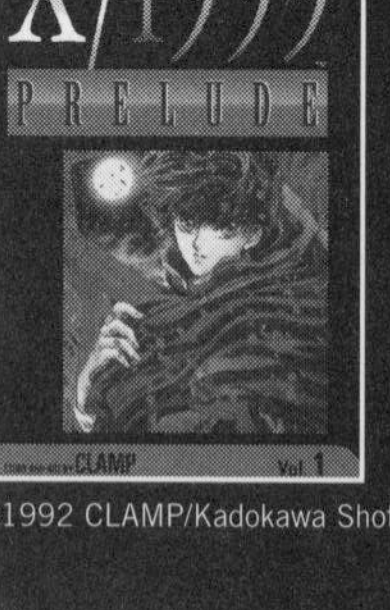
X/1999
PRELUDE
CLAMP
Vol. 1

X/1999

A supernatural st with breathtakin beautiful artwo X/1999 is a fantas shôjo melodrama cr ated by studio CLAM

OROCHI BLOO

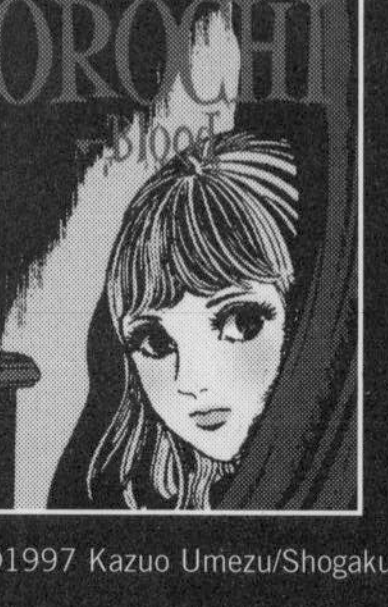
KAZUO UMEZU's
OROCHI
Blood

If you enjoy the dark a creepy elements in ***Cer*** and you're looking something even creepi then give manga mas of horror Kazuo Umez ***Orochi Blood*** a try. B be forewarned, it's r for the faint of heart a it's strictly for matu readers!

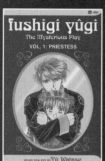

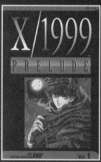

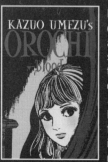

fushigi yûgi
The Mysterious Play

Seven Warriors... Four Gods...
Two Worlds... One Quest

Get drawn into the graphic novels today — only from VIZ!

"Yû Watase's art is lush and detailed." — Sequential Tart

COMPLETE OUR SURVEY AND LET
US KNOW WHAT YOU THINK!

☐ Please check here if you DO NOT wish to receive information or future offers from VIZ

Name: _____

Address: _____

City: _____ **State:** _____ **Zip:** _____

E-mail: _____

☐ **Male**　　☐ **Female**　　**Date of Birth** (mm/dd/yyyy): ___ / ___ / _____ (**Under 13? Parental consent required**)

What race/ethnicity do you consider yourself? (please check one)

☐ Asian/Pacific Islander　　☐ Black/African American　　☐ Hispanic/Latino

☐ Native American/Alaskan Native　　☐ White/Caucasian　　☐ Other: _____

What VIZ product did you purchase? (check all that apply and indicate title purchased)

☐ DVD/VHS _____

☐ Graphic Novel _____

☐ Magazines _____

☐ Merchandise _____

Reason for purchase: (check all that apply)

☐ Special offer　　☐ Favorite title　　☐ Gift

☐ Recommendation　　☐ Other _____

Where did you make your purchase? (please check one)

☐ Comic store　　☐ Bookstore　　☐ Mass/Grocery Store

☐ Newsstand　　☐ Video/Video Game Store　　☐ Other: _____

☐ Online (site: _____)

What other VIZ properties have you purchased/own? _____

_____

How many anime and/or manga titles have you purchased in the last year? How many were VIZ titles? (please check one from each column)

ANIME	MANGA	VIZ
☐ None	☐ None	☐ None
☐ 1-4	☐ 1-4	☐ 1-4
☐ 5-10	☐ 5-10	☐ 5-10
☐ 11+	☐ 11+	☐ 11+

I find the pricing of VIZ products to be: (please check one)

☐ Cheap ☐ Reasonable ☐ Expensive

What genre of manga and anime would you like to see from VIZ? (please check two)

☐ Adventure ☐ Comic Strip ☐ Detective ☐ Fighting

☐ Horror ☐ Romance ☐ Sci-Fi/Fantasy ☐ Sports

What do you think of VIZ's new look?

☐ Love It ☐ It's OK ☐ Hate It ☐ Didn't Notice ☐ No Opinion

THANK YOU! Please send the completed form to:

NJW Research
42 Catharine St.
Poughkeepsie, NY 12601

All information provided will be used for internal purposes only. We promise not to sell or otherwise divulge your information.